Praise for Previous

'It's a rich, diverse and sa
Starburst Magazine

'Horror is a wide church, supporting a wide variety of original ideas, and so it is here. *Elemental Forces* is another fine addition to an anthology series that is going from strength to strength.'
Concatenation

'A very impressive set of stories. Perfect for dark and cold evenings as we enter the more eerie part of the year. Strongly recommended!'
Runalong The Shelves on *Darkness Beckons*

'*Close to Midnight* illustrates what great shape the genre of horror is in… If you're a reader who enjoys quality fiction of the dark kind, this is a series to be cherished. There isn't a bad story in the entire book.'
Stephen Bacon

'*Close to Midnight* is a very solid collection of horror featuring stories of varied themes and content, and yet they all feel very comfortable inside the spine of one book. Worth a look if you like chills down your spine late at night as you lie in bed reading.'
Horror DNA

'Morris has assembled an especially strong group of stories with dazzling, diverse approaches to horror. Highly recommended.'
Cemetery Dance on *Close to Midnight*

'If you love short and sometimes shocking horror stories, you can't go wrong with this collection!'
On the Shelf Reviews on *Close to Midnight*

'I'm impressed with the imagination and variety coming from the writers. *Beyond the Veil* is another happy clump of ickiness... and I mean that in a good way.'
The Happy Horror Writer

'There is no end to the talent Mark Morris has brought together here. Fans of the genre will be pleased to see new work from such favorites as Nathan Ballingrud and Gemma Files, among others. So if you're ready for a long fall night, pick up a copy of this massive anthology and fall into the mysterious worlds *Beyond the Veil*.'
Phantastiqa

'Beautifully written pieces that lean into the intuitive and fantastic.'
Publishers Weekly on *After Sundown*

'This rich and masterful collection of horror highlighting both up-and-coming and established authors is an interesting twist on the standard anthology [...] Highly recommended for longstanding horror fans and those readers who may not think horror is for them. There is something for everyone in this one.'
Booklist on *After Sundown*

'This is a short story collection that does exactly what it sets out to, delight and scare. With stories from well-known authors in the genre as well as a few from emerging voices, *After Sundown* has something for everyone. Highly recommended.'
The British Fantasy Society

'An entertaining, slickly written, mainstream, fun, something-for-every-horror-fan anthology.'
HorrorTree on *After Sundown*

A FLAME TREE BOOK OF HORROR

FEVER DREAMS

An Anthology of New Short Stories

Edited by Mark Morris

This is a **FLAME TREE PRESS** book

Stories by modern authors are subject to international copyright law, and are licensed for publication in this volume.

All rights reserved. No part of this publication may be reproduced, stored in a retrieval system, or transmitted in any form or by any means, electronic, mechanical, photocopying, recording or otherwise, without the prior written permission of the publisher.

FLAME TREE PRESS
6 Melbray Mews, London, SW6 3NS, UK
flametreepress.com

US sales, distribution and warehouse:
Simon & Schuster
simonandschuster.biz

UK distribution and warehouse:
Hachette UK Distribution
hukdcustomerservice@hachette.co.uk

Publisher's Note: This is a work of fiction. Names, characters, places, and incidents are a product of the authors' imaginations. Locales and public names are sometimes used for atmospheric purposes. Any resemblance to actual people, living or dead, or to businesses, companies, events, institutions, or locales is completely coincidental.

Thanks to the Flame Tree Press team.

The cover is created by Flame Tree Studio
with elements courtesy of Shutterstock.com and Raggedstone.
The font families used are Avenir and Bembo.

Flame Tree Press is an imprint of Flame Tree Publishing Ltd
flametreepublishing.com

A copy of the CIP data for this book is available from the British Library and the Library of Congress.

1 3 5 7 9 8 6 4 2

HB ISBN: 978-1-78758-872-1
US PB ISBN: 978-1-78758-870-7
UK PB ISBN: 978-1-78758-871-4
ebook ISBN: 978-1-78758-874-5

Printed and bound in Great Britain by Clays Ltd, Elcograf S.p.A.

Represented in the EU for product safety and compliance by Authorised Rep Compliance Ltd., Ground Floor, 71 Lower Baggot Street, Dublin, D02 P593, Ireland. Contact us at www.arccompliance.com

A FLAME TREE BOOK OF HORROR
FEVER DREAMS

An Anthology of New Short Stories

Edited by Mark Morris

FLAME TREE PRESS
London & New York

CONTENTS

Introduction 1
Mark Morris

May I Borrow You for a Moment? . . 3
Tracy Fahey

Enter, Kill, Exit 22
Tim Waggoner

At Black Rock Beach. 32
Gary McMahon

Piglet. 43
Priya Sharma

The Mummified Corpse of Reese
Witherspoon 54
Philip Fracassi

The Wind Telephone 69
A.K. Benedict

All in the Game 77
Craig DiLouie

Not All Stones Mean Murder 93
Kaaron Warren

The Adjutant's Dinner Guest 106
Jeffrey Ford

CONTENTS

Sideways 115
Lucy A. Snyder

Forty Below 129
Caolán Mac an Aircinn

By the Skin of His Teeth 135
Chad Lutzke

The Shadow of His Vibrance 147
Kay Chronister

At the Bottom, She Rots 161
Ryan Cole

Silent Wounds 170
Clay McLeod Chapman

Agony Street 184
Rebecca Harrison

Watch the Skies 193
Alan Baxter

The Sitter 210
Rob Francis

It Has Eyes Now 220
Christopher Golden & Tanya Pell

Midnight Disease 236
C.J. Leede

Biographies 257

INTRODUCTION
Mark Morris

Is the world getting crazier?

It certainly seems so from many perspectives, but I suspect the same question has been asked by human beings since time immemorial. With the effects of climate crisis, unrest in the Middle East, the ongoing war in Ukraine, and even societal divisions in the USA dominating the news as I write these words, one can be forgiven for thinking planet Earth is currently on a collision course to oblivion.

Looking back, though, it seems that this insignificant ball of rock on which we all strut and fret our hour upon the stage has forever been on the brink. Our history is a relentless litany of wars, plagues, civil unrest, and, inevitably, the miserable by-products of all that – poverty, inequality, brutality, bigotry, and numerous instances of selfishness and stupidity.

Perhaps the difference between the past and the present, though, is that, via the internet, we now have almost constant access and exposure to the most mind-bogglingly awful events. This can become so all-pervading, so overwhelming, that there are times when it doesn't actually seem quite real; times when 'reality' appears more like a dream (or nightmare) – or even like a computer game that has run so far out of control, and reached such a crisis point, that the only solution seems to be to end the game and start again.

Stressful though all of this can be, it is in this febrile hinterland of human fears, phobias and anxieties where the inspiration for horror stories most commonly thrives, and where ideas gestate and develop. *Fever Dreams* marks the sixth annual anthology in the 'ABC of Horror' series, and the stories that have this year flooded in from contributors continue to be as relevant, inventive and varied as ever.

One thing that has particularly struck me this year is how *geographically* varied they are. Proving that nightmares are both global and uncontained, these twenty stories range from the USA and the UK to France, Greece, Australia, Antarctica, Syria and Iceland.

In terms of content, all human – and inhuman – life is here. Within these pages you'll find tales of cosmic awe, of human depravity, and of monsters conjured from the darkest recesses of our own souls. Thematically, the class of 2025 delve into the horrors of toxic masculinity and identity theft, mid-life disillusionment and lack of self-worth, intolerance and cruelty and deep-seated trauma. Revenge, incarceration, home invasion – all are explored within these pages. But if this all sounds rather grim, be assured that there is also humour here, to leaven the darkness, albeit admittedly the laughs do invariably come with a generous side order of body horror.

As editor, I continue to be enormously grateful to my contributors for knocking the ball out of the park again and again and again. In *After Sundown*, the first volume of this series, published five years ago, I announced my intention that these annual volumes should be a showcase for the sheer scope and inventiveness that the horror genre has to offer. Five years later, I believe whole-heartedly that these books are continuing to fulfil that brief.

Try not to have nightmares. But if you do, why not write them down and allow others to share them?

Mark Morris

MAY I BORROW YOU FOR A MOMENT?

Tracy Fahey

"You can't do this." My voice is rough, desperate. "I'll tell everyone."
You laugh. Shrug.
"Which of us do you think they'll believe?"

* * *

When I got the call for papers, I didn't even think of it as a viable option – too busy, too insolvent. But when you told me the department would pay, I hesitated.

There's a me that wanted to go, after all. To send out my ideas, spores in the air. To have my research witnessed and approved. To earn brownie points towards my PhD progression. Perhaps – even – to get a publication out of it. Yes. There's a me that *needed* to go.

And yet. Travelling with you. The proximity of it all, the closeness of lecture hall seats. Unwanted intimacies, breakfasting together. Your white hair, sticking up at the back from where you slept on it.

I shake my head, the image blurs.

You cough, cover your mouth with a white handkerchief. "No?"

I hesitate, irresolute, scroll down the page. The conference is in Paris. There's a tour of the Catacombs included. The amazing corridors of heaped bone and displaced bodies from eighteenth-century cemeteries. A slow thump of excitement.

"Maybe." A crazy dream-collage of Eiffel towers, a Champs-Élysées snaked with lines of traffic, the Mona Lisa's steady, shadowed gaze. Without meaning to, I'm smiling.

"I mean yes. Yes. I'll put in an abstract.'

You wipe your lips. "Good girl."

* * *

Outside the world peels away into sunlight, brilliant blue sky, wadded with soft masses of cloud. A flash of light far below; land, sea, I'm not sure which. I swallow. My hands are sweating.

You share my armrest. A vaguely unpleasant warmth as you press against me; I'm acutely aware of the bony line of your forearm. The air-con nozzle above me is on, but when I reach up to touch it, only the tiniest breath of air wheezes out. I don't like this. Being suspended in the air, being too warm, too hemmed in. Here and nowhere at the same time.

I put a hand on the window, to cool my palm. When I unpeel it, there's a handprint etched in frosty condensation. The engines thrum, a lift, the *clunk-clunk* of wheels folding up like birds' legs.

In the glass, a ghost of my face; pale, large-eyed.

The plane tilts, my insides tilt. I jog your elbow.

"Are you all right, my dear?"

"Kind of." I swallow. "I've only been on an aeroplane twice before." It's true. Once for a sun holiday with mates that we all got Credit Union loans out for, once for a family funeral in Manchester.

"Really?" you say, whiskery eyebrows raised. "You never cease to surprise me, Leonie."

I'm not in the mood to play Eliza Doolittle. I pick up my conference paper instead, now stippled with biro marks and crossings-out – *I must remember to try to print this out again at the conference hotel* – and start reading it over. When I sneak a look again, you're asleep. Linen suit perfectly creased; face collapsed into your chin.

I look down at my own velour tracksuit. I've seen celebrities wear these for travelling in, but, as usual, beside you I feel wrong. I know you don't mind it; on some level you find me quaint. Gauche. Amusing. Like when I asked too many questions in tutorials, and you called me Sisyphus. I had to look it up later. A god of persistent and futile tasks. Yes, you were laughing at me. But on some level, you *saw* me, and that was enough.

It's why I asked you to supervise me.

"So, you want to do a thesis on the fetch? Interesting." You ran a delicate fingertip over the print-out I'd brought for you – *email is vulgar.* "Why do you want to write about this?"

"Well, I always heard stories about it as a kid. About the fetch, coming to take you away."

You waited, head cocked to one side.

"And I had a really strange thing happen to me when I was younger. When my Nanna died, my ma covered the big mirror with a sheet, so she couldn't find her way back." Me and Jason, watching her, jostling each other. "My brother dared me to pull it back. So, I did."

"And then?" The window flickered; sunlight glitched on your gold signet ring.

"And then I saw myself and screamed in the dark room – I thought it was my Nanna, young again. Got smacked for it." The stinging brand, hard across the back of the legs. "And yeah, that's when I got really interested in the fetch."

You looked at me. The tiniest raise of an eyebrow.

I knew what you meant.

"*Right.* I mean... well, later I read other accounts of the fetch. There's a short story by the Banim brothers, and lots of descriptions of it in oral folklore collections."

A beat of silence.

"Maybe," you said, delicate as always. "Maybe avoid the autoethnographic approach. Perhaps a little" – you paused, coughed – "perhaps a little scholarly detachment?"

I nodded, ashamed.

"And when the research office asks at interview you'll say?"

I translated myself for you. "That I'm interested in the Banims' story, 'The Fetches', and its folkloric antecedents."

The plane's engines shift, change in tone. I look outside. Everything has disappeared in a drift of cloud. *Where am I?*

Beside me, you've started to snore, a light, rhythmic cadence. I dig my phone out of my tracksuit pocket. No emails. Of course not. And anyway, I checked it right before take-off.

I touch the silver pendant that Tommi gave me for Christmas. Gemini, the twins. A sharp pang of homesickness; to be on land, to be in our tatty apartment, my feet on Tommi's lap.

Outside the clouds rise, wreathe the plane in cotton-puffs of vapour. I close my eyes, imagine another version of my life down there where I stayed at home on our old estate.

A rattle of turbulence. I grip the pendant hard. When the shaking stops, I unpeel my fingers. Two girls facing each other, imprinted on my palm.

★ ★ ★

The conference hotel is fancy and intimidating. I poke around my dark room. A jumble of old and mismatched furniture – a tall wardrobe, a narrow bed, a scatter of small tables and chairs. I give the bidet an experimental flush, try to call Tommi. No answer. I put on a dress she helped me choose. Navy and plain, neither too tight nor too loose. Downstairs, a thin procession streams in. Chic, middle-aged women in black with interesting scarves and brooches, some men with equally interesting beards, some student types with square-framed glasses – underpaid PhD hopefuls, stealing opportunistic glances around the other attendees, calculating the advantage of introducing themselves.

I collect my badge, sign up for the Catacombs tour, collect a glass of red wine. As keynote speaker, you stand near the registration desk with the organisers, graciously greeting delegates.

I hold a glass of wine, watch new arrivals greet each other with noisy confidence.

"When did y'all get here?" Beards, big coats, American accents.

"Oh my, what a long flight!"

"Have you seen Peterson from Columbia? He's gotta great story about trying to get a cab here."

"Isn't there anything but wine? I can't drink alcohol, I have an allergy."

All eyes pass over me. I thread quiet paths through the clusters, forcing quick smiles as I squeeze myself past. The glass of red wine, a prop, grows warm and sticky in my hand. Desperation grows. I bump slightly into some of the chattier delegates, excusing myself. Nothing. They merely step back politely and continue their conversation. My skin pinpricks with perspiration.

I wish you were here. Tommi would roll her eyes at me. "Be yourself. Everyone else is already taken."

I feel your eyes on me. You bend forward, whisper in a dark-haired professor's ear. He smiles at me, a dazzle of white teeth. My cheeks bloom with red awkwardness. I put down my sweaty, undrinkable glass of wine and walk out. On the pavement I realise I've gone the wrong way – out of the hotel instead of upstairs. A cold wind carves into my dress.

There's a girl in the doorway, pausing to take a last drag of a cigarette. An illicit line of smoke arches into the foyer.

"Are you coming back in?" Her hair is a chic blonde bob.

"Me?"

"Yes. You look *human*," she says, her voice a perfect wash of short English vowels and precise consonants. Crisp and appraising. "Unlike those old fossils." She nods at the registration desk and the group of professors around you, woven in a close knot of gossip.

I touch my nametag. "I'm Leonie." We shake hands. Her nails are red and sharp.

"Julia. First time here?"

"Yes." It probably shows. Landing, I never quite got my bearings. Charles de Gaulle was impossibly huge and ant-lined with queues, signs in French and Mandarin – and, thankfully, English. The journey into Paris was confusing, the ugliness of the industrial suburbs, which dissolved in a few turns. And then, it was there, Paris, a plethora of graceful cream buildings, graffiti, bicycles, people, people, people.

She draws me back inside. "It's a bit much, isn't it?" She waves a hand at the ornate lobby, the grave waiters, the enormous glass chandelier. "Just soak up the wine, smile at everyone, avoid the boring papers, and you're good."

"Thanks." I'm grateful for these small wisdoms. My head is starting to spin, a combination of poor sleep, no food, and noise.

Julia picks up two glasses of wine, hands me one. "Are you here with anyone?"

"One of the fossils." I point at you. You move slightly apart from the crowd, cough into a handkerchief. "The keynote, Professor Atkinson."

"Atkinson... That old James Joyce fart? Book on the Hermetic Order of the Golden Dawn? Talking here about metempsychosis? Atkinson from Trinity?"

I'm laughing. "Yes to all the above."

Julia looks at you. "He doesn't look so well. Mind you, he must be ancient. You know him well?"

"Well enough. He's my advisor."

Julia leans towards me. "Careful," she says quietly. The hubbub in the room swells. "Careful of that one."

"Julia!" A handsome dark-haired man grasps her shoulders, kisses her on both cheeks.

"Antoine!"

I linger for a few minutes, but Julia is absorbed in talking. It's stuffy and airless. My head is starting to ache. I drain my glass, push through the crowd back to the door, through a drift of smoke and chatter at the entrance.

The rough stone of the wall pricks my back. Before me, the Seine is streaked with the buttery yellow of a low sun. I check my email. Nothing.

The soft *burr-burr* of the phone. Tommi's voicemail, lightly amused voice. "Don't leave a message. I hate that. Text like a normal person."

Oh Tommi. For a moment I see her, laughing, her purple hair, an undercut soft as suede under my fingers. My miracle girl who found me and gave me a home. *I wish you were here.*

I bypass the lobby, slink to the lift. In my dark and cavernous room, the thrum of voices and laughter below swells through the floor. I bump into the nightstand, further from the bed than I remembered from check-in. A red bump flowers on my knee.

I try Tommi's number again, click off before the recorded message.

In the bathroom, I'm confused. I can't work out the shower; a complex mix of levers and taps, settle for sluicing my face and hands under a large, antiquated tap. Coming out of the bathroom, I take a wrong turn, stumble over my suitcase. I flick on the TV, but I don't speak French. Lying on the duvet cover, I smooth out my paper:

Though there are many accounts of the doppelgänger – the exact double of a person – in oral folklore, its presence is regarded as a bad omen. Nowhere is this more acutely observed than in Irish lore with the trope of 'the fetch'.

God. That's bad. Stiff and pompous. I score an angry line through the sentences, put the paper back in my bag. My fingers brush my phone. I check it again. Three emails, all about upcoming research training seminars. I delete them, lie back on the bed, twisting the pendant between my fingers like a holy medal.

I wish you were here.

I took her home last Christmas. Tommi.

My mother's gaze slid across her. The hair. Her T-shirt slogan: *The Future Is Female.* The row of glinting earrings. I wound a strand of tinsel tight round my fingers till they creased white. Tommi leaned against the dirty worktop, piled with multipacks of crisps, huge bottles of cheap, off-brand cola, a doll in the wrong diorama.

"I'm sorry," I said, much later, squashed against her in one of the twin beds in my room. "For everything."

She pinched me. "Don't be a snob, Leonie."

I wander over to the hotel room window, queerly restless. In the glass I am an inky shape, a negative space, an absence.

Where am I?

Within me the city flowers in strings of lights.

★ ★ ★

"Mademoiselle?"

I've been practising. "Americano, *s'il vous plaît.*"

He looks doubtful. "Americano?"

"Oui." I shake a cigarette out of my pack, light it. In my head, I'm a louche Eva Green.

The young waiter shrugs. "Bon."

Paris is even prettier in the early morning sun. The street of tabacs, boulangeries and boucheries is striped with pedestrian crossings. I settle back in my wooden chair, blow a smoke ring upwards towards the red awning. A girl pauses in the street to my left; in my peripheral vision I see her from the back. Same black hair as me, same white shirt as me, same shoulder-bag bisecting her body.

Surely not? And then she turns. Her face is shockingly unlike mine, long nose, full lips, inky eyes.

My phone buzzes. I jump. When I look up the girl is gone.

"Hello, traveller!" *Tommi*.

"Babe, I miss you." I put the cigarette in the ashtray. I don't want her to hear me inhaling, scold me. "I've arrived safely, and it's all going OK. I even talked to someone last night at the reception."

"Ah, sweetie, I'm so happy for you." Her voice is warm. "Lucky old you, being in Paris. How is it?"

"Very *Paris*. I had a croissant earlier, just waiting on a black coffee. So far, so French."

"Any news?"

She doesn't have to specify.

"Hang on." I thumb open my email app, check. Nothing.

"No," I say. "And I can't think about it right now. I'm too nervous – I'm giving my paper this afternoon."

She makes a soothing sound. "I know, silly, that's why I called you. Don't worry. Be yourself."

"Mademoiselle?"

A sturdy tumbler of orange liquid swollen with ice. It smells of strong alcohol. I poke at it. "Americano?"

The waiter nods, drops a receipt tray on my table. The slip of paper printed faintly with 'Americano'.

What the hell? Tommi, oblivious, talks on. "So anyway, tell me—"

A hand on my shoulder. I grab my drink, hold it up. "Monsieur?" *Shit. You.*

"Ah, Leonie." Your face, amused. A cough. "A little Dutch courage for later?" You lift your Panama hat courteously, keep walking.

The phone crackles in my ear. "Who's that?"

I stare dumbly after you, put the glass down.

"No one. Well. You know. Atkinson. I have to go, Tommi."

I stub out my cigarette, glare at the drink glistening amber on my table. Wrong, wrong, always wrong.

She sighs. "Have a good time."

"It's Paris," I say. "How could I not?"

★ ★ ★

The day is a blur of panels, coffees, announcements by the organisers. You stand on the platform as keynote speaker, regally acknowledging applause in anticipation of your lecture tomorrow.
And then it's time. Almost time. We're the last panel of the day. The earnest young man beside me – Simon, the moderator said – is giving his paper. I reread my paper. *This is a load of rubbish.* I take out my pen and draw a line through the entire first page.
My phone buzzes. I sneak a look. New email. Subject line 'Your article is now online'. I let out a breath I didn't know I was holding in.
The earnest young man clears his throat. I'm up. I grip the lectern. Julia gives me a tiny wave. My heart knocks loud against my ribs. Before me, a blur of faces. I click on the first slide, an old-fashioned print of a woman on a country road.
You. Front row. Arms crossed, smile flickering across your face. I squeeze my eyes shut. Tommi's voice in my ear. *Be yourself.*
"Let me tell you a story," I say. "A story about my grandmother."

★ ★ ★

I sit down. My legs are shaking. I've left my paper on the rostrum. My phone vibrates on my lap. It doesn't matter. They're still applauding.
"Thank you to Leonie Burke, our last speaker," says the moderator. "We will now take questions for the panel."
A forest of arms, waving. A sea of questions. They're all for me.

★ ★ ★

The delegates who looked through me last night now swarm around.
"Have you published on this?" Simon, the earnest young man.
"Yes," I say, smooth and practised. "As a matter of fact, I have an article just out in the *Journal of Interdisciplinary Arts.*"
"So, you've conducted fieldwork as part of your analysis of fictional narratives?" A woman I vaguely recognise from University College Dublin. She smiles. "Come and see us in the Folklore Department when you're back, won't you?"
I nod. My phone buzzes in my pocket. Julia, from across the room, gives me a thumbs-up.

A warm hand on my elbow. You.

"Well, well, well." Your eyes are amused, but there's a flicker of something else. Interest? Challenge?

"I loved that story about your grandmother's wake." An American professor with a wild, white beard beams at me.

I daren't meet your eye.

You give the bearded professor a small, courtly bow, loop an arm in mine.

"May I borrow you for a moment?"

★   ★   ★

This is surreal. You squire me around the room. "Have you met my quite brilliant PhD student?" I keep nodding, keep smiling. My phone vibrates insistently, but the crush around me shows no signs of abating.

"And so young, Atkinson," says the professor with the huge white beard. "An original and a prodigy."

"Exactly, Braun. She has a very bright future ahead of her." You squeeze my arm, a little too tightly. "I'm sure of it."

I feel the phone buzz in my pocket. I disentangle my arm from yours. "I'm so sorry," I say. "I really need to get this." I pull the phone out, Tommi's face flashes up.

Your eyes are bright, avid. "The lady friend, I take it?"

The other professors raise their eyebrows. "How very *Colette*," says one, and you laugh until you cough.

"She likes the ladies," you say. "Can't blame her for that." They all chuckle.

"Tommi." I lurch over to the corner, press my burning cheek to the screen.

"I'm trying to FaceTime you, you idiot."

"Sorry." I pull away, grin stupidly at her. "The article—"

"I saw it's up! Great timing."

"Yeah." I shake my head slightly.

Tommi understands. "Babe," she says quietly. "No more worrying. You're safe now."

I can still feel your fingerprints on my arm.

"Maybe."

* * *

"Leonie." Julia materialises beside me. "You conference darling! Junk your fans and come join us." She waves a hand at Antoine, Simon and a group of postgrads. "We're off to get very drunk and trash-talk everyone."

I can't help it. A glow. *I'm part of the group.* "I'd love to."

The windows of Le Saint are fogged with condensation. We're on our third round of drinks. I clink glasses with Eve, a small, punky girl with a lip piercing.

Antoine smiles down at me. "You're with Professor Atkinson, aren't you?"

"Kind of." I inhale the first inch of my cold beer, lick my lips. "He's my advisor."

"He's pretty decent, no? He examined my PhD transfer last year."

"Yeah, right." Eve snorts. "He's one of those."

"One of those?" I put down my beer.

"You know," she says. "Fine with guys. But the female grapevine knows him. He's one of the creepy ones." Her face looms closer to me, she drops her voice. "You know. The ones that skate close to the line."

Your hand on my arm. *May I borrow you for a moment?* Your eyes on me, greedy, appraising.

I shiver.

"He's bad news," says Julia, draining a glass of wine. "Try asking Sophia Bell." Her lips are stained berry purple. "If that was possible."

The name sounds vaguely familiar. I lean forward, but Antoine wedges himself between us, brandishing a credit card.

A tray of tiny absinthe glasses glows green on the wooden counter. I shrug, pick one up, clink it with Eve's, toss it back.

"Good stuff," says Antoine. "To the Green Muse."

I slip out for a cigarette as they're all cheering. The light is fading, but the buttery limestone still glows. I want to tour around a little tomorrow. "I should go home," I say aloud, with tipsy dignity, then throw the half-smoked cigarette in the gutter.

At the door I pause. A dark haired woman in a white shirt sits at the bar between Eve and Julia. I can't see her face.

Is it the girl from the café? *Or?* I squeeze my eyes tight shut, so tight that stars spark behind my eyelids.

And she's gone.

The bar stool is empty, and so is the shot glass on the counter.

I push my way back to the bar. "Julia. Can we talk?"

She blinks at me. Her sleek, blonde hair is rumpled. "We just were. I told you to be careful, didn't I?"

I stare at our reflection in the bar mirror. "Who is Sophia Bell?" But she can't hear me anymore. She hands me another shot of absinthe.

"Careful," she repeats. Her eyes are unfocused. "You're just his type."

★ ★ ★

My night is a soup of dreams, muddy half-memories of running through dark rooms. Mirrors everywhere. I keep splitting, dividing, cartoon versions of me, white shirt and dark trousers, mouth a dark hole.

I wake in a tangle of sheets. *Where am I?* A beat, and then the fear descends. It pulses from my throbbing head around my body. Flashes of me laughing, my too-loud voice shouting nonsense at Julia and Eve. I pull the sweat-soaked duvet over my face. My leg hurts. Images unspool, faster and faster. More absinthe, twinkling green and malevolent. A blur and lurch, the sound of crashing glass. Antoine's laughing face bending over me. My own voice, magnified in my ears. "Don't let the bastards grind you down." Steadying myself on the street cleaners' green van.

My skin stings, flames with shame.

I lurch over to the window, rip the curtains back. Paris glares back in, the boulevard outside beautiful and haughty and alien. I'm still wearing my shirt and socks. There's a huge bruise on my shin. My throat is rough and sore from cigarettes.

I try everything. A shower. Coffee. Getting dressed. Putting on the incomprehensible TV. But all through these familiar motions, a dark underswell of dread – *What did I say? What did I do?* – beats a monotonous rhythm of horror.

Paris is ticking by and I'm missing it. A precious free morning, and of course I had to go and ruin it for myself. In the bathroom I scowl savagely at my pale, dry-skinned, wild-eyed double.

My phone bleeps. *You OK?* Julia.

I text back a bandaged face emoji, a thumbs-up one.

See you for the keynote. X

I don't reply. Instead, I rip my clothes off and crawl into bed in a T-shirt. The unfamiliar room eddies around me, settles.

★ ★ ★

I slip into the seat beside Julia and Eve. My throat is still raw. I raise my coffee cup and take a surreptitious sip. The coffee rolls forlornly around my empty stomach. I stoop and put the cup under my chair.

"I'm in pieces," whispers Eve. Her pixie face is wan. There's a streak of mascara under one eye. "I'm going to skip the Catacombs."

"Same," says Julia. "I'm feeling quite dead enough already." She pokes me in the shoulder. "*Le Saint* again? Hair of the dog that savaged you?"

My head thumps unpleasantly. "Um." I don't want to spurn her offer. "I'll see once this is over."

"Ah, Leonie, my dear." You're in front of me, smiling. "Come and sit with us."

I get up, give the girls a regretful smile. Eve looks unimpressed. Julia mouths something I can't catch.

"Hello." It's the old American guy from yesterday. *Brown? Braun?* "I'm very interested in getting you over to us in Chicago to share your research."

I'm overwhelmed. "Thank you, professor."

"Chad." He smiles at me through his bushy white beard, then holds a finger to his lips. You step up to the podium.

I've heard you speak before. And as you put up your first slide – a mosaic depicting Orpheus – I realise I've heard this speech before. At the Dublin conference last year.

"Metempsychosis – the migration of souls – is commonly believed to have its origins in Orphism." You pause, cough. "But to truly find its source, we must go back further, to Dionysian rites, to the celebration of Persephone."

You press your handkerchief to your mouth. "These cults celebrated those who descended to the underworld and managed to return. Those who survived, and even thrived as a result."

I sneak a look back at Julia. She rolls her eyes.

The familiar cadence of your voice; coughing, speaking. The click of the pointer. My eyes shutter down. Your words wash over me – *rites and rituals, the life of the soul after death.* The conference room dissolves. I'm in bed, heavy covers over my head, a hand grabs me in the dark – my head jerks.

I open my eyes, confused.

God. I nearly fell asleep. I slide my phone out of my pocket, check it furtively. A text from Tommi. *Proud of you, babe.* I send her back a flood of heart emojis. No emails. I pause, remember Julia on her bar stool, hair in her eyes. *Go ask Sophia Bell.*

I try Googling her. A number of hits, mostly young girls with pouting Instagram accounts. I pause, try Google Scholar. There's an affiliation. Same as mine. Trinity College Dublin. And there's something that looks promising. It's an article, 'Metempsychosis: a history of experimentation'.

I squint at the byline. She's a co-author. Before her name, there's another. *Professor S.J. Atkinson.*

As soon as the applause dies down, I wriggle past the delegates to Julia.

"Sophia Bell." I show Julia my phone screen. "You didn't say she wrote with Atkinson."

"She didn't." Julia looks around, draws in a breath. "He took her research."

I grip the seat back. "What happened to her?"

Julia shrugs. "She was never the same afterwards. Disappeared from the conference circuit. There were different rumours."

"I heard she went back to Canada," Eve offers.

"That's one story." Julia looks at me. "But—"

You catch my eye, beckon me forward. The organisers are marshalling a line of delegates for the Catacombs tour.

"Last chance," says Eve. "Wanna come with us?"

I ignore her. "But?" I prompt Julia.

"But I heard she killed herself." Her mouth is a thin line. "Sophia."

★ ★ ★

You find me in the line of delegates.

"Congratulations, professor," I say dutifully.

"Why, thank you." You are smiling but your eyes are cold. "Though I fear you – ahem – have forgotten to inform your advisor that you have an article published?"

"I… umm…" You've caught me out.

"A solo authored article, no less." You raise an eyebrow.

"It's the journal convention." Never mind that I chose to submit for precisely that reason.

You nod. I can't read your expression.

A bus pulls up. I'm confused. According to my phone, we're only a few metro stops away from the Catacombs.

Chad, beside me, sees my bewilderment. "It's a special tour," he explains. "We're going to a recently unearthed part of the complex. What a treat." I climb up the steps.

"Come sit with me." Chad pats the empty seat beside him.

"I think not." You shake your head at him. "You can't be allowed to poach my students, my dear fellow."

I stand, irresolute, in the gangway.

"Sit here." It's an order, not an invitation. "I like to keep an eye on my promising young students." Your eyes are hard, greedy. "And you, Leonie, are the most promising of all."

★ ★ ★

This looks nothing like the pictures I've seen online. We get off the bus at the bottom of a hill, somewhere in the suburbs. There's a large cave to one side, and a row of silent guides with headlamps and a basket of torches.

The main guide steps forward. "Stop," he says dramatically. "This is the Empire of Death." He introduces us to the Catacombs. There's a litany of cautions: *stay together, no loud noises, walk exactly where we do.* He shines a powerful lamp into the recess. A long tunnel unfolds. The light spills and wavers over a wet mass of yellow bones.

"Four hundred miles of tunnels," says Chad reverently.

I shiver.

"You don't have to go in," he says quietly. "You could wait on the bus."

You turn. "Nonsense," you say. "Full of *pluck*, aren't you, Leonie? An intrepid little adventuress?"

I don't reply. I pick up a torch from the basket, switch it on. The guide continues to talk. I play my torch-beam over a section of wall. A skull glitters. I touch it surreptitiously. It's gritty and slimy all at once, like half-melted salt.

"Limestone deposits." Your voice, close to me. I jump. "Fascinating, isn't it."

I tug my cardigan close to my body.

Your face, lit from underneath, is wolfish. "And the main event is yet to come."

We walk on. It's colder now. The bones are omnipresent, jumbled in heaps. Here and there, there's some kind of order. A mound of skulls. A nest of thighbones. The sheer number makes my head hurt. My sore throat throbs.

The guide halts. "Please pause," he says. "We have come now to a large complex of caves, unearthed during the recent excavation." He swings his torch around. The wall gives way to a succession of shadowy recesses.

Murmurs from the group.

The guide raises his hand. "We will only go inside one of the chambers," he says. "The structural integrity of the others has not been determined. Please follow me very precisely."

We shuffle behind him. I splash in an unseen puddle, swear quietly. The darkness extends softly upwards. Excited conversations break out; criss-crossing torch beams reveal a high ceiling, stippled with gleaming stalactites. We stand in a huddle.

"What have these caves been used for?" asks the folklore professor. She scribbles in a tiny notebook.

"Recently?" The guide shrugs. "Many things. Young people use the Catacombs to meet in. Sometimes to show films. Sometimes to have rave parties."

She looks up. "And before that?"

"We have yet to find a definitive answer." His torch catches a line of guttered wax candles, a startling purple against the rough grey limestone.

"Some weird stuff, I'd say." Chad examines the wall section nearest us, moving his torch beam slowly across the glistening walls. "There's some kind of writing here." Small lettering in a faded red.

"Yes." Your breath is warm on my cheek. "Potentially evidence of ritual practice." I hunch my shoulders. The hangover has kicked in again. I feel wretched. I want to go back to the warmth of the bus. If Tommi were here, she wouldn't hesitate.

"Intriguing," says the folklore professor, still writing busily.

You play your torch on the wall, start to recite slowly.

"Ah," says Chad. "Latin."

I'm jammed between you both.

Above us, a distant metal clang. "A truck," says the tour guide. "Hitting a manhole cover." I feel it all then. How far we are below. Surrounded by the dead. Sweat prickles on my forehead. I want to leave. I shouldn't leave.

Tommi's voice in my head: *Be yourself.*

Close beside me, you cough. A fine mist of spray hits my cheek. My stomach roils in revulsion.

"Apologies, my dear." You grip my arm firmly, continue reading aloud. I twist away.

"I'm sorry." My voice is rough, desperate. "I need to get out."

★ ★ ★

I'm the only person to wimp out on the tour of the Catacombs. I don't care. The bus is safe and warm and blasting dreadful French pop music. The bus driver is content to stand outside, smoking, and ignoring me.

My oesophagus is raw. *Stupid Gauloises.* I'm still cold. I shut off as many air-con nozzles as I can, rub my throat tenderly. Now my ears hurt too.

I imagine the waxy bones exuding tiny spores of disease, feel nauseated.

"Ah, you survived," says Chad cheerily, climbing on board.

"Yeah." I'm a bit sheepish. "Got a bit of agoraphobia there for a minute, I reckon." I clear my throat, cough slightly. "And I'm coming down with a bit of a cold too."

"I hope you feel better in the morning." Chad's kind face is concerned.

"Don't worry." You swing yourself onto the bus, smiling broadly at us both. "A good night's sleep and I'm sure we'll all feel much more ourselves."

★   ★   ★

What the hell? My head hurts. Everything hurts.

I slide my hand under the pillow. No phone. My bag? I stumble out of bed, hit an unexpected chair.

I bend over to rub my knee. The action makes me wheeze, hack, cough.

This isn't good. I've definitely caught something from the dank Catacombs. Still coughing, I move to push open the bathroom door. My arm slams against the wall.

"Ow!" I snatch my arm back, whirl around. The bathroom is on the opposite wall, a ring of light clearly visible around the doorframe. *What the hell?*

I grab around in the darkness, pull at the soft velvet mass of curtains. They jerk back in my hand. The city floods the room. But it's not the busy boulevard. This is the inner courtyard, the ornamental trees gilded with early sunlight.

Where am I?

This isn't my room. How the *fuck* did I end up here? My heart thuds hard in my ears. I put a hand to the doorknob, patting myself down to make sure I'm decent –

Instead of the jersey of my T-shirt, I pat soft, expensive flannel.

I open my mouth, but all that comes out is a tiny, airless croak.

Who's done this to me?

I struggle with the stiff handle, wrench it savagely. The door lurches open.

"Professor?" A voice, startled.

It's…

It's *me*.

This time there's no mistaking it. It's not the girl at the café with the wrong face. It's not the girl at the bar who drank my absinthe. No.

It's me.

"This isn't right." My words are swallowed by a bout of coughing. I clap my hand to my mouth, withdraw it. Stare. My hand. Wrinkled, mottled with brown spots. A flash of gold signet ring.

It's not me.

Somehow, impossibly, it's *you*.

"Good morning, professor," you say. Your lipstick is crooked, inexpertly applied.

A phone rings. Mine.

I slide a hand into my pocket looking for it. You pull it out of yours, a magic trick.

"Sorry, professor." You wink at me, hold up a finger. "Ah. *Tommi.*"

Your eyes on mine. That hard gleam. A slow smile that peels back over your teeth. "No, I can't wait to see you either."

★ ★ ★

"You can't do this." My voice is rough, desperate. *"I'll tell everyone."*

You laugh. Shrug.

"Which of us do you think they'll believe?"

ENTER, KILL, EXIT
Tim Waggoner

Someone's at the front door.

Julie was sitting upright in bed, surrounded by darkness, heart pounding, cold sweat beading her brow. She had no memory of waking, no memory of coming to bed, but she was up now – *Thanks, adrenaline* – and she held her breath and listened. Seconds-minutes-hours passed, bringing only silence. She'd decided that she must've been dreaming, but then she heard it again, the meaty sound of a fist pounding on the front door, three times, *hard*.

Thud-thud-THUD!

When she'd been a child and thought she'd heard something during the night, she'd grab her pillow, press it against her ears, then wriggle beneath the covers and hide until she fell back to sleep or the sun rose, whichever came first. But she was an adult – and nearly a middle-aged one, at that – and she lived alone. There was no one else to go investigate.

You don't have to do this. Who gives a shit how old you are? If you wanna hide, hide!

But she knew if she didn't check out the noise, she'd lie here afraid all night, and she'd stay afraid all day tomorrow, and *still* be afraid when night came again. *A coward dies a thousand deaths...*

Yeah, but she didn't want to die *any* deaths.

Still, she tossed back the covers and rose. She wore only a tank top and underwear, and the cool air in her bedroom raised gooseflesh on her skin. She liked to keep the temperature low when she slept, but she regretted that now. She wished she had her robe, but she couldn't remember the last time she'd worn it, and she didn't want to take the time to dig through her closet. She did, however, grab her phone off the nightstand and pick up the baseball bat she kept propped up in the corner. She didn't own a gun, had heard many times on the true-crime

TV programmes she was addicted to that most homeowners' guns were used against them during a home invasion, and she didn't want to risk that happening. It never occurred to her that an invader could snatch the bat from her hand and club her to death with it.

She quickly checked the time on her phone. 3:17 a.m.

Should she call 911 before leaving the bedroom? It would be the smart thing to do, but she'd already called twice this month, both times false alarms, and she feared the police were beginning to think she was a kook. Who was she kidding? They *definitely* thought that. If she called, and the police came and found nothing, they'd probably put her on a Do Not Respond list, and then when she *really* needed them, they wouldn't show up. She should at least verify there was an actual threat before she called.

Shouldn't she?

She opened her bedroom door and stepped into the hallway.

★ ★ ★

Seven months ago, she got a text from her brother Daryl while she was at work: *Check out AFTER THE MURDER on CrimeTV – they did an episode on Angie!!!!!*

Julie had been on her lunch hour at the bank when she read the message, and when she was finished, she felt a wave of dizziness coupled with intense nausea. She'd hurried to the women's room, sure she was going to vomit, but by the time she got there, the nausea had already started to subside. She splashed cold water on her face and returned to the break room, grateful she'd taken a late lunch and been eating alone. No one to ask her if anything was wrong, no one to explain to. She no longer had an appetite, so she tossed her Caesar salad in the trash.

Daryl was a true-crime *enthusiast*, to use his term, and CrimeTV was his favourite channel. She'd never understood the attraction those kinds of programmes held for him. As far as she was concerned, a steady diet of mini documentaries about murder, torture, rape and abduction warped a person's point of view, made them think the world was full of serial killers and sadists, that a long, painful death by mutilation, strangulation or immolation was not only inevitable but could occur at any moment. Sure, terrible things happened – she couldn't deny that – but she preferred to focus on the positive parts of life whenever she could. It was more psychologically healthy. Plus, she didn't want to remember... *that*.

She decided to forget about Daryl's text, but as soon as she got home that evening, she turned on the television, found *After the Murder* on CrimeTV and searched for the episode about Angie. It wasn't hard to find. It was in Season Two and titled 'Enter, Kill, Exit'. She selected it, but before she could hit play, nausea struck her again, and she hurried to the bathroom. This time she did throw up, and afterward she remained sitting on the floor next to the toilet, trembling. It took forty minutes for her to feel well enough to return to the living room and begin the programme.

As the story unfolded, she had the strange sense that she was falling backward in time. Angie Ingils had been in the same second grade class as Julie, and while they'd talked sometimes, and occasionally sat next to each other in the lunchroom, they hadn't been best friends. If they had, the producers of *After the Murder* would've likely tried to interview her for this episode. Thank Christ they hadn't.

Every summer Angie's family left town for their annual two-week vacation. They rented a cabin near Lake Erie, and they spent two weeks there, doing all sorts of outdoorsy things – swimming, riding jet skis, fishing, boating, hiking, and playing board games at night. On the morning of their last full day at the lake, everyone got up for breakfast – except Angie. Her parents decided to let her sleep a little longer, but when everyone else was almost finished eating and Angie still hadn't roused herself, her mother went into her room. She found the mutilated body of her child sprawled across a blood-soaked mattress, and people renting cabins within the vicinity swore they heard her anguished scream. Police came, as well as crime-scene techs and the county coroner – along with dozens of reporters from local TV stations and newspapers – but while the investigation was thorough and lengthy, in the end no one was charged for the crime. There were plenty of suspects, of course, and people had endlessly debated whodunnit on social media, podcasts and YouTube videos ever since. Julie knew about this continued fascination with Angie's case because Daryl told her. All these years, she'd avoided looking up any information about Angie's murder on the internet, not wishing to revisit that time in her life. But here she was, watching a goddamned TV show about it. Maybe enough time had passed for her to gain the emotional distance she needed to confront her feelings about the murder. Or maybe she had a morbid streak just like her brother and had finally given in to it. Whatever the reason, she congratulated herself for managing to make it through the entire programme without having a mental breakdown.

That was the first night she'd dreamed someone was trying to break into her house.

She'd woken, terrified, and almost called 911. But she told herself it was only a bad dream and went around the house, checking to make sure the doors were all locked and that none of the windows were broken. She peered outside to see if someone was lurking in the yard, but no one was there. No one she could *see*, anyway. There were trees to hide behind, and plenty of shadows…

She didn't have the dream every night, maybe once or twice a week. Each time she'd wake and check the doors and windows, and each time she'd find nothing to be worried about. Her house was secure, and she was safe. At least, that's what she tried to tell herself. But she knew if someone *really* wanted to get inside, nothing could stop them, and because of this, she knew safety was an illusion. No one was ever truly safe, not in any situation. People just pretended they were safe so they could get through their days with their sanity more or less intact. That's what she had been doing ever since Angie had been killed. And it had worked – until she'd made the mistake of watching that goddamn TV show. She'd tried therapy and anti-anxiety meds, and they'd helped. She'd never stopped having the dream, but it had become less intense, and she didn't always wake up anymore. She didn't imagine dying in a fatal car accident on her way to the bank, didn't worry that a robber would come in and shoot her when she worked the teller's station.

But eventually the meds stopped working, and the dream grew more vivid and started coming more often. She began losing sleep and suffering panic attacks throughout the day, and she'd missed so many days of work that she was surprised she hadn't been fired yet. The dreams became so real that she started calling 911, convinced someone was outside who wanted to enter, kill, and exit. The police never found anyone, of course. But as bad as her mental state became, she had never physically heard someone trying to break in.

Until tonight.

* * *

Julie watched every episode of *After the Murder* that was streaming, and then she moved on to other CrimeTV programmes, such as *Horror in the Heartland*, *The Children are Missing*, and *Death on the Beach*. From the moment she got home to the moment she went to bed, and for an hour in the morning before she got ready for work, she watched episodes of whatever show she was into right then. She became a worse true-crime addict than her brother ever had been. And with each episode she watched, the more dangerous the world became for her.

* * *

Julie moved slowly down the dark hallway, the wood floor cold beneath her bare feet. She didn't turn on the hall light because she didn't want to alert whoever was – no, *might be* – at the door. She walked slowly so the floor panels wouldn't creak, a ridiculous precaution since anyone outside couldn't possibly hear, but she was unable to stop herself. The hallway ended at the foyer, and she stopped when she reached its threshold, unable to make herself go any further. One more step, and she'd be in the foyer, and whoever had knocked would be able to see her through the glass panes in the upper half of the door. She felt the instinctive urge of prey not to reveal itself to a predator. *If I can't see you, you can't see me.*

She held her phone in her left hand. All she had to do was tuck the bat beneath her right arm, dial 911, and wait for the police to arrive. Maybe this time they'd catch whoever was harassing her, and she'd finally – *finally* – be safe.

Safety is an illusion, remember?

Stay here, take a step forward… neither action would prevent someone from breaking in if they were truly determined to do so. And what if someone was knocking for a perfectly innocent reason? A couple years ago, her garage door opener had stopped working, and she'd been forced to park her car in the driveway until she could get the opener repaired or, if necessary, replace it. One night, a loud knocking at the front door pulled her out of a deep sleep. She'd sat up, heart pounding, listening, hoping it had been a dream. It wasn't, though, and the knocking came again, only this time a muffled voice followed.

Police!

She knew it could be a trick, but the voice had a tone of authority that made her think it was legitimate. She got out of bed, went to the front door, looked through the peephole, and sure enough, a man in a patrol officer's uniform stood on her porch. She opened the door, and the man told her that her driver's side car door was open, and that there were coins scattered across the front seat and on the driveway. Julie kept her change in one of the vehicle's cupholders, and the officer said it looked like someone – teens, probably – had tried the driver's side door, found it unlocked, saw the coins in the cupholder and started to grab them. *Something probably scared them*, the officer said. *Likely a driver came down the road, and the kids ran off before they could be spotted.* The officer then lectured her about leaving her car doors unlocked – which she had a bad habit of doing – and then he had her check the car to make sure nothing else had been stolen. It hadn't, she locked the car, and the officer wished her a good night and left.

Her car was in the garage tonight, but what if there was something else wrong? Something serious this time. What if someone needed help? A neighbour who was sick or injured, or someone who'd been driving through the neighbourhood when they ran out of gas or their engine died. It could be anyone at the door, knocking for a thousand different reasons. But these thoughts weren't what made Julie finally step into the foyer. It was the thought of how Angie had died without anyone coming to her aid. Despite how scared Julie was, she had to check. For *her*.

She walked to the door, saw the deadbolt and chain were still in place, thank Christ, and then put her eye – her *closed* eye – to the peephole. A terrible thought occurred to her: what if it was *Angie* out there? She'd been thinking about her ever since watching that episode of *After the Murder*. Maybe Julie had thought about her so much that she'd called the girl here, and now she'd finally arrived. Any other time, Julie would've laughed at such a ludicrous thought. But not tonight.

She opened her eye and looked.

The outside light illuminated an empty porch, the front walkway, and part of the lawn. There was no sign of anyone. But there were no streetlights in her neighbourhood, and not all of the houses had their porchlights on. Plenty of dark for someone to hide in... for lots of someones.

A cold draught of air kissed the back of her neck, and she realised that just because she'd thought the knocking had come from the front door didn't make it so. The kitchen entrance was on the opposite side of the foyer, and that's where the back door was located. If it was open, a breeze could pass through the kitchen, into the foyer, and reach her. Panic gripped her, and she almost unlocked the front door, threw it open, and dashed out into the night. What stopped her was the thought of the darkness out there and all the things it might be concealing. At least in here there was light. She'd be able to see what came at her, would be able to defend herself, or find a place to hide. That was better... wasn't it?

She turned away from the front door, crossed to the kitchen entrance, stepped inside, and using her phone as an extension of her hand, flipped the wall switch. Bright light flooded the kitchen, dazzling her eyes, and for a second she couldn't see anything. This was it – the moment when the attack would occur. She let her phone drop to the floor, took hold of her bat with both hands, and started swinging wildly.

"Come on, motherfucker!" she shouted.

The bat passed back and forth through empty air, and when her eyes adjusted to the light, she saw the kitchen – like the front porch – was empty. She stopped swinging the bat, but she didn't lower it. The air in here was definitely cooler than it should be, and she felt air moving over and around her body. Gripping the bat so tight her knuckles ached, Julie walked further into the kitchen, past the refrigerator, then turned left when she reached the stove. She faced the back door now – and it was wide open. The backyard was enclosed by a wooden fence, and she'd put a padlock on the gate after the first time the dream had woken her in the middle of the night. But it wouldn't be hard for someone to climb over the fence if they wanted to.

She took her right hand off the bat and flipped on the patio light. The bulb wasn't any stronger than the one in the front porch light, but it was enough to show her that no one stood in the backyard. But that was no reassurance. She knew she hadn't left the back door unlocked before going to bed.

Maybe you were sleepwalking and opened the door for some reason, she thought.

She had no history of sleepwalking, so why would she start now, in her late thirties? Stress maybe? She supposed it was possible, but it didn't seem likely. That meant someone – maybe more than one – was already inside the house. But then why didn't whoever it was close the door behind them after they'd entered? To leave themselves a quick getaway? To scare her? If it was the latter, then mission fucking accomplished. She reached out to close the door, then hesitated. What if *she* needed to get out of the house fast? She thought she'd be able to climb the fence, especially with adrenaline surging through her body, but even if she couldn't, she knew the combination to the gate padlock and could open it quickly.

She lowered her hand and walked over to where she'd dropped her phone and picked it up. Fuck this noise. Time to call the cops. She input 911, held the phone to her ear, and waited. One ring, two, three… She heard a *click* as the call was answered, and she waited to hear *Nine-one-one, what's your emergency?* But that wasn't what the person on the other end said.

"*Julie? Are you there?*"

Her breath caught in her throat. This wasn't the bland, slightly bored voice of a 911 operator. It wasn't even the voice of an adult. It was a child's voice, a young girl's to be precise.

"*It's so lonely here. Please come visit me…*"

"You're not her!" Julie shouted, then hurled the phone at the refrigerator. The device dented the metal door when it hit, then fell to the floor, case cracked, screen shattered.

"*Come on, Julie. Pleeeeeeeeaaaaasssssse…*"

Julie dropped the bat, ran to a counter, and pulled a knife from the butcher block next to the stove. She then ran back to the phone, fell on her knees, and began stabbing the screen.

"Shut up, shut up, shut up, shut up, shut up!"

Glass shards flew into the air, and Julie kept stabbing, stabbing. At one point, her hand slipped, and she sliced her palm on the knife's edge. A bright flare of pain, and then blood pattered onto the broken phone like crimson rain. Julie didn't care that she was hurt. She grabbed the knife with her left hand and continued stabbing the phone.

"I hate you!" she screamed. "Hate-hate-hate-*hate*!"

In her mind, she saw Angie lying on a bed. She stood next to her, bringing the blade down in one vicious arc after another, ravaging the girl's flesh, blood flying everywhere – onto her clothes, hands, face... It was so *warm*. Angie's mouth was open wide, as if she was trying to scream, but no sound came out. The first thing Julie did after entering the room and closing the door quietly behind her was stab Angie in the throat so she couldn't make any noise. After all, she didn't want to wake Angie's family. They'd had so much fun on their vacation, and surely, they must be exhausted by this point. Plus, they were heading home tomorrow. They needed their sleep.

Everyone in their class *loved* Angie, even the teacher. They always smiled when they looked at her, and whenever she spoke, they listened intently, as if every word out of her mouth was a precious pearl of wisdom. They *oohed* and *ahhed* whenever she held up a drawing she'd done, and when the teacher called on her, which was often, Angie always had the right answer.

I wish I had an entire classroom of students like you, the teacher would say, and Angie's cheeks would redden with adorable embarrassment.

At first, Julie had loved her, too. But whenever she'd tried to talk to Angie, the girl's sweet disposition turned sour.

Leave me alone. I don't want to catch any of your Julie-cooties!

The other kids would laugh, and once after Angie said this during class, Julie had caught the teacher trying not to smile.

When April came around, Julie began talking to her parents, telling them how Angie's family always rented a cabin at Lake Erie every summer, and how much she wanted to do the same. Her birthday was in May, and the only present she wanted was to go to Lake Erie. Eventually, her parents gave in. Their cabin wasn't super close to Angie's, but it was close enough for Julie to pay a visit late one night.

Near the end of the school year, Angie couldn't stop talking about the trip. One detail in particular had caught Julie's attention.

"It's so nice at the lake. Mommy leaves the cabin door unlocked at night because Daddy and Grandpa like to go fishing late. 'That's when they're really biting,' Daddy says."

Julie washed off the blood at the edge of the lake, then she went to the hollow log where she'd left a clean T-shirt and shorts. She removed her bloody clothes, put on her fresh ones, then stuffed the stained ones into the log, and returned to her family's cabin. She was back in bed before sunrise.

"*Can you believe we were at the lake the same time Angie was killed?*" Daryl had said when he'd called to ask her what she'd thought of 'Enter, Kill, Exit.' "*It's so damn creepy... I mean, that could've been us.*"

Julie stood in the kitchen, breathing hard, skin slick with sweat, blood streaming from her palm. She looked at the scattered pieces of what had been her phone.

"I never should've watched that fucking video," she said. "It was easier when I could pretend I didn't remember."

She let the knife drop to the floor, and left the kitchen, leaving a trail of blood behind her. Good thing she hadn't cut herself that night in Angie's cabin. Otherwise, the police might've been able to track her.

She walked down the hall to her bedroom – except it wasn't hers anymore, was it – looked inside, and gazed upon a blood-soaked tableau that she hadn't seen for nearly thirty years. She could feel Angie's gaze on her, even though the girl no longer had eyes. Julie remained like that for some time, then left, gently closing the door behind her.

She headed to the foyer, unlocked the front door, opened it, stepped onto the porch. She didn't bother closing the door behind her. She didn't think she'd be coming back. The night air was cold on her skin, and the porch's concrete felt like ice beneath her bare feet. She began shivering, but as she looked at the dark expanse that stretched out before her – no porchlights anywhere, no silhouettes of trees against the night sky, no moon, no stars – she knew the cold wasn't the only reason she trembled. She was about to step off the porch when she heard a sound behind her, the soft *plap-plap-plap* of small feet walking on tile.

Small wet feet.

A moment later, she felt slick, sticky fingers grasp her injured hand.

"Ready?" Angie asked.

Julie expected to hear anger or satisfaction in the girl's voice, and there was some of both. But there was also sympathy and understanding.

Tears sliding down her face, Julie smiled, nodded, and together they walked into the dark.

AT BLACK ROCK BEACH
Gary McMahon

Outside, a dry heat nestled between mountains, and a muted sense of the unseen ocean extended towards a distant horizon. The sky stretched above them like a pale blue canvas. The sound of cicadas. The smell of the hot air. Dry grass. Pitiless sunshine.

Inside the car, the silence was heavy with so many things that had not been said, had never been said. Unspoken words gathered like cobwebs along the edges of the windows, on the backs of the seats, and among the empty drink cans and crisp packets littering the footwell.

Dave felt as if he were holding his breath as he steered the rented Nissan around yet another tight bend in the narrow mountainside road. Beside him, Hannah stared straight ahead, her sweaty face unreadable. In the back seat, Terry sat in a sullen teenage fug; he hadn't spoken since Hannah had pulled him up on his bad language about half a mile back, when the car had juddered into a pothole in the road.

The sun was hot on the skin of Dave's arm through the open driver's side window but he didn't move. It felt as if to do so might disturb something, like a small, heavy object dropped into a still pool of water. He continued driving in silence, the only noticeable movement that of his hands on the wheel, then his hand reaching to change down a gear as he navigated yet another hairpin bend.

"This damn road," said Hannah, breaking the spell. "It's crazy. I mean, what would we do if someone was coming the other way? There hasn't been a passing point at all."

Dave shook his head. "I don't know, but it's scary. I kind of wish we hadn't started along this route."

Terry sighed heavily, theatrically. Dave resisted the urge to respond; anger would only make things worse, just as the mood seemed to be lifting a little.

"My phone says we aren't far from the beach, but since when do beaches exist up mountains?"

"There's a track leading down to a cove," said Terry, softly. "The website said."

"Well, let's hope we see a sign soon," said Dave, before Hannah had the chance to respond.

"It is beautiful," she said, as if she were ignoring Terry's mopey interjection. "That view... spectacular."

"Greece is a beautiful place." Dave dropped down to second gear yet again as the car began to struggle up a particularly steep section of road. "Really gorgeous."

A tense silence enveloped them. Dave kept his focus on the road and was barely aware of Hannah at his side, the way she kept shifting in her seat, the occasional heavy sigh. He wished she would just relax; she never seemed to be able to shake off her anxieties and simply live in the moment.

"There!" Terry leaned forward in the back seat, pressing against the headrest.

"I see it," said Dave. There was a small sign attached to a crooked post at the side of the road. English words were daubed onto the rough wooden crossbar in flaking black paint, with an arrow indicating a left turn: *Black Rock Beach 1km*.

He almost missed the turning. It was a narrow track between two high boulders. He slowed the car, indicated despite there being nobody behind him, and eased into the steep bend.

The road was surfaced with loosely-packed hardcore. No Tarmac. He followed it upwards, keeping his speed down, and tried to act as if he wasn't nervous.

Near the top of the rise, the road turned sharply to the right and descended at a steep gradient. Another sign told him he was going the right way.

"Nearly there," said Terry, sounding excited.

Hannah sighed again, but said nothing.

The sun beat down upon the car, baking them like potatoes wrapped in tin foil. The windows were open and the air conditioning didn't work. For a moment, Dave felt as if he was on the verge of some kind of rage – and if he allowed it to take control, he might never come back from it. Just as suddenly, the moment passed; he felt calm again, but weirdly close to tears.

The road could best be described as a track. It was narrow and the surface was loose; Dave kept his speed low in case the wheels skidded. Each verge was a rock ledge, and beyond these were more rocks, with gorse and small bushes growing between. The gradient was such that as he looked ahead, he could see the ocean spread out somewhere far below them.

As the road wound down the mountain towards the sea, the landscape began to change. Trees appeared, and large grassy areas. The remains of a stone dwelling surrounded by windblown olive trees. The terrain was still rocky but it was less unwelcoming than before, higher up the mountain.

"Pull in here," said Terry. "Please... the view."

On a particularly tight bend, there was a flattened parking spot right at the cliff edge. Dave turned onto the compacted dirt and stopped the car close to the edge. The sea glittered; the sky was so blue that it made him long for something he didn't quite understand.

"Thanks, Dad!" Terry opened the door and rushed outside.

"Be careful..." Hannah fumbled at the lock, trying to open her door. "I'm coming too."

Dave switched off the engine. The car door slammed. It felt like a sign, or a signal – some kind of warning, perhaps. He sat in silence, watching his family as they edged towards the sheer drop. Terry had his phone out, pointing it towards the horizon, taking snapshots of the glorious view.

I could easily drive off, thought Dave. *Drive off and leave them here. Never see them again.*

The thought disturbed him. He wasn't sure where it had come from and he didn't want it inside his head. He swallowed hard, opened the door, and stepped out onto the dry, hard dirt, adjusting his olive-green baseball cap.

"Come and see," said Terry, smiling. "It's amazing."

He walked over and stood beside Hannah. He thought about putting his arm around her waist but didn't even try. Staring out to sea, beyond the sharp rocks that poked through the waves directly below them, and over the top of the taller, tower-like edifice that stood proud of the water like an ancient ossified sentinel, he wondered, not for the first time, what they were doing here in this ancient land, invaders on an island that didn't want them here.

Back in the car, they headed down towards the hidden beach. Cars began to appear at the side of the road, parked tight up against the rocks. Soon there were more of them, standing empty and huddled together like scared animals.

Dave found a spot and pulled in.

"Oh," said Terry. "There isn't a beach after all. Not really."

The cars were all parked above an area where a set of wide steps was carved into the bare rock face. The steps led down to a sort of natural landing area consisting of flat black rocks, where some people were lounging on towels and others were diving into the narrow sea inlet that resembled a fjord. They dove in, then climbed back out using the rusty ladders bolted to the side of the rock at sea level. They were so far below that Dave couldn't hear them. They moved like characters in a silent film.

"No," said Dave. "Not a real beach. Just more rocks."

"Black Rock Beach," said Hannah. "I suppose the clue was in the name."

"I'm going for a hike." Terry was already moving away, shrugging on his rucksack. "I won't be gone long. Be back in, say, an hour."

The road led upwards, of course, into the mountains. It became even narrower as it climbed, turning into more of a footpath than a road. It looked safe enough, if he stayed on the path.

"Be careful," said Dave. "Do you have any water?"

"I won't need it. Won't be gone that long."

"Here." He threw his water bottle and Terry caught it deftly in one hand.

"Ta. See ya."

Hannah nudged him with her elbow. "He can't go off on his own."

"He's eighteen. An adult. If he's careful, there's nothing to worry about." Then why was his stomach tying itself in knots? Why was he obscurely afraid?

Hannah turned away. "I'll sit in the car and read. It's too bright out here."

Dave felt trapped between them: his son, trudging up the mountain track towards the unknown and the unknowable; his wife, retreating to the safety of the vehicle.

"Okay," he said to nobody, or to both. "An hour!" he shouted at Terry's back. The boy raised a hand but didn't look back. He kept on walking, taking long, even strides. "I mean it!"

Dave kept watching until his son had turned a corner and vanished from sight. Even then, he found it difficult to look away.

He walked slowly back to the car. Up close, he noticed the bugs squashed on the windscreen and the light layer of dust on the bodywork. Hannah was sitting in the back seat wearing a white baseball cap. She had on her reading glasses and was staring at a paperback novel – one of several she'd brought with her.

"He'll be okay," said Dave. "Won't he?"

She turned to look at him, peering over her glasses. "You'd better hope so." Then she returned her attention to the book.

What if he didn't come back? Would it really be so bad? They could forget he'd ever existed and start again, just the two of them...

Dave leaned against the car, looking up at the sky, feeling guilty about his own thoughts – they felt like they belonged to someone else. There were no clouds. The sun was high and hot and bright in his eyes. He opened the door and took his sunglasses from the glove compartment. Even wearing them, he was unable to look directly at the sun.

He retraced their path along the road and approached the edge of the precipice, looking down again at the swimmers and the sunbathers. Miniature beings splashing in the water, basking in the afternoon sun, laughing, having fun. It unnerved him that the sound didn't carry; again, he was reminded of silent films he'd seen on TV in his youth. He stood there for a long time, simply watching them. He wished that someone might notice him there, perhaps wave at him. Do something to validate his presence here. Not one of them paid him any attention.

Turning away, he glanced at the car. The sun was shining on the smeary windscreen, blurring his vision. He couldn't make out Hannah but he knew she was still in the back of the car, reading – or pretending to. He thought about talking to her, speaking about the things that were swirling around in his mind. The unnamed thoughts. The dark undercurrents. Asking her what they were supposed to do with this life that frequently made them all so unhappy.

But, no. He could never do that. They didn't have that kind of relationship. They'd never discussed their inner lives, only shared what was on the surface of things.

He checked his watch: Terry had been gone for twenty minutes. Ten more, and he should be turning around to return to the car. He wished he'd spoken up and gone with the boy. It could have been an opportunity for them to bond. A slow walk in the heat, a long chat about football, college, Terry's thoughts about the future.

"*Damn*," he said, quietly. "*You idiot.*"

Dave had spent his entire life either acting too late or not acting at all, missing out on everything because of his emotional impotency. He wished he could be different, like other people he knew. He wished he could be a proper person. Then his family might be happy, their lives filled with sunshine – like the endless bright skies here, on this exquisite Greek island.

He walked back to the car and opened the front passenger door. Fumbling, he grabbed the other water bottle from the footwell. It was warm. He took off the lid and took a large gulp, wincing slightly at the metallic taste.

Hannah was no longer reading. She was leaning back on the seat with her baseball cap pulled down over her eyes. She must have dozed off in the heat. Perhaps the novel was boring. He watched as her chest rose and fell. Her breasts were saggy beneath the thin T-shirt. Her arms were fleshy these days; she hadn't been to the gym in years. He looked down at the beer belly hanging over the top of his shorts and smiled. *Yeah, right. Mr. Adonis.*

When he looked back at Hannah the cap had slipped and her eyes were open. She was staring at him.

"Want a drink?" He raised the plastic bottle and waggled it.

She shook her head. "What time is it?" Blinking at the sun, she adjusted her cap.

"Two o'clock."

"Is Terry back?"

"No, he'll be another half hour, if he sticks with what he said."

She shuffled on the seat, trying to get more comfortable. Wincing, she massaged the side of her neck with her fingers. "I'm not sure I like the fact that he's gone off on his own. Why didn't you go with him?"

He managed to stop the sigh before it manifested. "I don't know. I think he wanted some time alone."

"It might be dangerous..." She turned her head and looked out of the rear window. "Up there."

"He'll be fine. He's a sensible lad. I've not seen a single car either go up there or come down. He'll be trudging along sweating, wishing he'd brought more water with him."

"That's right," she said. "He doesn't have enough water... What was he thinking?"

"It's okay. That bottle I gave him was full. If he isn't back in half an hour I'll go up after him." He looked at his watch. "Twenty minutes, now."

That seemed to relax her a little; she slumped back in the seat and began to stretch. "I'm tired. I'm always tired."

He didn't know what she wanted him to say. "I know..." It wasn't enough. It was never enough.

She glared at him, lips tightening, eyes slitted like those of a cat. "I'm going to finish reading my book," she said, her tone cold and hostile.

Dave waited for a moment, then he slammed the car door and stalked away. He sat down on a large rock at the side of the road, drinking sun-warmed water and wishing he had a cool pint of beer instead. Once again, he hadn't reacted in the way he thought he should. He never knew how to counter Hannah's hostility, her passive aggressiveness. It made him feel small and powerless and less of a man.

He looked at his watch again. He'd give it another ten minutes, and then he'd follow Terry up the hill.

When Terry was a baby, he suffered from fits, seizures, strange episodes where he went completely stiff and unresponsive, apart from his eyes. While his body was as rigid as a length of timber, his eyes remained expressive – panicked, staring, looking around as if he were desperately trying to understand where he was and what was happening. The episodes didn't last long: just under six weeks, but it was the most terrifying period of their lives.

He knew that Hannah still worried in case there'd been some kind of hidden lasting impact on their son's health, or that the seizures might start up again. As for Dave, he feared other things, things that he could not even name. Those moments when his infant son was suffering, and he was unable to do anything to help him, had scarred him; and those scars, he knew, would never heal.

He wasn't sure why he was thinking about this now. There was no reason to dwell on the past. The present and the future were what was important now.

He checked his watch. Terry had now been gone for over an hour. Panic rose within him but he bit it down, trying to remain calm. He was a teenager, and they were always forgetting the time.

He stood and walked back to the car. The window was still open; Hannah was looking at her book but he could tell she wasn't reading.

"I'll go and look for him," he said.

She nodded. "Good." Her eyes didn't stray from the page.

Dave walked away, feeling a combination of regret and despondency. She always stirred within him emotions he struggled to express, even to himself. Had it always been this way, or had there been a time in their marriage when they'd communicated without such strange nuances? When he tried, he found that he was unable to remember the people they'd been when they first met, or as they'd embarked upon a life together.

The sun was hotter than before. He felt it burning the back of his neck as he trudged up the road. Adjusting his baseball cap, he leaned into the slope, trying to push himself forward.

He's probably on his way back now, he thought. *I'll meet him halfway.*

Looking to his right, he gazed out over the drop and the silvered waters below. The distant horizon looked razor sharp, a knife's edge. A vague terror flipped in his belly, like a fish caught on a line.

On either side of the road, the terrain was dangerous. To his right, the steep, rocky drop-off to the sea; to his left, a landscape of jagged boulders and sharp gorse-like growth. The land was dry, parched; it looked hard and unforgiving. He trusted that his son was sensible enough not to have strayed off the narrow road. He didn't want to entertain thoughts of seeing the red smear of his body smashed on the rocks below.

He was breathing hard now. Never a fit man, his body was ageing and his stamina was poor. What Hannah always called his "gammy foot" often flared up with pain. Ten years ago, he'd run the hundred metres in Terry's school sports day, despite the old injury that had healed badly and made one foot turn slightly inwards. These days, he struggled to run a bath. He smiled at his joke, then felt silly for doing so. Pushing himself onward, he tried not to slacken off his pace.

Looking over his shoulder, he realised that he'd covered a lot more ground than he'd thought. He could no longer see the car or the roadside parking spots beyond what was a long curve in the road, and he'd climbed quite a bit without realising. Now that he'd controlled his breathing, he felt good, as if the walking was opening his lungs and allowing his body to stretch out in a way that it hadn't done in years.

He paused, looked up at the bright sky, and then ahead, at the climb. He raised his hands and cupped them around his mouth, like he'd seen people do in movies, and shouted: "*Terry!*"

His voice echoed but not as much as he'd expected. Just a slight bounce; and then it returned to him flat and lifeless.

He pushed on, climbing, always climbing. Moving towards some distant and unachievable goal. The metaphor was not lost on him and he felt his life crumbling at the edges. What was it all for, this endless forward motion? Get married, have a kid you never wanted, buy a house you can't afford, fight for promotions that never seem to satisfy you. It was pointless, a game that he wished he hadn't started to play…

Where is that boy?

Surely, he should have encountered Terry by now, coming the other way? There was no sign of him. Ahead, the road was straight now: a long, unwavering climb to some unspecified peak. He could see so far ahead, in fact, that if Terry had turned back, Dave should be able to see him, even if he was just a small smudge on the landscape.

The panic welled up again, a wave, a surge. He tried to push it back down but it was stronger than ever. Memories of baby Terry's fits, his staring, accusing eyes. The way his arms and legs had felt so hard it was as if the blood had turned to solid ice in his veins.

"Terry…" he didn't even shout. Not this time. "Where are you, son?"

He walked for another twenty minutes. That meant Terry had been gone for an hour and a half. It seemed impossible that they had not met on the road; it made no sense. The boy had his faults – they all did – but he was usually reliable because he knew how much his mother worried.

Decision time: should he continue (and if he did, for how long?), or should he call it quits and turn back, hoping that somehow Terry had found an alternative way down – some hidden track or dry gulley to follow?

He chose the latter, purely because it was so hot and he was so tired and the sweat was blinding him. He turned around and headed downhill at a slightly faster pace, trying to convince himself that they'd somehow missed each other and Terry was sitting in the car with his mother, both laughing at Dave's wasted efforts.

One foot in front of the other, a fast march. Breathing heavily. Sweating bullets. Legs aching, arms slack, feet slapping on the dry road and making a sound like raw meat dropping onto a slaughterhouse floor. For the first time he noticed the silence. It was total, like a pressure inside his head. There were no birds in the sky. The clouds were motionless, like a photograph. When he glanced down at the oddly still sea, the small figures were frozen in place. Everything around him was static: nothing moved. He felt trapped in a frozen moment.

His vision began to blur; there was a strange tingling behind his eyes. He stumbled, his old injury causing him to lose his footing. He didn't fall but he took several staggering steps before bringing his legs under control.

He stood there, feeling empty and bewildered. This place seemed different somehow, as if something had shifted… But now the clouds were moving again, and a single bird wheeled across the sky above him. He could hear the world again as the air rushed back into his ears. He started moving, wanting to get back, to return to the reality of the car, his family, the promise of a cold drink at a bar somewhere.

Before long he reached the bend in the road. He knew that once he made it around the long curve, and the cars came into view, he'd see Terry approaching the spot where they'd parked… his son, his boy, the person he now realised that he'd blamed for so long for holding him back in life.

There… up ahead. There he was.

But it wasn't a single person: there were two of them. Roughly a quarter of a mile ahead of him, a couple of figures were strolling towards the car. He recognised his son's narrow shoulders and pale legs, the silly bucket hat he'd been wearing all holiday, his creased football shirt. The other figure was familiar too, but in a way that his mind fought to deny. A man of average height, wearing a light green polo shirt, khaki shorts, and a sweaty olive-green baseball cap. His awkward gait. The way his left foot was turned slightly inwards from a childhood accident. The two were talking. There was an easy familiarity between them, as if they belonged together.

"Terry!" His voice was strained but they must have heard him.

The figures did not respond.

The rear door of the car opened and Hannah climbed out. She was bound to react – surely, she'd send the other away and protect their son?

But, no: she was smiling. It was the kind of smile she'd saved for Dave, many years ago, before the rot set in.

Hannah approached the strange man and threw her arms around him. She was laughing. He was laughing. The three of them were laughing. The stationary sun beat down upon Dave's face; his eyes were streaming; his throat was dry and ragged. He tried to call out again but nothing came.

He started to run, at least as fast as his tired legs would carry him.

The man got into the driver's seat. Hannah sat next to him, brushing something from his shoulder with the back of her hand. Terry slid onto the back seat. The windows were all open. As he drew closer, ever closer to the car, the engine started up and the wheels spat gravel as they spun on the road surface. Music from the radio. Laughter.

The man behind the wheel turned his head and leaned slightly out of the window. He smiled. Waved a thin hand. Unable to help himself, Dave smiled back at the man whose features he still refused to process.

He stopped running. Fell to his knees in the dust and the dirt. Watched in mute horror mingled with acute sadness as the car pulled slowly away, negotiated the tight bend, and set off back down the mountain road: to the small villa, perhaps a meal out, drinks, an ice cream, then back to the villa and to bed, where this man might make love to his wife as their son slept peacefully in the bedroom down the hall.

The car was gone. He could no longer hear the engine, or the radio. All he heard was the static inside his head; a low, flat hissing, behind which lay a truth he did not want to face.

Standing on the cliff edge under a picture-book sun, he thought about the life that used to be his and the place where he'd once thought he belonged. It all seemed such a long, long way from here.

PIGLET
Priya Sharma

Piglet was tall for sixteen. He wore Blouchon's cast-off jeans, which were ill-fitting, and work boots. His jersey was stained at the armpits, and his hair, which he cut himself, made an unflattering frame for his face. His short nose was upturned, revealing too much nostril. Piglet's lips disappeared when he grimaced.

He'd worked on Blouchon's farm since he was eight. He'd arrived in a truckload of pigs, travelling from Dieppe. He remembered the noise and the press of their bodies, like the journey with his mother when they'd escaped Britain, packed in with the others in the dark. He had to be prised from her cold body when the lorry had been opened, somewhere outside the port. He saw the distant harbour lights briefly before he was put in the boot of a car, and then the truck.

Blouchon sighed heavily when he saw Piglet. "What am I supposed to do with this one?"

"Louis thought you could use an extra pair of hands."

"Tell my brother not to do me any favours in future. I need larger hands than these."

"We can't take him back."

"Put him in there then." Blouchon pointed to one of the outbuildings. There was an old mattress on the floor with a blanket on it, and a sink in the corner.

The men stood talking about the pigs, Blouchon leaning against the doorframe, looking in. Piglet sat on the mattress, staring at a spider crawling across the wall.

"Tell my brother if this particular piglet doesn't work out, I'll fatten him up and send him off with the others to be slaughtered."

Piglet's eyes widened and Blouchon chuckled. He switched to English. "You understand French. Who taught you?"

"My mother."

"Can you read and write?"

"No." The schools closed just before the second English Civil War.

"Good. Remember that I'm not stupid, like these fools, so watch yourself."

★ ★ ★

Piglet gained lean bulk from carting pig feed about. He marked time by the animals coming and going. The sound of the piglets' squeals from the back of the truck brought bile to his throat.

He cared for them in the vast barn until they were in their prime. Their pinkness was thrilling. It was a similar shade to the small plastic doll he'd found in one of the old sheds. It was naked, one of its blue eyes worn away. Its rubbery bumps and curves, and the pale nylon hair, made him feel strange when he ran his fingers over them. It confused him. The last woman he'd seen was his mum. She'd been limp, then rigid in death, as the days ticked by. Her face was lost to him.

It was easier to think about the pigs' pink innocence, before the burgeoning adultness of coarse white hair and dirt.

Blouchon found Piglet in the barn one day with a piglet on his lap. He'd taken it from its compatriots. It lay on its side and Piglet scratched its belly and behind its ears. The animal wore an approximation of a grin and Piglet smiled back at it.

Blouchon crouched down before them.

"She likes that, doesn't she? Is that one your favourite?"

Piglet stiffened, unaccustomed to the mildness in Blouchon's voice.

"You know what happens when they're grown. Tell me, Piglet, what happens?"

"The lorry comes for them."

"And after that?"

"I don't know."

The air was cooling and the fluorescent strip lights came on, casting out the dusk.

"Pigs are born with teeth and working legs, but look at them." Piglet averted his gaze. He'd no idea what Blouchon expected of him. "They're born ready to fight." His fingers made a nasty snapping sound as they flicked Piglet between the eyes. "But they're docile and stupid."

Piglet thought better than to try and correct him.

"I'm going to do this as a kindness to you. You're nearly a man." Piglet was twelve. "Stay right here. Don't move."

Blouchon returned with a large kitchen knife. He put it in Piglet's hand and took the snuffling creature and held it down on the floor. It started to squirm.

"Kill it."

"What?"

"Kill it."

Piglet hesitated.

"Don't make me repeat myself."

Piglet looked at the blade that was an extension of his hand, this thing of flesh and metal fused. He put his other hand on the pig to steady it, as it was now writhing and squealing. He was suddenly aware of the life under its skin. It was more vivid to him than his own. Blouchon loomed over them, excited. It shocked him more than Blouchon's fury, which was commonplace.

"Do it."

The murder took much longer than anticipated. Piglet's hands shook and his breath came in fast. The baby pig thrashed and screamed so that Blouchon put a knee on it in the end. Piglet sawed at its neck ineffectually. Blood splashed his hands and face. The give of flesh to metal sickened him. He felt the resistance of the tendons and windpipe to the blade's edge.

The animal's suffering was magnified by Piglet's tenderness. The kill was botched by his reluctance.

"Will you finish it?" he begged Blouchon.

"No."

Once it was over the only sound was of Piglet panting. The pigs were silent.

"Well," Blouchon spat, "you made a pig's ear of that, as you English say. Now I will show you how to butcher it."

Piglet never held the animals again.

★ ★ ★

Piglet woke often, the night constricting his chest, stealing his breath, and deadening his fingertips. He was clammy, even though it was cold. The outhouse walls were lost in blackness. He could be anywhere. He could be eight and in the back of a lorry, or he could be dead. He reached out to touch the wall, the crumbling mortar and brick grounding him.

As Piglet returned to himself he was aware of the pigs. Either they too had bad dreams that shredded sleep or something had disturbed them.

He knew he should investigate. Blouchon would give him a hiding if anything happened to the livestock.

Then Piglet heard the deliberate step of hooves on cobbles. They paused outside, snuffling heavily. Piglet sat up and felt for his torch. He craved the light but was too afraid to switch it on. Its weight in his hand would have to suffice. Blouchon had once told him: *Stay on the farm. There's a devil living in the trees.*

What if the devil had come down here to find him?

The devil's breath punctuated Piglet's heartbeat. Then it fell silent but Piglet knew it was still there, waiting. The moment stretched until Piglet broke and let out a sob.

The devil-in-the-night sighed and then it was away, hooves moving at a pace.

★ ★ ★

Piglet marked time by cycles of rearing pigs for unseen slaughter. He settled in the new livestock with feed and water. They jostled one another, unhappy to be away from the teat and traumatised by the journey.

When he went back outside mist still clung to the morning, making everything damp and chilly. Water droplets decorated the spiders' webs and softened the crumbling blown-brick buildings. Amid the missing tiles and peeling paint, only the farmhouse of thick pale stone blocks had been built to last.

Piglet walked around the now empty truck parked in the yard, treading as lightly as he could. He tried the rear doors, but they were locked. His heart raced, imagining the void within. No, he couldn't face that. He crouched down to look at the underside, then climbed up to peep at the cab. He could hear Blouchon talking to Henri, the driver.

"Louis wants you to do something. It's a fun thing he's got into. He wants you to host it here."

Piglet took a step back from the cab, stones crunching under his boot-heel. The men came around from the far side of the cab.

"You're a sneaky little bastard," said Henri.

Blouchon stared at Piglet. "Don't mind him. He's a bit touched in the head. And his French isn't that great. Come on, come in and have a drink with me."

The pair went into the farmhouse.

By lunchtime Henri had gone and Blouchon came out with a bowl of cereal. Piglet leant against the wall, shivering as he ate it. Afterwards he rinsed the bowl and spoon at the outside standpipe and left them on the kitchen step. Blouchon came to the open doorway, cigarette in hand. He took a drag and then blew a line of smoke from the corner of his mouth.

"I know what you were doing."

Piglet pulled his sleeves over his knuckles.

"You're thinking about running off."

Piglet shook his head.

"You can get up to the main highway on foot, easy, no problem. The hard part comes after. Do you know what's out there?"

Piglet looked to the main gate, as if the answer were there. His world for the last eight years, within the confines of safer memory, was the farm, Blouchon, the pigs, and the long stretch of grass beyond the boundary that ran into the trees. Only the sky changed, and that was a gift. Sometimes it was heavy with rain, and sometimes it was piled with pale clouds.

"There's nothing for you out there. Run, if you want, but it'll be worse for you. You're not meant to be in this country. You have no rights. You're illegal." Blouchon tapped a piece of paper on the corkboard beside the door. "You've not got any paperwork. They'll lock you up, tighter than the pigs, or send you back to England. You definitely don't want to go back there. You've got it easy here with me, Piglet. There are much worse places that Louis could've sent you."

* * *

The devil had started to visit the farm more frequently. Piglet lay awake, listening for it. He heard it stop in the yard, sniffing the air. It waited for him with expectation, then walked on, disappointed.

Its hooves fell silent as it went from the yard, through the gate and out onto the field. Piglet was tired of fear. He got up. His breath was visible in the cold night. He went out, scanning for a dark shape in motion. There it was, a shadow low to the ground. It disappeared into the body of the woods. A sound pierced him, a high-pitched call to combat.

He crossed the field, heading for the treeline. The oaks were always the last to shed in autumn. Their dead leaves were still clinging to the boughs. The wind picked up, bringing them down in great gusts. Piglet considered lying down and letting them settle on him until he ceased to exist.

* * *

Piglet spent the following few days helping Blouchon clear one of the larger breeze block sheds of twisted tools, empty crates and pallets. They dumped them in the paddock, beside the old tractor that was gripped by ivy and weeds.

The floor was wet in places, leaking from the corrugated roof. Piglet swept it as best he could. He and Blouchon dragged in hay bales and lined the room with them. They carried in chairs that Henri had delivered and arranged them in an arc at one end of the room.

Blouchon had no time to chastise or bully Piglet. He kept checking his phone.

"There are going to be a lot of people here tonight. Keep your mouth shut and do as you're told."

When night fell it wasn't a soft envelope of darkness, but dense and unremitting. The farm was the only reprieve for miles around, a pocket of huddled lights.

Piglet went out to watch the cars arrive. A rangy man in tight jeans and gold chains directed them to park in the field by the gate. It was an egalitarian collection of vehicles. Luxury SUVs lined up beside dented Renault Clios. Rowdy young men with crew cuts and tracksuits piled out of them. A variety of tattoos were on display, marking their tribalism and vanity. And women. There were women.

He'd never seen so many people in one place, not since he was a boy. The memory sucked his mouth dry and brought him out in a sweat. He hung back in the shadows and listened to their strident voices.

A car was parked apart from the others, right outside the farmhouse door. It was a sleek machine. The engine idled and then died. The driver got out and opened the nearside passenger door. Piglet had never seen a creature like the one who emerged. His blond hair was short and clean. His wire-rimmed glasses looked delicate. He wore a long woollen black coat and a rollneck jumper. To Piglet's eye he was sleek and regal.

Blouchon stood above this stranger on the kitchen step. This version of Blouchon was new to Piglet. Clean, clean-shaven, and wearing a shirt and trousers. He never looked like that, not even when he brought a woman back.

"Welcome, Louis," Blouchon said.

"It's good to see the old place again, big brother."

They embraced but Blouchon stayed above him on the step.

"You should come to Paris again. I'll look forward to entertaining you. You had fun last time, no? The ladies loved you."

The driver opened the other doors. The two women who stepped out were young. Louis took one of them by the hand and raised it above her head. She twirled around and Louis passed her to Blouchon.

The other woman hung back, cradling a bottle in her arms. She glanced over at Piglet as if suddenly aware of being watched. He shrank back.

"You like the look of her? So you're red-blooded after all." Henri, the trucker, stepped from the shadows. Piglet had been so intent on Blouchon's guests that he'd missed him. He sported a burgundy velour tracksuit and a baseball cap. Piglet would've coveted those clothes had he not seen Louis' splendour. "Don't let King Louis catch you staring at her. She's his favourite."

★ ★ ★

It took about an hour for the shed to fill up. Piglet lingered in the doorway, but it was too much for him. Too many bodies jostled for space, climbing or sitting on the hay bales.

He staggered to the safety of the barn, leaning against the pens, the rail pressing into his knotted stomach. The pigs grunted their greetings. It didn't soothe him. His panic was mounting to a pitch. He couldn't stand it anymore. Not this feeling or this place.

Something moved in his peripheral vision. It was the girl. Louis' favourite.

"Breathe slowly," she ordered. Then: "Watch!"

Her chest rose and fell by demonstration. It was a struggle to slow himself to match her but he tried. The jarring scent of her shocked him back to himself. It was sweet and chemical. A memory washed over him, one he didn't know he had. His mother painting her toenails orange, the sun through the window drenching them both.

"Better?"

She waited silently while he gained control of himself. When he was finally still, she said, "If this ever happens again, I want you to remember this moment."

Her eyes eclipsed everything.

"Where are Blouchon and King Louis?" he asked.

"Don't let him hear you call him that." Her laugh was a sharp bark.

"No?"

"Definitely not." She slipped from French to English. His mother tongue. "You have an accent. You're British too. How long have you been here?"

"I'm not sure. A long time. What about you?"

"About three years. After the schools and universities closed, my parents and friends lived on a commune. They tried to teach us everything they knew. French, Spanish, history, and politics. They were arrested for being radicals, so their friends helped get me out."

Piglet didn't recognise all the words but he was entranced. To be spoken to at length without derision was precious. School. He recalled it, vaguely. There was a teacher and there were books. Living in a house. Piglet saw that his concerns had become those of the beasts; that of the belly, of sleep and warmth, the labour of his bowels, and at best, the needs of the herd. He had no other way to express himself, so it came out as, "I'm not an animal."

"No, I know you're not. Neither am I. What's your name?"
"This little runt is Piglet." Piglet turned at Blouchon's voice. "He shovels pigshit. Go on, boy, get out."
"No." Louis took his hands from his coat pockets. The girl moved between them. "We were just talking. That's all." King Louis was casual. He put his arm around Piglet's neck, making him stoop. "So, Blouchon, here's the solution to our problem. We need a fighter. Piglet can oblige. How does that sound?"

★   ★   ★

"Ladies and gentlemen, and the rest of you ugly bastards," at which the crowd booed the compère, "I'm assured that Gabriel the Destroyer is on his way, but as he's been delayed—" the crowd booed louder. "Now, now, we've arranged a bit of light entertainment for you while we're waiting. Our normal rules apply. That is, *no* rules, and to continue until someone taps out or is dead. Got it?"

Piglet shivered. The mob writhed and jeered. Only the occasional face was bored and indifferent, more concerned with the money passing through their hands.

His opponent was stripped to the waist. The man bounced on the balls of his feet and shook out his limbs. He rolled his dark-fuzzed head from side to side. He was agile and energetic for such a large man.

Piglet started to gulp air. He couldn't get it far down enough into his lungs. There was no way out, every turn blocked by the rabble. The girl, now sat beside Louis, was the only stillness in the room. Piglet wanted to live in that stillness. He wanted to live.

Blouchon sidled up to him.

"That's Adrien. He's going to play with you for a while. Nothing too bad. It's just for show. When he gets you on the floor and it's too much, give in."

Louis beckoned to Adrien, who went over, bending down to listen. Louis' hand covered his mouth and Adrien's ear as he talked. A slow grin spread across Adrien's face and he nodded.

"But not too soon," Blouchon continued. "Don't show me up."

Piglet realised that he hadn't asked the girl's name.

"Begin." The compère clapped and slid back into the crowd.

It was too late. Too late for anything. It didn't matter. He'd taken plenty of beatings from Blouchon when he'd been thwarted, drunk, or in a fit of despair.

"Go on." Blouchon gave him a shove.

Adrien circled him, skipping sideways. Piglet turned on his heel to face him, his fists raised in imitation. He was overcome with an absurd need to laugh. A foolish impulse. Adrien's first jab was so fast that Piglet didn't register it landing on his side. It left him winded but he moved back in time to avoid the follow-up blow to the mouth.

Piglet realised this would be different to Blouchon's indiscriminate fury. This man was discerning in how he doled out hurt.

Adrien kept him moving around the floor, herding him, tiring him. His punches were efficient. The crowd appreciated his conciseness. Piglet's wild swings flew wide. When Piglet fell back, many hands pushed him forward, screaming: *Hit him back, you idiot! Fight, for fuck's sake!*

Adrien came in close. They were grappling now. Piglet was shocked by the forced closeness to his naked torso. They were both breathing hard.

Something seared the side of Piglet's head, then a slick, wet feeling down his neck. There was the patter of blood on the floor. Adrien's grin was red. He spat out flesh.

Part of Piglet's ear landed on the floor. The audience were giddy at the bloody morsel.

The girl covered her face with both hands. Louis gently removed them, speaking quietly to her, but his mouth was contorted into an ugly shape.

Piglet felt Adrien's hands on him and the world was upended. He was thrown across the floor. All he could see were shoes and legs. Blouchon came into view. "Get up!"

Adrien's boot landed on his chest and he felt ribs crack. He curled up into a ball, his hands over his head.

Blouchon dropped to the ground. His advice to Piglet changed. "Give in. Just give in!"

Piglet rolled onto his back. "Please. Stop."

Adrien grabbed Piglet's arm and dragged him to the centre of the room. Piglet screamed as his shoulder muscles were wrenched and torn. Adrien straddled him, putting his full weight on Piglet's chest. The pain from his ribs changed to something sharp and more insistent. His lung was on fire. He couldn't throw him off.

Piglet felt something under his good hand. It was a nail that he'd missed when sweeping. The animal in him clamoured to live. He drove the nail towards Adrien's neck but the man was fast and leant back from his waist so that it landed in the meat of Adrien's arm. He pulled out the nail with a flourish and put it between his fingers. Both his hands were fists. They rained down on Piglet, pounding and piercing and tearing until Piglet lay still.

★ ★ ★

The fighting continued long into the night. Once the scheduled fight between Adrien and Gabriel was over, men lined up to take an impromptu battering. The consequences were less serious but they still wanted to feel the crunch of bone and the splitting of skin for themselves.

Rebecca sat beside Louis, rigid, until she couldn't take it anymore. She excused herself. He waved his hand, a cold dismissal. She'd lost his graces but knew he'd still have uses for her.

She noticed Blouchon's sour expression, but he remained silent. Blood will out, after all.

Rebecca turned up her coat collar and kept walking until she was at the gate. She watched the movement of glowing cigarette tips and heard the men's grunts as they dumped Piglet's body in a hole.

She went off in the other direction, towards the forest. The trees parted for her. There was safety between the trunks. She stopped when she was weary and lay down between the roots of an oak tree and pulled armfuls of dry leaves over her.

When Rebecca woke, colour was seeping into the dawn. She wasn't alone. The boar's breath was steam in the red bracken. Its body was leaner than a pig's, its bulk carried on shorter legs. Maned and bristled, it watched her with dark, deep-set eyes. The boar was a warrior. It was a berserker on four legs. She followed it, two free things into a new day.

THE MUMMIFIED CORPSE OF REESE WITHERSPOON

Philip Fracassi

Jack can't believe his luck.

He's never won *anything*.

He reads the email twice, just to make sure it isn't a hoax. Or spam. Maybe the database of entries had been hacked, and all the hopefuls would now be asked to supply their social security and credit card numbers to some darknet criminal hacker. But the address seems legit. Bursting with excitement, he scans the email a third time.

SUBJECT: CONGRATULATIONS!
FROM: RW CONTEST <contest.admin@amazon.com>
TO: Jack Hillson

Greetings!

We are thrilled to inform you that you are this month's winner of the *Reese Witherspoon Book Club's* A WEEK WITH REESE contest.

Please respond to this email with confirmation of your home address, email, cell, and a minimum of six socials.

As specified in the contest guidelines, REESE will be delivered by an Amazon Guardian. Please comply with any requests of the Guardian during delivery and retrieval.

Please click the link below to confirm all your information and schedule delivery and retrieval of REESE.

Congratulations again, and enjoy your time with REESE.

HAPPY READING!

Jack clicks the link and sure enough, it's virus-free and nested within the Amazon web domain.

This is real.

This is *happening*.

Giddy, he fills out the forms, sets a delivery date for the following Monday, and sends the information along.

Mere seconds later, a confirmation pings his Inbox and he can't help doing a little dance around his apartment, wondering who he should call to share the good news.

No one in particular comes to mind.

MONDAY

The man at the door wears all black – black pants, black shirt, black suit coat. Even a black hat that Jack knows is an old style not many people wear anymore.

A top hat, he thinks, a tiny explosion of synapses deep in his subconscious alerting him of the trivial fact.

"Jack Hillson?"

Jack nods. "Are you the Guardian?"

"I'm here with Reese," the man says, and steps aside to reveal a tall, narrow, wooden crate. It has four wheels at its bottom and stands no more than five feet high.

"May we come in?" the Guardian asks.

Jack moves back from the door and the man wheels in the crate, which rolls smoothly and effortlessly over the apartment's thin industrial carpeting.

"Where would you like her setup during her visit?"

Jack looks around urgently, a small shiver of panic rising inside him. He hadn't given that any thought, and now he isn't sure. His apartment is small – a one bedroom with a tiny kitchen, an even tinier balcony (that's technically a fire escape), and a bathroom. The living room, where they now stand as Jack gapes and the man in black waits patiently for a response, is the only place he can think of. The only option there is.

"Here," he says, and points to a corner next to the small couch. "Can she sit? Or, I don't know... bend?"

Without answering, the man gestures across the room, toward a sunlit window and Jack's makeshift painting space. A half-finished abstract faces them, uncovered, but Jack doesn't mind. He isn't sensitive or embarrassed about his art. Besides, it's really more of a hobby.

"You an artist?" the man asks, then starts snapping open a series of clasps affixed along the edges of the wooden crate.

"I paint," Jack says with a shy smile. "I think there's a difference."

The man grunts – whether in dismissal or acknowledgment Jack has no idea – and continues opening the crate. "I see you read books, which makes sense considering. I'm a comics man, myself."

Jack glances at the tall, broad shelf of books along one wall; well-worn paperbacks and hardcovers with tattered or missing dust jackets are crammed into each nook and cranny. "Yes, of course. That's how I knew about the contest. I always buy what Reese recommends. Always."

"That's good," the man says, and sets his hands on the loosened front panel of the crate. "Even if you do buy them secondhand."

Jack swallows, but says nothing.

"You ready to meet her?"

"Sure."

The Guardian smiles broadly and pulls away the wooden panel, the interior of which is coated in a thick, molded padding.

"Oh," is all Jack can think to say.

The man takes a step back to study the mummified corpse of Reese Witherspoon along with the contest winner. "Yeah, it takes a minute to get used to her."

"She's smaller than I thought," Jack says quietly. "Very small."

"That shrinkage comes with age and the mummification process. You know, there's no organs in there, and the flesh without moisture turns that caramel colour and sort of sucks into itself," the man says. "Like an old sponge when you let it dry out."

"No lips?"

"Always smiling. But seriously, they're just stretched back. See there?" he says, pointing to a thin, worm-like upper lip.

"Of course," Jack replies, feeling bad for drawing attention to her stature and more bizarre features. "And is that hair…"

"Real? Hell yeah, that's the real deal, Jack."

"But the eyes…"

"Ah yes, those are fake. Glass. But they're cool, right? Better than a couple dark sockets. I mean, if you kind of squint, she's goddamn pretty."

"She is, for sure," Jack replies uncertainly.

Reese is set up on a delicate metal stand, one that supports her corpse without worry of it falling over. She smells, Jack thinks, like one of his old paperbacks.

Pleasantly musty.

The Guardian gathers the disassembled crate, then pulls a gold-coloured business card from his pocket. "I'll be back in exactly one week to pick her up. If anything happens in the meantime, call me."

Jack studies the card, nods. "Of course."

"We ask that you don't move Reese, as she's delicate..." He gives Jack a quick wink. "But not as delicate as you'd think. Still, I'd just leave her on the display stand, to avoid damage."

"Of course," Jack says, feeling like an idiot for repeating himself. "I mean, I likely won't move her around."

"She's a wonderful human being, and she means a lot to people," the man says, walking to the door. "Her book club has over ten million followers around the world, can you believe that?"

"I know!" Jack says excitedly. "My mother was such a fan, so I'm really thrilled I'll have this time with her."

"Good, good," the man says. "No hanky panky now!"

He laughs loudly and Jack shakes his head, studying the mummy's beef jerky skin, the thin blonde hair, the rather elegant black dress tugged tightly over her body. "No, I..."

"I'm just messing with you, Jack. We'll see you in a week. Remember, if you have a problem, call me."

Jack looks at the business card once more, then stuffs it into his pocket as the man opens the front door and steps into the hall.

"I can't imagine I'll have any problems."

The man pauses, and his smile fades. "Well, in the past, with other winners, I mean... there's been some issues."

"Issues?"

The man looks at Jack closely, meeting his eye for a moment, a troubled look on his face. Then, as if he'd flipped a switch in his head – or come to a decision – he smiles brightly. "Nothing you need to worry about, Jack. You seem... just fine."

And with that, he closes the door, leaving Jack alone, in his small living room, with a corpse.

* * *

The rest of Jack's first day with Reese is uneventful.

He works on his painting, makes dinner, and finds himself casually talking to his temporary new housemate.

"I've got all the books you've recommended the last few years," he says, pulling a few beat-up hardcovers from the shelf. "They even have that yellow sticker, see?"

He holds up a book to show the corpse, who stares back, beaming at him with wide blue eyes, a toothy grin.

"I know you've been gone for a while, but it must be nice to still be making a difference, you know? Helping authors, helping readers..."

For a while Jack lies on the couch with a book, taking comfort in not being alone. He finds himself continually glancing toward the mummy, as if assuring himself she's really there with him. He reads a passage of the book aloud to her, one he found particularly touching.

That first night, Jack sleeps better than he has in months.

TUESDAY

Jack is briefly taken off guard when Reese, quite impossibly, begins to speak.

After working on the painting – what he feels are the finishing touches – he stands back to study it, pride running through him like a warm current.

He turns to see Reese, watching him from the far side of the room.

"You like it?" he asks, chuckling at her glassy stare.

As he starts toward the kitchen to wash his brushes, she replies.

"Not really," she says, her voice bright and youthful, a mild Southern twang at its core.

Jack freezes... then slowly turns around, and gasps.

Reese's head has *turned* to look at him, her lidless blue eyes boring into his own.

"How... is this a joke?"

"No," she replies, her petrified teeth unmoving, her withered face completely still. "But that painting is."

"Now hold on…" Jack replies, the strangeness of a talking corpse overridden by a flash of anger. He takes a step toward her, extends the point of one long brush in her direction. "Take that back."

"I'll take it back if you take that painting back to whatever thrift shop dumpster you pulled it from," she says, then giggles.

Jack looks at his new painting, then back at the mummified corpse of Reese Witherspoon. "Okay, smartass, what's wrong with it? Art is subjective, you know."

For the next several minutes, Reese explains to Jack that his use of negative space implies an emptiness he didn't intend, how his choice of colours creates confusion for the eye and disrupts any emotions he may have been trying to convey, how it's technically proficient, but ultimately feels like more of an homage than something actually original.

Jack doesn't reply to the critique but knows in his heart that she's right. Instead of debating her opinions, however, he leaves the room silently to take a shower and get ready for work – serving tables at a touristy restaurant chain that, most months, barely covers his bills.

★ ★ ★

When he returns that night, exhausted, his feet aching from having to cover two shifts thanks to another server not showing up, he finds all the books from his shelf piled in the middle of the living room floor.

Actually, there are *two* piles.

"What the hell are you doing?" he asks.

Reese had somehow moved to the middle of the living room, her support pedestal still in the corner, now empty. Her mummified corpse kneels over the two large piles of books, as if studying them. With bony fingers, tanned skin stretched tightly over each digit, she sorts through the titles. "I'm separating your books, Jack. This is a good pile," she says. "And this is, well, the not so good. Honestly, Jack, some of these are just awful. Why do you have them?"

"Because I enjoy them. Why are you going through my stuff?"

"My pick for next month's book club is going to be amazing," she says, ignoring his question. "It follows a family of horse thieves over decades of time, a dramatic saga about crime and the hidden bonds between generations…"

"I don't care, Reese!" Jack yells. "I'm tired, and you've made a mess, and I didn't have time to eat. So please just pick all those up and return them to the shelf. You're a guest here, for god sakes."

Jack storms from the room to make himself a peanut butter and jelly sandwich, ignoring Reese's mumbling voice as she continues to pick through the books.

WEDNESDAY

"What do you think?" Jack asks, spreading his arms wide, feeling sheepish as a teenager on prom night.

"Why so dressed up?" Reese asks, all innocence.

Jack stands before a full-length mirror in his bedroom wearing blue jeans, a white button-down dress shirt, and a navy blue sport coat. He shakes a finger at her. "You know perfectly well why. Just tell me if you like the outfit. I'm going for casual elegance."

"No tie?"

"Too formal. It's a first date, and the restaurant isn't that nice."

"You mean it's all you can afford," Reese says, but her tone is light and he laughs at himself.

"Exactly."

"You look fine, Jack. Maybe not the sneakers, though."

Jack nods. He'd been thinking the same thing. "Agreed. I have some black boots that'll be better. And hey, don't forget about later."

"Later?"

"Assuming nothing goes horribly wrong, I'm gonna bring her over. She wants to meet you."

★ ★ ★

After dinner and a cocktail at a nearby bar, Jack and his date, Sandy, go back to his place. He mixes them a couple drinks while Sandy *oohs* and *aahs* over the corpse of Reese Witherspoon.

"She's so tiny!" Sandy exclaims, taking a huge gulp of her gin and tonic.

Reese doesn't talk with Sandy around, which is just fine by Jack. After the novelty wears off, he shows her some of his paintings, and they end up making out on the couch, their mashed faces only inches from the blonde-haired corpse.

Three drinks later, Jack is about to climb into bed where Sandy, very drunk and very naked, waits for him.

"Hope you wear protection," a voice says.

Jack turns his head to see Reese standing at the bedroom door, her slight figure a dark shadow against the dimly lit apartment beyond. He crosses the room in two quick steps and does his best to ignore the wet sheen of those bulbous glass eyes staring at him as he shuts the door in her face.

"What are you doing?" Sandy murmurs from the bed.

"Just wanted it darker in here."

"Who was that at the door? Do you have a roommate?"

"No, there was no one."

Wanting to change the subject, Jack begins kissing parts of Sandy's flesh as she runs her fingers through his hair, sighing in the darkness. "I can't believe Reese Witherspoon's corpse is here," she whispers. "It's so hot."

"I guess," he mutters, moving to her stomach.

"I heard her next book selection is about an interracial autistic couple who are denied love by their over-worrying parents. Sort of a modern-day retelling of Romeo and Juliet, you know… if they were autistic."

"Uh-huh," Jack mumbles, and shifts his mouth even lower, hoping it will finally distract Sandy enough to keep her mind on him, and not the leathery corpse listening intently at the door.

THURSDAY

The next day Jack takes his new painting, and three others he'd finished in recent months, and tosses them out onto the fire escape.

"Why did you do that?"

"Because you were right and they suck."

"So you're throwing them away?"

"Just... I just want them out of my space, so I can start something new. Something better."

"I see."

They stand in awkward silence for a moment, Jack unable to meet her blue eyes, Reese fidgeting with the folds of her dress. "Let me ask you something," he says, hoping to soothe things between them. "Who picks your books now that you're dead?"

Reese sighs. "Oh, there's a committee of sorts. But my granddaughter has final say. She and I always had similar tastes in fiction. You'd like her."

"Uh-huh. She an actress?"

"No, she's a writer. She wrote a wonderful book about two young New York City couples who are really into the party scene. But then one of them gets cancer and wants to be buried in Central Park. It's a dark comedy."

FRIDAY

"I feel like you're angry with me."

Jack paces, eyes haunted as he glares at the drop cloth spread across his living room floor; the mess on top of it.

"Jack, please..." she says, her withered, warped body leaning against the kitchen doorway. "I didn't know it was going to rain! And besides, I never told you to put them out there."

On the drop cloth lay four canvases, the paint on them running off the edges, having blended mercilessly with rainwater, the colours smeared into one another in diluted, reckless chaos.

"They're ruined because of you," Jack mutters.

"Well, one could argue there wasn't much there to ruin in the first place," she replies snappily, as if she were peeling off a line of dialogue from one of her old movies.

"I guess you don't care that it hurts me when you say things like that," Jack says. "That it *hurts* me to see my work ruined."

The mummified corpse simply stares and grins, her tight black dress clinging to the stretched, formless skin beneath.

"No quippy reply to that?" he says, anger growing. "Have you forgotten what it is to hurt someone? Fine, let me show you pain."

Jack goes into the kitchen, rummages through a drawer. When he returns, Reese stands quiet and still on her metal perch, staring blankly at nothing. At everything.

"Let me know how this feels, Reese Witherspoon."

Jack holds a lighter. He thumbs the spark wheel and a finger of flame licks upward. He holds it beneath the corpse's dry hand.

"Can you feel *that*?" he says, tears streaming down his face. "Does that feel good to you? Or does it hurt?"

Reese stays perfectly still, saying nothing, as her skin blackens and smokes. The stink of burning flesh fills Jack's nostrils, and he gags.

"Art is *fucking subjective!*" he screams, spraying her face in spit. Then he throws the lighter across the room and drops onto the couch, face in his hands. "Months of work ruined," he says weakly, the words disrupted by a sob. "And now I have to go wait tables for tourists!"

★ ★ ★

Outside the restaurant where Jack works, the mummified corpse of Reese Witherspoon watches from a bus shelter, staring through the broad windows of the themed restaurant as Jack brings food to clapping tables, sings birthday songs, and smiles like a madman while taking orders. It's still pouring rain and her dress is soaked through. At one point, she wonders if Jack will notice her, but hour after hour he simply continues on with his work, giddily delivering trays of cheeseburgers and soft drinks, beer and desserts. Reese wonders whether the people in the restaurant follow her book club selections, but then dismisses the thought. It's not important right now.

If this were one of her movies, she thinks, she'd march right in there, rain-drenched, and kiss him on the lips. Everyone in the restaurant would clap.

When it begins getting late, she makes her way back to Jack's apartment, her hand stinging from the burn, her heart breaking from his words.

SATURDAY

"It's about a German rocket scientist who is forced to immigrate to America after World War II in order to design a top-secret plane but ends up falling in love with the test pilot who must fly it," Reese says breathlessly. "Of course, the pilot doesn't realise that the plane's been sabotaged due to the scientist's secret Nazi beliefs."

Jack doesn't reply, but simply paints on a new canvas, his back to the corpse across the room. The ruined paintings had been taken to the dumpster that morning, the work unsalvageable, the canvases beyond repair.

"It's a story of having to choose between love and loyal..."

"Yeah, I get it," Jack snaps. "Can you stop talking, please? I'm working."

The room is silent for a few minutes, until Jack sighs heavily, slumping on his painting stool. "Can you go into the kitchen or something? I'd like to be alone. Besides, having you stare at my back with those creepy glass eyes is freaking me out."

"I thought we'd have a nice weekend," Reese says. "I was hoping you'd take me to the park. I love the outdoors."

"Yeah, that's not gonna happen," Jack mutters, his brush attacking the canvas in broad, heavy strokes. "I want you out of here, Reese. We just need to get through these next couple days."

Reese lets out a sigh of disappointment. "I see."

Jack ignores the soft sounds of her frail corpse shuffling from the room, the gentle scrape of a chair as she sits at the kitchen table.

When he's finished working for the day, Jack covers the painting with an old sheet. He doesn't want her telling him whether it's good or not.

* * *

Late that night, Reese slips into Jack's bed, and holds him while he sleeps.

SUNDAY

The next morning, Jack takes an old wooden broom and rests it across the kitchen table. He then goes into the bedroom, pulls a cardboard box from the closet, and begins to dig through it.

"What are you doing?" Reese asks from the living room, where she's perched on her display stand.

"You'll see," Jack says, and then exclaims happily. "Yes! I still have it."

He walks back into the kitchen, lays something down on the table. He pulls a tacked picture from a wall, tosses the image aside, and bends over the broom.

"Hopefully these thumbtacks will hold it in place," he says, his back to Reese's lidless, inquiring eyes, her brown-toothed grimace.

When Jack comes into the living room, he sets his creation next to Reese; leans it gently against a wall.

"What the hell is that?" she asks nervously.

"It's a clown mask from Halloween a few years ago. One of those cheap plastic ones. It's cracked, and the rubber band is broken, but it'll do the job."

"Why is it attached to the broom handle?"

"That's not just a broom handle, Reese. That's your new friend. *Our* new friend. Let's call him... Broomy. Funny, right?"

Jack turns the bristles at the base of Broomy so the empty-eyed clown mask stares blankly at the living room. "There," he says. "Now he can see everything."

"I don't understand..."

"What's to understand?" Broomy asks brusquely, his voice high-pitched and wavering.

"Jack, this is silly!"

Jack grins, strides across the room, and pulls the old sheet off his work-in-progress.

Reese audibly gasps.

"What's wrong?" he says, still smiling.

"Jack... what have you done?"

Jack folds his arms across his chest, cocks a thumb at his new painting. "You don't like it?" he asks, raising an eyebrow. "It's not quite finished, but it's close."

"I..."

"Well, *I love it!*" Broomy exclaims, followed by a happy chuckle. "It's fanny-fan-fan-*fantastic!*"

"Thank you, Broomy," Jack says.

Reese scoffs. "Is that what you want? A Yes-Man? Or do you want honesty?"

"I *am* being honest!" Broomy squeals, the red smear of lips across the bottom of the white mask stuck in a constant smile, the blue diamonds painted around his empty eye sockets seemingly aglow with earnest pleasure.

"See, Reese. You don't know everything."

"I never said I did!" she yells, then takes a deep breath. "Look, let's get out of here. Go see a movie or something."

Jack shakes his head, then slips his earbuds from a pocket and puts them in. "You two hash it out, I have work to do."

As Broomy and Reese continue to argue with each other, Jack plays his favourite album, picks up his brush, and goes back to his painting.

MONDAY

On the day the Guardian arrives to pick up Reese, she's stopped talking to Jack altogether – which is just fine with him.

With Broomy's encouragement, Jack has finished his new painting, and spends a good part of the morning studying it, wondering what it all means.

"I was telling Reese about my idea for a novel!" Broomy exclaims giddily while Jack eats a light breakfast. "It's about a clown private detective who solves crimes that happen at the circus!"

"Sounds great, Broomy," Jack mumbles, dipping a corner of buttered toast into his coffee.

"I think you should write it, Broomy," Reese says quietly, almost sadly.

Jack grimaces, hating her tone of congeniality. Of kindness.

When the knock finally comes at the door, he walks through the living room, stopping for only a moment to look into those shining blue eyes one last time, the chewed-bubblegum bump of a nose, the dry, thin blonde hair. "Goodbye, Reese."

"Jack, please…"

Then he continues to the door, and lets the man inside.

"Hey there, Jack. I'm here to pick up."

"Of course," he says, stepping aside.

The man starts a bit when he sees Broomy grinning madly back at him from the corner, but says nothing as he sets the crate pieces onto the floor, gently begins enclosing the mummified corpse of Reese Witherspoon inside.

"What happened to her hand?" he asks, fitting the back of her into the formed foam padding.

"Don't know," Jack says, and walks across the room, toward his painting.

"Fair enough," the man mumbles, then affixes the two crate pieces together and begins to secure the clasps, one by one.

As he rolls Reese toward the door, he glances in Jack's direction, perhaps to say goodbye, perhaps to ask about the hand again. "Oh, dear God!"

Jack turns. The man is staring, open-mouthed, at his painting.

"What's wrong?"

"That... you painted *that*?" the man says. "On purpose?"

Jack shrugs. "It's a self-portrait. I feel it really captures who I am inside."

The man shakes his head, grumbles something under his breath, then wheels the crate out the door and into the hallway.

"Don't you like it?" Jack calls after him.

"It's horrible. Goodbye, Jack," the man says, then pulls the door shut.

Reese is gone.

Jack tries to laugh off the Guardian's words, but the critique cuts deep. Besides, he knows.

Deep down, he knows.

"Well, I for one think your painting is *wonderful!*" Broomy yells, screeching from the corner.

Jack sits on the stool before his painting and stares at the image of himself he'd created. He picks up a small jar of paint thinner and pours it over the canvas, then runs his fingers through the colours, the lines. He smears the paint onto his face, hoping to bring the two disparate pieces of himself together, and winces at the sharp reek of the paint thinner, tries to ignore the way it stings his skin.

Then Jack takes a lighter – the same one he'd used to burn Reese's dead hand – and holds it to the corner of the canvas, where it catches the flammable liquid, spreads quickly across the painting.

As black smoke broils up from the flaming easel, flowing against the apartment's ceiling, Broomy shrieks madly.

"Don't worry, Jack! You can always paint another!"
"Thank you, Broomy," Jack says. "You're very kind."
Then he sits back, and watches himself burn.

THE WIND TELEPHONE
A.K. Benedict

There was nothing insubstantial about Yorkshire air. It barged into the side of Erin's car, buffeting her across the road. Nan, a self-declared psychic, used to say, while opening all the doors in her house, that, "The wind, like wraiths, must be welcomed. Let it, and them, wander through your home, bringing fortune. Or else they'll bring death."

Erin wound down the windows, letting the wind in. Carrying the ghosts of gorse, sheep shit, and the brine of a distant sea, it charged round the car and topped up her courage. As strong as the county's brew, it marked her soul like tea stains on a mug. Born and raised in Scarborough, she'd even holidayed as a child in Robin Hood's Bay, and then, as a teenager, camped on the moors with Sam, her twin sister.

Erin hadn't been back to North Yorkshire since Sam's funeral, one year ago today. She'd left halfway through the wake, unable to stand the sight of Nathan, Sam's widower, weeping over the buffet. The only thing he grieved was the loss of his punchbag. The police couldn't prove his involvement in Sam's stabbing and death, even though his alibi for her murder, as tasteless as the prawn vol-au-vents, had flaked away via the strip club's CCTV. With no weapon or witness, he couldn't be charged.

Erin knew, though, DNA deep, that Nathan was to blame.

"You have reached your destination," the satnav lass said.

Getting out of her car, Erin zipped her parka up to her neck. Her heart clenched when she saw the small sign, in black letters, that Sam had hand-burned into wood. 'WIND TELEPHONE'.

Sam had set it up five years ago, after their three years studying together in Japan. Nan had died while they were in Osaka. Unable to speak to her before she passed, their friend, Himari, took them to the first wind phone, or *kaze no denwa*, on a hill outside Ōtsuchi. Erin and Sam whispered goodbyes to Nan into the disconnected receiver and felt like their words were somehow received. The wind took their words of love and loss and breathed them to her ghost.

Both twins brought something back with them from Japan when they returned to the UK. Whereas Erin had brought back a suitcase of sweet mochi, Sam had returned with an idea. She applied for and won arts funding to transform an old red telephone box on the moors into a wind phone. She had repainted it white, as if it'd had a fright. "When one of us dies," Sam said, leaning against the box, "the other one can find them down the line. After all, where else are we going to haunt than these moors?" Days later, she'd met Nathan. Erin had then begun to lose Sam while she was still alive.

Now, the wind grabbed at Erin's hood, flipping it back like a Pez dispenser. Holding the hood by its floof, she pulled it forward and walked on, fixing her gaze on the shingle path leading up a hill away from the road, tiny pebbles bleeding into the heather. As she turned the corner, the wind phone stood stark white against the moors. It looked like a box made of bones.

A sob surged from Erin. A sparrowhawk hung in the bruising sky.

Trying to steady her breathing, Erin reached for the handle. It was cool and seemed to vibrate. But it wouldn't budge. The wind was trying to keep her out. She had to use both hands and lean back against the buffeting just to get the door ajar. Wedging her wellie in the crack, she managed to edge her way in before a strong gust slammed the door shut.

Once inside, she knocked back her hood. Everything was hushed. If it weren't for the swaying and flattened grasses outside, she'd never have known it was blowing a gale. The glass panels tamed the darkening moor into boxes, frames of a silent movie. Her heartbeat slowed. She became claustrophobic in small spaces but in here she felt calm. Held.

In front of her, an old-fashioned black telephone sat on a silver shelf. Next to it was a notebook, opened on a page-long message, written in Sam's looping hand:

Welcome to the Moors Wind Telephone! This phone is not connected, not in the usual way, anyway. It is here to link you to those who have died, to connect you with your grief. It can be hard to find the words, so maybe just sit in silence for a while, let it be a shared silence, a shared space, protected by the box and yoked by the wind. If you can, tell your loved one the big things – what you loved and still love about them; what you wish you'd said, and what you wish you hadn't; what you should have done, and what you shouldn't have. Tell them how they made a difference in your life.

Tell them about the little things, too. The shoes you got for a bargain on Vinted. How your road's being dug up by yet another broadband company. What you fancy for tea. Your ghosts are hungry for your life, so feed it to them.

Every time I come here, I thank my beloved Nan for teaching me how to sail, in every way. I was gouged by grief when she died. I was hollowed out, a beached hull. Talking to her on the Ōtsuchi wind phone let me feel like I could sail on.

If you don't have anyone to talk to, talk anyway. Someone will be listening. The wind takes your words to where they belong, and they, and you, will be heard.

Erin tried to quash another sob, but it was like trying to wrestle a tent back into its bag. At least in this box, she could cry as much as she liked, instead of stoppering her sobs with her sleeve.

A year on from Sam's death, people expected Erin to be over it. They didn't say so explicitly, but she could feel it. They'd given her extra time as 'it must be awful to lose a twin, like you've lost half of you', as if loss worked like that, but after six months the looks went from pitying to frustration. Anger, even.

But Erin *couldn't* get over it. Or around it. Or under it. It took up too much room. Gouged was the right verb for grief, as it was so active. Grief was an attack. There should be more physical signs of its assault, other than changes in weight and dark circles doodled by nightmares. 'Friends' said how great she was looking: "Have you been on a diet?" they asked.

"Yes. I've lost a sister," she always replied.

Erin picked up the receiver with one hand, gripping the disconnected spiral cord with the other. What number did you use for lost ones? There were no directory enquiries for the dead.

She held the phone to her ear. No dialling tone, but there was *something*. A faint, jagged exhale, like hissing through a closing throat. A trick of the ear. There must be a name for the phenomenon, like when listening to a shell and hearing the sea exhale over stones. Maybe the brain faked soundwaves to drown silence. Ever since Sam died, Erin always needed a soundtrack. Music, radio drama, sketches, neighbours' sex sounds through the flimsy wall… anything. Silence was an open grave; noise the soil that filled it.

She was supposed to be making noise right now, but nowt came out. She'd thought she'd know the right words, but she had nothing. Speaking out loud in public was hard enough, but by herself was even more difficult. But that was the point, wasn't it? She had to believe she was no longer alone.

"I'm going to start with little things," Erin said, closing her eyes. "Else I won't get words out for crying. I'm staying in the Grand, which I thought you'd appreciate. The smell of fishfingers still haunts the corridors. I went into the old ballroom and was thrown like a fish back into the memory of Mum pissed, on stage, singing karaoke Meatloaf, then falling into the audience, flashing her Spanx."

She stopped to take a breath. Was she supposed to leave gaps in her monologue with the dead, as if it were a conversation? Or keep speaking, like Auntie Van who only shut up when ten-gins-in to Christmas Day?

The hissing down the phone grew louder.

"I'm only booked in for two nights, though. I've got our old tent in the car and I'm thinking of camping out in her old spot, not far from here. Other little things? I bought a blow-up pirate at the fancy dress shop on the front to replace the one you punctured. And I felt so lonely in Scarborough without you that I tried to hang out with the chainsaw clown in the Tower of Terror. I think I scared him."

The hissing was less mechanical now, more human.

"And that's how little things turn into big ones, I suppose," Erin said, tears forming. "Eveything is about missing you."

Slowly, in drawn-out bursts that sounded painful, in a voice that was Sam and not-Sam, the hiss said, "Erin."

Erin dropped the receiver. It swung by its cord, hissing filling the box like smog. She was imagining her twin's voice, her brain hearing what it needed. It made sense: she'd love to hear Sam again, see her, put her to bed after a night on the piss. She took a deep breath. Her exhale made ghosts on the glass.

"I'm making up your voice, Sam," Erin said. "Shows you how well things have been going for me since you left."

But what if it wasn't imagination?

"I know you're not really there, that this is a way of soothing myself that doesn't involve Baileys and a bucket of crispy chicken, but, if it's you, there's so much I want to say, and ask."

"Erin." The whisper slid from the receiver. "Let me in." Words formed from the hiss like birds joining a mumuration. "Let me in. I must come in."

Erin rubbed away the condensation and stared through the glass. The sky was heather-purple with dusk. There was nobody outside the box to allow inside. Only the wind.

"Let me in." The voice swung back and forth by Erin's shins.

She picked up the receiver again, held it close to her ear. "Sam? Please? Is that you? I need to know."

"All that is left," the hiss fizzed.

"All that's left of what? Of Sam?"

The hiss stopped for a second, then resurged louder.

"All that is left. Let me in."

"I don't understand, please, help me."

"Help me," the voice echoed.

The wind picked up speed, charging at the phone box, rocking it on its base. All went silent, then the gust blasted at the glass. One panel shattered. Skin hit with glass sleet, Erin shrieked, and the wind fisted into her mouth and down her throat.

Burning and creaking, her lungs expanded like stretching fingers as the wind pushed against her ribs, finding more room till her first rib broke. The blood-tinged scream in her throat carried with it a hiss.

Pain seized her sides as she threw her shoulder at the door and lurched out of the telephone box. She had to get off the moor. Get to a place she could be sane.

The wind rushed at her as she stumbled back down the path, searching her face and stinging her eyes as her feet found the path. It was dark. The kind of dark that swallowed. Shingle shifted beneath her. The ground tilted away. She walked but couldn't feel her legs. Of course, she couldn't. She was numb, in shock. Retriggered. She should never have come.

On the road back, her headlights showed only slices of road. The moors pressed in on either side. The wind, though, was at her back, pushing the car on. Maybe it was helping her back to the hotel.

Her ribs flared again. The sound of splintering came from her chest. She could hardly breathe as she held her side with one hand, the other trying to keep control of the car.

At the junction, she indicated to head to the city centre. Nothing happened. Her hand stayed on the wheel, steering her on. She tried to move her fingers. Nothing. Not even a twitch. She wasn't alone in the car. Or her own body.

For one moment, her loneliness was blown away and she was whole, twinned within, again. Then something swelled inside her and her foot slammed down on the accelerator. The car jolted forwards and another rib ripped, a kindling twig readied for campfire. Her eyes were eclipsed by the blackness at the heart of flames.

★ ★ ★

Erin woke. Car horn sounding, hiss trickling from her lips.

Opening the car door, she climbed out, slowly. She was in a cul-de-sac, in a suburb by the look of the *Edward Scissorhands* houses, the Volvos and run-arounds in identikit driveways, the working streetlights with their pumpkin pools of light. She'd never been here before, didn't know how she'd driven here or what happened on the way. Somehow, though, she shook with the nausea of recognition.

Unable to see inside the boot, she took something cool and pointed from a bag and slipped it into her pocket. Her hood was flipped up by the wind. Walking up to one of the houses, she stopped by a dying hanging basket beside the door and, without knowing why, rubbed a geranium leaf between her fingers. She sniffed her fingertips. The lemon-green scent meant nothing, but she was crying. They weren't her tears.

Bending down, she tilted one of the terracotta pots and picked up a house key. Put it in the lock. It fitted, but only just. She gave the key a wiggle till it turned, as if she knew how. Something else was driving her.

Erin tried to run, to turn, to cry for help, but couldn't change her direction. Walking into the hallway of a warm, bright house, keeping the door wide open, she slipped off her wellies, leaving them on an immaculate mat. On the walls were marks where photos once hung. Her mouth opened and words stretched their way out – "I'm back."

Nathan walked into the hallway, a fire iron in his hands. His hair may have been longer than the last time they'd met but the ice in his eyes was the same.

The young woman had big, haunted eyes, a small body and a heather-purple bruise on her wrist. She shrank, trembling, into the wall.

"Get out now," Erin's mouth told her. "You know what he is."

The young woman moved towards the open door.

He stepped forward, blocking her and grabbing her injured wrist. "You're not going anywhere."

"Let her go, Nathan." Erin's throat was worked from the inside.

"Take down your fucking hood, Erin," Nathan said. "You invade my house and talk shit to my fiancée. Turn around and leave or I'll get my gun. Who the fuck do you think you are?"

"I'm not who you think," Erin's lips said. "And you don't have a gun. Hours in hunting shops and you never had the nerve to buy one." A ventriloquist had her larynx, although it wasn't her voice. It was softer, deeper. Sam's but not. Its words carried the hiss of another world. "The back door is locked, right?" she asked the young woman, who nodded. "Good. Because we don't want the wind, ghosts, murderers or death to get out."

Nathan was now as pale as the telephone box. One hand gripped the young woman, the other raised the fire iron. "Sam?"

"You don't get to hurt anyone else, Nathan." Erin's jaw was loose, and moving. Her panic was smothered by a sheet of calm as her legs were moved towards him.

"What the fuck is that?" Nathan stared at Erin's hand.

Erin looked down at the sharpened tent peg in her left fist. She must have taken it from the boot.

Nathan's smug laugh was sugar glass brittle. "You and your sister always did love camping, didn't you? So pathetic."

Pushing the young woman away, he loomed towards Erin, grabbing her neck. The wind of the moors hissed in her throat and her chest.

Her hand raised and she tried to jam the peg into Nathan's side, but he knocked it away.

He laughed. "Is that it?" he asked. Then he blinked, over and over. His head jerked down to his chest. A knife with a green wooden handle was stuck between his ribs. His eyes widened. "How did you... find it?" His words jerked out slowly, hissing like a slow puncture.

"Where you left it," Erin's ventriloquist said, stretching her mouth into a smile.

Nathan slumped, a cut puppet, to the floor. Eyes fixed.

"Thank you," the young woman said.

★ ★ ★

The next days were a held breath of police questioning and confusion. CCTV showed Erin driving up to and breaking into Nathan's lock-up and locating Sam's ashes and the knife he'd used to kill her. She couldn't explain it. Or her broken ribs. Or her glazed glare. Or how, two days later, when the testimony of Nathan's fiancée freed her, she opened the window of her sea view room and exhaled the north wind. Like the tide, Erin breathed herself back in again.

Picking up the bone white box of Sam's cremains, Erin opened it and held the ashes up to the gorse-yellow sun. She tipped them, a murmuration of memories, and said, "Let her in," to the waiting wind.

ALL IN THE GAME
Craig DiLouie

Doug pounds up the basement stairs, making every second count.

Right now, seconds are life.

Panting, he seizes a cardboard box loaded with bottled water and stomps back down to drop it onto the hard floor. Then up again, sweating and red-faced.

He should have done more cardio. He should have made the time. For years, he worked hard to take care of everyone and everything except himself.

Gritting his teeth, Doug powers through it. People are counting on him. Right now, every box is survival.

He freezes at a distant scream. The grating shriek seems to leap from the background gunfire booming outside like the Fourth of July.

"Honey?" he calls out. "Katherine, are you all right?"

"They're outside!" she yells from upstairs.

"Hurry up!"

His voice sounds tinny and breathless. Doug forces a few deep breaths but cannot seem to get enough air in his lungs. For days, the threat circled his home, and now it is on his doorstep.

He grabs a box and lunges down the stairs to toss it alongside the others and then bolts back. One by one, he heaves bulging suitcases and sends them tumbling and banging down the stairs.

Katherine squeezes past carrying Chloe and bustles down to disappear into the dim basement. Wearing a backpack, Nate peers up at Doug.

"Can I help, Daddy?"

"Just get downstairs."

"What's going on?"

Another scream, closer. Doug glares at the wall, as if it might part for him so he can see what is happening out there.

"They're, uh…"

"It sounds like a movie or something," his seven-year-old son says.

"Go downstairs and give your mom a hand," Doug tells him.

This usually works. Nate loves to help.

"Awww. Can't I go see?"

A window shatters. The living room. A table lamp bursts with a loud pop. An animal howl of pain and rage fills the hallway.

Nate gapes in awe. "What was *that*?"

Doug hands over the last suitcase. "Take this to your mother, Nathan. Go!"

He rushes into the den where he keeps his safe. The roaring cascades in the living room. Something crashes in another room in the house. The kitchen. Closer. His wild eyes take in everything but cannot seem to focus on anything.

Then the old civil defence air raid siren at City Hall blares with a deafening wail, blotting out all other sound. It galvanises him to move even faster.

Fumbling with his keys, Doug opens the safe and removes the AR-15 rifle and ammo. He never owned a gun and did not even like guns until he bought this home and became a father.

The window blinds are raised, and that is when he spots one of his neighbours backing away from a pack of men across the street. She turns and bolts straight into the arms of another man, who wraps her in a tight hug and starts gnawing.

His stomach turning over, Doug looks away as people emerge from everywhere to form a squirming, bloody dogpile.

He loads a magazine and racks a round. Levelling the weapon, he re-emerges into the hallway and sweeps for threats.

The siren is still blasting. He senses rather than hears more crashes in the kitchen. Vibrations in the walls. Whoever is in there is tearing the place apart.

For most of his life, Doug feared physical conflict. Always ready to back away from confrontation, unwilling to risk losing a tooth or worse over a stupid fight.

Not when it comes to his kids, however. Not when it comes to his home.

His terror becomes rage.

Growling, he advances with the rifle ready to shoot. As if sensing his presence, whoever is in the kitchen stops moving. Goes still, waiting.

At the end of the hall, Doug stomps on a stuffed bear on the carpet. He stares at it for a few moments. He recognises it as Mr. Tickles. Chloe cannot sleep without the stuffie.

He scoops up Mr. Tickles and shoves it into his back pocket.

Then he retreats back to the basement, gets inside, and slams the door.

★ ★ ★

DAY 1

Doug gets to work buttoning up his Alamo to survive here as long as it takes. He appreciates being busy. Breaking survival down into a series of chores.

He turns on the taps in the bathroom to fill the tub with a water reserve. He cuts cardboard to tape over the basement windows. He pushes all the old family junk to the sides of the storage room so that Katherine can turn it into a larder.

These are all things he can do, things over which he still has control. Moments he does not think about the world ending right outside.

Ending inside, too. Right upstairs, in fact, in his kitchen.

Too late now to hammer planks over the doors and window frames. The noise would only draw more of the things into the house and straight to the door.

He does not know how strong they are. Whether the planks would even hold.

The air raid siren cut out an hour ago. The police sirens stopped long before that. Now even the popcorn pop of gunfire has faded to the odd jarring boom.

The silence struck Doug with relief until he realised it meant the battle was over, a grand battle the living lost.

In the storage room, Katherine emptied half the boxes, organised the food, and now busies herself storing them. Cans, boxes, and bottles line the shelves.

Doug starts chipping in.

"No," his wife says crossly. "I have a system."

Katherine winces as she blinks away the needles of tears. She is shaking. Something else Doug can do, comfort her.

When he reaches to stroke her back, his wife growls. It reminds him of the things outside, how like animals they are. He drops his hand and watches her smash a pasta box down on a shelf. Her breath hitches in her chest.

"What are we going to do?" Katherine asks him.

"We're going to stay put and keep quiet."

She has her system, he has his.

"I thought we were going to defend the house," she says.

An unspoken accusation. Doug gave up the upstairs without a fight. Yes, they had a plan to try to hold the entire house, but it didn't work out that way. It would have been a fight he'd have lost, and his children would have lost a protector.

"We're better off down here," he says. "Safer."

"My cellphone isn't working."

"The power's out. The network is crashing. We expected this."

"I can't reach Mom. I don't know what's going on."

Doug says nothing. As far as he is concerned, they know everything they need to know. It is all happening right outside. There is no other useful news.

Katherine's mother lives in Colorado in a region that was still free of infection as of this morning. He resists the temptation to take stock of his own scattered relatives. Doug has his own people to worry about right now. Katherine, Nate, and Chloe.

He does not mention that he bought a battery-powered radio but left it upstairs during the pell-mell rush to get into the basement.

"She could be *dead*," Katherine says.

"I'm sure she's fine."

Katherine flinches at his words, his offhand tone.

"Listen. We're okay," he adds. "That's the important thing."

The words come out so lame he does not even convince himself.

Katherine's wince turns into an all-out grimace as she goes on stocking, slamming soup cans into place. They have always dealt with crises very differently. Doug postpones processing so he can act. After it is over, he can have his freakout. His wife always gets hers out of the way at the start, and then she is right as rain.

When the outbreak engulfed a chain of big cities, Doug prepared. On the first day, while the government promised a swift end to the emergency, he drove to the supermarket with a long list Katherine wrote for him balled in his fist. Ramming his cart down the aisles, he trusted his intimidating height and stature to see him through without any fights over who got to loot the last box of Captain Crunch.

Friends, neighbours, none of them matter anymore. They will fend for themselves. This is the type of crisis that rapidly pares society down to the individual. Every man for himself.

No. Every *family* for itself.

"We're okay here," Doug says again, this time with total conviction. "We stay hidden, and we stay quiet. We're going to live. All of us. I'll protect us."

"Sure," Katherine says, though he does not like the way she says it.

Shoulders clenched and teeth gritted, she goes on filling the shelves. He wonders if he said the wrong thing and should try a different approach, but his instincts tell him to leave her alone and let her process. Right now, organising their supplies is something she can control.

There is still the propane stove and sleeping bags. He can get those sorted.

"Mommy?"

Doug forces a smile for his five-year-old daughter, who is peeking her head around the corner. "Mommy's busy. I can help you, sweetie. What do you need?"

Chloe walks into the storage room and looks up at him with wide eyes.

"There's a man in our house," she says. "I'm scared."

Doug squints at the ceiling, and then he hears it. The creak of footsteps. Chloe swivels her wide eyes from him to her mother, expecting an explanation.

"It's okay," he says. "He'll go away soon."

He made a rule never to lie to his kids. Even when Nate reached an age where he started to question whether Santa Claus was real, Doug hedged his answer, telling his son that some people believe there is a Santa and others don't.

Doug will have to learn how to lie now, however. There is no explaining this.

"When are we going back upstairs?" Chloe says.

"Soon, sweetie." A white lie, as he hopes this is true. "Real soon."

"But who is the man?"

"Don't worry about him. Hey. I was wondering if you've seen Mr. Tickles."

Chloe responds with a glum wag. "I can't find him."

Doug turns around to make a show of searching for the stuffie, exposing Mr. Tickles sticking out of his back pocket for her to see.

"He's right there!" his daughter cries.

He wheels. "What? Where? I don't see him."

"He's behind you, Daddy!"

Another dramatic turnaround. "Huh? I don't see him!"

Finally, Doug relents and lets Chloe have her favourite stuffie back. They are both laughing now. A small moment of happiness for him, and then the terror and anxiety and survivor's guilt returns like a sucker punch.

Smile fading, he leaves the storage room to survey his defences. The idea was to convert the house into a fortress, but the plague rapidly reached Dalton like a wave that spilled straight into his home. Now these friends and neighbours want to tear him and his family to shreds and eat them.

The basement is thankfully finished, something Doug insisted on when buying the house, picturing a man-cave complete with massive flatscreen, fully stocked bar, and pool table. Instead, it quickly became a sprawling playroom, toys and games everywhere, the couch cushions plundered to make a blanket fort.

The only way in or out is the door at the top of the stairs, where he'd installed a deadbolt, and two windows near the ceiling now taped over with cardboard. His next task will be to nail two-by-fours over—

"Who are these people in our yard?" Nate calls out.

The boy has shoved an old side table under a window and now stands tiptoe on it while gripping the windowsill. A piece of cardboard dangles by a strand of tape.

Doug's first instinct is to shout bloody murder. Instead, he remembers himself and uses his warning voice.

"Get down from there before you fall," Doug says.

Or they see you, he thinks but does not add.

Nate stiffens and climbs down. "Sorry, Daddy."

Doug walks over for a peek himself, hoping he does not see a repeat of the bloody dogpile. He spots Hank, one of his neighbours, skulking through Katherine's flower beds wearing an expression of perpetual rage and astonishment, hands clenched over his mangled chest.

Terrified to the point of being sick, Doug expects Hank's head to swivel toward him with a hateful glare.

Once spotted, you're dead.

"Hell's bells," he mutters, the most he will allow himself to curse around his kids. After fitting the cardboard back over the window, he retapes it to the surrounding frame. "This stays closed at all times."

"Why?" Nate asks.

His son is at that age when this is his response to everything. *Because I said so*, Doug thinks, but he knows this will not cut it.

As a father, he is used to improvising.

"Because we're glamping," he says.

Behind Nate, Chloe laughs. "What's *glamping*?"

"Camping with glamour."

The kids gawk at this fresh pearl of adult mystery.

"We're taking a camping trip right here in our basement," he explains. "The adventure of camping with all the comforts of home. Ignore the rest of the world for a while and recharge our batteries. Get some really good family time."

Nate looks at his sister and then back to Doug. "Okay."

"Now," says Doug, his smile widening. "Who wants to play a game?"

★ ★ ★

DAY 3

Doug draws a card and tosses it down with feigned horror.

"Daddy has the worst luck," he says. "Back four spaces."

"You'll do better, Daddy," Chloe comforts him.

"Thank you, sweetie. I'm not ready to throw in the towel yet. Your turn, Nate."

His son delivers a cunning look and flips a card. A five, allowing him to traipse one of his pieces straight onto Doug's square and knock him back home.

"Sometimes the towel throws you, Daddy!" Nate announces.

"It ain't over 'til it's over, boy."

Chloe glares at her brother's moment of triumph. Her face turns sulky. "I don't want to play anymore," she says with theatrical regret.

"Because I'm winning!" Nate yells. "You always do this."

The girl starts bawling. *"I want to go upstairs!"*

For help, Doug turns to Katherine, but she is focused on preparing their supper at the propane stove under one of the windows. Another night of canned ravioli.

For three days, they stuck to the plan. Stay hidden, stay silent, stay alive. The only problem is children's brains need constant engagement and grow bored easily.

Nate is inquisitive and physical, already talking about becoming an engineer like his dad when he grows up. Chloe is creative and always thinking about others' feelings. They were too little during the Covid lockdowns to remember that time. Doug wonders how other parents managed it with older kids. In desperation, they probably let their young ones run amok on their screens.

Not an option now, with no power grid.

Still bawling: *"I don't like this room anymore!"*

The house rustles over their heads. Feet tramp across the floor. A piece of furniture topples over with a loud thump.

"It's a game," Doug says. "This is all a game. Do you want to know a secret?"

At the edge of an all-out meltdown, Chloe's brain switches gears. "What secret?"

"It's a special game. Like hide and seek, but we'll be on TV."

Still improvising, desperate.

Nate regards him with an exaggerated frown. "Are you kidding, Daddy?"

"It's true," Doug says with a shrug that says *don't believe me if you want, that's fine.* "It's a game show where the contestants hide and then other people have to try and find them."

At the stove, Katherine wheels.

"Doug! Stop it."

"Mommy's not happy I told you. It's against the rules. Right, hon?" Her confused and angry glare does not waver.

"Your father's right," she says. "He was not supposed to tell you that."

"So, it's like one of those reality TV shows?" Nate asks him.

Doug glances side to side before answering with a conspiratorial whisper. "There are hidden *cameras* all over the basement *recording* us."

Both kids look all around, hoping to spot the hidden cameras.

"I *knew* it," Nate says.

"Don't look," Doug scolds. "You're not supposed to know, remember?"

"We get a prize if we win," Chloe says. "Right, Daddy?"

Another glance side to side.

"That's right," Doug answers.

The kids erupt with a loud cheer.

Instantly, the house comes to life again. Pounding feet. A seething snarl from a dozen mouths.

Chloe yelps as a fist bangs against the door at the top of the stairs. Another snarl, louder. Doug stiffens but stays calm.

"Shhh," he says, wearing a smile he hopes does not look as forced as it feels. "We have to be quiet as a mouse."

The kids giggle but otherwise keep silent.

"It's all part of the game," Doug says.

★ ★ ★

DAY 5

Doug sits up bleary-eyed in the sleeping bag and props his back against the wall with a sigh. Next to him, Katherine stirs with a dazed look, once again confused about why she is waking on the floor in the basement.

He rubs his hands over his stubbled face and then through his greasy hair. All night, he dreamed he was alone and could not find his family, while something awful hunted him in the dark.

"Every day's a win," he mumbles.

"If you call this winning," she says.

"We're all alive. I'd call that a very big win."

"I wonder if we're just dying slower than everyone else."

The floorboards above them creak as the infected move around. Doug is curious if they ever sleep, what they dream.

Katherine glares at the ceiling. "Why don't they leave?"

She has puffy dark circles under her eyes. Her face looks gaunt, her hair stringy. Like him, she is wasting away down here.

"I think they can hear us," Doug says. "They know we're in the house. They just don't know where."

"We need a plan."

He frowns. "We have a plan. Stay hidden, stay alive, and wait for rescue."

"How do you know help is coming? What if this is it?"

"We'll be okay, hon," he says. "I promise."

"Don't do that." She sits up with her arms crossed over her chest. "You can lie to the kids and pretend everything's all right, but don't bullshit me."

"That's not fair, and you know it."

"You telling them it's all a game," Katherine says. "It's not a game."

For over a week, the kids have sensed something is wrong. Cooped up in the house, tension among their parents, too young to understand what is happening. Now this. Trapped in the basement. It could be a living nightmare for them, or Doug could at least delay the trauma and let them live by inventing a story.

"What if today was our last day with them?" he asks. "Would you want to see them terrified or having fun, living life?"

She blanches with a flash of rage. "Damn you, Doug."

"I'm sorry—"

"All you want to do is sit here and pretend this isn't happening. I'm so terrified, I'm losing my mind. We should be getting out of here."

"How?"

"We have the rifle," Katherine says. "We both know how to shoot. We should get in our car and go!"

Doug feels an overwhelming urge to do just that. Charge up the stairs blasting at anything that moves. Get these monsters out of his house once and for all. Recover the radio and find out what is happening.

Do *something*.

"I'm scared too," he admits. "If it was just us, I'd say let's go. But I'm really scared that I won't be able to protect our kids. If anything happened to them…"

Her anger softens. "I know."

"I'd give up."

He does not rule out leaving, though. At some point, they may have to bug out. He does not want to face the prospect that they are trapped.

Katherine takes his hand and squeezes it tight. "At least I know you're human."

"What? What do you mean?"

"You putting up such a strong, happy front. I was actually starting to think a part of you was enjoying all this. It was really pissing me off."

Doug lets out a bitter chuckle.

"Hon, I'm barely holding it together. Every second, I'm about to lose my—"

A piercing scream sounds in the main area. Electrified, Doug scrambles out of the sleeping bag for the rifle as Chloe rushes into the room and straight into her mother's arms.

"Nate hit me in the leg!"

Her brother stomps in after her. "I didn't do anything!"

Overhead, the house trembles to life. Snarls join to become a single bestial roar. Furniture scrapes and spills in loud bangs. Glass pops and shatters. Scores of feet stomp. Hands slap the basement door.

Doug waves to silence the kids, but they are already quietly gaping at the ceiling with their mouths hanging open.

He glances at Katherine, who stares back with wide, watery eyes. They are not getting out of here through the house. No radio, no shooting their way to the garage.

The windows are now their only exit. Doug pictures it, hauling the kids out one by one in plain view of the infected. Shooting the entire time to stay alive. Every shot drawing more, racing to the sound.

They would be slaughtered.

Doug forces a smile.

"They are really looking for us," he says. "But we're going to win."

Chloe turns in her mother's arms to glare at him. "I don't like this game, Daddy!"

Nate flops on the floor and sags. "I hate it too."

"Why don't you guys bring me a book, and we can read it together?"

"I don't feel like reading."

"We could play I Spy—"

"I want to go upstairs!"

"Shh," Katherine pleads. "Please be quiet."

Upstairs, the noise begins to abate as the infected settle.

"Mommy, I'm scared," Chloe says.

"It's okay to be scared, baby girl. But we're going to be fine. We'll go upstairs soon. I promise."

"As soon as this stupid game is over," Nate grouses.

Katherine looks at Doug in a mute appeal for help.

He asks, "Did I ever tell you kids what we're going to get if we win?"

They stare at him. He has their full attention.

"There are two types of people looking for us," he explains. "One is the zombies. The other is the Army. We have to make sure the bad guys don't see us and that the good guys find us first."

"But what if we win?" Nate asks him.

Chloe chimes in. "You said they'll give us a prize. Right, Daddy?"

Doug musters a grin, which he hopes appears happy instead of frightening.

"We get a free trip to Disney World for two weeks," he says.

Their eyes go wide. Mouths stretch into Os.

"Wow," Nate says. "Hell's bells!"

"Shh," says Doug. "I wasn't supposed to tell you. It's our secret."

"When can we go?" Chloe asks him.

"As soon as we win. We just have to wait for the good guys to find us."

"The Army?"

"That's right. In the meantime, the bad guys are going to try to scare us."

Doug punctuates this with a wry chuckle, as if he pities them for trying. Nate responds with a conspiratorial grin. *Yeah, those zombies are dumb*, the grin says.

Nate's punch and the racket overhead forgotten, Chloe plants a loud kiss on her mother's cheek. "Mommy, we're going to Disney World!"

Fighting tears, Katherine says, "That's right, honey. We sure are."

"But only if we win," Doug reminds them.

★ ★ ★

DAY 7

Doug marches into the storage room, where Katherine takes inventory of their dwindling provisions. Behind him, Nate and Chloe go on bawling.

"What happened this time?" she asks him.

"I caught Nate sneaking up the stairs again." He rummages around the piles of junk for the planks he knows are here somewhere. "I'm going to have to board it."

"He hates this." Katherine does too, he can tell. The idea of being trapped.

Doug gives the emptier shelves a quick inspection. "Food's not looking too terrible. The problem is water. We're using it up faster than I thought we would."

"And then what?"

"What do you mean, 'and then what'?"

Practically snarling the words. He saves all his patience for his kids. He has to be careful about bottling it up and then taking it out on her.

Doug takes a deep breath. "If the water runs out, we'll think of something."

"We could still leave. Try to find safety instead of waiting for it to come to us."

"We won't make it. Those things are like animals."

"We have the gun—"

"Do you know Allison, lives with Greg three doors down? Never cleans up after her dog?"

"Of course I know her," Katherine says. "We had them over. And yes, she does clean up after her dog, it was just that one time—"

"I saw them get her. I *watched*, helpless. They didn't just bite her. They tore her apart with their hands." He stretches his hands into claws. "Like…" The full memory of the dogpile comes back to him, and he winces. "Like she was tissue paper. She was still alive and screaming when—"

Katherine's hands are clapped over her ears. "Stop it."

"We're staying put as long as we can, and that's final."

"I married a man, Doug."

"What?" A burning heat floods his chest.

She glares back at him. "I said you're a man, Doug. So do something!"

"I am doing something!" he roars. "I'm keeping you and our kids safe as well as I can!"

Their eyes go wide. Doug does not even breathe.

A strange growl permeates the basement, rising in volume. A mechanical sound accompanied by the screech of tracks. Then the house trembles as some big armoured vehicle rolls past.

A loud drumming pierces the air. A heavy machine gun.

"Jesus Christ," Doug breathes. "That's the Army."

Katherine bursts into tears. "We made it?"

He slowly nods. "We—"

She hurls herself at him, and he catches her in a twirling embrace. Doug hugs his wife for all he is worth while she alternately cries and laughs.

"We made it," he says.

"Oh God, I love you, Doug. You were right."

Outside, a second vehicle approaches, already shooting. The thuds of bullet impacts splash overhead. The loud rumbling fills the basement as the big vehicle slowly grinds past the house.

In the main area, his little girl lets out a terrified screech.

"Chloe?" Electrified, he bolts into the room and falls to his knees in time to catch her flying at him with a high-pitched scream. "What's...?"

The infected are in the basement.

They spill down the stairs, a squirming avalanche of bloated bodies, vacant eyes, and gaping maws chomping, always chomping. The house must have been full of them. They tumble down in a rolling pile of living corpses, still trailing shards of flesh and gnawed limbs that snap off and become part of the flood.

They bring with them an overwhelming stench. At the stairs' bottom, a small hill of bodies writhes while the rest stand and shamble toward Doug.

"Nate let them in," Chloe cries against his chest. "I'm sorry, Daddy!"

"What?" His voice cracks. "*Nate?*"

Katherine marches past him, yanking the AR-15's charging bolt.

"*Goddamn it, motherfucker—*"

She levels the rifle and opens fire with a deafening report. The nearest infected spins away while the rest continue their advance.

"Nate!"

Bang, bang, bang, bang.

Blood and bits of flesh and bone fly through the air in a noxious mist. Katherine lets out a banshee scream as she drains the magazine. Bodies topple, only to be replaced by others pouring down the stairs. The rifle clicks dry, leaving a haze of gun smoke.

"Naaaaaaate!"

Katherine charges and slams the rifle stock into the nearest face. The man stumbles backward. She wades into the mob swinging the rifle like a bat.

The zombies crowd around, snarling.

"Katherine," Doug sobs. "Oh, God. *Katherine!*"

He takes a step forward to help his wife but remembers his little girl in his arms and that he is responsible for keeping her alive at all costs. Backing away, he retreats to the storage room and turns one last time to see his wife shoving at the bodies, still trying to reach their son, screaming as one of the infected grabs a fistful of her long hair and yanks it from her scalp with a sickening *rip*. The dead continue to press in, grabbing and scratching.

The rest lurch toward Doug.

There is nothing he can do.

He brings Chloe inside the storage room and slams the door. They hug each other while Katherine howls Nate's name until it morphs into a bloodcurdling scream.

The infected start pounding on the door.

"N-N-Nate o-opened the d-door," Chloe sobs. "He said the good guys were here. He wanted to win the game."

"It's okay." He squeezes her tight. "You're okay."

At last, she settles down enough for him to tuck her into her sleeping bag with Mr. Tickles. The room is dark except for the glow of an LED lantern. Doug lies close to her, their faces only inches apart.

"Are Mommy and Nate going to be okay?" she asks him.

He musters a reassuring smile. Outside the house, a vehicle grinds down the street on clacking tracks. A machine gun chatters.

Inside, the dead wander around the basement, thumping into walls.

"Of course," Doug says.

"Are you sure?"

"Oh, I'm sure. Daddy knows."

"I don't know what happened."

"Were you scared?"

"Yeah."

"It's okay," Doug says. "Even big, brave girls get scared. Okay?"

"Okay."

"Mommy and Nate are fine. The bad guys caught them, that's all."

"You mean in the game?"

"That's right. It's all in the game."

"Did we lose? Are we still playing?"

Doug smiles again.

"We're still in the game," he says. "That's why we have to be super quiet. Quiet as a mouse. I know the game isn't very fun for you, but we made it this far, didn't we? Most don't. We can't give up now. The good guys are almost here. You'll see. Then we'll win. We'll all go to Disney World. We'll ride the rides. We'll eat ice cream in the sun. We'll visit Mickey and see all the princesses you like. It'll be you and me, Nate, and Mommy. All of us together. As soon as the good guys find us. We'll all go to Disney World as a family."

At last, Chloe produces a small smile of her own.

"I love my family," she says sleepily.

"I know you do, sweetie. We love you back. More than we love ourselves. And we'll go on protecting you, because you're so special to us."

"We'll be very quiet."

"Quiet as a mouse."

"And they'll never catch us."

The little girl closes her eyes. Doug kisses her forehead goodnight and then, at last, he allows himself to weep.

"No." His voice hitches in his chest, around his aching heart. "They never will. I won't let them."

NOT ALL STONES MEAN MURDER
Kaaron Warren

While others told scary stories of the Mill House and who haunted it, it was always the Mill itself that fascinated me. We could see it from the derelict hut on our side of the river where we used to party as teens. The roof was safe enough and we'd sit up there with our cheap wine and view the river and all upon it. We'd smoke drugs if we had them and go wild about that river, the high moon reflecting a path on the water. The house loomed large, alone on the other shore, remnants of fruit trees dead and strange, even then. The Mill attracted me, changing in the light, looming in the shadows. It was the sort of thing you forgot about the minute you turned away, like most dreams the moment you awaken.

So when my photography lecturer set us the task of doing something brave, of photographing what we were scared of, the Mill had to be it. "You have to get it close up," the lecturer said. "Look your fear in the face."

"I don't know if he'll give me permission," I said, meaning Mr. Miller, who still lived in the house itself, and who was known to shout at anyone he caught near the Mill. His family had lived there for decades, but he was alone now.

"Don't quote me," my lecturer said quietly, "but asking permission isn't brave. You need to get over there."

I asked myself: Is it safer in the light or in the dark? But that didn't matter.

I undertook to photograph the old Mill every hour, on the hour, for a full day. Staying up all night for a project was not unusual for me. Sometimes you needed to wait for that magical moment to appear.

I set up my small tent, high enough for me to stand and wide enough to keep my equipment protected. The mist would rise throughout the early morning and I wanted to keep as much moisture out of the camera as possible. The mist itself would become a feature, I was sure.

I began at 4:00 p.m. Already there was a chill in the air, but I had chosen the warmest part of the year. I didn't want to freeze to death, become a pointless martyr to the arts. Perhaps no one would find me for weeks and by then the equipment would be destroyed and I'd be eaten by the stray dogs and cats that roamed around… I amused myself with this thought. I decided that if I was close to death, I would set the digital camera to automatic and stumble out there, so that I would be photographed every hour, on the hour, until someone found me.

The contrast of dark and light is part of what frightened me. The second floor of the Mill building filled with light, and I could see the idea of furniture up there, perhaps a desk, perhaps a floor lamp for evening work. The outside walls were patchy with damage, chipped, stained with moss both dry and new. Below, there was a pitch black space. My eyes started to find features and shapes where none existed, the longer I looked. That was where my fascination lay.

Nearby there was a two-wheel wagon, tipped diagonally, and a white metal bucket, to catch what exactly? Blood, I thought, or the rain.

At five in the evening came a wild calling of the birds claiming their sleeping spots. I captured them in motion, the windows obscured by bird flesh. I wouldn't change focus or zoom on my old school camera, but out of boredom I would use my digital camera to observe close up.

The black space beneath the Mill darkened even further, if that was possible. I took a sip of my coffee, still warm, but bitter. There was such a fresh smell in the air my nostrils stung.

At 8:00 p.m. moonlight swamped the Mill. There were shifting shadows but no one to cause them. Nearby trees casting shade, perhaps, or the last flights of the birds unable to settle.

At midnight, I snapped a person outside the Mill. They sat with their legs dangling over the dark space, disappearing into it. The dark covered them like a blanket. I zipped up my jacket, planning to warn this person, *pull your legs up before you are enveloped.* By the time I neared the Mill the person was gone and I knew I had imagined them.

I stood on the lip of the dark place. There were small rustling sounds, insects having a life in there. Rats. I shone my torch in but the light was eaten up. I tried my camera flash, pointing in and clicking. In that moment of illumination, many jars were revealed, filled with apricots or whatever. I wouldn't eat them even if I was starving, unless the liquid was brandy, but I didn't think it was.

I stretched in, reluctant to go all the way inside. Swinging my hand around to find a jar and draw it out. I'd photograph it.

My foot caught. Stuck. Using my flashlight I saw the under Mill area was filled with old bits of equipment, metal boxes, jars. None of it had been touched in decades, it seemed.

A spider web, or a spider, or something, brushed the back of my hand and I recoiled. Truth told, I turned and ran. Finding refuge in my tent, I took a dozen or more photos from afar before curling up to take a nap before my next shot.

★ ★ ★

She was the first person Timmy Miller had seen near the Mill for a while. Most people had lost interest, had better things to do and places to go. He assumed she'd come the long way, over the bridge and then the pathway through the forest. Quickest to cross the river by boat, if you had one. Or take a swim, quickest of all.

When he was younger, on his day off he would swim from the house side of the river to the other. He would rest a while on the muddy banks, enjoying the difference in the sensory elements. He could see his own house, but the air smelled and felt different.

Each time he did this he picked up a small river stone, as evidence he'd been there. These he stacked on the kitchen windowsill. They stood ten deep and twenty across; a lot of swims across the river. He had not added to the stack for a long time and he was wistful. He took short swims, even when the water was freezing (some days the swims were a few strokes, it is to be admitted) but hadn't thought about reaching the other side in an age.

Today, though, after the funeral of his last surviving childhood friend, loneliness overwhelmed him. He sat on the garden bench he had built from flotsam, feeling the sun on his face and the ants at his feet. His dress shoes fell discarded at the back door; he would never wear those cruel, uncomfortable things again. They could bury him barefoot for all he cared. He would use these as planters. There were some marigolds that could be moved.

He wouldn't need those shoes for another funeral. His only friend had passed, and his mother, and his brother Micky long sleeping. His mother's funeral had been a sad affair. Only he and his brother, the milkman and the priest in attendance, and on the street a crowd of ill-wishers, wanting to be sure their mother hit the dirt – "And you next," they called out to the brothers. Following them to the cemetery to make sure she was buried deep.

He could hear the grinding of the mill wheels, although they were long past movement.

He dug out the marigolds. He didn't change out of his suit, not just 'best' but one and only, and he smiled to think of what his mother would have said. She'd been gone twenty years, though.

Those spectators, those haters, did they care about her at all? Had they watched her die from the inside out, as he and his brother had done? Had they dug their own mother's grave, had they spat on it, had they danced and sung Good Riddance, as the boys had done, free from her cruelties, her sharp tongue, her sharp knife marking them each time they disappointed her?

The feel of dirt as he dug up the marigolds with his bare hands, and the joy of seeing worms at work, lifted his spirits. He nestled the flowers into his best shoes. These he placed on a patch of concrete near the back door, thinking they could spread their colour, bring him joy, perhaps.

He heard someone call his name. A distant call, across the water. "Come! Swim!"

His cat, who was not his but kept him company some nights, pressed against his toes, purring and taking a gentle nip. He laughed. She always wanted food. He had the chicken carcass he was planning to bury. Let her gnaw on that. It would keep her happy for a few minutes, at least, by which time he would be away and she would have forgotten his existence.

"Come! Swim!" It could be the grinders shifting in the old Mill, that back and forth movement. But he thought the voice was high, a woman's. Not his mother; her voice was low and sharp, a mean dog barking. She was more like the grinding wheel, harsh and damaging.

He had not done this swim for two years at least. It was probably more; time passed strangely when you lived alone. His brother had never been lonely. The house was still filled with mementoes and memories. He did not feel right simply throwing the items away. Each one represented a real person who had lived, breathed and died. Partly he kept them because he should feel guilty. He would never lose that regret, that guilt at not stopping his brother.

Was he as bad as Micky had been?

He wasn't.

He wasn't.

But had he tolerated, if not encouraged? Had he kept that façade up, so needed for his brother to get away with it for so long?

Perhaps.

As a young man, under the influence, Timmy would swim naked across and back, although always at night and not in full moonlight. Sometimes he'd visit women – 'your little girlfriends', his brother had called them.

Now, he pulled on a wetsuit. The water was cold, even the summer heat couldn't take that chill off.

He walked a few steps in, his feet unsteady on river stones. He wore rubber shoes and knew he looked a sight. If there was a woman waiting on the other side, she'd laugh in his face.

The water suddenly rose, and he began to swim. Stroke by stroke. He loved this, powering forward, the water refreshing him, making him feel young again.

It took longer than it used to. By the time he could stand on the opposite river edge, he was puffing, his breath catching, his heart racing. He needed to exercise more.

The stones on the other side were smaller and paler in colour. He collected one to carry back with him. "Hello?" he called. There was no answer. The silence was dense. He couldn't hear a cricket, a frog, a bat. Nor distant traffic, nor trees rustling, nor voices.

He turned, thinking he would rest once he was home.

The lights were on in his house. Surely he'd set off in daylight, so no lights left on. Time passed strangely, now it was night.

And the lights were on.

He was sure he hadn't left them that way but there it was. A sense of relief filled him. If his mother was alive, he and Micky would be beaten for leaving the lights on. The glow didn't reach the Mill, but he could see a tiny pinprick of light, that young woman's lamp? He would ask her to leave, one way or another, when he got back. He'd left her a warning but she hadn't taken heed.

Over the thick crop of trees he saw lights glowing, at least one sign of life. He wanted to hear voices, suddenly. To sit in a pub with beer, and listen to people talk. Once, he had worked over there, in a butcher's shop, helping the customers, making the sausages. All the cats near his house knew about him, all right, and the dogs, the lot of them with a sixth sense of when he'd arrive home with meat scraps for them all.

At least one of the cats still alive today was a part of his brother's death three years earlier. The first he knew of the trouble was after a swim. He was towelling himself off and heard a low, collective yowling, and Micky there on the back step, naked, skin shining, blood-red, bloodied. One cat latched on to his shoulder, one to his stomach, one to his calf, biting, scratching, hysterical. None on his penis, lucky for him. They dropped to the ground and leapt up again, licking and biting, excited by the blood. Micky had shaken them off and stepped into the house. Fresh blood from a wound seeped out, running in rivulets in the blood dried on his skin.

"Nice swim?" Micky had asked him.

"Jump in the shower, I'll get something for those wounds."

Micky had nodded. Elated. When he was clean and in his pyjamas, he sat upstairs to watch the Mill.

"Can you see anything crawling out?"

"Only the dark," Timmy had said as he placed the river stone he'd collected with the others.

The next day Micky was sluggish, his skin reddened around the lesions, his eyes puffy. The animals wouldn't go near him.

"We should go to the doctor," Timmy had said.

Micky had touched his wounds. "Don't want to talk about it." He took a salt water bath to clean the wounds, swallowed antibiotics left in their mother's bathroom cabinet. He washed in the river when Timmy told him to, *fresh water cures all*. But within a day, he couldn't get out of bed.

"I'm tired," Micky said. "I'll sleep. Don't wake me, Timmy. Leave me to sleep a long time." He said, "Put me with my darlings. No one will know. Put me with my dream girls." And when Micky died, that's what Timmy did, dragged him under the Mill where he could dream all he wanted.

Timmy spread the word that his brother had self-banished and no one was sorry about that. People knew he wasn't right. It didn't mean they didn't like him. He was gregarious, generous, always handing out gifts. What's mine is yours, for the asking, but don't ask for the house. What he gave belonged to the dead but no one knew that. Gold chains, cigarette cases, earrings, small bottles. Sometimes he'd ask, *Can you name me one object that should represent you?* He didn't give it all away.

Timmy wanted to wake him so many times. When the bank or the police asked bad questions. When the butchers closed down. When a girl said no. But he never did go under the Mill.

Those Mill noises; Micky turning over in his sleep.

For the first few days after his brother went under the Mill, Timmy left food out, but that was eaten by the cats and dogs. For the first few months, he'd sit at the lip and talk, but his own voice echoed back at him.

He felt a sense of peace, which brought guilt. He travelled to work and back. He spent days in the town sometimes, lovers, dining out, no one to protect or tell otherwise. He played those ordinary people games. He sat at the railway station, watching the trains come and go, wishing he was brave enough to jump on one. Knowing he wouldn't. He couldn't.

Then the pleasures of the quiet home. The cats. The river.

He shuddered. The wetsuit was clammy and uncomfortable. He unzipped it as he walked towards an old hut near the water's edge. Behind it, years ago he'd learned to stash some clothing. Just simple pants and a shirt, slip-on shoes. Enough that he could wander unnoticed in town. Peer in windows if he wanted. Perhaps buy a beer, if his credit was good.

The clothing was there. It was stiff from the weather (and other things, he now remembered) but warm enough, so he changed there in the twilight. Pulled on the shoes after banging them against the ground to shake any spiders or other creatures out. And wandered.

The town was quiet, preparing for the evening meal and bed. Street lights glowed and mist in the air softened this light. Trees had shed their leaves and these pale things covered the ground like snow. As Timmy stood on the crest of the main square, a dark path through the leaves, trod by many dozens of people in the day, looked like a river. It looked like a snake and as his eyes misted, the river snake lifted and reared towards him. He laughed at this fancy and walked on. At the centre of the square stood an old, deformed tree, and partway up pressed a statue of the Madonna. Someone had built her a wooden surround, long since rotted, but she herself rested clean and pure, shining over the town, her expression sad, scared, loving. Timmy knew that at closing time, some would stagger past and pray to her. Others would wave. And some would wave bare arses, pants down, cocks out, all bravado after whisky and beer.

He would never, himself.

The more he gazed at ordinary things, filled his heart with them, the better it would be once he was home. He could close his eyes and picture: the path of footsteps in the leaves, the family meal, Madonna watching over.

★ ★ ★

I woke up, picked up the digital to snap a few off, that mist! And saw a picture of me sleeping. I must have set it up, somehow? Before? I was tired. I went back to sleep/woke/took photos until the sun came up.

★ ★ ★

Timmy wandered on. Home was in the back of his mind. Those lights on. And it'd be chilly without the fire lit. And the girl there, cold in her tent, but he wasn't going near her. He passed houses, curtains closed or ajar, glowing with warmth. This house had a large crack, the plaster caking off. The wood frame was untreated and damaged, although the glass was surrounded by a newer wood frame, recently replaced perhaps. A large hook hung there for shutters that no longer existed.

Along the window, a child's farm playset. Cow, chickens, farmhouse, trees and a stile. Behind them, three large plant pots crowded each other, the leaves dry and dead.

He would look after it all better if it were his. But it wasn't. None of it was. His cats would want their dinner and his dogs, too, none of them his, so he headed back to the river. He saw a park bench, on a nearby small hill. Lovers would go there to watch the world pass and have a sneaky grope. As young as 15 they went there, 14. Built by a long-ago walking group, it sat here, paint peeling, in case someone came by again.

But this seat, and the stretch of land nearby, had too many stories of ghosts attached to it. Firstly, it was the disappearance of 15 year-old Dianna Smith, who, thinking to have a romantic afternoon with Jack Brown, 16, which to her meant holding hands and talking about favourite things. To Jack, it meant this as well but perhaps he would put his arm over her shoulder, perhaps there was some breast he could feel.

She waited for him for over an hour. She knew his parents must have delayed him; he always had to do chores as payment for going anywhere but school.

After an hour passed she realised he would think she was desperate or in love with him for having waited so long. She stood up, brushed off crumbs (after half an hour she had eaten all the cake she brought), and felt a hand on her shoulder…

"About time," she said, turning, trying to smile not frown. The hand on her shoulder was heavy. It pinched as she turned to see a man who was not her boyfriend.

Timmy walked up to this bench as he had before to see initials carved there. MM and DS.

His brother called Dianna Cake Tin when he told her story. Because that was what they had at home of hers.

Timmy thought, "I should get back." His brother was long asleep but that girl was over there and who knew what she'd find?

★   ★   ★

I really wanted to leave once daylight struck, creeped out by that photo I didn't remember setting up, but I could almost feel my lecturer's hand on my back, pushing me forward. Him listing the bravest photos, "Tiananmen Square, anyone? To name a recent one!" The Mill was just a dark space. I heard the wheels grinding, shifting back and forwards as the building creaked side to side, like a lumbering giant trying to walk. It smelled wet, it smelled *dark*, if that's even possible.

I used the flash and saw piles of animal bones. Scraps of material. I heard those bones shifting and scraping, and heard a low moan, a cow in pain somewhere? I felt that sound, the echo and vibration, in my feet, my ankles, and I stepped back outside, knowing I had my shot. I wouldn't know until later *what* I had. But an image sprung into my mind unasked, unphotographed, of a human face turning to look at me.

The sun was bright on this cloudless day. I could leave now, ride twenty minutes and I'd be on the outskirts of town. I walked quickly to my tent, trying not to feel pursued.

I leant in to pack my camera, roll up my sleeping bag.

An odd, old smell filled the tent. I must have trodden in something, caught mud on my soles. There was that smell... it wasn't rot, it was infection, shit, like the time my ear piercings went bad. Packing faster now, leaving a lot of it behind, I'd come back later, heard that grinding sound, bone on stone, then the tent flap opened and my ankles, something vice-like around both ankles and dragging me, I'm face down, face in the dirt, I'm trying to turn around, to scream, to see, and the shock and the agony, the *sound* of my ankles cracking as I'm dragged into the dark—

★ ★ ★

Slapping his face to bolster himself, Timmy stepped back into the river. Hopefully the light in the house was an illusion and he would step out of the other side to darkness.

Not only were the lights on, there was movement. Thieves. He shook himself dry then pulled on his loose warm pants, his thick knitted jumper, his beanie. He'd be winning no fashion parade, not unless he could judge himself.

He walked around the side of his house and selected an iron bar from the pile of debris there. Swinging it, his own strength surprised him.

A shadow passed across the kitchen window. Who was in there? Rather than rush-attack, he slowly crept to the window and peered in.

A tall man inside looked so much like his brother, Timmy said his name aloud. This must be a cousin, surely? His dad had eleven siblings and between them, dozens of children. Who were they to push into his house, turning on lights and using his kitchen?

He went in through the front door, thinking to sneak up on the intruder.

The smell of dirt (of under the Mill), and of infection, filled the house. A trail of mud led from the back door to the kitchen, smeared like a dog had dragged its shitty arse. Timmy hefted the iron bar, ready to hit first at the person who would filthy his house like this, ask questions later.

On the kitchen table; a camera.

Standing at the sink, tall, slumped, hair clumped and knotted, the man who looked like his brother. Peeling potatoes.

Timmy lifted his weapon. It couldn't be.

But the figure turned, a terrible smile of welcome on his green-tinged, pustule-ridden face. "Nice swim, Timmy?" he said. "Are you hungry?" He said, "I've been asleep a long time."

Micky always cooked a feast when Timmy got back from a swim.

"Get the good plates," Micky said. The fleshy part of his hand was dark with decay. His eyes yellow and oozing pus. His elbows worn down to bone and that bone splintered.

Timmy was in a daze, although he had known deep down, otherwise why spend so long peeping around town?

The good plates were in the sideboard in the front room. He never went in there, never opened the doors. On the sideboard was his father's last glass of whisky, just a sludge in the bottom now. Sitting next to the old phone and don't you dare touch it, that was the last place she'd thought of him alive. Standing there getting the news and her eyes on the boys as if somehow they'd caused the accident that killed their father. Her frozen stiff then turning with a face of such utter fury they ran and hid for a day.

When Timmy returned with the plates, Micky'd opened up a cake tin. Full of bits and pieces; buttons, pins. Hair clips. A tiny pencil and a half-knitted baby bootee.

His large hand encircled a beer mug. His hands covered with scars from molten metal, when he used to work in the big industrial sites. Timmy at the butcher's, with his cuts and slices, Micky at the big place, wielding a massive hammer, tipping up those huge pots of metal. In each pockmark now, tiny gardens of mould, some kind of growth. Each scar a world in itself.

Timmy picked up the camera. "Where's the photographer?" He checked; the photo he'd taken of her was still there. Not a bad shot. Her fault she hadn't taken heed.

"The flash woke me up," Micky said. "Stupid girl."

Micky moved slowly. He shed skin like pale fallen leaves. He said, "Where are my dream girls?" He said, "I've been asleep a long time."

Timmy could see the tent from the attic window. Its door flapped in the wind; he fancied it waved at him, sending a message. He would need to walk down there to see if the girl was all right, but he was scared to do this. He wanted to believe it was a dream, that he had dreamt his brother was awake, and that the girl had taken her photos and left. That she'd simply forgotten her camera.

A crash from downstairs, a shelf of glasses broken? Chair thrown through the window? He took the stairs two at a time, as fast as he was able to go.

Micky was there, real as the nose on Timmy's face. He'd smashed some of their mother's crystal, standing there laughing amongst the shards. He handed Timmy a parfait bowl. How they'd hated her nasty desserts; old fruit, custard with a skin. And she'd sit there with them, making small talk, until they ate every last awful mouthful. Timmy smashed a dish, too.

Timmy took the river stone from his pocket and added it to the pile on the windowsill. His brother nodded. "You better throw her bike in the river," he said. "I'm still gathering my strength. Bury everything else. Whatever the hell she had in that tent. And the tent, too. Get digging."

Timmy turned away. Would he, this time? Be brave enough to say no? Micky put a hand on Timmy's shoulder. It felt gelid, loose, but heavy. "Bury the rest of it," Micky said. "She won't need it in dreamland. No one sleeps there." He closed his eyes. "No one sleeps. They just look beautiful for me. They help me sleep easy. Sleep sweet."

Timmy thought, what about me? My dreams? He looked at his pile of stones. He'd collected one for every swim, but not all of them meant murder.

A weird silence hung over the place, an emptiness of sound. It was the animals. No barks, no snuffles, no miaows. No calls for food, none greeting him as he walked the path.

His brother stood in the darkness under the Mill, holding on to the concrete ceiling, leaning in and out, in and out, like he was made of rubber, bending backwards and forwards. "Nice swim?" he said. It was then Timmy noticed the great pile of animals, necks broken, stacked near the old wagon. "That'll teach those fuckers to bite me," Micky said.

Micky slept under the Mill and crawled out when he couldn't rest. He'd say, "You tell me when you want to go for a swim and I'll know it's time. Same as always."

And he was right. He was. Every swim was avoidance, an excuse not to help. Timmy liked the dream girls, too; they kept him feeling loved, each time he closed his eyes Micky moved like a dreamer, a sleepwalker, like a monster in your dreams. He'd wade through the river, glide over the water, he'd walk until he found his next dream girl.

And Timmy would swim, and peep at ordinary lives. He felt an awkward sense of pride; I know what you don't, he'd think, looking in at those people.

He thought, what if I don't go back? To find what I will find and clean it up? He sat at the railway station, past eight in the evening. The lights glowing around him. He hung his head low, his shoulders slumped. He was tired, so tired.

"Trains running late, must be the weather," a man said to him. Timmy nodded politely but willed him to go away. He watched people on and off the trains, imagining himself getting on one. He watched young girls alone, lost in their dreams, beautiful and sweet and he felt happy for them, fluttering away, free and safe. He would never be his brother. He would never gather a dream girl.

But he'd clean up after. That he would have to live with; he couldn't bear it, but couldn't stop it. He'd clean up, stay quiet, and watch over Micky as he slept.

THE ADJUTANT'S DINNER GUEST
Jeffrey Ford

Every evening, we waited for the Adjutant in order to begin eating. He had rank on us, and we owed him our patience and goodwill. Not one of us had an atom of either to spare, though, when the meat went cold and the mashed potatoes mixed with the gravy to leave a brown molten puddle on the plate. Sometimes, it was minutes, more often we starved deep into the night. While waiting, we smoked cigarettes and jawed about the work of planning the coming war – tedious hours, calculating the cheapest method of removing the dead from the battlefield, weighing hearts against minds, composing the primer for torture. We were told that if we wanted to win, we had to think of everything.

There was always a warning as he approached the old barn where we sat at a long dining table aglow with lanterns. We'd hear the 'Adjutant's Call'. There was a young private who knew something about the bugle and learned the march at the insistence of the Adjutant. From the pompous sound of it, when he eventually arrived you'd have thought he'd show up on a white horse, clad in armour, sword drawn and glinting in the sun. Not for a second. It was Asgof the Adjutant, a bulbous potato of a man – a bald head of a nose, weak eyes and heavy lids, mere tumbleweeds of hair, such a fine jumble, moving in the breeze. It had been posited by Ebberrand, from Munitions Storage, that Asgof's moustache and eyebrows were fake. We'd all heard the story about the Adjutant's run-in with the locals.

As Ebberrand told it, Asgof was stopped in the street by a small crowd of hard-up locals, the type due to be mowed down like summer wheat in a matter of months. They appealed to him to halt the insane rush to war. The Adjutant lifted the riding crop he always had in his hand and waylaid the crowd, beating them back out of arm's reach.

There didn't appear to be malice in his actions, as judged by the grim, unwavering straight line of his mouth. On the other hand, neither did he seem to have any regrets for taking the stick to them. Just when it seemed the matter was settled, and he was about to continue on his way, the crowd surged forward, parted, and an old woman stepped forward. From a large blue jug, she doused him with a wave of green something. The smell of whatever it was made him gag. Death and shit all green, ripe, and juiced. He fell on the pavement, the crowd set upon him, and beat him unmercifully, breaking a dozen bones, kicking the eyebrows clean off his face, and vanquishing his flimsy hair.

He was in the hospital for weeks afterward. Penten, from Cheese Ration Distribution, had a girlfriend who was a nurse in the ward where the Adjutant was convalescing. She said that every time Asgof struggled to his feet and tottered toward the toilet, the bugler played the 'Adjutant's Call'. She said he looked pale green, broken. After he'd healed, the big brass decided to use him for some experiments before sending him back to work. The last thing the nurse said about Asgof, before Penten found her in the bedroom of their apartment with her left eye shot out, was that the doctors 'put something in him'.

In Asgof's absence we dined every evening with the Adjutant's Adjutant. His name was Misrimol Piliteen and he was one agitated Adjutant. He never shut up – endless, blithering sad-sack stories that dissipated into a grey miasma. War stories wherein everyone died but it was glorious and morally righteous. He was ever concerned about his rank, and whether we respected him or not. Many a night he ordered Pincer's Gold Label for all, had a few too many drinks, and then inquired of us individually, moving around the long table, specialist to specialist, as to whether we liked him more as a person or in his official capacity. His embarrassing antics were my first inkling that we could lose the war.

Sure, we gave him that he was nearly always on time for dinner. Not even a month went by, though, before we longed for the return of the Adjutant, his Adjutant be damned. After a month and a half of Piliteen's spit drivel, Marge, from the Department of Battlefield Humour, one late gin night after Misrimol had gone off to bed, suggested we kill him and make it look like he'd been murdered by a mob of locals.

It took a while for the idea of doing away with Piliteen to gain traction among the specialist staff, but just as it started to catch on, the sound of a bugle poked the twilight and we knew Asgof had returned. I hold with my general description of him, both pre- and post-stay in the intensive care unit – the man was a tuber. We specialists stood to attention and saluted as the Adjutant passed our chairs, riding crop tucked under his arm, a vacant look on his turnip face. He'd traded his official uniform for a contraption of flowing green robes and an ankle length cape made of green satin. On his diminutive feet, he wore emerald embossed slippers. The outfit enveloped him like a sick cloud, and to top it off, instead of his smart little cap, now he wore the hood of the cape pulled up, so he peered at us as if from within a cave.

The specialists believed that when he returned, he'd inquire of each of us what progress we'd made in our provisions and calculations concerning the coming battle. We thought it a certainty that he'd go up one side of the table and down the other, hurling difficult questions and belabouring our faults the way Piliteen badgered us for a sign of respect. We'd worked hard and formed our answers in preparation for his return. Instead, he settled into the chair, grunted, and they brought out the first course.

We ate in silence, all eyes on Asgof. There was obviously something wrong with him. His head jostled with frequent tremors, and the hue of his flesh, what we could see of his face and hands, was like an overcast autumn day. His eyes had yellowed like ancient ivory. Every time he took a forkful of meat to his mouth there was a billowing of his garments, like a wave rushing up toward his throat, and then that forkful disappeared, never touching his lips, in a confused event too sudden for me to follow. We tracked the tidal flow beneath pastel layers of chiffon as one might the efforts of a ghost ensnared in the window drapes. Eventually he noticed our focused attention and he growled viciously at us. A most disconcerting dinner.

When they brought the dessert, a small, malformed chocolate cookie with a suspicious spurt of cream, he was the last to be served. We waited for him. His was no sooner laid upon the table than it vanished. Marge, who'd floated the idea of doing away with Piliteen, screamed and pointed at the Adjutant. She cried out, overwhelmed by surprise, "A hairy little arm and clawed hand shot out and snatched away the cookie." Those around her begged her to calm down and by all means stifle her comments. Meanwhile, the Adjutant had snapped his fingers and his personal retinue of guards came out of the shadows and headed in her direction. We knew there would be a lot less humour on the battlefield in the coming war when Marge's head appeared the following morning on a post just inside the gates to the compound.

In the specialists' barracks, we discussed in whispers the comportment of our superior. It seemed to me to be the opinion of my colleagues that Marge stepped over the line and more or less deserved her sentence. Not a stranger to it myself, I could smell their spineless fear, but still I asked, "What is going on with Asgof?" No one had a ready answer. Ebberrand suggested that we lay a trap for Piliteen, get him drunk and see if we might get some answers from him. Symms, specialist in charge of Rain Making, said his office was right next to the storeroom where they kept the bottles of Pincer's Gold Label, the libation our annoying sub-Adjutant craved. Symms said it might take a few days, waiting for the head clerk to leave the room unattended.

At our second meeting with Asgof after his return, he entered as usual to the bugle's call, and again, once he set upon the meal, his green enclosure came to life, undulating across his form as if a great snake was moving through tall grass. Again, his food never made it to his mouth, but in a sudden disturbance of a precise moment, disappeared. We did our damndest not to notice. It was impossible not to recognise that we were witnessing a dark event, bordering on the obscene, an invisible explosion of wrong, but we saw precisely nothing, not even a scrawny arm darting out and back like the tongue of a snake.

After the dishes of the main course were removed, Asgof snapped for dessert. A waiter came in with only one small plate. In a white waistcoat and black bow tie, the fellow walked along one side of the table and set what appeared to be a green turd down in front of Ferdis Mews, the overseer of Victory Analytics. I watched from some distance down the other side of the table, the acrimonious expressions of the analyst and those nearby to the confection's rank aroma.

From within the Adjutant's hood, there came a high scratchy voice, unlike the one we'd come to know. It said, "I saw your latest calculations, Mews. You have the enemy winning by 30 percent."

"A mere preliminary finding," said the analyst, his lips trembling, tears forming in his eyes.

"Eat your dessert," came the command.

We watched in silence as the poor man cut, skewered, lifted and chewed a full third of his treat. By then, the smell had permeated the barn, and with each of his nibbles, he gained the sympathy of a martyr. Before the second third could be begun, he fell forward across the table, no doubt poisoned, squashing the remainder of his dessert with his chin. With Mews's last shudder, life fleeing for the exit, the Adjutant's cocoon erupted with the usual rough and tumble, only this time accompanied by a soft whistling sound like a blocked nostril, a tired tea kettle. I stole a glimpse at Asgof. Within the dark recess of his hood, I watched something eclipse his face, creating a momentary blur. This effect continued and I couldn't look away. His mordant visage phased in and out of clarity, as something orbited his head at phenomenal speed. The satin hood ballooning and falling slack in turn with each revolution.

That night, Symms lured sub-Adjutant Piliteen to the Recreation Room of our dormitory with three glistening bottles of Pincer's Gold Label. None of us drank, but we gathered round the man, gave him mighty pours of the tawdry gin and put questions forth as if he were a prophet. Ebberrand began the investigation after Piliteen's third tumbler. He said, "You better bone up on your adjutantation. It looks like your boss is ready to give up the ghost, if you know what I mean."

We each told him that we agreed with what Ebberrand had said. We went on to claim we believed that Asgof's final instant was in the offing, and that the sub-Adjutant would be called into service at the drop of a hat. He got a roomful of the respect he'd been craving when we let it be known that we had full faith he would be fit for the new position.

"Well, well," said Piliteen. "Let's not rush things. Adjutant Asgof is still in charge of all logistics. He does look less than well, though, I'll admit that. He went into the hospital a sharp-eyed military man and came out a dimwitted green effluvium. Have you watched him eat?"

"I don't think the food is ever arriving on his tongue," said Symms.

"That's what I mean. He's sharing his private cloud with some other entity. I heard at a sub-officers meeting that he participated in Commander Gull's project to create an undefeatable soldier, Project Skitterby."

The specialists gathered couldn't help but laugh. At that moment, I realised the war was already lost.

We let Piliteen carry on for a while more, fed him drinks upon drinks, and at midnight we kicked him out. He staggered across the compound, falling in rain puddles more than once. After we got rid of him, we sat for a while and had a quiet drink ourselves. Most of the specialists were present. The young woman who'd taken over Mews's group of Victory Analytics, Shasa Boeth, lit a cigarette and said, "I feel it's my duty to inform you all that the 30 percent defeat Asgof murdered my old boss over was a ruse. In reality, it was 60 percent. On day one we're looking at a massacre of our own forces."

"It does seem that the Adjutant's condition might be a metaphor for the well-being of the entire effort," I added.

"Are you saying we should flee?" asked Symms.

"I'm not saying that," I said. "Saying that would mean I just ordered the green turd for dessert. I'm just saying what I'm saying."

"Don't you think Commander Gull has everything in order?" asked Ebberrand. "What about this secret, undefeatable soldier project? I've got to believe he's prepared for everything."

The next night, we waited for what seemed a month of nights. Some time less than an hour before dawn the bugle sounded. What was left upon our plates was by then inedible. We'd talked and smoked away the hours as if in limbo. By then we'd reached a point where half the specialists had their heads upon the table, dozing, and the others sat upright, dreaming wide awake of a violent death at the hands of the enemy. 'The Adjutant's Call' drew us from our torpor and we managed to shake off the lethargy.

My first view of Asgof in the lantern's glow gave me a shiver. Inside the lair of his hood, his face drooped, his mouth hung agape and froth spilled over his bottom lip. His eyes were black holes, and blood ran from his porcine nostrils. He appeared most assuredly dead, and yet he moved erratically toward his chair, every few steps, turning in tight circles. The dinner guest within his garments roiled and rolled about so quickly its frantic actions were obviously the only thing that kept the Adjutant on his feet. When he reached his chair, he turned one last time and fell backwards into it. There was an enormous release of air, the sound of breaking bones, and a ferocious gasp that might have been Asgof's last order.

We sat in awe of the fact that the Adjutant was defunct. He'd not been accompanied by his guards. The cooks and the waiters were all asleep in the kitchen. A long silent pause followed, and just when the first rays of the red sun sliced through the cracks in the barn's wall, Victory Analyst Boeth stood up and carefully approached the slumped, green pile. She eventually leaned over him, moving her hands above his layers of fabric, trying to decide where to touch. She turned around and glared at the crowd of cowed specialists. "Somebody help me," she ordered. Symms and I were the only ones who went to her aid.

For starters, she pulled back the hood. Lumpen and besotted with boils, it looked as if his skull had melted in spots and the loose flesh of his cheeks and forehead had sunken in. Mews's green turd dessert had nothing on Asgof's stench. I knew that if I gagged once, I would never stop, a test of my willpower. Imagine a grey jack-o'-lantern left on the steps until February. From his head, we set about unwinding his voluminous layers of green chiffon. They peeled off like giant sheets of toilet paper from a man-sized roll. A morning breeze blew in the open doors of the barn and lifted into flight the dozens of airy wraps like a murmuration.

"It's like Christmas," said Shasa, just before divesting Asgof of his last garment. Where we expected to see his failing old torso and sunken chest, there was something entirely different. Those trademarks of the human body, flesh, muscle, organs, hair, were all gone and replaced with what looked like a large birdcage. The door of the cage was open, and a small creature, something between a lizard and a marmoset, lay asleep, a diminutive iron clasp around its neck, and attached to it a long, fine chain of golden links.

"Surprise," I murmured.

Symms backed away.

Shasa stared with a look of nausea, and said, "How did the golden chain not snarl as the thing ran around and around Asgof's remains?"

"Never thought of that," I said. "But yes, its properties are as shocking as the current state of the Adjutant."

By then specialists had risen from their seats and moved cautiously toward the door. It was hard to believe in those days that there wasn't a machine gun constantly trained upon you. When they managed to get outside, they bolted through the early rays of sunrise for the fence. The possible success of the war effort had disappeared like the Adjutant's chocolate cookie. I could tell they were panicked and meant to escape the compound. Two minutes later we heard the reports of the machine guns picking them off the high fences topped with barbed wire and dropping them into a bloody pile this side of freedom.

Shasa reached into the already open birdcage and removed the sleeping creature. It nearly fit in her palm. The golden chain seemed to grow as the creature was taken from its home. With her thumb, she petted the white fur. We drew close and inspected its lime-green scaly parts – hands and face and a large portion of its tiny paunch, the tips of its ears. "A Skitterby?" she asked. We nodded. "I can feel its heartbeat increasing. It might be waking up."

"Put it back," said Symms, and that was the last thing he said. The Adjutant's dinner guest leaped out of Shasa's hands and onto our Rain Making colleague's neck, where it dug its fangs and claws down to the artery and severed it. The poor fellow listed side to side as the creature feasted on flesh and blood at a frantic pace. Only for a second did it rear back and chortle before diving in headfirst again. In that moment, I saw its blue saucer eyes and they showed me a hundred percent victory.

Shasa lifted a nearby lantern off the wall and threw it at Symms and his passenger. With the crash of glass, the flames leaped up his legs and engulfed him. He had just enough left to cry out once, and that was followed by the Skitterby's screech. The next I knew, we were outside, running toward the back of the compound. She held my hand and dragged me along, telling me when to duck to avoid the searchlights. All the commotion was at the front gate, but where we were, in among the trees and shrubs of a far-flung corner of the compound, had been left unguarded. There, she led me to a hole in the fence, obviously made by wire cutters.

We escaped to the nearby town. As we walked the early morning streets, pretending to be hard-up locals, Shasa told me that after determining the war was already lost, Mews had snuck out one night and cut himself an escape hatch in the fence for if things went awry. "He only told me about it the day he died," she said. Luckily, she was sharper than myself, and when Mews told her of his escape plan, she decided to always carry a large sum of cash with her. She divided it between us, and we went our separate ways.

No one came after us, because the fire we started in the barn spread to all of the buildings in the compound, turning the entire area into an inferno fed by explosions of ammunition and rockets and phosphorus bombs that tore through and melted the flesh of those trapped by the locked gates. The citizens of the nearby town, where I got a job as a street sweeper, shook their heads and laughed and breathed a sigh of relief. On warm quiet days, clearing the cobblestones, I wondered what it was that made us want to be part of that war insanity. The people who passed me by seemed utterly content with no fever dreams of domination, whereas we, specialists and commanders alike, each harboured a small vicious creature that snatched away any sense of beauty or peace before it reached our hearts.

When the bodies of two young girls near the abandoned movie house in the poorer part of town were found with their throats missing, their blood drained, the local newspaper surmised the killers might be a new ferocious strain of rat arrived on a ship from some far away port. I knew then, of course, that not everything had perished in the compound. A war, once imagined, can have a life of its own.

SIDEWAYS
Lucy A. Snyder

"I know it's a big ask, but Wren is hellbent on going to the protest. Locke has been talking her ear off about it all week. And... I'm worried things will go sideways."

I arched an eyebrow at my boyfriend over my morning coffee. "*Sideways.*"

Jon squirmed in his seat, but still gave me a sad puppy dog look with his big brown eyes. "Please?"

Ugh. He was being cute at me, and I am *such* a sucker for cute. "What kind of 'sideways'?"

"I... uh. I don't know, exactly? There are all these crazy rumours about the police deploying new anti-protestor tactics, and it's all probably nothing... but. If there's any truth there, I don't know that Locke and his crew can look out for Wren like she needs."

I dumped a spoonful of sugar in my cup and stirred once. Having a little syrup at the bottom when I finished my coffee was a nice, tiny dessert when I was otherwise having to watch my carbs. "Locke's too busy being a rock star community organiser, huh?"

"I mean, yeah." Looking uncomfortable, Jon nibbled on his English muffin.

My heart told me I was being needlessly snarky. I wasn't an Orson Locke fangirl – Wren *clearly* was – but god knows we needed 'get it done, and get it done *loud*' leaders right then. The confidence you need to be that kind of organiser *always* comes with an ego. So expecting driven-snow purity from a guy with a charismatic agenda inevitably results in tiny shards of shattered belief sooner or later. But all evidence so far indicated that Locke was the real deal when it came to walking his talk.

And his talk was great. Even I at my most cynical had to admit that. He was a long tall drink of water – no trouble seeing him in a crowd even if he didn't have a Pilates box to stand on – and masculine good looks that made him seem older and more statesmanlike than most sociology PhD students. A striking Utah blond, and you can't discount the profound appeal of that when white supremacy riddles the bones of the country like tertiary syphilis. Great voice, too: deep, resonant, earnest. Obama had that kind of voice, but he could be boring. Locke's delivery had *fire*. He could read from the phone book and it'd be compelling. In a year or two, odds were he'd run for city council, or maybe a state representative seat. And then, the Senate? A lot of us could see him running for President in a decade.

If, of course, his truth-to-power tactics didn't get him killed in the meantime.

"If shit gets real," Jon said, "then Locke's going to be in the middle of it all with a bullhorn. Obviously. That's what he lives for. But Wren…"

"…who is a grown-ass thirty-year-old woman? Fully capable of making her own decisions?"

Jon groaned like he was forcing open a rusty gate in his throat. "Yes, she's an adult, but our IPO is dead in the water if we lose her as our lead coder."

"Ope, there it is."

It wasn't that I disagreed with Jon on any particular point he was making. Nor with the worthiness of the protest: ICE had teamed up with local police and brown immigrant kids were just… disappearing. Snatched off sidewalks and roadways and out of yards. The local school bus drivers collectively told ICE to go gargle Drano and refused to let that shit happen on their watch, but it wasn't enough. Parents were desperate and terrified, as intended. Ten years ago I'd have laughed at the scenario and been all, "Naw, really? Snatching little kids? That's some Scooby Doo villain shit." But here we were.

And, obviously, yes: we as a larger community had to publicly protest that kind of authoritarian bullshit. *Obviously*. We had to protest that *hard*.

But asking me to drop out of my club's Saturday match against the Cleveland Iron Maidens and babysit *his* coworker? For the sake of *his* project? Much as I loved him and wanted to support him, much as I thought his company's new ADHD- and dementia-friendly life-management software was cool and worthy… there was a wafting patriarchal stink in the air that annoyed me. So I wasn't above making him squirm a little before I said yes.

"Look, this isn't the Twin Cities," Jon continued, "but you *saw* what happened to Linda Tirado."

"Yeah." I swallowed a bitter mouthful of coffee. "I damn sure did."

I'd followed Tirado's reporting before a Minneapolis cop shot her with a 'nonlethal' round while she was covering the George Floyd protests. A man who had promised to protect the public saw her press credentials, clearly saw she was a peaceful truth-teller working for the public, and very deliberately aimed at her head and shot her. The police projectile destroyed her eye and left her with brain damage that became progressive, severe dementia. A bright light snuffed out by a dull bully with a badge. A life worth far more than the $600,000 the city paid out, a settlement that wouldn't even cover her medical expenses as she slowly died.

"I'm not, like, asking you to put yourself in harm's way," he insisted. "I wouldn't *do* that. I just want you to get her out of there if the police start closing in or they start chucking tear gas. Just make sure she wears her respirator, and make sure she keeps her head down."

"And if she doesn't listen to me?"

"Oh, come on, Ellie, how many years have you been practicing jujitsu and playing rugby? You're a foot taller than Wren. She's *maybe* ninety pounds soaking wet. You could tuck her under your arm and run down an alley with her if you had to."

A smile twitched up my cheeks despite my best efforts. "True."

"Look, I would not ask just *any* girlfriend to do this. I'm asking you because of your situational awareness and extreme competence."

"And because of your extreme situational need to be in Pittsburg."

His face scrunched. "The project's investors—"

I raised my palms. "I know, I know. I'm just busting your balls, babe. I'll do it. I don't want to see Wren get hurt, either."

Because in addition to being a wizard with Python code and a motherfucking sorceress when it came to illicit information extraction... Wren was so damn cute I really did want to just pick her up and carry her around like a kitten. (Not that I ever had. I actually do make an effort to *not* make things weird at other people's office parties.) Wren's general adorability wasn't a physical thing, or at least not *entirely* a physical thing. I mean, sure: red bouncy pigtails, freckles, dimples, her Mrs. Frizzle Meets the Muppets wardrobe – all so kawaii! It was her radiant optimism and the joy she found in doing the things she loved, especially when they were just a little messed up, that warmed my tiny icy heart. She, too, was a very bright light in the world.

Jon let out his breath and ran his fingers through his thick mop of brown curls. "Thank you."

"But you're gonna owe me big for this, Mister." I waggled my finger at him. "Like four days in a luxury suite in Chicago big."

"Anything for my strong, brave, exceptionally helpful sweetheart."

He stood, leaned over the table and gave me a buttery, sticky marmalade kiss.

★ ★ ★

Law enforcement types often refer to 'nonlethal' rounds such as bags of metal pellets, hard foam or rubber-coated steel bullets, as 'kinetic impact projectiles.' Which is a deeply annoying bit of technical jargon. 'Kinetic' just means… it moves. Cool, you just described literally any projectile! 'Impact' means the thing hits something else. Hey, Luigi! That's a projectile!

A bullet.

They're all fucking bullets.

They blast from the barrel of a gun and hit human flesh, causing pain and injury that may be far from temporary.

But if cops call them kinetic impact projectiles, they get to use a nifty, obfuscating acronym: KIP. Which probably sounds cool in a crossfitty kind of way to the right set of ears. It certainly sounds damn near harmless to a twenty-year-old small town reporter dutifully writing down everything Officer Friendly says as true facts: "Oh, heavens to Betsy, no, we would never use bullets on crowds of unarmed civilians! We only use KIPs. When our officers feel it is absolutely necessary."

When do cops think KIPs are necessary? When people are out protesting injustice. KIPs weren't a thing in the US before the civil rights marches in the 1960s when authorities decided they needed better 'riot control.' And that's not just about dispersing crowds. It's about punishing them for showing up in the first place. It's about small men with big bodies who are itching for an excuse to gun down people who got brave and decided to make some public noise… and getting to claim plausible deniability afterward when some of those gunned-down people die.

* * *

"No justice! No peace!" Locke's voice booms. His back is a solid wall of green Army surplus wool a few feet ahead of me and Wren. He's flanked by his friends Freddy and Bull, both dressed in antifa black jeans and tees and checkered keffiyeh scarves wrapped around the lower halves of their faces. Despite the near-freezing drizzle, Freddy's in short sleeves. He always complains about being hot. If I were him, I'd cover up my tattoos, at least, because I'm sure there are hundreds of electronic eyes on us right now.

Wren is wearing a long lavender raincoat over a pink cotton maxi dress and stompy silver Doc Martens boots with rainbow socks. Her respirator mask matches her dress. At least I convinced her to tone down her colour palette a little.

Aside from a pink KN95 from Wren's stash, my sturdiest pair of leather running sneakers and an old pair of jeans, I'm wearing a tie-dyed zippered hoodie that has a yellow smiley-faced cartoon bee and the words 'BEE KIND' on the back. It is hella twee, and assuredly not something I ever would have gotten for myself. But Jon gave it to me early in our relationship before he'd really gotten to know me, so I charitably dubbed it a good luck charm. Not stylish, but useful. It's big and it's cotton — natural fabrics protect your skin from corrosive chemicals better than plastic fabrics — and the colours are all cool, so it sort of fades into a roughly pavement-coloured greyish blob from more than twenty feet away. Apart from the cartoon bee, anyhow. And it nicely hides the crossbody bag I'm wearing beneath it, which is loaded with water and milk bottles and a couple of elastomeric respirators for me and Wren that will be at least temporarily effective against tear gas.

I am very much hoping we won't need the elastomerics, but the volume of cops lining High Street is… concerning. They're all wearing urban soldier gear, and the ones that aren't armed with riot shields and steel batons have chunky black KIP launchers of some kind strapped to their bullet-proofed chests. Tear gas is almost certainly on today's menu, and they might have something worse. I'm seeing bandoliers with Mountain Dew-coloured shells I don't recognise. Beanbags? Might be. I unzip my hoodie halfway, just to make it easier to get to the respirators if we suddenly need them.

"Oh shit!" Wren's turned pale, and is gaping, horrified at something down the street to our right.

A boxy black armoured police SUV is just casually trundling down Main Street. Right through the crowd of protestors. People are screaming, panicking, trying to push onto the packed sidewalks to get out of the way. But there's not many places to go.

"Bearcat! Three o'clock!" I yell at Locke. "They're running people over with a fuckin' Bearcat!"

Locke swears and lifts his bullhorn… and his head snaps back as a neon yellow blob slaps into the side of his head, sticking hard to his scalp through the velvety blond fade above his ear. The jackass cops to our left took advantage of the distraction to open fire.

"Drop!" I try to yell to Wren, but one of the sticky, heavy KIPs punches into a patch of exposed skin below my left collarbone, and what comes out is a D-shaped scream.

The pain is white hot, and my heart starts pounding like I just got a shot of pure norepinephrine straight in my vena cava. I am filled with absolute unadulterated rage, and I black out for a minute or two.

When the rational part of my brain comes back online, I'm over on the left side of the street, standing over the unconscious body of a riot cop lying halfway over the curb. I *hope* he's just unconscious, anyway. His helmet is in my blood-wet right hand, and his nose, cheeks and mouth are a gory hamburger hash. Looks like I yanked his lid off and beat the shit out of him with it. His KIP launcher and ammunition bandolier are in my left hand. His blood is spattered all over the front of my jeans and my tie-dye hoodie.

Wren is tugging on my sleeve. "I can't find Locke! We gotta go, we gotta go, oh shit we gotta go!"

I toss the helmet, zip the gun and ammo under my hoodie, and we go.

★ ★ ★

Before Locke's van driver Eliot dropped us off for the protest, he gave the address of a nearby safe house in Vienna Village where we could regroup if things went south. Things have absolutely gone south. I don't know what the hell is in these new sticky KIPs, but the people who've been hit with them have lost their damn minds. Clearly, they're loaded with some kind of drug. Maybe the cops hoped that, once they had a *real* riot on their hands, they'd have an excuse to use overt deadly force? Or wanted a riot to cover up the casual street murders they committed with their Bearcat? Either way, this was an obviously terrible idea and it is *not* going very well for law enforcement. At least not in the short term.

"They're gonna declare martial law," Wren mutters beside me as we duck down an alley. "They're gonna use this as an excuse to round up everyone they don't like."

The sticky KIP hurts like a motherfucker, and it is welded firmly to my flesh. It's got a strong plasticky chemical stink, and it's hot, like when you mix cyanoacrylate glue with baking soda to make a rock-hard resin. My skin's red and blistering around the blob, but not blistering enough to make the KIP lose its hold.

I do feel a little better about the cop I maybe-murdered after I see a fifty-something woman in blue-and-gold choir robes curb-stomping an officer between two parked cars. Her gold kitten heels are doing awful things to his eyes. A neon yellow KIP bulges from her neck like an alien parasite. The look on her face says she is *gone* gone. And if this nice churchy middle-class lady couldn't keep her shit together, what prayer did my white trash ass ever have?

And I wonder: am I doing comparatively better because of my combat training, or simply because my KIP isn't implanted right over a major blood vessel? Either way, I'll take it.

The safehouse is a late nineteenth-century brick Craftsman with a broad front porch and iron-barred windows. It has an abandoned, forbidding look to it, but the front yard is tidy. A black and red sign on the four-foot-tall hurricane wire fence protecting the yard says BEWARE OF DOG. But there's no doghouse or any other evidence that a dangerous canine patrols the premises.

Wren and I hop the fence, scurry around to the back porch, and do a shave-and-a-haircut knock at the door.

Eliot cracks open the door, looks past us to make sure we didn't bring company, then hauls us into the kitchen. Freddy is pacing in a tight circle on the old yellow linoleum, clearly tweaked out of his damn mind, tugging at the sticky KIP superglued to his left forearm. Locke and Bull hover near him, concerned.

"Just... just leave it alone, bro." Wincing, Locke rubs at the blisters around the KIP above his ear.

Freddy shakes his head and starts digging his strong, wiry fingers into the flesh around the blob. "Gotta get it off."

"Stop, you'll fuck up your tattoo!" Bull says.

Freddy's flesh is bleeding freely under his digging fingertips. The muscles of his right forearm stand out like cords as he grips, twists... and the blob rips wetly free. Wren gags and turns her head away. Freddy's eyes are glassy, and he gives me a wide, exhilarated grin as he holds the bloody blob aloft—

—but then his face goes slack. He sways, knees wobbly. Pitches straight backward. Locke just barely manages to catch him and keep him from cracking his head open on the marble countertop.

"Jesus, bro, are you okay?" Locke gently sets him down and slaps his cheek. No response. Locke presses two fingers against his neck, and apparently doesn't like what he feels.

"Shit, his pulse is weak as hell. Bull, Eliot, take my car, get him to the ER at Saint Michael's."

"Shouldn't we call the squad?" I ask as Locke's boys hustle to get Freddy off the floor.

Locke frowns at the blood on my jeans. "No, we should not call the fucking squad. The cops would be all over us."

He nods toward a door off the kitchen. "Laundry room. Probably some clean clothes you can wear hanging in there. Get out of that evidence and wash it on cold, then wash it again, hot with bleach. Do your shoes, too."

Everything he's telling me to do is perfectly reasonable, but it pisses me off just the same. "Aye, aye."

I step out of Bull and Eliot's way as they carry Freddy out the back door. Unzip my hoodie and pull out the KIP launcher and its ammunition. "I got these. Where do you want 'em?"

"Wren, take that shit upstairs and see what you can find out about it," Locke tells her. "We need to find out what these slugs are made of, who makes them, who approved the local cops using them. There's a computer in the second bedroom on the left. I'll give you the password."

I hand the gun and ammo to Wren, then go into the laundry room to change out of my bloody clothes and get my laundry started. Only my jeans and hoodie need to be washed. My grey leather sneakers have some spots on them, but I'm able to clean them off in the laundry sink with a little bleach and a lot of hot water. The sporty black tank top I have on under the hoodie is fine, as are my undies. So at least I'm not having to rawdog the pair of men's medium grey sweatpants I find on a wire hanger. The risk of catching a raging yeast infection from someone else's unwashed crotch is low but never zero.

I finish getting dressed, sling my bag over my shoulder and head to the living room to see what Locke's up to. He's slouched in a dark leather easy chair, focused on his cellphone. That's where he does most of his work, whether it's messaging people or making social media posts or recording videos.

But something weird's going on in his lap, and it takes me way too long to realise that he's sitting there with his dick fully out. Close-cropped balls flopped across his open jeans zipper, and his rod at veiny attention. It is some impressive gear. I absolutely neither expected nor wanted to be seeing it right now.

And it makes me sick. Makes me want to run away. I *hate* feeling like this. It's been *years*. Locke's got me flashing back on all the times my parents sent me to check on grandpa in his backyard shack. That nasty old creep would be sitting there in his underwear, dick out, asking me to come sit in his lap. He never did make me do anything, but my parents never did believe me about it, either, so I had to see his gnarly purple grossness over and over, with him grinning like it was the best joke ever.

I am *not* that scared little girl anymore, goddamn it. I haven't been her for a long, long time. I took hardcore steps to be the woman I am now. Could all my work on personal bravery really just go flying out the window over *this*?

So I take a deep breath and plant my feet in the entryway. "Am I interrupting something?"

"Huh?" He glances up at me. "Nah. Sit down."

"…okaaay…" I too-casually perch on the sofa on the other side of the room. "What in the Louis C.K. are you doing, my dude?"

"Eh, just horny." He pauses to scroll through his screen. "Really, really, *really* horny. Figure it's the drugs in whatever these nonlethals are. You horny? We could, like, bang it out before everyone gets back."

Another surge of nausea, but then I can feel the rage creeping back in, and it steadies my stomach. "Dude. *No.* Also, *hello*, I'm not a cheater."

He *humphs* and rolls his eyes. "Yeah, like Jon would have the balls to do anything about it if I fucked you."

His words feel like an actual slap. "I beg your fucking pardon?"

"Sorry." He shrugs and touches his blob, wincing. "I think there's some kind of truth serum in these things. Which would make sense, right? Because right about now they'll have a bunch of people in custody. Cuffed to tables in interrogation rooms. Bet some of the cops are running some hard trains on the bitches who don't have any intel. All that hot, tweaked-out leftist ass chained down and bent over tables… those cops are some lucky fucks. Damn, but I'd like to be in their boots right about now."

It's getting hard to breathe. These are not words I *ever* expected to come out of his mouth. I was there at the University Union when Locke made an eloquent, moving speech about the horror of sexual assault for National Women's Day. He talked about what it did to his *aunt*, for god's sake! And here he is fantasising about raping his comrades? Here he is fantasising about enjoying the violent patriarchal power he's supposed to have dedicated his life to destroying?

Am I hearing this right? Or am I the one who's lost her mind?

It's just the drugs, I tell myself. *He can't have fooled me like this for so long. I knew he wasn't gonna be Mr. Perfect but I'd have known if he were a monster under it all. Wouldn't I?*

He laughs. "Anyway, my filters are all off. It's a straight line from my brain to my mouth. I'd apologise, but I'm not *actually* sorry, so… whatever, right?"

My every instinct is screaming something bad will happen if I stay here. I stand up, appalled that my legs are shaking just a little. "Yeah, so, I'm gonna go upstairs and keep Wren company."

The message app on his phone dings, and he holds up a hand to stop me while he reads his screen. "Wait. Aw, dammit. Freddy died."

A shock runs through me. "He *died?*"

Locke shrugs, frowning like he just found out the pizzeria down the street ran out of anchovies. He and Freddy have known each other for *years.* How can he be this detached, this cold? Is it *really* the drugs making him act this way?

Or do I have to admit that yes, this guy had me fooled, and now I'm seeing his exceptionally well-crafted mask drop?

"Massive heart attack. I guess taking these things off is bad for your health." He sets his phone down on the coffee table. "Look, I really need to bust a nut so I can concentrate. Come here and blow me."

"Blow yourself, asshole."

He laughs. "Yeah, sorry, I don't bend that way. Come here and get on your knees. It's what you girls are good for."

It's what you girls are good for. Grandpa said nearly the same goddamned thing to me when I was twelve. I'm not sure how I maintain a semblance of calm, but I do, even though my blob is itching so bad I want to tear it off. Even though I know what doing that would cost me.

"Are you fucking kidding me?" I stare at him. "After all your talk of being a feminist, *this* is how you act when your filters are off?"

"Oh, grow up. You *know* I'm an alpha."

"Jesus Jizzling Christ, alpha males aren't real! Just go in the bathroom and rub one out! Stop being a gross psychopath!"

"Why should I have to resort to gooning like a loser when there are two perfectly good pussies in the house?" He pauses, looking me up and down. "I mean, Wren *is* a lot prettier than you. Maybe I should just go upstairs and say hi. Maybe I can get her to start crying. I'll cum a lot faster if she does."

Like my high school guidance counsellor always said: When someone tells you who they really are, believe them.

I apply maximum effort to keep my voice steady. "Leave. Wren. Alone."

He meets my gaze. I see no human warmth behind his eyes. Just hard, sober calculation.

"Why should I?" His tone is calm, but it's an unmistakeable challenge.

"Because I have a better idea," I reply.

* * *

Most people in my circles know I went to *The* Very Large State University on a rugby scholarship. And they probably assume that the scholarship paid for my undergraduate degree. If you know anything about the funding situation for women's sports in red states, of course, you already know that I wasn't getting anywhere near enough to pay for everything. I held some odd, unsatisfying jobs until I started dating Tara, who was one of the other women on the team.

Turned out, Tara had a side gig as a dominatrix. A very lucrative gig, in fact, and she had more client requests than she could handle. Having enough money to live on certainly appealed to me… but so did the idea of learning how to have sexual power over men. Working with her seemed like a solid way to get over the fears my grandpa had planted and the shame my parents fostered. A whole flock of birdies to kill with that one stone. She took me on as her apprentice, and that's actually how I met Jon.

Tara quickly realised that I have a talent for extreme pegging and fisting. It helps to have strength and flexibility in your fingers and wrists, but also patience, and a sense of how much will be too much for sensitive areas of the human body. I'll grant you that some masochistic guys are genuinely thrilled about prolapse situations… but they're a tiny minority. Nobody ever had to visit the ER after a scene with me.

Which is to say: I'm an actual pro at working improbably large objects into other people's orifices.

* * *

Unfortunately, feeding Locke his cellphone ends up being much louder and more strenuous than I expected. But I do shove the flat glassy slab down his throat, and twist it sideways, and it *is* incredibly satisfying. But his muscles seize as he's suffocating, and my right fist gets stuck in his gullet. In the process of getting my hand out I snap his lower jaw and rip out some of his teeth. And so I get blood all over the borrowed sweatpants. It's just been one of those days.

Wren, of course, hears the unmistakable sounds of a struggle, and comes down to investigate. She's got the KIP launcher locked and loaded. I have to take two cartoonishly large steps to the entryway to meet her. Block her. Try to prevent her from seeing the body. But of course she can perfectly well see my hands, which are wet with spit and blood and vomit, and the fresh stains on my clothes.

"Jesus Christ, Ellie, what did you do?" The gun shakes in her hands, but she doesn't point it at me.

"So, you know how every time some godawful guy rises to power, like Hitler, people are all, 'Well, surely there were signs when he was young. Surely *someone* saw *something* wrong with that guy. Surely *someone* could have done *something* before he had so much power nobody could get rid of him'? Well, Locke showed me his *something*, and I seized the opportunity to stop him."

"But what signs..?"

"Did you find out what's in the blobs we got shot with?"

"Yeah? More or less?"

"And they're laced with truth serum, right?"

"Yeah, how did you... oh. *Oh.*" Wren's eyes are very big.

"Locke wasn't honest with us about... well, maybe anything. He wanted to hurt you."

"Thank you for, uh, not letting him do that."

"Glad I was here to help. Did you find out who's responsible for all this?" I touch the blob under my collarbone. It still burns and itches like a motherfucker.

"Yes. I need to double-check some addresses, but yes. I have a list."

"Do you have home addresses, or just office addresses?"

"Both."

"*Score.*"

At that moment, Bull and Eliot come through the back door, looking miserable and shell-shocked.

"I'm really sorry about Freddy," I say. "Unfortunately, Locke is dead, too. He started making threats and one thing led to another. But the good news is, Wren here has figured out who's responsible for this mess. And I'd like to pay them all a visit. But we're going to need a few more people to help out, people who have the equipment and social media reach for effective livestreams."

"You're... you're not going to kill them, are you?" Wren asks.

"Oh no," I assure her. "Well, not on purpose, anyway. But they're *definitely* going to get a taste of their own medicine. They're going to learn what it's like to get shot in the head with one of these fun KIPs they decided we civil malcontents deserve. And then we're going to tie them to a chair, put a camera on them, and see if any interesting truths come out under the influence of their own drugs. I suspect one or two of them have some details that they'll just be *dying* to share."

I look at Bull and Eliot. "You guys in?"

They look at each other.

"Hell yeah," Bull replies softly.

Eliot nods gravely.

"All right." I clap my bloody hands together like a chef. "Let's go show these fascist bastards what happens when they make a protest go sideways..."

FORTY BELOW
Caolán Mac an Aircinn

The first thing the guard did every morning – religiously, without fail – was check the thermometer display on his wrist. Today, it was thirty degrees Celsius below zero. Once he had satisfied himself of this temperature, the guard dressed himself in his outside gear – parka, boots, snowshoes; wrapped up warm as warm could be – and poured himself a bowl of nutrient paste. Thus equipped, he went to see the man in the mask.

Outside his bunker stretched the snowfields of Adélie Land, the French concession in Antarctica. This early winter morning, the sky was a bright, aching blue and the white sun glimmered on the snowdrifts and gilded the ocean waves, some miles away but still visible. The snow crunched under the guard's boots as he made his way to the cave. He knew – it had been his job to know; he'd been a meteorologist before he came here – that often the snow in Antarctica was immeasurably ancient, that the flakes on the ground had frozen uncounted thousands of years ago and would lie frozen for uncounted thousands more; that is, unless some lout in clunking boots were to traipse across them with a bowl of nutrient paste. For this reason, he tried always to retrace the same route, to retrace even his exact footsteps, so that his route only ever showed two sets of footprints: one going to the cave, one going back. He did this even when he knew there was a snowstorm coming. The guard knew that others before him had not been so careful, and if others came after him, they would not be so careful either. But the guard knew that he had been chosen for this work for his punctilious nature; and so, every morning, his foot landed in the exact same spot.

Every time he reached the cave, he tested the bars, even though the thermometer reading had been satisfactory. He did this because he was careful, but more so because he was nervous. The thing in the cave scared him.

It was an Antarctic ice cave in the side of a hill, which became cliffs a way inland; it was distinguished by the fact that it had two sets of bars blocking its entrance. The first was at the very mouth, the other was just where the light began to fade. Set across from the cave on a pole was a camera, so that Control, at the base on the coast, would know if the man in the mask ever escaped.

When the guard arrived, the man in the mask came to the second, inner set of bars to wait for his meal. Even so close to the mouth of the cave, the light was not good, and the guard could not make out details of the man in the mask. What he could see looked like a perfectly normal human being in a grey fabric jumpsuit, with black rubber gloves, black boots, and the mask which had led Peterson – in Control, apparently referring to some hammy movie, or maybe it was a French legend – to call him 'the man in the iron mask'. The mask wasn't iron, obviously; the guard understood that it was some sort of titanium alloy, designed to be strong, flexible, and above all, never, ever able to break. It covered the man's face, leaving slits at the nose, mouth and eyes. The guard had often looked, but the man in the mask seemed to keep his eyes in shadow, and the guard had never once seen them.

There was a control panel by the first set of bars, and trepidatiously the guard punched in his code. A section in the middle swung wide, admitting the guard to the gap between the first and second sets of bars. Once he had stepped inside, he carefully set down the bowl of nutrient paste precisely in the centre of the space created. He didn't know whether the man in the mask cared about this precision, in fact he was sure he didn't, but it was important to the guard. All the while, though it was cold beyond words, he was sweating profusely. If he didn't make it back to his bunker soon, the sweat would freeze, and then he would have other things to worry about than the man in the mask.

Once he had set the bowl down, he scurried back outside the cage and punched a different code into the keypad. This caused the first section of bars to close and then the second to open, admitting the man in the mask to his nutrient paste. The guard watched him step in, and thought of how wrong, how jerky and inefficient, how *alien*, his movements were. The man in the mask picked up the bowl of nutrient paste and turned to regard the guard, his eyes still shadowed. Normally the guard would hurry away, but he had checked his thermometer and today he was feeling brave, and he met the gaze of the masked man. Though his eyes were hooded in shadow and his nature was entirely inscrutable, the guard held his gaze.

Then the man in the mask did something he had never done before: he bowed stiffly. Though the masked man's grasp of normal human gestures seemed to be limited at best, the guard could see, in the fussy precision and military rigidity with which the prisoner executed his bow, more than a touch of mockery. Only once the prisoner had held this pose for a minute did he retreat into the darkness of his cave with his bowl of nutrient paste.

The guard tried not to hurry back to his bunker, but the exchange had unnerved him and, worse still, there was now a ribbon of iron-coloured cloud at the base of the seaward horizon. Control, in one of their terse, one-way messages, had warned him that a blizzard was on the way, and the thought scared the guard so much that if he considered it for more than thirty seconds he was liable to piss himself. For Peterson had warned him, when he sent him out here, that the electronics that held the man in the mask's prison closed would work only down to forty degrees below Celsius. Any colder than that, and the two sets of bars would simply cease to function, and the man in the mask – whoever, *whatever* he was – would be free to roam.

The guard made it back to his bunker and put on an old English comedy show – *Porridge*, today. This, too, was a routine – in his time here he'd already finished all of *Only Fools and Horses* – but today he couldn't focus on the episode. His mind kept drifting back to his prisoner, circling around him like a probe around some alien planet.

He had been recruited from the civil service, where he had had a dreary job in an agency with a three-letter acronym helping calculate blizzard risks. No one had ever told him why he had been chosen for this posting – his career was not exactly stellar; indeed, no one had singled him out for anything before, except for occasional meetings about 'taking the initiative' or 'appropriate workplace etiquette' – but he knew that he was meticulous and, naturally, assumed that this quality had finally been recognised. He had neither spouse nor children, so he had told his parents via a brief phone call that he had been selected to go to Antarctica for a very important mission; they had politely congratulated him.

He had touched down by helicopter in Adélie Land three days later, head abuzz with his own importance and with the thoughts of the hundred-and-fifty-grand salary he was to receive. Here, he had met Peterson, whom he had taken for a smiling nonentity. Nevertheless, the nonentity briefed him on his one and only task: make sure that the man in the mask did not escape.

Everyone at the coastal base in Adélie Land, from which Control operated, knew about the man in the mask, and they all had their pet theories about him. The guard, in the three days he had spent there prior to his assignment, had been introduced to them all. The least imaginative held that the prisoner was a freak of nature, or that he had stepped off a spaceship into a cornfield somewhere and that the government had captured him. Others suggested that he was some kind of political prisoner, who had been subjected to horrible experiments, or even something that had been fished out of Mengele's laboratory after the war. They all agreed on one thing: the man in the mask was not human, not in the broadly accepted sense of the word.

Peterson did little enough to clear up this morass of mysteries. The man in the mask, he said, was very sick, and his illness made him both nearly immortal and very, very dangerous. How either of these should be the case, Peterson did not explain. He was being held in Antarctica to minimise the risk to human life in case he should escape, and he was to be held until the government had devised some sort of cure for his condition. In the interim, they needed someone loyal, someone trustworthy, someone *careful* – someone, in fact, like the guard. The guard preened a little before accepting his commission.

In the months since he had accepted, the guard had found out little more about the man in the mask. He did, indeed, appear to be a man in a mask; and the fact that he was able to endure who knew how many months and years of confinement in an ice cave with only two bowls of nutrient paste a day would seem to indicate that he was, indeed, not a normal human. Yet there was nothing else to be discovered. The guard had combed his bunker from top to bottom, and had found no documents, not even handwritten notes from his predecessors guessing what the man in the mask might be. He had tried to speak to the man in the mask, but the prisoner had not replied, and when the guard had returned to his bunker, he found that he had been telegraphed a terse message warning him not to try communicating with his charge again.

So, what the creature in the cave was remained obscure; and, after turning the problem this way and that like a Rubik's cube in his mind, the guard concluded that there was no answering the question and focused on his programme. Outside, the wind began to howl, and the snow — there would be fresh prints in the morning — began to fall.

At five o'clock, a little alarm went off, reminding the guard to feed the man in the mask. Reflexively, he looked at his thermometer — and tensed. The thermometer display read forty degrees below. The guard stayed glued to his seat, unable to move. Then, miraculously, the display ticked up to thirty-nine degrees below. He glanced out of his window. The blizzard had arrived now, and it obscured everything. Quickly, he girded himself for the outside, poured his bowl of nutrient paste, then went out.

The storm howled around him and the greedy winter winds snatched at the bowl in his hand, threatening to send it spinning off into the untimely darkness. But the guard had been out in storms before, albeit not this bad, and knew to keep a tight grip on the bowl. He struggled towards the cave, chagrined that the snowstorm meant he could not keep to his self-approved route, and heaved a sigh of relief when he saw that the bars were intact. But when he made it to the outer set of bars, his relief changed to horror, for the inner set of bars was swinging wide open. His only relief was that the man in the mask was nowhere to be seen.

He wiped the rime from the thermometer display on his wrist. Sure enough: thirty-nine degrees below. The bars should work! The guard remembered a protocol for dealing with this situation. Carefully, he punched the code Peterson had given him for this situation into the keypad.

The outer set of bars swung open. The guard had a second to register terror before the man in the mask came sprinting out of the darkness, through the unlocked inner bars, through the unlocked outer bars, and barrelled into the guard, sending him flying. He crashed into a snowdrift, crushing who knew how many thousands of ancient snowflakes, and was just struggling to his feet when the man in the mask appeared out of the snowstorm and placed a black rubber boot on his chest. When the guard was thus immobilised, the man peeled off his titanium mask. And when the guard saw the rows and rows of teeth, the smile that reached so much wider than any smile should reach, the piggy red eyes that never looked out of any human countenance, he screamed, and screamed, and screamed. But the blizzard wind took with it his screams; and in any case, they cut off abruptly.

★ ★ ★

On the other end of the camera, the guard's screaming was noted by a man in a white coat – Peterson – who watched until the man in the mask had finished with his victim. Afterwards, he wrote neatly in a notebook the following words: *Feeding concluded successfully. Subject 773 died 12th October, endured 143 days.*

He paused a moment, then added: *The weapon appeared to enjoy him.*

BY THE SKIN OF HIS TEETH
Chad Lutzke

I was sitting in my car, sucking on a piece of jerky and watching 112 Seaside Ave – an impressive, yet quaint, adobe house near Laurel Canyon. It's where Sonny Hanover lived. He wasn't home yet, but I had a tail on him, making sure he headed straight there after his visit across the border.

Sonny was a pimp who also muled heroin from Mexico once a month. He ran his own operation. Nothing big, but enough to ruffle feathers. Some of those feathers were Charlie Cavanaugh's. Charlie was a pimp too, but he didn't run drugs, wouldn't have anything to do with them. And if a girl wasn't clean, he wouldn't go anywhere near her. Drug addiction was a deal breaker. He hated the idea of a girl whoring herself out because she's a slave to something she can't control. He wanted whores who loved their job. Some for the money, and some for the sex, like nymphos. So, Charlie was just there to line up safe johns, not take advantage of the ladies. If there was ever a pimp with morals, it was him.

And he hated Sonny Hanover more than anyone.

Sonny beat his girls, kept them on a tether made of meth and needles. Early on in his career, he got comfortable with the role of pimp, checking every box in the stereotype. But I remember him as a kid – complexion like road rash and about as charismatic as a windowsill wasp. His old man was a stoolie at the local dive, and his mom checked out before Sonny could even walk – spent all her time in front of the TV, sporting sweatpants, no bra, a scowl, and a ponytail that never came down, just so she didn't have to bother with a brush. You know the type.

Sonny was raised on fish sticks and TV Guide. Things like a home-cooked meal or a brand-new bike were exotics. But becoming a product of your environment is a fallacy. You get to be a certain age, we're all capable of choosing a different path. That's what Charlie Cavanaugh did. Sort of. Charlie's upbringing wasn't much different, though his mother was fond of chicken nuggets over fish sticks, and his dad's addiction was whores and pills, not booze. It's a wonder Charlie didn't come from under the skirt of a stranger downtown instead of his father's wife.

A couple months ago, Charlie and I had a few beers at The Dolphin, and he told me he wanted Sonny out of the picture. He wasn't talking about killing the guy, which I'd never do, seeing how I wear a badge. He wanted him locked up.

Despite being a cop who gets paid to weed out the bad, I owed Charlie a favour. We were in sixth grade. I had a dangerous crush on Beth McGee and would have done anything to impress her, so one summer, when I found myself looking down at the Kalamazoo River from thirty feet above, I jumped from Krickett Bridge, while Beth and her friends stood on the embankment and cheered me on. Charlie Cavanaugh was there too, shaking his head. Seconds later, I'm sucking in a lungful of Michigan water after being caught in the river's current. I was half dead by the time Charlie pulled me out.

"He'll be toting powder up his butt," Charlie had told me, while sipping his beer. "Just samples from a bigger delivery expected in August."

I told him small packets of H wasn't enough to put anyone away for long.

"Trust me, you catch him with that, and it'll be plenty."

We argued about the law and how it works, trafficking drugs versus possession. I explained the whole process through another beer, and he just sat there grinning, one tooth sticking out further than the others, glistening in the dim bar. Finally, he said, "Just trust me."

I told him, "You know I'm not dirty, right? Don't get me caught up in some trouble."

"It ain't like that. You've got nothing to worry about. Just show up *where* I tell you, *when* I tell you. Hell, bring your partner if you want." He reached into his pocket, then slid a burner across the table. "And hang onto this. I won't call until a week from tomorrow, but keep it on you just in case."

"No trouble, Charlie."

"You know me better than that, Meyer. Have a little faith."

★ ★ ★

I did bring in my partner. Wagner. He was the tail. He followed Sonny through the airport and into the restroom, made sure he didn't empty in the stall, and that no trades or handoffs were made along the way.

Wagner called me with updates that night. "We're headed downtown. Looks like he's going straight to Seaside. We nabbing him first thing?"

I didn't have an answer. Charlie was calling the shots on this one, and I needed him to give the word. Strange taking orders from a pimp. I told Wagner I'd get back to him, then grabbed the burner from the empty seat and rang Charlie. He picked up right away.

"He there yet?" he asked.

"Not yet."

"Okay, listen. When he gets there, tell him you need to talk about some allegations. Take him inside and start asking about Tijuana, what he was doing down there. The whole interrogation thing. The key here is to let the clock run out, because I guarantee he's got a laxative workin' through him as we speak."

"That stuff doesn't pass that quick, Charlie."

"He doesn't eat the cargo. He shoves it up the back door for the plane ride. One of my girls used to work for him. She told me all kinds of stuff. Hell, she's packed him up before, said he likes it. But he won't eat the cargo. It freaks him out. And he doesn't like holding it any longer than he has to. Wants it out the second he's at a safe place and in the clear, which is where you intercept."

"So, you want me to keep him company until he shits his pants?"

"Basically. Call me when you think he's touching cotton."

We ended the call, and I filled Wagner in.

Wagner had a real good question. "You're sure this guy's on the level?"

I began to wonder that myself.

★ ★ ★

Ten minutes later, Sonny pulled up. Wagner parked down the street around the corner, ran through some yards and stuck to the shadows, then slid into the passenger seat of my car. He was a rookie detective, the youngest we had. But he was spry. Alert. I'd seen him embarrass more than one suit when pointing out a detail that went overlooked by veteran eyes. He was easy to trust, and probably a hell of a lot quicker with his piece than me if it came down to it.

"He's got a girl with him, looks like a junkie," he said.

"She's probably carrying too."

We watched Sonny get out of his car and tug at the seat of his pants like he had a wedgie. I threw the binoculars in the backseat. "Let's grab him before he gets inside."

We got out of the car, and I saw Sonny grab the girl by the arm and yank her. Then he yelled at her, and I heard the word "bitch". He didn't see us until we were on him.

"Sonny Hanover?" I said.

He turned with saucer-wide eyes. Looked us up and down. The guy was lit on something. "The hell you want?"

"Let's go inside."

"I ain't going anywhere until you tell me who you are." His arm was creeping to his side, like he had a gun he meant to show us.

I flashed him my badge. Wagner did the same. At this point, the girl made a run for it, got about ten feet before one of her high heels betrayed her ankle, twisting it with an audible snap.

I made for Sonny, while Wagner grabbed the girl, helped her walk toward the front door of Sonny's house.

"Okay... all right. What the hell you want from us?" Sonny asked.

"Just to answer some questions, maybe grab a cup of coffee. Wagner, you up for some coffee?"

My partner nodded. "Always."

"Well, you're outta luck. I don't drink coffee, especially with pigs."

Sonny toyed with the keys in his hand until he found the one for the house. His hands were shaking. He unlocked the door, then stepped inside and fiddled with the alarm. I kept a close eye on him, with my hand wrapped around his arm the whole time. I couldn't afford to have him bolt for the bathroom.

He flicked a switch, and the room lit up with sixty watts of dim light, then flicked another switch and a glass amber globe in the corner of the room turned on. Cozy.

He had a nice place. Clean. Expensive furniture. Light beige suede. The walls were decorated with giant black and white photos framed in steel. Most of the photos were of naked women, but tasteful. One of the frames held a cityscape I recognised as Denver.

"Pretty nice place for being unemployed," I said.

"I work."

"If that's what you wanna call it."

"I gotta sit down," the girl whined.

It was hard to tell her age. Drugs had ravaged her, as had a thousand tricks, I figured. She could have been twenty. Could have been forty. When she sat on the couch, her dress rode up her legs, and I could see a palette of blues and purples across her knees and down her shins. But her feet. They were the most beautiful I'd ever seen – like the kind you'd find in a magazine ad for soap or bubble bath – with the exception of one toe. It was missing. The middle one on her left foot. I surmised she'd lost it shooting up. I've seen that before, especially in beginners. They don't want the tracks on their arms, so they pick a spot that's hidden. After a while, they stop caring and will shoot in their eyeballs if they have to.

"And I gotta piss, so your meeting's gonna have to wait a minute." Sonny pulled away, and I lost my grip.

"Hit that bathroom, and I'll consider it resisting arrest," I said. "Might have to get ugly."

He turned back to me, his face scrunched. "Arrest? For what?"

"Sit down, asshole!" Wagner wasn't having it.

Sonny lingered at the end of the couch for a moment, then found his way to a cushion and sat down next to the girl, like it was all his idea. I sat down in one of the chairs across from the couch. There was a glass coffee table between us that held a wooden bowl and a metal sculpture of an elk. Gaudy as hell. I expected more, considering the rest of the place was something I wouldn't mind waking up to every morning.

Wagner made his way to the kitchen and opened the fridge. He moved a few things, then pulled out a carton of milk and emptied it in the sink.

Sonny was swinging his head back and forth between Wagner and myself. "Okay… just what in the hell—"

"How was Tijuana?" I said.

He fixed on me, face made of stone. "Hot." Then he leaned back, tried to look comfortable. Tried not to look nervous.

Wagner came back with the empty carton, tossed it in Sonny's lap. "You can piss in that."

"I read an article once about this married couple." I lit a cigarette and pulled the coffee table closer to me. "They ended up in the ER because she stuck something up her snatch she couldn't get out." I grabbed the wooden bowl from the table and flicked some ash in it. "You know why the husband went to the ER too? He didn't go because he was a good man... a supportive hubby. He went because his head was what was stuck in her snatch, like some reversal-birth roleplay. I found out a few years later the story was fake. But there's others that aren't. Men with Barbie dolls stuck up their ass. Hot dogs, carrots, even a jar of peanut butter. True story. My nephew, he's a medical transcriptionist, told me all about it. Can you imagine? Shoving stuff up where it don't belong?"

The girl's face broke, and her chin quivered. She knew where this was going.

Sonny, on the other hand... "The hell you guys want?"

"I wanna know about Tijuana," I said. "What were you doing down there?"

"Vacation. She's got family there." Sonny pointed a thumb toward his woman. "They put us up for the weekend."

Wagner sat in a chair next to mine, and we watched them, these two folks with foreign objects stuffed all up inside them. Sonny glared back. The girl's eyes climbed the walls like two beetles searching for a way out. This was the worst day of her miserable life.

I asked what her name was.

"Maria." Her lips stuck together when she said it.

"You want something to drink, Maria?" Wagner asked. "Might be a little something left in that carton."

She shook her head and kept her eyes on the wall, the ceiling, anywhere but us.

"What family's down in Tijuana, Maria?" I asked.

"A cousin," Sonny blurted out, like it was a race to answer.

"You always speak for her?"

"She don't feel good."

"I'll bet."

"She drank the water down there. You know what they say."

The room was quiet for a full minute. Must have felt like a lifetime to someone with drugs up inside them, those birth pangs rumbling.

Sonny couldn't sit still anymore and shot up off the couch, started pacing the room. "Either get to the point or get out!"

"Sit down."

"You can't keep us here like this. It's kidnapping," he said.

"We're in your house, Sonny. We haven't taken you anywhere."

"Then we're hostages. You can't do that." He was rubbing his hands together like he was cold, or on the verge of filling his pants.

"You're right," Wagner said. "Let's head to the station instead."

"Aww… come on, man!" He threw himself on the couch. "We went to Tijuana to visit her cousin. We ate a ton of authentic, she drank the water, and now we just wanna take a shower and get in bed. That's it. That's what we did."

I said nothing. If I'm honest, I was enjoying it. I was getting a real kick out of watching them writhe, trying so hard to play it cool. Trying to hold the cargo in.

"Oh… and I smoked a joint Saturday night after dinner. Is that what you want to hear? I got high. We both did."

Then Maria turned pale-white and burped – a sign of things to come.

Sonny scooted away from her. "Yo… you need to let her get to the bath—"

Before he could finish, Maria grabbed the milk carton and ripped the top wider, then stuck her lips around it and did her best to make it all in. She was mostly successful. Some of the vomit shot out the sides of her mouth and splashed onto the couch.

"Dammit, Maria. On the suede?" Sonny said, scooching away from her.

That's when my phone vibrated. It was a text from Charlie: *He dump it yet?*

I texted back that he hadn't.

He will soon enough. In the meantime, ask him about Gerdy Sanchez.

More riddles. I'd debated all day on whether or not to take orders from a pimp, but seeing how I knew the *real* Charlie, I'd decided early on I was all in. Just this once. But going in blind, especially with this new talk of Gerdy. I didn't like it. I was shooting from the hip without seeing my target. And if it didn't pan out, we're not talking a verbal lashing from my superiors. This was my job on the line. My career. And potentially Wagner's too.

I stared at my phone and let the screen go black, then looked at the couch across from me – the girl with perfect (almost) feet, with puke on her lap and a swollen ankle, and the dirtbag next to her, both of them stuffed like Thanksgiving turkeys.

I took a deep breath and said it. "Now tell us about Gerdy Sanchez."

When I saw the fear sweep across his face, it took everything I had to hold back a sudden burst of laughter, being pushed out by my relief that somehow this was going somewhere. Charlie was right. As for the girl, the question didn't faze her. And I began to doubt she was ever privy to most of what went on behind Sonny's curtain. When it came down to it, she was nothing more than a piece of ass and a mule. Not a business partner.

"Never heard of him." Sonny did his very best to look me straight in the eye, but the uneasiness was there and shone like the sun.

"Come on now, Sonny. You don't need to be a detective to tell you're lyin' out your ass. How do you know Sanchez?"

"Sanchez... Sanchez. He that dude that sells tacos outta the truck down on Los Feliz?"

If he was, I didn't know. I needed more info from Charlie. It was time he told me everything.

"Wagner. Babysit the kids a minute, will ya?"

As I walked outside with the burner, I could hear Sonny whining again about being a hostage and how we can't do what we're doing. Wagner set him straight.

I dialled Charlie. "Listen, man. We're at a point where you're gonna have to lay everything out. Who's Gerdy Sanchez?"

"Yeah, all right," he said. "Up until this weekend, he was a small-time slinger in Tijuana. Used to live here in LA until a few years ago, when Sonny ran him out. But now he's dead, and it's by Sonny's hand."

"How do—"

"How do I know? Same way I knew Sonny was headed down there in the first place. Same way I know he's got an ass full of heroin. But if you're asking who told me, our bromance ends there. You and I... we may be in bed together, but you're never getting to home plate."

"Fair enough. But if you know he killed Sanchez, why not use your connection to handle it down there? I mean... the hell am I supposed to do with the intel? We've got no body. No witness."

"Trust me," Charlie said. "You've got more than you need. The truth will come pouring out. Just wait for it."

I hung the phone up and went back in. Sonny hadn't moved, and the girl was doubled over, rubbing her ankle. Wagner was watching them, a big grin on his face.

"Your partner's a sado," Sonny said to me. "My eyeballs are swimmin' in piss, my girl's sick with a screwed-up ankle, and he thinks this is some kinda party."

I decided to move things along, see if I couldn't get Sonny to give up the goods early. "There's one of three reasons why your girlfriend's sick, Sonny. One, she's scared to death of going to prison. Two, the laxatives kicked in. Or three, the pack of heroin shoved in her cooch popped open and she's about to get a high she ain't ever coming down from."

This time Maria didn't make it in the carton. Vomit sprayed through her nose, onto the suede and those beautiful feet. Sonny didn't seem as bothered by the suede as he was before. His face went slack with terror, eyes locked on mine. I thought he might puke, too.

I let a smile come through. "Now, we can sit here all night until you crap your pants. Or we can take care of business right now. Either way it's coming out, and you're screwed."

As if on cue, Maria stood up, hiked her dress, yanked her underwear down, and squatted on the carpet. "Ohhh... please, God! I don't wanna die!"

Sonny buried his face in his hands. "You stupid whore."

Maria started in on Sonny, going on about how much she hates him for what he's done, that he's ruined her life and hopes he rots for it all. In the middle of the tirade, a ribbon of excrement hit the floor, followed by another, swirling on top of the first like a cobra ready to strike.

"Get it outta me!" she screamed, then held her breath, while her face burned red and a vein popped from her forehead like a parasite stuck under the skin. Sonny watched in horror as his girlfriend laid the egg that would land them both in prison.

"Maria!" Sonny said, giving me a sideways glance. "You're carrying drugs?"

"Cut the bull, Sonny."

"I had no idea," he said.

"You're in a hell of a lot deeper than she is," I said. "We know you took care of Gerdy Sanchez while you were in Tijuana."

"Huh?"

"You're going down for murder, Sonny. Say goodbye to that suede, and everything else you treasure."

"You got a body?" he said.

I didn't. And it showed.

"No body. No murder."

I started thinking about the pension I'd never get, about what I'd tell the wife. Maybe I wouldn't altogether lose my job. Maybe they'd keep me on as a desk jockey. I'd keep the ruse going, tell the wife I clock in as Detective Meyer every day. She'd never have to find out about the paperwork I pushed from here on out. Sure, I'd be dead inside. But I'd have a job. My mind wandered like this for what seemed like hours, while Sonny kept on.

"Ain't that what they say? No body, no murder?" He had a weak smile on his face that was suddenly wiped away by what looked like an urgent need to empty his bowels. He grabbed his stomach, squeezed it.

"In your pants, or on the floor, Sonny. We got you... and we'll get you for that murder too."

It was the biggest bluff I'd ever pulled. I was holding a pair of deuces but was told by Charlie I had a full house. Sure didn't look like it from here.

"Ahh, screw it." Sonny undid his pants, went behind the couch, and squatted. All I could see was his head, changing colour while he grunted.

Wagner pulled his gun. "You even think about throwing it at us, I'll put a bullet in your head."

Good call.

Maria was back on the couch, head in her hands and crying. Life, as she knew it, was over. I was hoping she had no priors and that the system would have mercy. Maybe she could cut a deal and get some help, make herself brand new.

"How many eggs you laying there, Sonny?" I asked him.

"Just one. I'm not bigtime." He paused to hold his breath, then pushed. "It was just for me." I could hear a strong stream of piss hit the carpet. May as well. Two birds, one stone.

"A sample of what's to come, is what I'm told," I said. "You know... there's a whole lot of people out there that'll be glad to see you behind bars."

He chuckled. "Shiiit... This ain't nothin'. I'll be out before the year's up."

"Not for the murder you won't be."

"Like I said... no body, no murder." He stood up, pants around his ankles, a smile on his face. "I'm done, if you wanna come wipe me."

I headed to the kitchen, grabbed a roll of paper towel, and tossed it to him. "Wipe it yourself."

Wagner pulled a pair of rubber gloves from his pocket. I did the same, then cuffed Sonny. "Have a seat."

Wagner cuffed the girl, gave her the courtesy of hands in front. We collected the cargo from the floor and rinsed them off. They were condoms. One red and one green, like Sonny and his girl were in the Christmas spirit when they packed up. The rubbers were half filled, knotted, then doubled over and knotted again.

We threw the packs on the coffee table, and I texted Charlie, told him we had the goods. I asked him about proof of murder, because we still had nothing.

He texted back: *Open them. My friend in Tijuana. He personally packed your boy something special.*

I looked at the bulbous packs, pulled out a pocketknife and poked at one.

Open them?

Not exactly protocol. This was no Eighties crime film, where the cop splits the goods open and runs a coke-covered finger across his gums, waiting for the tingly numb.

Finally, I grabbed the green one, the one Sonny had carried. I held it tight, then ran my blade across the top. Heroin fell like snow onto the glass table, as four wide eyes gazed at the drug, wishing they could tie off and boot up.

Then the glass table tinked, as something that wasn't heroin fell from the condom and bounced to the carpet. Then another. And another. Then several more.

They were teeth, the roots intact and meaty red. Trusty little capsules filled with DNA.

"What in the hell?" Sonny said, clearly unaware of what he'd been toting.

I smiled. "How's that for a body, Sonny? Hand delivered, even."

I wrote Charlie back. *I think I owe you a beer, old friend.*

THE SHADOW OF HIS VIBRANCE
Kay Chronister

Her father's apartment was not what she had expected, though Miranda could not have said what she did expect. Miranda had not been a guest in her father's home in twenty-four years, since she was thirteen and her parents were still going through the motions of following their custody agreement. Back then, her father had been renting a bungalow in central Texas that was filled with boxes of product from a multi-level-marketing scheme (shakes, or powders for shakes, something with an approaching expiration date that emitted a faint odour of banana). He had been ignoring a series of increasingly stern notices from the electric company about missed payments. On Miranda's fourth day with him, the lights – and, more significantly, the air conditioning – had powered down with a soft resigned *whoosh*. She had watched her father chain-drink smoothies from his warming fridge while they waited for the cab that his neighbour had called to take her to the airport. "They're going bad anyway, you want one?" he'd said, and Miranda had said, acidly, "I don't really like fake banana," and there had been hurt on her father's face, but it had been fleeting, barely there.

Sometime between then and his death last month, her father's fortunes had taken a turn, though Miranda couldn't say what that turn was towards exactly. His address was the left half of a tall and narrow brick house, the fourth in a row of tall and narrow brick houses on a side street in a town called Moon's Bed, which appeared only on very zoomed-in maps of south-central Washington state. To get there, Miranda had flown into the Boise airport and rented a car and driven for three hours. She had taken the whole week off from work.

"I don't see why it should be me and not you," she'd said to her mother when the letter arrived in the mailbox of the house where they both lived. *Please make arrangements to empty the residence of personal effects within thirty days*, was the polite demand. *Outstanding items will be discarded or offered for public auction.* There was no name in the salutation, only a blank space after *Dear* and before a comma.

"You're his next of kin," her mother had said. "*You* have his forehead. I was just stupid enough to procreate with him."

"How did they even get our address?" The last time Miranda had heard from her father, a few years ago now, he had been living in Lawrence, Kansas and looking for investors to split the cost of a share in something truly revolutionary. Miranda couldn't remember what. VR timeshares?

"When there's outstanding debts, they always find you," her mother said. "Don't let them try to tell you that you're liable for anything."

At the mention of the word *debt*, Miranda had decided she wasn't going. Miranda made twenty-seven thousand dollars a year as a customer service associate for a pharmaceutical company and saved half of it; Miranda had never opened a store credit card or taken out a loan or paid a bill late. Miranda had moved back into her mother's house three years ago when her landlord raised the rent for her apartment above 30 percent of her monthly income. Miranda made a habit, even an art, of moving through life unencumbered by liability or risk.

And yet, for reasons she could not explain even to herself, two weeks later she got on a westbound plane.

On the shared porch of the duplex where her father had spent his last days, a middle-aged woman was sitting in a wicker chair, smoking. Miranda could feel the woman's eyes following her as she parallel-parked, then walked down the sidewalk, but she kept her own eyes averted.

Her father's half of the narrow porch was unfurnished but swept clean. An ashtray sat on the porch railing. Miranda had never known her father to smoke, when she had known him. On the other side of the porch, the woman in the wicker chair was resolutely facing the street, as if she had never been looking at Miranda but only at the place where Miranda happened to be for a moment. The smoke that came out of her cigarette smelled vegetal and wet, as if the woman was smoking moss.

"He's not there," she said to Miranda.

"I know," Miranda said. "I'm supposed to be cleaning out his apartment. His landlord sent a letter. Do you know how to reach the landlord?"

The woman looked at Miranda with sudden interest. "You're the ex-wife," she said.

"Daughter," said Miranda.

The woman shook her head. "It's not fair," she said. "Three sons, birthed them and raised them, and not one of them would do it for me."

She stamped out her cigarette, then went inside and slammed the door.

Miranda stood on the porch for a minute, hoping without much expectation that the woman would come back out, and trying to decide what to do. It did not seem as if there was any hope of finding the landlord. Eventually, she tried the door to her father's apartment. To her relief, it was open.

The apartment was uncomfortably warm, as if the heat had been left running. Miranda made a mental note to turn the thermostat down, wary of being stuck with the heating bill. A patchwork of jewel-toned Oriental rugs covered the floor – expensive-looking, she noticed half-guiltily – and the left side of the room was crowded with sofas and loveseats, all covered in age-faded silk upholstery. A far cry from the sagging faux-leather sidewalk find that Miranda remembered from the bungalow in central Texas. And yet also not *that* far a cry. She thought there was roughly the same chance that something had made a nest in the cushions.

She walked the house, getting the lay of the land. She looked into the single bathroom with its old pull-cord toilet, the astonishingly numerous bedrooms, the checkerboard-tiled kitchen. She decided the apartment must have come furnished. It was decidedly not her father's home. There was no way he had sourced all that old furniture, those four-poster beds with their moth-eaten canopies, those cherry wood armoires. *Her* father, formerly the owner of one mattress on the floor, could not possibly be the owner of those velvet curtains or porcelain dishes. And in that case, how could she possibly determine which things were his personal effects? Were any of them? The demand from the letter felt like a joke. She began to question whether she had the right apartment.

But her father had left his tracks in the attic. A can of Arizona iced tea still sat open on a mahogany desk beside an ashtray and lighter. The jacket from a royal blue tracksuit hung from the back of a desk chair. And there were papers everywhere – evidence of the debt her mother had predicted. Carbon-thin pink sheets, unopened envelopes bearing red stamps. *Second Notice. Final Notice.* Miranda stared at them for a minute, then turned around and descended the ladder.

Downstairs, she noticed for the first time a note taped to the back of the front door.

Please go to The Moated Grange on High Street. Mention my name to Jerry. Yours, even still, Jonathan.

Miranda considered this weird directive for a moment. The uncharacteristic *please*. What did it mean, *yours, even still?*

She felt a tightness between her ribs. Hunger, she decided.

She would try The Moated Grange, not because of what her father had said but because it sounded like a restaurant. If they didn't serve food, she wouldn't stay. She was not in Moon's Bed to mourn him.

★ ★ ★

The Moated Grange turned out to be a low-ceilinged, orangely lit cave of an establishment cloaked in the damp odour of the cigarettes her father's neighbour had been smoking. The parking lot was almost empty, but the sunken dining room was crowded. The leather banquettes lining the wall were filled; so were most of the seats at the bar.

Miranda sat down at the first empty bar stool she saw, between an elderly man with an oxygen tank seated behind him and a thin, nervous-looking woman with a scarf wrapped around her head. They did not seem to be there together, but it was hard to tell. Both had cups of coffee set in front of them. Across the bar, a middle-aged man in a flannel shirt stood facing a smudged mirror that ran the length of the bar back. She thought he must be able to see her in the mirror, but he betrayed no awareness of her presence until Miranda got up the nerve to say loudly, "Do you serve food here?"

The bartender turned slowly towards her, as if the effort pained him.

He had a conspicuous scarlet growth on the side of his neck that went to the collar of his shirt. "What kind of food do you want?" he said.

This did not feel like a question that should be asked at a food-serving establishment. Miranda searched futilely for a menu or signboard. "What do you have?"

The bartender fingered the growth on his neck. "We don't cook ahead," he said. "It will have to be made special."

Miranda had the distinct impression that he did not want her to order. "Fine," she said. "Is there a grocery store around here?"

The man mouthed the word *grocery* as if it was unfamiliar to him. "Yes," he said, after a torturously long moment of consideration. "Percy's. Down the road some."

"Thanks," Miranda said, and she slid down from the bar stool with the intent of leaving. But halfway to the door, something – obligation, curiosity – held her, and she turned back. "Are you Jerry?" she said to the bartender.

He looked suspicious. "Who's asking?"

"Jonathan Fishburne's daughter."

The man's entire demeanor changed, then. "Johnny's *daughter!*" he said, and he reached out to shake Miranda's hand. Miranda shook back. His hand was cold and very dry. "We all love your father. Respect and admire him. Say, Stephen, this is Johnny's daughter," the bartender went on, addressing the man to Miranda's left. "Don't you see the likeness?"

Respect and *admire* was not what Miranda had been expecting. Neither was the present tense. *Love* him?

"I could have told you," said the woman to Miranda's right. "She has his nose."

"Taller than I would have guessed," said the man to her left. "Not like him, in that aspect."

Miranda realised she couldn't remember if her father was a tall man or a short one – if her height, tallish though not exceptional, had come from him.

"Stanley will want to meet you," the bartender said. "Ellen too. Practically everyone. We respect your father. He has such a quality to him, a – what would you call it, Stephen?"

"Serenity," contributed someone behind them: a woman sitting in one of the banquettes. "He's a serene man."

"He was always peaceful," the man to Miranda's left decided. "Like he could see past the horizon."

Miranda didn't know what to say. "What did he... do here?" she ventured, dreading the answer. She did not want to hear that her father had spent the last years of his life fleecing the whole population of Moon's Bed, and yet – what else could he possibly have been doing?

The bartender seemed taken aback by the question. "Same as all of us," he said. "Lived in the shadow of their vibrance."

"Whose vibrance?"

"We don't name them," admonished the woman sitting at her right. "It would be presumptuous."

"How do we know she's really Johnny's child?" said the man to her left, crossing his arms. "*I* don't see any resemblance. Not even the nose."

"Look at her straight-on," said the woman to her right. "You'll see it."

He craned his neck to look Miranda in the face.

"You got an ID on you?" he said.

Miranda looked incredulously at the bartender, who only muttered reluctantly, "It would firm things up a little, for us."

Miranda decided she'd had enough. "I'm not showing ID," she said. "I don't care who you think I am. All I want is – does anyone know how to reach my father's landlord?"

Everyone at the counter looked bewildered.

"Dear," the woman with the headscarf said, "no one has a landlord here."

★ ★ ★

Miranda had decided, as she left The Moated Grange, that she was going to get in the car and drive away from Moon's Bed and forget about her father's personal effects, but instead she walked past her parked car and up the porch steps into the apartment. There was no reason to drive all night to reach the airport when there would be no flight waiting for her, she told herself.

She had not ended up going to the grocery store, reluctant to show her face anywhere else in Moon's Bed, so she searched the cabinets and the fridge for something to eat, but there was nothing. The cabinets were bare besides a canister of instant coffee and stacks of dusty antique dishes. The fridge held only, bafflingly, half-a-dozen Tupperware containers of hand-rolled cigarettes. Miranda opened one and was blasted by a wet vegetal odour. She unrolled it on the counter and found a little pile of what appeared to be loamy earth inside.

Miranda was not a smoker and never had been – why risk taking off years of your life, she had always thought, when you could simply *not* – but something compelled her. She took a cigarette from the Tupperware and climbed up to the attic, where she used the lighter on the desk to ignite the end. She didn't know how to get the smoke down into her lungs and realised almost immediately that she was not going to figure it out, but stubbornly she held the end between her lips, getting a fetid, mossy whisper of what her father had apparently enjoyed. After a few minutes, bored and sour-mouthed but not willing yet to relinquish the experience, she began flipping through the clutter on the desk.

The clutter was not only debt notices, as Miranda had thought at first. It was something worse: a paper trail that meandered back through her father's whole adult life, gathered by either no logic or indecipherable logic into binder-clipped stacks and stained manila folders. There were instructions for setting up and using a variety of As-Seen-on-TV gadgets comingled with letters from collection agencies. Welcome packets and incentive structures for at least four different pyramid schemes. One folder contained nothing but star charts done by three different astrologers (two in Texas, one in Kansas) and a kindergarten art project that Miranda supposed must be her own, stick figures on construction paper, *Daddy* and *me* scrawled above their heads. Had she ever had that much faith in him? Or maybe her father had another child, an equally near living relative with an equal claim to the contents of his apartment. Miranda set the construction paper aside, handling it delicately. In case it was hers. In case it wasn't.

Then, in a folder that had fallen off the desk and spewed its contents onto the floor, she found a sober-looking printout, *Navigating Your Diagnosis of Mid-Stage Colo-Rectal Cancer*, and blurry scans of library book pages. *Accessing the Astral Plane*, *The Immortality of the Soul*, *Nootropics: Extending Your Life Through the Latest Findings in Food Science*. Then, beneath those, a photocopy of a photocopy. *Secrets of the Moon's Bed* read ribbony cursive lettering. Beneath, half-decipherable through the distortion and grit of the photocopier, an illustration of a deep crater with fir trees on either side and a beam of light poised above.

The rest of the pamphlet was not there. The scan had only captured the cover. Miranda turned the paper over and back, willing something more to appear. She felt the shape of her father's life in Moon's Bed resolving into something shadowed and vast, far beyond her comprehension but unnervingly slipping into the bounds of her awareness. Her father had come to Moon's Bed, he had lived in these dingy rooms that bore almost no mark of him, and he had befriended the sickly weirdos who frequented The Moated Grange, probably not in spite of their weirdness but *because* of it. There was something he had wanted from them. And something they had gotten out of being with him.

It occurred to her that she didn't know how he'd died and where he'd been buried.

In the absence of anything better to do, Miranda called her mother. She found some comfort in hearing her mother's usual salutation – the word *what?* Which was her address to anyone who called the house phone, whether friend or telemarketer or her own daughter – in its usual tone, comprehensible and firm.

"Mom," said Miranda, and realised she didn't know the answer to the one-word question. *What.* "It's really weird here."

On the other end, there was a scrounging sound. Plastic rustling. She imagined her mother digging in the garage or the pantry for something, the phone propped between her shoulder and her chin. "Sounds about right for your father," her mother said.

"But it's not his usual weird. It's…" How could she explain any of it – the dirt cigarettes, the masses of antique furniture, *the shadow of their vibrance,* the picture of the crater? "He had all these papers," Miranda said finally, though this did not really convey the sinister quality of things. "About extending your life. I think he was dying."

"Well," her mother said, with equanimity, "he's dead, so. Probably."

"Do you know anything about Moon's Bed?"

"Moon's Bed?"

"The town. The secrets of the moon's bed. Have you heard of this? Dad had a pamphlet."

"How should I know? We didn't talk. You know that."

But her parents *had* talked – at length, for months – before Miranda was conceived and her father accused her mother of trying to entrap him and then fled, migratory-bird-like, from the cold demands of the northeast to the safe anonymity of central Texas. Miranda's mother just preferred not to acknowledge that she had once liked Miranda's father as much as you needed to like someone to co-sign on their high interest car loan, support their doomed business ventures, open a joint bank account with them. Whenever her mother spoke of her ex-husband, she did so as if he was a storm that had blown through and left a trail of unavoidable, only half-foreseeable devastation behind him. This had always annoyed Miranda; from her perspective her father was inescapably the kind of person who thought he could achieve fabulous wealth selling exotic birds door-to-door, but her mother should have known better than to believe him. Her mother had been the mark of a mark, and that was even worse than being a regular mark. The least she could do was admit it.

"You have no idea why he would have come out here?" Miranda said.

"I didn't know he *was* out there," said her mother. "Listen, your father was always getting himself involved in something. Don't you remember when he was in that UFO cult? For a solid six months you couldn't have a conversation with him without hearing about how he would get airlifted if he only went up enough levels in his classes. It's probably something like that. Get what you want out of that apartment, and get out."

In fact, Miranda had forgotten her father's old dream of getting airlifted, which he had described to her in letters that so captured the imagination of her seven-year-old self she'd ended up in the school counsellor's office after spending a week of recesses standing on the top of the jungle gym, arms outstretched and eyes closed, waiting to be taken up into the stars.

Remembering that, Miranda felt disgusted with herself the same way she felt disgusted with her mother. But she'd only been a child. That was the difference.

"I'm leaving tomorrow," she said. "They can throw away all his junk if they want."

Her mother had already hung up. Her usual way of ending conversations.

* * *

Miranda was reluctant to sleep in any of the beds in the house, all of which looked and felt like exhibits in a half-forgotten museum, so she made a bed out of spare blankets from the linen closet and lay down on the floor of the living room. She prided herself on being an unfussy sleeper, but the apartment was intolerably warm; she had not found the thermostat, and she was beginning to suspect there wasn't one.

No thermostat, no personal effects, no landlord.

The floor creaked beneath her every time she rolled over.

Miranda laid there for a few hours, then abandoned hope of sleeping and got up and changed her clothes and stepped out into the cold fog-shrouded night with a sensation of relief.

Her father's neighbour was standing on the other half of the porch, looking up at the horizon.

"Oh," she said, turning to see Miranda. "Forgot you were still here."

"Sorry," Miranda said.

The woman leaned on her cane and lit a cigarette, then lifted it to her lips. Miranda watched as she took a deep, practiced drag, then exhaled.

"You want one?" the woman said, seeing her look.

"No," Miranda said decisively. She still hadn't gotten the taste of the last one out of her mouth, even after two vigorous teeth-brushings. "Thank you, though."

The woman nodded, as if she had expected this answer, and took another drag.

"Why does everyone smoke those here?" Miranda said. "What's in them?"

"Earth from the crater," the woman said. "Supposed to make us live longer."

Miranda stepped forward and leaned on the porch railing, following the woman's gaze to the layer of fog hanging ten or twenty feet above them. She could see no stars, only the faint insinuation of moon. She could not guess what the woman was looking at.

"Is everyone in this town dying?" she said.

"Trying not to," the woman said. "That's the idea."

It occurred to Miranda that her father had come to Moon's Bed not to con the people living there but to con death itself. She thought he probably could have convinced himself that living near a crater could counter the effects of colorectal cancer. It was not more insane than any other thing he had believed. Her father was a serial monogamist when it came to his schemes, her mother used to say. He believed wholly and without question in what he was saying while he said it. And when he stopped believing, he forgot the thing completely, thought of it with neither bitterness nor remorse, looked at its consequences with a kind of hapless bewilderment and assiduously learned nothing. For him, the *big* one, the *real* one, the thing that would let him transcend the mean work of survival and arrive at wholeness, was always just ahead.

"I thought it was bunk, myself, at first," the woman said, seeing Miranda's expression. "But the doctors gave me three months, and it's been almost two years."

"Oh," Miranda said.

"Of course, living here, it's only a way of suspending things. Everyone here does die, sooner or later," she continued. "Unless they are lucky like your dad."

"He's not dead?"

"Did you not know?"

There were two possibilities, Miranda thought. The first was that her father was dead and he had conned everyone in Moon's Bed into thinking he wasn't, though she could not guess what he stood to gain from that. The second was that her father was not dead and she was the one being conned; that he'd written that letter himself because he'd wanted Miranda to believe he was dead but he'd also wanted her to come to Moon's Bed – though, here, too, she could not see what he stood to gain.

Had he thought she wouldn't come if she knew he was still alive?

It made her sad, almost.

"Can I see him?" she said.

An unreadable expression came across the woman's face. "I thought that's what you'd come here for," she said.

"Where is he?"

The woman stubbed out her cigarette with her cane. "We only approach the fullness of their vibrance at midnight, on clear nights," she said. "You missed it tonight. But tomorrow, you could go. We meet at The Moated Grange."

* * *

Miranda spent her second day in Moon's Bed carrying her bag to the car and getting in and driving down the street, then turning around and driving back. All the way out of Moon's Bed, and then back. Almost fifty miles east, then back again. Because although Miranda was almost certain her father was dead and very certain that she had no good reason to see him if he wasn't, she could not make herself leave Moon's Bed with the possibility still dangling before her that something had yet to be revealed, that there was some meaning to the note which read *yours, even still* and the adulations of the people in The Moated Grange and the stupid impenetrable beam of hope that had surrounded her father, even when he was chain-drinking boxed smoothies from a warm fridge in central Texas.

So, an hour before midnight, she went to The Moated Grange.

There were two cars in the parking lot and a crowd of a few dozen packed inside the restaurant. The mood in the room was not lethargic as it had been the night before but buzzy with anticipation. When Miranda stepped down into the sunken dining room, conversation died only for a second and then restarted.

There was no hope of getting a seat without insinuating herself into one of the groups at the banquettes, so Miranda stood at the bar until the bartender noticed her. He greeted her with a glass of pale ale – on the house, he said. It was what her father always used to drink. "I'm sorry about that confusion with Stephen yesterday," he added. "He's a crank, that's all. And, well, it's not hard to admit that most of us are a little jealous. We all lived in longing for what he achieved, and few of us have anyone so devoted to us as Johnny obviously did."

"I don't know if I really am," Miranda began, "so devoted," but the bartender had already been called away by someone else and she didn't think he heard her.

Ten minutes before midnight, by unspoken consensus, the diners in The Moated Grange poured out into the floodlit parking lot, where others were already waiting. A faint, damp snow had begun falling. Miranda let herself flow out with the crowd down High Street, their walkers and wheeled oxygen tanks and slow laboured strides commanding the whole breadth of the two-lane road. They turned into a public park, then followed a dirt path through rows of towering firs, and by the time Miranda realised that people were letting her through, falling back, she was almost at the mouth of the crater.

The crater resembled the picture on the pamphlet, a wide flat basin with ragged earthen edges. It was unremarkable, except that a faint blue phosphorescent glow seemed to come from within. Paint, Miranda thought. Or some natural phenomenon. Mould, or something. Someone had hung a ladder from the edge. As she lowered herself onto the first rungs, she faced the crowd and saw with vicarious embarrassment that there were tears shining on some of their faces.

She trembled as she descended, but she had always been nervous around heights.

When her feet hit the ground, she stood in the blue glow and felt slightly dizzy. Her ears were ringing. She began to wonder if she was not going to see her father either dead or alive, if there was nothing here but the phosphorescent light and the jealous, eager crowd above, who thought she was experiencing something otherworldly only because her father had believed there was something otherworldly here.

Her eyes sensed movement, and she realised the blue light in the crater was emanating not from the earth but from dozens of pale, smooth, slug-like figures clinging to the walls of the crater. The walls were covered with them, but in front of her some of the figures were shifting slowly away from each other, parting. After a period of ten or twelve seconds, they parted enough to reveal Miranda's father.

He lay prone with his back on the wall, held there by some tie that Miranda could not see. His face was still recognisable enough, but there was an unnerving smoothness to him. He had no hair, no eyebrows.

"Dad," said Miranda.

His eyes focused on her, and a look of dismay came across his face. "Where's your mother?" he said.

His voice was higher pitched than she remembered, softer, and she didn't know whether it was because of the crater, or the cancer, or if he had always sounded like that.

"At home," Miranda said. "Dad – what is this?"

"It was not supposed to be you, it was supposed to be your mother," said her father. "Why did you come here?"

Much to her own irritation, Miranda was hurt by her father's obvious disappointment. "What do you mean?" she said. "You sent a letter."

"To your *mother*, I sent a letter," said her father. "I would never have asked this of you."

Miranda became aware that the pale figures on the walls were again moving, this time down towards the floor of the crater. Their bodies were the length of adult human bodies but they were narrower. They had few distinguishing features – no eyes that she could make out, no limbs – but she could see that they had mouths.

"Asked what of me?" she said.

"They are going to make me one of them," said her father. "I am going to live forever. But they need someone healthy to help them absorb my sickness. It was supposed to be your mother, it wasn't going to be you."

"I don't understand," Miranda said, although dimly, faintly, horribly, she was starting to think she did. "What do you mean, need someone?"

Her father didn't answer at first, and she wondered if he didn't know or if he knew perfectly well and didn't want to say. "Listen, they are benignant, they are *perfectly* benignant," he managed, at last. "They told me that it won't hurt. It may be good for you, in fact."

The figures were advancing across the floor of the crater, getting closer. They had gotten between her and the ladder.

"How could you do this?" Miranda asked. A pointless question; didn't she already know the answer? The same way he had done the protein shakes and timeshares and sound healing.

He didn't answer.

As the figures reached her and her father retreated silently into his limbless transcendence, she realised that really the appalling thing was this: some part of her had always stayed standing on the jungle gym with her arms above her head, waiting to be taken up, wanting desperately to believe. The mark of a mark.

AT THE BOTTOM, SHE ROTS
Ryan Cole

Jolene has already moulted three times since waking up, yet she still hasn't had a chance to sit down and eat breakfast.

The first time is in the shower, when she scrubs at what's left of her greying black hair, trying not to notice as it comes out in clumps, the long strands gathering in a puddle at her feet. The next is in the closet when she picks out her clothes, watching as her arms start to peel at the elbow; the skin curls off and blankets the carpet she vacuumed just yesterday, the lint bag still clogged up with her pale skin-ribbons. The last is by the still-locked door of her bedroom, when she thinks of the wine-dark freckles on her stomach – or what started as freckles – each of them now about the size of her thumbprint. She thinks of the insults that caused them to appear, the parasitic words digging into her body, now deeper and darker than they've ever been before. Thinks of the person who continues to feed them, whose voice she can hear from the other end of the hallway.

Her mother-in-law. Who Jolene will have to live with for the next five days.

Carefully, she picks at the skin on her neck, and she pulls at the film with the tips of her fingernails. Just like she did on her last trip to the beach, for her fortieth birthday, only two years ago. Back before the wedding. Before Daphne's belly had swollen to bursting, and Crispin had been born. That trip to the beach, and the fight that came after, was the last time Jolene had seen Daphne moult, the last time words had infected her wife. Now, it seems Jolene is the only one hurting, the only one losing the pieces of herself in a desperate attempt for her body to heal, to push out the layers that have started to fester.

There are only so many layers a person can lose, only so many before you hit blood and bone. And Jolene has come to worry that she's close to the bottom.

A secret she keeps. A secret she doesn't dare share with Daphne, or even worse, Barbara. Jolene wants to be strong, to have the family she lost, her mother-in-law the only parent she has left. She wants for her son to have the love that she didn't, alone at eighteen without a dollar to her name. Her silence is worth more than picking a fight. Worth more than proving Barbara's true nature, when Daphne won't listen. When all it will do is bring them back to the beach, reliving the things they should never have said.

Which doesn't do much for the heat, or the pain. There is a burning sensation as the skin-layer detaches. She stifles a shiver as her arms turn to goosebumps, prickling and pink from the newly exposed flesh. She covers this up with a chunky blue sweater, combs out the wig she's been wearing for months. Then a fresh layer of make-up, a plastered-on smile, and she is ready to go, to deflect, to pretend. All for the six-month-old bundle of joy whose shrieks of excitement now creep from the kitchen.

But first, the evidence.

She scoops up the skin flakes scattered on the carpet and throws them in the toilet. Then, she folds up the rest of the pale skin-ribbons, presses them into a tight mushy ball, and she hides them in the back of the underwear drawer, where no one will see them. Just for this morning, until Daphne has to leave.

Only then, with a last-minute glance in the mirror, a few deep breaths, does Jolene feel ready to unlock the door, walk down the hallway, and say hello to the woman who she knows still hates her.

★ ★ ★

"Well, look who it is," says Barbara from the kitchen table. Her fingertip is white with a dollop of ointment that she smears in a circular motion on Crispin's cheek. Eczema and winter in Connecticut aren't a match, and even though Jolene knows her son's condition well, taking care of his rashes every morning and night, Barbara makes it seem like Jolene has been absent, has been shirking her duties as a stay-at-home mother. "Shouldn't you have gotten out of bed before now?" Hiding the question that clings to her lips, that underlines each of their forced conversations: *Why can't you do more?*

Each of them knows that she'll never be satisfied. Jolene can never give her what Barbara really wants.

An issue Jolene squashes as she leans across the table, kisses Crispin on the forehead, and rearranges her sweater around the freckles on her stomach, each of them prickling as her skin begins to moult. "Thanks for coming," she manages to say through her teeth. She bends down to lay an awkward hand on Barbara's shoulder, a gesture Barbara returns with a one-armed hug, too much space left between them. "We're so glad to have you here."

Barbara smiles back, and her jawline tugs at the cracks in her face, the crinkle-lines coating her most recent layer of skin – and maybe her last. Jolene often thinks of when that final layer will come, for herself, and for Barbara. And which one of them would be first.

But there isn't time to worry. She can hear the garage door, and before she can say what she'd like to Barbara's face – what she'd always been afraid to – Daphne appears in a fitted grey blazer, her silk blouse stretched over the dregs of baby weight. Daphne dabs at her lipstick and the pristine skin that her body retains, that she doesn't have to purge. Which makes Jolene dwell on how different they are, how jealous she is that she can't be like her wife.

"Morning, Jo," says Daphne as she slips through the kitchen, squeezing Jolene's hand in a sign of reassurance. "Meet me on the porch?" A whisper she gives before hugging her mother and cuddling Crispin for several long moments. Jolene understands. Work-trips are hard – she knows this from serving as a flight attendant pre-Crispin – but this will be the first time Daphne has travelled since Crispin was born.

Hence, the reinforcements.

"You okay?" says Daphne once the two of them are alone. She runs a smooth hand through the hair of Jolene's wig, doesn't mention the bald spots or the crusty skin below. The truth, for now, is better left unsaid. At least until she's back. "I know it'll be difficult, but she loves you, believe me. She just needs time. It's a lot to adjust to."

Jolene just nods, too worried that something she says will start a fight, will nourish the rot buried deep in her layers. That she won't sound grateful for the help they're receiving. "I'll be fine," says Jolene, as the prickling intensifies, and her stomach starts to tear. Doing her best not to show her desperation, to grab Daphne's hand and tell her to stay, for God's sake just *stay*, that she can't handle Crispin and Barbara on her own, that she'll peel to the bone before Daphne returns.

Instead, she says, "Have a good trip," and hugs Daphne. Brushes Daphne's cheek with what's left of her lips.

Daphne does the same. And as Jolene quietly watches her get in the car, pull out of the driveway, and disappear into the neighbourhood, she can't stop thinking: would this be their last kiss?

★ ★ ★

The day wears on. Jolene makes coffee for Barbara and herself, she feeds Crispin breakfast as Barbara inspects her, drowning Jolene in unasked-for suggestions. "Shouldn't he be eating more than fruit?" says Barbara. "When Daphne was his age, I was feeding her eggs. Do you not feed him eggs?" Each question laced with: *Do you even know what you're doing?*

Jolene just smiles like Daphne taught her to. "He's allergic to eggs. It makes his eczema worse." She says this while wiping at a scab on Crispin's cheek, the rash a sunburn-red. "It looks like I might have to take him to the doctor."

Barbara quirks an unbelieving eyebrow at Jolene, as if Jolene is the one who is making Crispin worse. As if being a man would help her cure Crispin's eczema.

Her skin all a-prickle, Jolene leaves the kitchen; she uses the excuse that she's going to call the doctor. But in the safety of the bathroom, she picks at the film that has started to moult, sending a chill down her goose-pimpled arms. She places this layer – all speckled with black – in the pocket of her purse so that Barbara doesn't see, doesn't have another reason to view her as weak, doesn't have another word that she can use to kill Jolene.

Jolene picks up the phone, and she dials the office. Thankfully, there's an appointment for later that afternoon.

"Careful," says Barbara as Jolene tries to buckle Crispin into his car seat. Crispin keeps squirming, and from all of the skin-layers Jolene has lost, her fingers are still raw, they can't clip the buckle.

"Are you sure you can take him alone?" says Barbara. "Too bad we don't have a man's hands around here. A man's hands can fix everything." Jolene can hear Barbara's wicked grin in those words as she finally clips the buckle.

When they arrive at the doctor's office – just Jolene and Crispin, with Barbara back at the house – Crispin is in tears. Jolene wants to cry too, but she doesn't let it show. She takes full note of the receptionist's face – how it's starting to crinkle, how ribbon-like bits of skin dangle from her cheeks, crumbling away as a new layer emerges. Like everyone else in the silent waiting room.

Jolene sighs in relief when they're finally called back. The sooner they're done, the sooner she can go home, the sooner she can peel off the dots on her stomach that are now as big as fists.

"What seems to be the problem?" says the doctor soon after. Dr. Fogarty is young, her skin unblemished, her reddish hair tied into a carefree ponytail – everything Jolene wants to be, and never will.

Jolene sits fidgeting as the doctor looks at Crispin, applies a bit of ointment that soothes the irritation. They speak of Daphne's trip, how anxious Jolene has been, how Barbara's looming presence has made Jolene tense.

"This is likely a result of that pressure," says Dr. Fogarty, writing a prescription for Crispin's new medicine. "Stress can make everything worse, especially skin."

Which doubles the guilt Jolene already feels. This, as well as everything else, is her fault. Her child, her marriage, her relationship with Barbara – they would all be better off if Jolene could just cope, could not be so affected by the things that people say, that are making her rot from the inside out.

"Can I show you something?" says Jolene. Knowing she shouldn't, that she won't like the answer. She pulls out the skin-layers crammed into her purse. Then she lifts her sweater, and she points at the freckles-turned-fists on her stomach, now a midnight black.

Dr. Fogarty frowns as she rubs at the skin. "How long has this been here?"

"A few months," says Jolene, the lie coming easy. Too damn embarrassed to tell her the truth. Two years of hiding, of trying to believe that it was just one more layer – nothing big, nothing scary – is all that keeps her sane.

Dr. Fogarty nods; she doesn't meet Jolene's eyes. "I'm not a dermatologist, but I'd get that checked out if it lasts too much longer. The infection is deep. We'd want to make sure it doesn't go any deeper. Otherwise, you might not have much left to shed." She chuckles at this, as if to lighten the mood. Crispin catches on, and he starts to laugh too.

Jolene tries to smile, but her lips won't let her.

★ ★ ★

"Hey, Jo," says Daphne on the phone that evening, her voice coming choppy all the way from Minnesota. There is chatter in the background, the clinking of silverware, the ho-hum laughter of a formal client dinner. "Everything okay?"

Jolene wants to say yes. She wants to say Daphne has nothing to worry about. But even more, she wants to share what Dr. Fogarty told her, the fear of her condition now picking her apart. What if she's closer than she thought to rock-bottom? She wants to come clean, but as always, she's afraid – of what Daphne might say, of what it will do to Jolene. So, she says something else. "It's Barbara – she won't even look at me, Daph." Thinking of the way Barbara casually ignores her. Thinking of the way she walks right past her, as if looking at Jolene, as if acknowledging her presence, will solidify the fact that Daphne's married to a woman. She is tired of feeling unwanted in her own house.

"Jo," says Daphne, "we've been over this already. It's only four more days. Can't you try to push through?"

There's a break in the call while Daphne goes muted; the chatter and silverware briefly disappear. Then the noise floods in. "Sorry," she says, "I have to get back to the table." An uncomfortable pause. "Can you promise me you'll try to make it work? For Crispin?"

Jolene's fingers creep to the spots on her stomach. "I'll try, Daph," she whispers, hiding the pain.

"Great, I'll call you back when I'm done," says Daphne.

The call clicks off before Jolene can say goodbye.

★ ★ ★

In the middle of the night, Crispin wakes up crying. Jolene hears him scream, but before she can summon the energy to move, Barbara is there, her head in the doorway, her grey hair pinned as if she never went to sleep. As if she's waited for hours just to prove Jolene's laziness. "Don't worry," says Barbara, "let me handle it this time." Her lips quirk into a smile of disdain; or maybe that's only in Jolene's mind, seeing what she fears, what she can't let go of. "Where's the medication?"

Jolene points at her purse. She wants to reach over and grab it herself, but she's caught in the skin that lay wrapped around her ankles, the pale wet ribbons she shed the night before. Reminded of Daphne, how she didn't call back, how she doesn't take anything Jolene says seriously, the two of them never more distant than now.

Barbara takes the purse, and she closes the door.

Several moments pass. Crispin stops crying.

Braced for the now-constant burning sensation, Jolene rolls out of bed. The hallway is dark when she opens the door. She peeks into Crispin's room to see if he's okay, but his blankets are empty, his crib-door open. "Barbara?" says Jolene as she creeps down the hallway. No answer comes.

Quickly, she covers the length of the hallway, and she sighs in relief as she sees Crispin there, strapped into his highchair, his red cheeks wet with a dollop of ointment, the medication bottle still open on the table.

Barbara is there, too; she sits facing the hallway. Jolene's empty purse lay open in her lap. And in the palm of her hand, she holds a wad of blackened skin, dry bits floating like ash to the floor.

"Care to explain?" says Barbara with a smile.

Jolene's mouth is dry, her throat gone tight. She wants to deflect, wants to tell her it's nothing, but she can't, and now everyone will know Jolene's secret. They'll know that Jolene is as weak as she appears, that she's half-dead from words, she's not fit to be a mother.

Barbara's condescending smile digs into her skin, deeper than Daphne's rotten words ever could, and it ricochets all the way down to her stomach, the fist-prints throbbing, her skin white-hot like it's never been before.

Jolene can't speak. So, she panics. She runs.

★ ★ ★

Sweaty bare legs on the cold bathroom floor, her breath coming ragged, Jolene starts to pick at the skin on her stomach. She doesn't look up as the doorknob rattles, doesn't tell Barbara to go the hell away as she yells at Jolene to open up, to come out, to stop being fake and start talking for once. Jolene would have laughed if she weren't doubled over, her muscles on fire, her tender skin prickling. *Jolene* is the one who is fake, who won't talk? Which only intensifies the near-blinding pain, her whole body squeezing as it presses out the rot.

The outermost layer of her skin starts to rip. The flesh curls off. But this time, it isn't as thin as a ribbon. This time, it doesn't just snap when she pulls. And when she tugs at the tissue-flesh under her skin, and she tries to yank it free, she sees that the layer is as wide as her pinkie, as soft as new leather, and it throbs at her touch. The more that she pulls, the more it unfurls, the less of the black that remains underneath.

For two years, this is the layer she has needed. This is the layer that has caused so much pain. And this is the layer that will steadily kill her if it doesn't come off.

But it's stubborn, it sticks. She pulls at the skin, her fingers slippery with blood, and she's able to get it all the way to her waist. She wiggles her legs to try to slide her way out, but the burning gets worse, it only gets worse, and why can't it just stop, oh God *please make it stop.*

Trembling, slipping and sliding on her layers, she calls out for Daphne, for Crispin, for Barbara, for anyone out there who can help pull her free.

Then, the lock pin snaps; the door swings open.

Jolene pulls away, hunched over by the bathtub. She hides her face in embarrassment as Barbara tries to roll her over.

"You have to trust me," says Barbara. "I know what to do."

Jolene's heart crumples at being so helpless, at being seen as so weak, so vulnerable by Barbara. But she doesn't have a choice. If she doesn't take the help, she might never leave this bathroom.

Barbara doesn't cringe, doesn't gasp, doesn't judge. She leans over Jolene, and with meticulous fingers, she catches the skin layer and delicately rolls it, tearing the tissue at just the right angles. She is calm, *too* calm. Silent and methodical. She handles the skin as if she's done this before, as if Barbara herself has peeled raw to the bottom. Jolene starts to wonder if she even knows the woman, if Barbara has layers that she may not have shown, that she keeps from Jolene as Jolene has kept from her.

"Don't give up," says Barbara, as Jolene starts to scream. "You're almost there, keep going."

With one final tug, the skin detaches at the ankle, more black-rot than not. Jolene kicks it off into a pile on the floor. The layer that remains – the new layer that she wears – doesn't show any sign of the two-year-infection, isn't speckled with words that are too long ignored. It glistens in the dim yellow lights above the sink, still birth-wet with blood.

Jolene is smooth again. A new version of herself. A better version, she hopes. One that she doesn't have to hide anymore.

"Now, clean yourself up," says Barbara. One hand lingering too long on Jolene's shoulder, for the first time looking Jolene in the eyes.

And there, Jolene hopes, is the start of their truce.

★ ★ ★

The sun has just risen when Daphne comes home. She arrives as Jolene is feeding Crispin breakfast, with Barbara at her side, their shoulders almost touching. Barbara doesn't say what Jolene should do better, how Crispin would prefer it if she fed him more than fruit, or wouldn't it be nice if Jolene's voice was deeper? The kitchen is silent. For although they haven't spoken of that night in the bathroom, things have been different. Less like Jolene has something to prove.

Jolene takes Daphne and leads her into the bedroom, sits her down on the bed. She pulls out the wadded-up skin in her purse. Rolls out the black and bloated flesh from the bathroom. She places them both into Daphne's empty lap.

Jolene tenses up from the pain she fears will come. Hoping, and praying she's stronger this time. But she has to say it now, before she loses her courage. "I need to tell you something, Daph."

Daphne doesn't smirk, doesn't try to pull away. She sits there quietly as Jolene starts to speak. And for the first time in over two years, she just listens.

SILENT WOUNDS
Clay McLeod Chapman

(Inspired by 'The Gunners Who Came Home Damaged' by Dave Phillips, The New York Times, November 5, 2023)

Mama Arab was cradling her baby in the corner of my bedroom again last night. The kid's legs dangled against her chest, limp little things, like dust-covered chicken wings.

I knew that baby wasn't breathing. That's okay, 'cause neither was she. Not that that's kept her from staring back at me while I'm in bed for the last five fucking nights in a row, just trying to get some sleep. Any sleep. She's been following me for about a week now, hauling that crushed corpse of her kid, bouncing his jangly body in her arms wherever we go – the grocery store, the gas station, the drive-thru at McDonald's – this kid's loose limbs flopping at his sides like he's an empty sock puppet. That boy's bones are all shattered to shit. His ribs are nothing but a nest of Pick Up Sticks poking up from beneath his skin. One arm is snapped backwards. But mom still holds him, rocking her kid to sleep, never letting go, staring me down the whole goddamn time like I'm supposed to do something about it.

What do you want from me? I ask. Out loud. *What the fuck am I supposed to do?*

Never heard that baby cry. Not once. But his wailing fills my head, as shrill as an RPG launching right at my shoulder, that missile tearing straight through my sleep. This kid's eyelids are half-sealed, all gummed up with concrete dust. His lips are pale as chalk. Nostrils plugged with clumps of dirt. Yeah – that baby's never opening his eyes ever again. Never taking another breath. So why does he sound like a fucking rocket launcher to me?

Where's that missile coming from? His *mouth*? That hollow thing?

Mama holds him out, outstretching her arms at her chest, palms up and cupping this pulverised seven-pound sack of skin and splintered bones, the boy's pulped skull in one hand, his snapped back in the other, as an offering. A poorly wrapped present just for me.

Mama says something in Arabic. One word, repeated over and over again. *Take.*

No, I say. *I don't want it.*

Take. Take.

Please. Just – just stop. Go away.

Take. Take. Take.

It was the gun. The fucking Widowlicker. We brought back all its ghosts with us. Everyone we killed. Our whole unit – Alpha Battery, 3rd Battalion, 9th Marines – came home cursed. Other soldiers have been seeing the same goddamn thing I have. Different ghosts, same fucking gun. You can't tell me this many marines are experiencing the exact same symptoms – seeing this shit wherever we go – and not know what caused it. The DoD knows it, I know it, every last grunt in the artillery gun crew knows what the hell this is.

The Carl Gustaf M3 long-range cannon. A two-person 84mm calibre shoulder-mounted rocket launcher. One loads, the other fires, a hundred pound round hurled over fifteen miles. Twenty miles. Wherever that spider-hole our target is curled up in is.

A ghost gun.

Our mission was to push back the Islamic State. Get ISIS out of the cities. Deliver every last jihadi straight to hell. We sent an endless torrent of fire all day, every day. Morning, noon and night. Bring the fucking thunder. Just pummel everything under the sun.

I never once saw the eyes of my targets. Not a goddamn one.

Not until I came home.

Now I see them all the time. They're everywhere I go. In my shitty apartment. My bedroom. The streets. It's easy to tell them apart from civvies, because of the dust. They're covered in crushed concrete. Makes them look all white, pale as sheets. Boogedy boo.

You've been seeing them, too? Private Noah Hendricks asked me over the phone, sounding all needy and shit, like a couple kids talking about seeing spooks for the first time.

Yeah, I see them. Noah loaded the Gustaf while I pulled the trigger, then we'd swap. Noah was the one who came up with the badass name. Said it was from some song – *Widowlicker* – but I'd never heard it. Can't remember the name of the band now. Everybody uses *widowmaker* – but fuck that, Noah wanted to slip under these wives' burkas. Run his tongue up their asses. We're not supposed to give nicknames to our weapons, but we did.

Of course we did.

How many do you have following you? he asked me.

Couple? Maybe four or five?

Shit, man... I'm up to a dozen of these motherfuckers. They won't let me sleep.

They won't let me sleep, either. Won't let me eat. Won't let me drink.

I'm never alone now.

I thought I was the only one who saw them, Noah said. I could hear the relief in his voice, faint through the phone, knowing that he wasn't alone. That I saw them, too.

Lucky, lucky us.

Private Jenna Ortiz called them *demons* – which, I'm sorry, that's just her Catholic ass putting her own religious spin on this shit. Didn't matter what pew you parked your keister in. Pull the trigger on the Widowlicker and you were cursed. Marked for life.

Firing a weapon like that takes a toll, she told me, hiding out in her parents' basement somewhere down in South Carolina. She never said where, exactly. I never asked. *We all signed our souls away to that gun.*

Says you, Ortiz. I'm not seeing demons. The whole point was we never had to see who was on the receiving end of the Widowlicker. That didn't mean we weren't dragging their spirits back home with us. No – these were ghosts, straight up. Every target, intentional or not, tagging along.

I tried telling my wife about them, Noah told me. *She thinks I'm crazy.*

Maybe you are.

Fuck that. He laughed, all air. *I told her I'd get my head checked, but I haven't yet.*

How are you dealing with it?

Drinking, mostly. You?

Smoking up does the trick. For a bit, anyway. Talking to Noah helped, too. He lives in Michigan. Got a wife and a five-year-old. We've been calling each other nearly every night for a week now. I'm like his spiritual sponsor. Whenever he starts to get this particular itch that he's being followed, he picks up the phone. Calls me. We've been comparing spooks, like we're telling ghost stories. All we need is a campfire and some fucking marshmallows.

You tried talking to one of them yet?

Nah, I lied. I talk to them all the time. I got no one else. My girlfriend left me after she caught me shouting at myself in the kitchen. She didn't see the broken baby, her mother holding him up for me to take, *take, take*, while all I wanted was to eat my cereal in peace.

Get the fuck away from me, I shouted, throwing my bowl at her. Hit the wall instead. Milk and Frosted Flakes dribbled to the floor, puddling up at Mama Arab's feet.

My girlfriend thought I'd been aiming at her. She didn't know any better. Didn't see.

You need to get help, were her last words to me before packing it in.

Yeah, I thought. Help. I'll get right on that. You want to know how many times I've been on the hold with the VA? Just to schedule a checkup? Takes for fucking ever just to get a living, breathing human being on the other end of the line. I've had an easier time chatting with the dead people crashing on my couch than with my designated medical specialist.

Noah up and asked me over the phone – *What do you think they want?*

Fuck if I know.

You think they'll stop?

Stop, what? I asked, acting like I didn't already know.

Haunting us, bro.

There's this boy. Always stands outside my apartment building. Can't be older than ten, maybe eleven. He wears the same soccer jersey every damn day. Number eleven. The shirt's torn right down the centre of his chest. This kid could be coming home from practice. It's not entirely out of the realm of possibility that he tripped on the field, tore his shirt, fell in mud, caked himself up in shit and now it's all dry and crackling across his skin.

Then why's he always waiting outside my window? Staring me down? *The hell are you looking at?* I asked once. *Go home. Go. Get.*

He didn't move. Just stood there, glaring back at me. This kid looked royally pissed. Like he wanted to throw a punch. All ten years of himself. Big man. His lips were pinched so tight, they went all white. His eyes were so dark, practically black, contrasted against the brittle film of dried dirt covering his body. His skin.

But something was off about him. He almost looked out of focus. Fuzzy. I couldn't focus on his features. There was a hum coming off his body. The tiniest vibrations.

I said go home. I stepped up. Lunged like I was about to run him, you know? Just one foot forward. Bringing my hand up, I wanted to scare him off and—

Oh.

Now I can see through that hole in his shirt. See how far – how deep – that hole goes.

All the way through.

War changes your body. I'm not talking mentally. Yeah, it does that, too – but physiologically, it alters you. You come home like, a different person. Inside and out.

This gun disrupted us, somehow. Rearranged our insides. The Widowlicker threw our bodies all out of whack. Nobody told us that a gun could do that. Change us.

I remember the first time I slung that motherfucker onto my shoulder. Not those test runs back in Camp Lejeune. I'm talking the real deal. In combat. Syria, baby. I'm feeling the weight of that launcher at my neck, the outright majesty of it. I'm strapped in, mounted up. Ready to roll. Noah loads a round in, types in the coordinates – and I squeeze the trigger.

I swear, it's like the heavens opened up. A fucking jet airplane blasts right off at my ear. This shockwave ripples through my body – my mind – and everything goes pitch black.

There's a tear. A rift between our world and beyond. Between the living and dead.

It's so cold here.

So empty.

So—

Target hit, Noah said, slapping my back. I must've blacked out. I don't know how long I was gone. Couldn't have been more than a couple seconds, but I swear, it felt longer. I lost consciousness. Lost time. There's a temporary gap in my memory where I'm seeing nothing but stars. Not like on a clear night. This was different. This was another fucking galaxy altogether. I was somewhere else. Not in my body. My whole skeleton felt like a tuning fork, bones vibrating with the aftershock, humming in this high-pitched frequency.

Holy shit, I said. *This motherfucker really rings your bell...*

My turn, bro, Noah said, all giddy and shit. *Saddle me up.*

Every last cannon blast radiated out from the Widowlicker and into the atmosphere, passing through us first, our muscle tissue, our bones, absorbing every cell in its path.

Private John Watkins called it The Ripple. The shockwave. When it washes over you, that sonic aftershock passing through your body, you come out the other end all different.

You come out cursed, was what Watkins actually said. Took a few calls before he finally picked up. There's no telling where he was. I hadn't seen him for months, but talking to him on the phone brought our deployment right on back. *That gun put a hex on us all...*

You listening to yourself? You sound like a gypsy or some shit. Cursed, my ass.

What would you call it then?

That weapon broke all the laws of man. Of God. Of whatever the fuck you want to believe in. I never prayed a day in my life, but after making a pact with that cannon and pulling the trigger, I tore a rift through space and time. That's some cosmic fucking shit.

When you were in high school, Noah asked the last time we talked, *you ever choke yourself? Get dizzy for shits and giggles?*

Like pass out on purpose?

Yeah, we called it space monkey.

Whip-its were my style.

I did it all the time, he said. *I'd cinch a belt around my neck, hang myself by just a few inches from the rod in my closet, getting all euphoric and shit. Blacking out. Seeing stars.*

I knew where he was going with all this.

That's what it felt like that first time, he said. *Pulling the trigger on the Widowlicker. I blacked out. Went somewhere else, man... Saw some stars I'd never seen before.*

I saw them, too. Travelled there, too, whatever galaxy it was. Definitely wasn't ours. None of these constellations looked familiar to me. A totally different celestial pattern.

I think, Noah started, then stopped, like he was trying to figure out how best to say this. To articulate himself. *I think, maybe, we crossed over, you know? To the other side.*

What other side?

You know what side. Beyond the veil. To the dead...

I laughed, playing all tough. *Fuck that.*

I'm serious, bro. Something came back with us. Followed us home. That gun's a bridge. We're bound by a bullet. Those ghosts are connected to us forever now.

You really want to know what it feels like to fire the Widowlicker? Pull the trigger? Ever been kicked in the chest? Your lungs lock so you can't breathe? Ever been smacked in the ears by a pair of open hands, that cymbal crash of palms sucking all the sound out so fast, you think your eardrums just burst? Ever feel your bones quake within your own body, like the fucking framework of your skeleton is literally rattling, losing all of its shape? Just jelly? Ever feel your eyeballs squash in their sockets? Your field of vision blurs because your eyeballs flatten for just a split second? Then the shockwave reaches your brain, The Ripple seeping into your cerebral matter, making scrambled eggs out of everything in your skull.

We were told to anticipate migraines.

Nobody said anything about ghosts.

I have this family of four following me through the VA whenever I come in. I've been seeking help for about a month now, but everybody here sounds like a broken record. Too much red tape. Too much waiting. And this family – Daddy Arab's head cleaved in half, Mom's missing an arm, and their kids can't even stand anymore, their legs all crushed, like a boulder fell on their feet or something, smashing everything from the knees on down – they're always staring at me in the waiting room, like they're expecting me to help them.

It's not my fault, I said. Out loud. A little too loud. *How was I supposed to know?*

Our targets were always hideouts. Never homes. Never hospitals. Never schools.

That's what we were told, anyway. How would we know, miles away?

All we ever got were coordinates. We only knew that on the other side of those numbers were some bad fucking dudes. That's all. We never saw them. Never knew their names. Never needed to. It was so easy. So fucking easy. Pulling that trigger. Kaboom.

Our airstrikes pounded the shit out of ISIS positions. Hundreds of rounds fired. *Thousands.* Zero American casualties. Not one fatality on our side. Mission accomplished.

You think they blame us? Lance Corporal Kelvin Linquist asked me over drinks. *I think they do. I think they want us to pay for what we did to them. To atone or some shit.*

You can't keep thinking like that, man…

I'm serious. My body's shaking all the time. Here — look. I'll prove it to you. He held out his arm, quivering in the air over all our empties. *I can't stop my wrists from trembling.*

I've got the same shakes. Vibrations in my wrist. That tuning fork in my forearm.

The Ripple. The endless aftershock.

Only way I know how to make the shaking stop is to grip a pistol, he said.

Fuck's sake, man…

It's true. He made a fist, squeezing it so tight, his knuckles went white. *Try it.*

You know what they'll do to you if they hear you talking about drawing a firearm?

I'm serious, Lance said, finally lowering his hand, hiding it under the table. *It's like — like The Ripple needs a weapon. A gun's the only thing that's gonna silence these ghosts.*

I know how to spot them now. The spirits. Tell the difference between them and civilians. Other folks don't even notice them. That's a dead giveaway. These ghosts are just for us. Our unit. We're left to deal with them. They'll tag along whenever I head to Safeway, following me through the cereal aisle, no cart, no basket, just dragging their heels behind me. Carrying their dead babies like they're nothing but a dirty Perdue chicken. Like they're going to lay their fucking kid to rest on the conveyor belt in the checkout line. Nine items or less. I wonder if the girl behind the cash register will ask for a price-check on dead babies.

Take. Take.

The biggest difference is that if you can get close to them, real close, you'll notice their bodies are vibrating. Just the slightest reverberations. Makes them look like they're out of focus, almost, but it's really because they're quivering. Oscillating in the tiniest waves.

The Ripple. Noah was right. It's dragged them back from the other side, riding that shockwave.

I've learned I can't react to them. If I panic, other people will notice. That's what gets me into a pile of shit. I have to keep these ghosts to myself. Nobody understands. None of the people around me know what the fuck I'm going through. Not my friends. My family.

Only family I have now are these ghosts. I talk to them more than my own parents. Who else is going to understand what I'm going through? At least these ghosts get it.

I started reaching out to the rest of my unit weeks ago, right around the time the third or fourth ghost found me. The soldiers I served with were bound to be going through the same shit as me, right? Seeing them? We each brought home our own ghosts. A little keepsake from our deployment overseas. Supernatural tchotchkes.

I reached out to Noah first. Then Ortiz. Watkins. Linquist.

You think Pete's seeing the same shit we are? Pete Simmonds was our first lieutenant. He oversaw our unit, doling out coordinates. Not people. Just numbers.

You didn't hear? Noah asked, all serious and shit.

Hear what?

Noah didn't say anything for a moment.

Dude. Hear what?

Pete blew his brains out.

The fuck? When?

Two days ago.

Tell me, tell all of us: How do we get rid of our ghosts? How do we make them stop?

How do we make the shaking stop?

By the time I finally got an appointment with a medical specialist on the books, I was dragging a half dozen spirits into the checkup room with me. I had to keep my eyes on the doc as he's talking. Try hard not to pay attention to that mother holding up her broken baby – *Take.*

Take. Try hard not to notice the boy with the hole in his chest. Try hard not to—
I'd like to run a few tests if that's okay, the doc said.
What kind of tests?
CT scan, for starters.
Why?
Just want to rule a few things out before we go any further. We can schedule one—
When?
About a week, he said.
I got to wait another fucking week? I don't know if I'm going to be alive that long...
There's no test for seeing ghosts, but sure thing, go to town. Run those tests, doc. Be my fucking guest. The VA is just going to keep giving us the runaround, saying we all suffered from TBIs. Concussions. That's it. An ol' knock on the noggin'. We'll become nothing but a statistic for the DoD. Data on a spreadsheet. Not flesh and blood. Not people.

We're all getting headaches. Experiencing memory loss. Patches of our day, just gone. Black holes swallowed hours of our lives. I'd snap back and suddenly discover I was somewhere I've never been before, no idea how I even got here in the first fucking place.

What's an MRI going to show me that I didn't already know?

We've got ghosts, man. Not brain injuries.

I hit my kid, Noah told me the last time we talked. *My own flesh and blood, man...*

What the hell happened?

I thought he was a ghost.

You got to stop doing this to yourself. Get your shit together.

You think I haven't tried? I called the goddamn DoD and they're just jerking me around. TBIs. That's all this is to them. Nobody wants to help. Nobody believes me.

I believed him, even if I didn't say so on the phone. I should've said so.

We're all seeing them.

The DoD never told us what this weapon would do to our bodies. Our minds. We believed we were safe because they told us we were safe, but that was just bullshit.

We're cursed. Cursed by a goddamn gun. The Ripple's finally turning back around, I can feel it. Coming back for us. Every last one. A sonic boomerang, rebounding my way.

You want to tell me Private First Class Noah Hendricks wasn't seeing spirits? He brought his ghosts home. Every last target he took down followed him back. He was up to ten, twenty ghosts a day before he shot himself. *The Ripple's getting worse. I need my gun.*

You want me to drive up there? See if we can get you some help, together?

He wasn't listening to me, just talking to himself. *Drinking does nothing for me. Drugs do nothing. Only a gun. I need to hold it. Get my hands on it. Pull the trigger again.*

Cross back over. Into that black. Noah wanted to get his ass dragged off by the tide of the cannon's aftershock, sent into that blissful distance where life and death intersect.

Shuttle into the great beyond all over again and never come back.

No wonder Noah slipped his service revolver into his mouth. Severed his spinal column at the back of his throat. One last blast before entering the void, riding The Ripple.

I tried calling him a couple times even when I knew he wouldn't answer. There was a part of me, I guess, just a bone fragment of hope, that wished I'd get his ghost to haunt me.

I miss him.

I keep reaching out to as many members of our unit as I can. Which ones are still left. The ones that'll talk to me say they're experiencing the same symptoms. Insomnia. Nightmares. Panic attacks. Depression. Hallucinations. Not to mention chest pains. Shortness of breath. The shakes. Headaches. Common combat stress reactions, all of it.

The VA is saying it's TBIs. Traumatic brain injuries. Blast exposure. Fire off a weapon like the Widowlicker and it'll fuck you up. They're covering it up, calling it a concussion.

This isn't PTSD, I keep saying. These are ghosts.

I killed these people.

We all did.

This is The Ripple bouncing back, rebounding our way. The Widowlicker is hungry for more, lapping at the back of my brain. You think any of us would've pulled that fucking trigger if we knew we'd be dragging these spirits home with us? Haunted by a fucking gun?

Guess how many marines have committed suicide? Eight of us. *Eight*. Half my squad. John Watkins. Jenna Ortiz. Kelvin Linquist. Gone. By the time the brass decides to get off their fat asses and do something, we'll all be dead. I'll be dead. A fucking bullet in my head. That's the only way to make the shaking stop. Ride The Ripple right into oblivion.

The great beyond.

You want to tell me the DoD doesn't know what's going on here? They're covering this all up and calling it delayed onset of PTSD. But that's just bullshit. They know what's happening to us and they're not doing a goddamn thing to help us. To stop it from happening to someone else. They're still using the Gustaf right now, I bet. Who's to say they aren't aiming a fucking rocket launcher at my apartment right now, huh? Who's to say there isn't some grunt just like me, miles away, wrapping his finger around the trigger, sending his payload to my apartment? Who's to say the roof of this place isn't going to crumble?

I'm next, aren't I? They're trying to silence me.

Am I the Widowlicker's target?

You got to stop using the Gustaf. Discontinue it altogether. That weapon's haunted. Look – I know you don't believe me. Nobody believes me. I know how stupid this all sounds. A goddamn ghost gun. We were firing that rifle from miles away. We sent hell to those people. Then the Widowlicker dragged something back. A vacuum across the void.

It cursed us, I know it. That fucking rifle cursed us all. Our whole unit.

The gun did this to me. Our own weapon. Taking us all to hell, one marine at a time.

I'm the only one left now.

I'm all alone.

I've been thinking a lot about my brain lately. What it must look like, all littered with lesions. I don't need a CT scan to show me how scrambled my mind is. I wonder, when I'm gone, taken away by The Ripple, if the DoD will try to claim my body. Do an autopsy. Somebody will cut my skull open and scoop my brain out, just to see what happened to me.

Ghosts don't show up on MRIs. Only I see them.

Linquist was right. The only way to reach The Ripple and cut it off, keep those vibrations away, is to hold a gun. As soon as I held my service revolver in my hand, it softened the aftershock. A piddly little pistol isn't worth shit, but at least it's something. Deadens the vibrations a bit. Mutes them for a little while. I'll take whatever help I can get.

Anything to keep the oscillating ghosts away. Just for a little while.

Time to ride.

Mama Arab is here. Like always. She's fluctuating in the far corner of my bedroom, her frame out of focus, juddering in the shadows. She holds out her dead baby for me.

Take. Take.

I can't right now, I want to tell her. I've got my hands full.

I tighten my grip around my revolver. It softens The Ripple in my wrist by just a bit. I can still feel it, that ache reverberating through my bones. Only one way to make it stop.

Take, this mother keeps saying to me, holding out her dead son. *Take. Take.*

I can't. I'm sorry, I can't.

You want to know what the biggest difference between us and them is? We wouldn't look at them. Wouldn't see. We were miles away from their eyes. And we decimated them. Wiped them off the face of this earth.

This woman, though, this mother, she's looking right at me. Only a few feet away.

I see her eyes. I see them now. The white of them.

Take. She's looking straight at me, dead on in the eyes. She doesn't blink. Not once.

I can't. I have to end this. Stop the shakes. The Ripple. *I'm sorry. I'm so sorry, I can't...*

Take.

I'm crying now. Sobbing now. *Please. Make it stop. Please.*

Take.

I don't want to look at that baby.

Take.

I don't want to see...

Take.

I put my pistol down on the bed next to me. Release it.

I can't do it.

I'm sorry. I'm so sorry. I hold out my hands to her, trembling. The vibrations grow louder, resounding in my wrists, arms humming like a tuning fork. *Forgive me. Please.*

This mother, she gives me her child.

Take.

I take her baby into my quaking arms. I hold him, cradling him against my chest. I look down, look into this child's half-lidded eyes, the clumps of dust gumming them all up.

I wipe the sediment from his eyes as best I can. Brush the dust from his cheek.

The baby looks up at me. I see his eyes for the first time, the endless depths of them.

The vibrations finally, *finally*, stop.

AGONY STREET
Rebecca Harrison

When Granny came back as a house, Pa didn't talk to me for a week. But I wasn't a bit sorry.

"You brought shame on us," he said to his beer. That was unfair. The beer hadn't done nothing. It was all me. See, Pa'd been too busy pawing Granny's limp hand, too busy crying, "Ma, Ma," to hear the creak of the latch. I climbed on a chair to reach the window as Granny's spirit lifted right out of her. She was all shine and smile. I knew I was doing right. Granny didn't want heaven, she wanted here. So, I opened the window, and her spirit went right out, right over the rooftops. Proper eager like. She didn't mind one bit. See, Granny wasn't no snob. She flew smiling over my school. She shone in the windows of the chip factory. She was a buttery glow over the town. And I was right proud as folk pointed. See, Granny was always church smart. So, she didn't look dying or sad, she had her handbag and her Sunday shoes, and her hair was just so. I shut the window. Pa swung round. He was on his feet and shaking me till I nearly fell off the chair.

"What'd you do, Sally?" he bellowed.

"It won't be Agony Street if Granny's there," I shouted. I squirreled out of his grip and jumped off the chair. He flung the window open.

"Ma! Ma!" he yelled. Granny looked back but she didn't wave. She was too busy. She was on her way to Agony Street. And Pa couldn't do nothing about it. "Heaven was waiting for her," he said, his forehead on the pane.

"But she didn't wanna go. See." I pointed to Granny. Her green coat flapped like the wind was in it. Her face was peaceful as pudding.

"That's not how it works, Sally. If the window's open, you go to Agony Street. Sure as." But what was wrong with that? Sure, Mr. Graddax had turned into a house ugly as ugly with smoking chimneys all over his roof and higgledy-piggledy floors and black scowling windows, but that was 'cos he was a wrong'un. Granny was the best woman in town. She couldn't be an ugly house if she tried. I was proud as proud just thinking how pretty she'd be – if she'd have window boxes of yellow pansies or a green gable.

"Let's go watch her grow, Pa," I said, tugging his sleeve.

"Watch her grow?" He spun round and his face was all grizzly. "Don't you get it, Sally? Folk'll think we did this 'cos heaven wouldn't have her." I looked past him. Granny had gone so far, she was just a pinch of shine.

"I'm gonna watch her," I said. I darted out the room and down the stairs. Pa thundered after me. I yanked the front door. Pa got his hand on it. "I'm going to see Granny and you can't stop me." I tugged at the door. He slammed it shut.

"You don't go near Agony Street."

"You can't stop me," I yelled. But his face went full of bear, so I ran upstairs. I crouched by Granny and held her cooling hand. "You're going to be the prettiest house there ever was, Granny."

Pa didn't let me out. So, I couldn't visit Granny. But she wasn't alone 'cos the whole town had gone to see her. When Mrs. Stocker brought over a chicken stew, that weasel Rupert came too.

"I've seen your Gran. Twice," Rupert whispered to me. His Ma was all sympathy and eyelashes at Pa.

"What she look like?" I whispered back.

"Like this." And he drew a house shape in the air with his fingers. I flicked his forehead.

"Tell me proper or I'll do it again."

"Real nice. Got flowers 'bout her door. Whole town's been to look at her." Well, I was right jealous, so I flicked him again.

I brushed my hair shimmery for the funeral. But what with Ma long gone and Pa not talking and Granny being a house, there was no one to tell me I was pretty but the mirror. I put my best blue bow in my hair. Granny called me Strawberry Sally cos of my hair. And we ate strawberry shortbread just the two of us and she said we were ladies at the races. And my horse always came in first.

"You ready, Sally?" Pa called. It was the first thing he'd said to me since I let Granny out the window. So, I snatched it up like a lemon sherbet. I ran downstairs. Pa was smart but his shoulders were sad. He didn't say nothing else.

All the town folk were standing by the church just waiting for us. All polished up like toffee apples. But they didn't have weeping eyes, they had snooping eyes. Bet they'd been peering in Granny's windows or trying her front door. I wanted to flick the lot of them. But I walked past proper proud, and when Pastor Perry welcomed us in, I even nodded at him. I didn't look at Granny's box. I sat with my hands in my lap, real ladylike. And I sang *All Things Bright and Beautiful* loudest of all. Then Mrs. McKellar got up. She was Granny-smart, with shoes so shiny you could tell fortunes on them, and a hat that looked box new.

"Seems like only yesterday me and Bernice were picking berries in the fields out back of our schoolhouse. Only yesterday I stood in this church as her maid of honour. We've all our own memories of Bernice. She was the best cook in town, and well, she was the best woman in town, too." She glanced at Granny's box and her lips went tight. She shook her head. "It's not right. Not right at all. What's a woman like Bernice doing in Agony Street? Why'd you do it, Samuel? She was my best friend." She stared right at Pa. A gasp went round the church. Pa got shuddery to his feet. Like fighting, but his face was full of sheep. I didn't wait to see what happened next. I jumped up and I ran. I ran down the aisle, out the door and along the road. I didn't stop. I ran and I ran. I ran across town. All the way to Agony Street. I stood at the top. No one had followed me. It was just me and the wind, though I'd rather have been alone 'cos that wind was messing my hair. And I wanted to look nice for Granny.

Agony Street is long. And it can be noisy. And not just from jackdaws. Some of the house folks are pretty howly. House Albert Nannock, for starters, him with that roof that narrows into a lone chimney – his door always swings wide, and he goes *woooooo*. You can't tiptoe past quietly enough to stop him. Then there's House Prissy Dale – she's got windows like spiteful stars, and when you walk past, she hisses, and her chimneys puff out black coughs. Mean ladies and nasty men. I had no time for none of them, so I walked business-like with my hands in my pockets and my nose in the air.

I walked all the way to the bottom of the street.

And there was Granny. Pretty as pretty and cosy as cosy. Like a picture on a puzzle box. Her windows shone like toffee wrappers. She had beams and a thatch roof and two friendly chimneys with silver smoke. Her front door was the colour of the lavender she grew in our garden. She even had her own little path lined with pansies.

I smoothed the wind out of my hair, and I tiptoed up the path.

"It's me, Strawberry Sally," I said. The roses round the door nodded. There was a cooing sound. The door opened all gently. Inside glowed sunset-y. Oh, it smelled of handbag mints and the radio guide and rock cakes. I slipped my shoes off and set them on the welcome mat. The hall rug was soft as soft. Along the walls were painting of penguins – Granny's favourite animal. Magic pictures that moved. The penguins were all merry and waddling about on slabs of ice. You grinned just looking at them. "You happy here, Granny?" There was more cooing. "Pa ain't best pleased you're a house now, but he's always been set in his ways." The roses rustled like laughter and the front door swung shut behind me. "Pa ain't stopped weeping. But he's not going hungry. Hasn't got a chance, 'cos that Mrs. Stocker has been over most nights with stew. She says it's chicken, but I reckon it's boots." I pulled a face. Suddenly a door at the end of the hall flung wide and dinner smells gusted. My mouth watered. I was in the kitchen and lifting the lid of the pot before you could say goulash. And that's what it was. I ladled a big helping into the daintiest white and green china bowl and sat down for eating. It was right pretty in here. White and green with flowers painted all about. And those painted flowers dropped painted petals and then grew new blooms. When I finished, my bowl magicked clean. I thanked Granny and then I went exploring.

But I didn't get far 'cos the living room had a big cushiony sofa that floated when you curled up. There was a reading lamp with wings and talons that held books for you. The grandfather clock blew snowflakes when it chimed. And the windows didn't show Agony Street. They showed meadows with bending poppies. But the sun still got to evening and so I had to go.

Pa was waiting for me. And he had a tale of woe.

"How'd you think I felt with all their eyes on me? Accusing me of doing wrong by my ma?"

"But Granny's real happy," I said.

"Pastor Perry took me aside and asked me, real confidential, if Ma had done something so heinous heaven wouldn't let her in." He shook his head. "That's down to you, Sally." But I wasn't a bit sorry.

I wasn't a bit sorry at school when those wallies sniggered at me.

"How many lavatories has your Gran got?" Sarah Dillow laughed.

"Five, and each one of them cleaner than that pigsty you call home," I said, and I flicked her.

I ran to Agony Street soon as the lunch bell rang.

"Pa's griping something awful, Granny," I said as I took my shoes off. The roses rustled behind me. "But he'll come round once the beer runs out."

Lunch was strawberry shortbread on dainty china. Then I curled up on the sofa, it floated high, and in the windows were the races. Horse races. Just like we pretended. Suddenly, a ticket appeared in my lap. "Strawberry Storm!" I read. Well, the horse at the front, he was the same colour as my hair. And I could tell from the dust at his hooves, he was just like me. I could tell it even more when he won. I did a victory lap round the living room. But then I had to go.

Pa was drinking and muttering all evening. But I wanted to mutter after another dinner of Mrs. Stocker's boot stew.

"You been back there?" His eyes were bleary and growly.

"Course I have. I'm Granny's favourite," I said, and I ran to my room.

I went back the next day and the next. If anyone in class dared asked me about Granny's plumbing, I flicked them good. And I took rock cakes home and ate them while Pa struggled down Mrs. Stocker's boot stew. But then it was Saturday, and Pa was looking at me all wolf and telling me to get my shoes on. He didn't say nothing else, but I knew we were going to Agony Street from the way his eyebrows went into one scowling line. He proper strode, so I had to skip to keep up with him. Folk eyed us like we were strange things in jars. But I didn't mind. I just waved at them. That put a stop to their staring. The wind strode along with us too. And it blew dust on me, so I pretended I was Strawberry Storm, and I shook my mane. Then we were at Agony Street.

"See here, Sally," Pa said. "This was Jimmy Blessing." Well, I always ran past House Jimmy Blessing, so I didn't want to stop, but Pa put his heavy hand on my shoulder. "Only he wasn't nothing like a blessing. Not to his victims. And now look at him." He was ugly as ugly. His round windows didn't sit still in his walls but were always on the move. Like big staring spiders. They clustered about to watch you. His smoking chimneys bended over so much they almost touched the ground.

Pa walked me to the next house.

"That there was Silvie Fathom. Don't need me to tell you she was a sinner." He gestured at the scarlet smoke chugging from her chimneys. Well, I didn't mind House Silvie Fathom. She was right interesting with her five purple doors that opened and played sour songs. But Pa grunted and moved me on. He stopped at each of the house folk and told me they were bad. It wasn't news.

"Dorothy Ivy." I didn't need him to tell me she was the first of the lot. "Couldn't just burn quietly, could she? Had to curse the town." He shook his head. House Dorothy Ivy was all dark and tower-y. With lightning always raging inside and windows that opened and poured out hailstones. Real Biblical hailstones, like oranges. "Well, I ain't one for repeating a witch's words." He rubbed his forehead. House Dorothy Ivy's front door flung open with a great bellow of thunder. "And now Ma is under her curse." Pa was turning into a real bellyache. I shrugged his hand off my shoulder and walked up to the door. I did a proper curtsy.

"House Dorothy Ivy, thank you for making my Granny the prettiest house there ever was." The lightning paused. I looked at Pa all triumphant. Then I ran to Granny.

I didn't go home till it was late enough for Pa to be asleep in his easy chair. He even snored displeased. And he woke displeased, too. He marched me to church with his heavy hand on my shoulder.

"Let them talk some sense into you," he said.

"Let them try," I said, and I walked with my arms folded.

Church was full of folks trying. They tried with hymns and wailings. They said "Why, Bernice?" so much it was like 'Why' was her Christian name. And Pastor Perry listened like a mountain listens. Well, he wasn't beyond flicking if it came to it. It started getting clamour-y with all the folk shouting over each other, and old Bessie Waddell sobbing so hard the pew shook. Pastor Perry held up his palms until silence shuttered down. A silence with porcupine spines. I didn't like it one bit.

"The Lord has not forsaken our sister, Bernice. There's a place in heaven for her still," he said.

"But what good is a seat up there if she's on Agony Street?" Mrs. McKellar said.

"You can't reach heaven when you've got foundations," said Mrs. Stocker.

"You just need wings," Pastor Perry said, and he tapped his bible.

I don't know who started it but suddenly there was a stampede. I ran alongside my Pa. The whole lot of them were going to Agony Street. Pastor Perry clutched his bible and old Bessie Waddell sang like a toad on a bonfire.

When we reached House Granny, everyone stood round gawping. She'd grown two apple trees with golden fruit and blossom that turned to fizzing colours in the breeze. Pastor Perry walked up to her front door.

"It's me, Bernice. Thought one of our chats was overdue." The door opened. He stepped inside. I started after him, but it swung shut on me. I turned the handle, but Granny didn't let me in. I pushed and I pushed, but the door didn't budge. Pastor Perry was in there with his bible. Well, he'd been to pastor school, and I reckoned they did lessons on breaking curses.

"Sally, it's time now." Pa's hand was on my shoulder.

"Don't let him send Granny away."

"Bernice is going to a better place." Mrs. McKellar nodded.

"But there ain't no place better than being together." I wiped my eyes with my sleeve.

There was another porcupine silence that had all the folk stuck on its spines. So, no one said nothing. Too busy waiting and expecting. Expecting House Granny to vanish in a big puff of silver sparkle. Or to shrink and spin until she was Granny-shaped again, and then fly up through the clouds with her handbag swinging. I plucked a golden apple off a low branch and put it in my pocket. I wanted a bit of Granny to keep. Then the front door opened. Pastor Perry was holding a dainty plate piled with rock cakes.

"Well, Bernice, it's been real pleasant. I'll be over Thursday for another of our chats," he said. The roses round the door nodded. He walked up the pansy path and the door closed behind him.

"Well?" Pa said.

"Seems there's nothing in the scripture against it. The commandments don't say 'thou shalt not be a house', do they? And Bernice is as good a house as she was a woman." He put his hand on Pa's arm and looked at him direct. "Honour thy father and thy mother." Then he handed the china to Bessie Waddell. She took a cake and passed the plate on. There was munching and gossiping.

"I ain't above admitting I'm a silly goose," Mrs. McKellar said. The front door opened and there was a cooing sound. She went inside. Pastor Perry started back up Agony Street.

"You can't leave Ma here," Pa shouted. But Pastor Perry just kept going.

Pa didn't stop being a bellyache. He didn't need the beer to help him be miserable. He did it all by himself. And so well, even Mrs. Stocker stopped bringing her boot stew. I carried a pot of House Granny's goulash home, but he wouldn't even have a teaspoonful. He snatched up the pot and tipped it over the sink. Well, it was a never-ending pot, so it didn't stop pouring. There was goulash all over and then some. We waded in it. The only way to clean up was to let the neighbourhood dogs in to eat their fill. I stopped going home for dinner after that. And then I stopped going home to sleep, too. Why would I? At House Granny, I slept on a cloud. It sure was comfier than any bed. And it bobbed up against the window and the moon smiled at me and sang me lullabies. The stars flew past on their itsy-bitsy wings, and if I pretended to be slumbering, they peered right in at me. Pa could've moved in. There was a room for him with a window that always showed steam trains whistling into the far away. But he was too busy being miserable.

Then one day, he was bellyaching at House Granny's front door. I was curled up on my cloud bed with a book about a princess who lived in a castle on a frog's back. I was just at a real good bit where that frog hopped onto the moon. So, I wasn't in the mood for putting down my reading. Well, the front door had swung and now Pa was inside and all jabbering.

"Ain't right. Ain't right," he kept on. Well, what wasn't right was my reading being disturbed. I shut my book and I got off my cloud. I went to the top of the stairs and looked down on him. He had a big canister and was sloshing water over the penguin pictures and the rug. He disappeared into the kitchen, and I heard more sloshing. An engine smell stung my nose. Well, it wasn't water at all! Then he was sloshing up the stairs, till he was just a couple steps below me. He looked at me all snake. He tossed the empty canister and pulled a matchbox out of his jacket.

"Leave Granny alone!" I yelled at him.

"It's the only way, Sally." He pushed the box open and took out a match. His bleary eyes were on me. He lifted his hand to strike the match.

I pushed him with all of me. He wobbled. He reached for the banister, but it vanished. He gripped at nothing. I shoved him again. I shoved him till he fell. The hall rug rolled back, and he landed on stone with a mighty thwack. I went downstairs. He looked real uncomfortable lying all contorted.

"You playing, Pa?" I nudged him with my foot. But he didn't move. Then his spirit started lifting out of him. Well, he wasn't best pleased: his face was yelling, and his arms were flailing at his body. Then the front door swung wide open. Pa started shaking his head. He tried to grab hold of the penguin paintings, but his hands went right through. "You can't fight it, Pa," I said. He floated along the hall and out the door. I ran after him, but he didn't go far: just to the empty plot next door. He was stood on the dirt. His face was full of running but he couldn't move 'cos his feet were sinking into the ground. They were turning into foundations. Then his head got bigger and bigger and the rest of him shrunk right down. His body got smaller and smaller until it was all gone. His screaming mouth became a flapping door. His rolling eyes were two windows with shutters that opened and slammed, over and over. He had a row of chimneys that shot bullets of black smoke. He was all grey bricks and green moss. There were no two ways about it: Pa was an ugly house. He fit right in on Agony Street.

Pa didn't stop his bellyaching just 'cos he became a house. He howled and then some. But I didn't care, 'cos in House Granny I only heard the moon's lullabies and the horses races. And that piano that lived in the spare room, that strutted on the landing and played ragtime. I lived real happy in House Granny. But I didn't forget Pa. Sometimes I went up to his door and said, "It's me, Strawberry Sally," and I howled right back at him.

WATCH THE SKIES

Alan Baxter

As the dirt road became ever more corrugated and potholes began to resemble ponds, Steph Bennett hoped her Mazda 2 would hold together. The small hatchback had been perfect for travelling around Hobart's city streets, rarely ever seeing a highway for more than half an hour. Unsealed roads into the wilds of southern Tasmania had never really been on her radar. And on the occasions they'd ventured beyond the city, Jed would drive. Jed would insist on driving, his SUV chewing up the bumps with barely a shudder. But that was before.

She'd never dreamed of ending up like this. Of being alone, untethered. Although unprepared certainly didn't mean incapable, and she had every intention of reinvention. Assuming she made it to the cabin before her car rattled itself to pieces or her bones shook out of her skin.

Steph gasped as the small car clanged into a pothole she couldn't avoid and her teeth clacked together. Holding her breath, she waited for the inevitable grind of broken metal, but it didn't come.

"Attagirl." She patted the steering wheel. "Not far now."

The GPS on her phone said another 2.1 km. She could manage that. Gum trees hung over the road, an occasional letterbox in between with dirt driveways leading to weatherboard houses. The one she headed towards apparently promised all the home comforts despite its isolation. Except internet, which put her on edge.

"It'll be dusty and full of cobwebs, I expect," her downstairs neighbour had said. "I haven't been down to the place in the last few years. I'm getting old."

Funny that her salvation had turned out to be an almost-stranger she'd barely said more than good morning to. But when the old woman, only ever known as Mrs. Beaumont, even now, had seen her crying in the apartment building lobby, she'd been kind. When Steph said she just needed to be somewhere else for a little while, the kindly neighbour had offered up the remote cabin.

"I holidayed with Harold there all the time, but since he died... I should probably sell it." Mrs. Beaumont had smiled sadly. "There's a neighbour a few hundred metres back up the road. She has satellite internet if you need it in an emergency. Her name's Tracy and she's friendly. You might get a bit of mobile reception, but don't count on it. There is a landline, which you're welcome to use, but no international calls, please."

Steph didn't have international friends. Hell, since everything went down, she wondered if she had any friends at all. How many people knew but said nothing? How many friends had she ever really had? Didn't matter. She didn't need anyone else. Certainly not Jed with his half-adult, half-child sensibilities. She needed herself right now and, to find herself, she'd left everything else behind.

The road curved slowly and she passed another driveway as the GPS clicked over to three hundred metres remaining. She glanced back at the gate she'd passed. *Must have been Tracy's place.* She couldn't see the house through the trees. How would it be to live as remotely as this? She supposed she was about to find out. The thought of living all the way out here permanently made her shiver.

The road angled down a little and she saw the shimmer of weak autumn sunlight on water. Then there it was. The little house she'd be in for three weeks. Dark wooden weatherboards under a metal roof painted olive green. It was set back from the road a bit with a short drive and a scruffy, overgrown garden in front, right at the end of the spit of land she'd slowly travelled along. Windows at the cabin's front overlooked the ocean, only fifty metres away. Ocean that disappeared to the horizon and didn't see land again until Antarctica.

"Here we are then," she said, guiding the Mazda onto the drive. "Arse-end of the world. Thank you, Mrs. Beaumont."

The cabin was simple. A large central room with small kitchenette off to one side. A sofa in front of the large windows to sit and take in that expansive view, only interrupted by a few gum trees. At the back of the main living space were two doors, one to a bathroom, the other to a bedroom with a surprisingly large and firm double bed. And that was it. All she needed. The place smelled musty and there was a lot of dust, but it wasn't nearly as decrepit as she'd feared. She would clean and tidy while she was here to partially return the favour.

The day was quickly sinking into the gloom of twilight, shadows gathering, but she opened up all the windows to start airing the place and returned to her car to unpack the groceries she'd brought. Footsteps crunched on the dirt road behind her.

"Oo-roo!" someone called out.

Steph turned to see a middle-aged woman, well-rounded and smiling, with iron grey hair pulled back in a loose ponytail that seemed to hang almost to her waist. "Hello."

"Thought I'd come and say hi. I saw you drive past and if you passed my place you could only be coming here. Unless you planned to keep going right into the drink, of course."

"That would be a strange way to suicide." The words seemed unusually bleak the moment she said them and the woman's smile faltered.

"Well, yes. It would at that. I'm Tracy."

"Steph."

"Good to meet you. Friend of Mary's?"

So that was her first name. "Upstairs neighbour. In Hobart."

"I haven't seen her in a long while. You staying long?"

"Three weeks, I think. Use up my accrued leave from work."

"Three weeks here? What'll you do? You'll be bored after three days."

"Boredom is what I'm after." At Tracy's raised eyebrow, Steph felt the truth bubbling up inside her. The need to vent, that she'd been denied. "My husband is a prick and was having an affair with this dopey twenty-something from his work and it seems everyone knew about it, even my best friends. Who I thought were my friends. 'I'm friends with you both, I didn't know what to do!' You know what, Stella? You tell the woman being cheated on. You tell your friend of twenty years that her husband is making a fool of her." Steph sucked in a breath, suddenly embarrassed. "Sorry. Anyway, I need solitude."

Tracy nodded, lips pressed into a gentle line. "Understandable. Well, I'm just a short walk up there. If you need to talk, I'd be happy to listen. And if you need internet, I've got satellite. But otherwise I'll respect your wish to be alone."

"Sorry," Steph said again.

"No need to apologise."

"Are you here alone?"

Tracy smiled, but there was a sadness in it. "I have my boy, Xavier. He needs a lot of care. We keep each other company though."

"Just you and him..?"

"Yes, just us."

"Must be hard, caring for someone here, so far from anything else."

"We like it here. It's the best place for us."

Steph smiled. "I'm glad it works for you."

"Watch the skies."

Steph blinked at the non-sequitur. "The skies?"

"We're due some pretty good aurora tonight. Big solar storm happening at the moment."

"Oh, that's cool."

"So if you're looking outside at night, keep your eyes up."

It sounded more like a warning than a suggestion but Steph couldn't put her finger on why.

"Just along there, if you need anything." Tracy gestured back up the road, and turned to walk that way. "Enjoy your stay."

"Thanks."

Tracy raised a hand over her shoulder without looking back and was soon lost behind the trees. Steph watched where she'd gone for a moment, a little nonplussed, then shrugged and carried her things inside.

Night fell quickly. Steph made herself some simple eggs and toast for dinner. What a relief it had been to stop thinking about satisfying Jed's needs for interesting dinners. To simply eat to survive most days, then please only herself when she felt like it. Much as she'd resisted the dutiful housewife role, especially given they both worked full-time, she'd still somehow fallen into the trap of doing most of the cooking, most of the housework, most of the emotional lifting. And all the time he'd been busy with a girl ten years younger than her and half as capable.

In some ways it made it worse that Steph had liked Lou. They'd met at a couple of Jed's work socials and got along. Not nearly as well as Lou and Jed got along, as it turned out. And Lou had been pretending too, just like Stella and all the other so-called friends. Everyone had known but her, and the knowledge of that was an ice dagger in her guts every time she thought of it.

As she ate, the big windows became black mirrors, reflecting herself and the room back at her. *I'm like a stunned mullet in a fish tank to anyone outside*, she thought. Then wondered who the hell would be outside to see her. Someone on a boat, maybe, zooming in with a telescope, spying from some insurmountable distance. The thought gave her a chill and she quickly pushed it away. It was just so damned dark and quiet.

She took her plate to the sink and then went around the place closing the windows and turning off all the lights except a bedside lamp, leaving the bedroom door ajar as she went back into the living space. She stilled, awed.

The sky was alive with coruscating ribbons of red and green. Eyes and mouth wide, she went out the front door and walked a short distance from the house to stare up at the heavens.

Watch the skies.

The colours were brightest on the peripheries of her vision but perfectly visible when she stared directly at them. They seemed to ripple side to side sometimes, other times pulse directly upwards. She turned slowly and they covered the sky as far as she could see in either direction, far out over the water to where it disappeared at the horizon, lost in darkness. The sea lapped gently at the shore some thirty metres away, the tide low and calm.

Tears of wonder trickled over her cheeks, stretched in a grin of absolute joy. No surprise ancient people had to invent gods to explain this phenomenon. It was equal parts delightful and terrifying. She'd never felt so small.

She had no idea how long she stood there, staring up. Her neck began to ache, but she didn't care. Early autumn in southern Tasmania could get cold and her toes were numb, each hand tucked under the opposite armpit, but she didn't care about that either.

Movement below caught her eye. Steph looked down at the water and saw a branch sticking out. Long, at least two metres, black against the silvered surface. It seemed to have emerged upwards at an angle. She frowned. Was it pushed by the tide, fetched up against the sea bed or a rock? But the ocean was calm, hardly moving. Strangely calm. Long and thin, the branch split into two smaller limbs at the end. As she watched, it snapped halfway along its length, the bifurcated end dropping back to the water. As another branch thrust upwards beside it, Steph realised it hadn't broken. It had bent. Like a joint. The second long, black branch bent the same way as a third and fourth broke the almost still surface.

Steph's heart raced and her mouth dried. She sucked quick, short breaths as two more branches – legs, they're fucking legs! – broke the surface. Each more than two metres long, spread across a span of some three metres. What did those legs support? What was about to lift itself, dripping, from the calm, cold waters?

"No, no, no." Steph walked backwards up the gravelly slope, shaking her head but unable to take her eyes from the thing.

More movement, this time up the slope to her left, and Steph cried out. Ripping her gaze from the ocean, she saw Tracy striding down towards the water. She wore tatty UGG boots and a fluffy bath robe.

"What..?" Steph managed.

"Go back inside," Tracy called out, not looking at her. "Watch the skies."

When she reached the damp stones at the water's edge, Tracy opened her arms and shook off the robe. She stood naked but for her sheepskin-covered feet, facing the water and the thing emerging from it. She put her arms out to either side, cruciform, iron grey hair a fan across her back. Slight rolls of flesh made a dark line above each hip, her upper arms hung a little loose, her butt round and lightly dimpled, and she looked strong. Proud.

"Inside," she called again, firmly but not angry or scared.

Water ran in cascades as the long black legs heaved and something bulged from the surface. Dark and rough and spiny, long and wide, crab-like, lobster-like, unlike anything that could possibly be real, it lifted itself higher than Tracy stood, a soft chattering sound audible over the sluicing of seawater.

Steph's bladder threatened to let go as she saw more long, brittle-looking legs poke up to the left and right of the first creature. Then more behind. With a sob of confusion and terror, she turned and ran.

The house was dark but for the soft glow of the bedside lamp leaking through the gap in the door. The sky outside still shifted and moved with curtains of red and green. But Steph only had eyes for the beach, fifty metres away. Tracy stood there, a silhouette against the pastel shades of night. The spindly-limbed things surrounded her, loomed high over her, heavy bodies swinging in the cradles of their legs. Tracy remained motionless, arms out to either side, as they moved closer. Each extended one many-jointed limb and pressed its tip against her body somewhere, legs, back, buttocks, shoulders, some in front where Steph couldn't see. Tracy jerked, stiffened at their touch, and lifted. The toes of her sheepskin boots pointed down at the rough sand as she hung between them.

Steph's breathing came in ragged fits and starts, her hands shook, her knees trembled. What was she watching? How could it be possible?

The aurora faded slightly, colours lessening to paler shades only mildly discernible from the starry sky. The gloom through the few trees between her and the beach seemed to thicken. Steph blinked, strained to see, but the creatures with Tracy suspended between them were hard to make out against the darker tones.

She staggered back from the window. "I have to go." She looked around, cataloguing her stuff. Suitcase, half-unpacked. She could repack that in minutes. Travel holdall, barely opened yet. Food in a couple of boxes and bags, some put away, some yet to find a home. She could leave all that, it was only groceries. Then she thought about the road leading down to the cabin, the rough edges, the wheel-wrecking potholes. That would be terrifying in the dark.

In the morning. She would leave at first light.

But they were out there. Was she safe inside? Tracy had told her to go inside.

She double-checked all the doors and windows were locked then went back to the front to look out. The aurora was back, but at a fraction of its previous brightness. Despite its presence, her sense of wonder had shattered at the far more disturbing phenomena so close to home. She peered through the dark again, but the beach seemed empty. No evidence of Tracy or the huge, chitinous things that had lifted her up. No evidence they'd ever even been there.

Taking one last look at the rippling colours, Steph sucked in a ragged breath that did little to steady her, and drew the heavy curtains. All the windows had curtains or blinds, and she closed them all. She turned on every light she could find, bathing herself in the glow of earthly, human, electrical luminescence, then went into the bedroom and closed the door. She climbed into bed and thought she would never sleep. That she would never stop shaking. But despite it all, fatigue drew her down.

She woke with a start soon after dawn, startled by some half-remembered dream of giant crab-like things crawling out of the ocean. She barely even remembered going to bed the night before. The bedroom light and bedside lamp were on. When she opened the door she saw every light in the place was on, even in the range hood over the small electric cooker. What the hell?

Steph blinked, trying to recall her dream. Something about Tracy too, the friendly yet slightly off-kilter neighbour. What had the woman said to her the day before? *Watch the skies.* What had that even meant?

The aurora! She'd seen such amazing colours in the sky the night before. Why had she gone to bed with all the lights on? She must have been far more exhausted than she'd realised. The trauma of recent weeks, probably. Discovering the truth, realising her friends had been complicit, the shouting, the crying, the slamming doors. The final scream as she chased Jed out of the apartment and his poisoned parting barbs, tearing into her heart.

Presumably finally arriving at the cabin, somewhere to lick her wounds, had allowed all that to crash down on her. Despite the wonder of seeing the aurora, she had still collapsed into dreamless slumber.

No, not dreamless. The images that had startled her awake faded further, but she remembered something about Tracy... shadowed lines above her hips and the crack of her full butt. What the hell? And some black lobster-like monstrosities, bigger than cars with legs too long, jointed too many times.

She frowned, trembling as the memory flitted and skittered around her mind, refusing to be held and observed. Then it was gone again. Dreams were so weird. She went into the kitchen area to fix some food and make a desperately needed coffee.

As Steph stood at the window, a warm mug between her hands, looking out over the ocean, wisps and tatters of her dream kept coming back to her. She looked between the scrubby trees to the gravelly beach and frowned.

She sipped coffee and watched gulls wheeling high over the water, rougher now than it had been in the night. That's right, the sea had been almost preternaturally calm as she'd stood staring up at the southern lights.

She went outside, mug still gripped between her palms, and walked slowly down the slope towards the lapping waves. Small white crests were whipped by a soft but persistent breeze. The waves crashed and sucked at the shoreline, big enough that they'd reach her knees before she was a metre in if she decided to wade. Yet last night it had seemed still as a lake.

She shook her head. Changeable weather was nothing unexpected in Tasmania so she supposed there was no reason that wouldn't apply to the tides too. She turned to head back to the cabin and barked a noise of surprise at Tracy standing not three paces behind her.

"Oh, I'm sorry! I didn't mean to startle you."

Steph let out a confused laugh. "I didn't hear you coming." On such stony ground that seemed unlikely.

"The wind, maybe?"

It wasn't that strong. She heard the leaves nearby rustling, after all. "Maybe," she said anyway.

Tracy watched her a moment, seemed to search her eyes. The woman's scrutiny quickly became uncomfortable. As Steph opened her mouth to say something, anything, Tracy said, "Settling in?"

Steph gaped like a fish for a moment, then nodded. "Sure. It's quite the place here."

"You saw the aurora last night?"

"I did! It was amazing. I've caught glimpses before from Hobart, but nothing like that. It was so clear." *Tracy's naked back as those huge, chitinous creatures surrounded her, lifted her.* Steph shuddered, quickly tried to steady suddenly raw nerves.

"Are you all right, dear?"

It wasn't a dream. Seeing the woman now, everything flooded back. It had been real, all of it. And she'd almost forgotten. Had she been hypnotised? Drugged?

A dark look passed over Tracy's face. Was it disgust? Contempt?

"You remember," the woman said. A statement, not a question.

"What..? How..?" Steph's tongue felt thick and clumsy. She couldn't organise her thoughts any more than she could form words.

Tracy sighed. "A shame. Xavier will be disappointed again."

"What?"

Tracy reached out, put one warm, dry palm against Steph's cheek.

The touch was simultaneously caring and disquieting. Strangely invasive.

"I have to go!" Steph said, her hands shaking. She remembered her panic of the night before, her need to leave. Her decision to wait for daytime. That's why all the lights had been on. "I have to go," she said again and hurried past Tracy, back towards the cabin, hot coffee slopping over her fingers as she walked so fast she was almost running.

She gulped the last of her coffee, wincing as it seared her throat, and left the mug in the sink. She would leave the groceries too. Just pack her things and go. Pay a cleaner to come in or something.

Five minutes later, suitcase in one hand, heavy sports holdall over her shoulder, she hurried back outside. Tracy was nowhere to be seen. Steph pressed the button on her key to unlock her car, opened the boot and started dumping her bags in, then realised the back tyre was flat. Muttering random negatives, she moved around and saw the front tyre deflated too, both with slash marks in the walls. She ran to the other side. All four tyres, slashed and empty.

Sobs rose. "No. Because I saw? Because I remembered?"

Tracy had to have done the damage, but why? If she didn't want Steph to leave, what did she plan? Steph turned and ran her bags back inside, then looked around the kitchen. She would defend herself. She grabbed the biggest knife from the block beside the cooker and left the cabin again, striding back up the road towards the neighbour's house. She would take Tracy's car if she had to, at knifepoint if necessary. She would be a victim no longer. She would be other people's fool no longer.

Tracy's house was set back a little deeper into the trees than the cabin, but otherwise quite similar in design, only a little bigger.

I have my boy, Xavier. He needs a lot of care. We keep each other company.

Steph paused, breathing hard, knuckles white on the hilt of the carving knife. Was there a child inside?

She went to the door and banged with the side of her fist. "Are you in there? What the fuck did you do to my car?"

Waiting only a moment, she tried to open the door but it was locked. No car on the short drive, no garage. Had Tracy gone? Where to? Steph imagined all kinds of nightmare scenarios, Tracy returning with neighbours as crazy as she was... to do what? Feed her to the giant crab things?

Sobs rose again and Steph swallowed them down. How could this be happening?

She moved around the house, cupping her hands at her face to peer in the windows. There was a lounge, then a kitchen area. Then frosted glass that presumably had a bathroom beyond. The next window showed her a bedroom, rumpled doona on a double bed, clothes thrown over an easy chair, wardrobe half-open. She moved to the next window and her breath locked up in her throat.

Another bedroom. Another double bed, wardrobe, but tidier than the other. And occupied. On the bed was a person and Steph blinked, trying to figure out what she saw. The size of a grown man, broad in the shoulder, but clearly a child. Soft features, wide eyes, sparse hair wispy across his scalp. Not even a child, more baby than toddler, but bigger than she was. As she stared, he lifted one arm, pointed a pudgy finger at her and his eyes widened further. His mouth fell open, lots of small, rounded teeth, each with a gap between it and the next as wide as the tooth itself. He started a keening wail, rising in pitch and volume, wordless but filled with fear.

Steph staggered back from the window, shaking her head. "What the fuck? What the actual fuck?"

She turned in a circle, lost, confused. What could she do? She just needed to get away from this insane place, but her car was not an option. It was too far to walk. She pulled out her phone and had no reception, as expected.

There is a landline, which you're welcome to use, but no international calls, please.

She could call for help. Call a mobile mechanic and have new tyres fitted. Was that even possible? Fuck it, she could just call a taxi and get the hell out, worry about her car later. Send a tow truck to collect it from the sane safety of Hobart. She turned and ran for the cabin.

The phone was on the counter in the kitchen, an old plastic thing with black rubber push buttons. She grabbed the handset and put it to her ear, pressed the six-digit number for the cab company she'd used so many times after nights out in Hobart. She'd never trusted the idea of Uber, believed in protecting existing industries. It took a second to realise there was no sound. No dial tone. Landlines were supposed to have a dial tone, weren't they?

Fear manifesting again, she rattled the button to hang up and stabbed 0 three times. Call the police, simple as that. But no, not simple. Because nothing happened. Because there was no dial tone. Because the phone was not working. Cut off. Disconnected. Slashed like her tyres?

Movement outside the big window caught her eye and she turned to see Tracy, naked, walking towards the water. The woman's large breasts shifted side to side as she walked, unselfconscious. This time her feet were bare too.

Steph ran outside. "What are you doing? Why did you trash my car?"

"Your turn now."

"What?"

Tracy didn't turn, kept walking. "Your turn now. I was happy to carry on, you know. I wasn't the first, but I'd have carried on. Remember that. I didn't want this."

"Want what?"

Tracy reached the water's edge and walked in up to her knees. Waves broke around her thighs and hips. She put her arms out to either side.

"What are you doing?"

Tracy tipped her head back and Steph saw tears on the woman's cheeks.

Something long and black and spiny broke through the water. Then another and another, and like before, the huge things heaved themselves up. Their stony, clattering sound rose. Steph stumbled backwards, making space between herself and the impossible sight, but couldn't stop watching.

Again, the things surrounded Tracy. Again, they each pressed a spiky, bifurcated foot somewhere against her body. They were more rounded than long, Steph saw. Each with ten long, many-jointed limbs. Where she had expected mandibles of some kind and eyes on stalks she instead saw wide maws with backwards-facing teeth like shards of glass. They had three glossy green-black, rounded eyes in a line above their bristling mouths, each swivelling independently. Some of those eyes, she realised, were looking at her even as others within the same hideous faces looked at Tracy.

Again, they lifted the woman and Tracy hung suspended between them. Then a slight shudder and every limb that touched her punched right through, blood and bone and viscera bursting in every direction.

Tracy flapped like seaweed then tore apart to splatter into the ocean all around.

Steph screamed, fell back and scrambled on hands and heels to make more space, to get away. She twisted and pushed up to run, sprinted back to the cabin. She fell inside the door and slammed it, locked it, slid down against it, and cried. Every part of her shook. What to do? What to do?

She needed to get away. She didn't need to understand despite the questions that howled and bit at her mind. She just needed to go. But how?

Our neighbour has satellite internet if you need it in an emergency. Her name's Tracy and she's friendly.

Friendly! Maybe she would have been if Steph hadn't seen what she'd seen the night before. Or if she hadn't remembered, thought it all a twisted dream. Too late for that now. But there was satellite internet at Tracy's house. Did that mean a phone too? Then again, with internet she could forget her disposition towards Uber and organise a ride online.

The manchild thing on the bed made her shudder, but she wouldn't need to go in there. Was that Xavier? How long had he been there? Was he helpless now? She would send help once she got out. Call the police, tell them to come and investigate. Not her problem.

She sucked in a deep breath and pushed herself up a little, risked a look out the window. The creatures had gone, presumably back into the depths. There was no sign of Tracy's remains.

Steph left, back to Tracy's house. She knew the front was locked, but there had been a back door too. She tried that and it opened into the kitchen. The bedrooms were to her right, she would avoid those. She went into the main living area and saw an old Dell desktop computer on a small hutch desk. She ran over, pressed the power button and it hummed into life.

"Thank fuck."

She waited as the hard drive spun and the fan hissed.

"Mummy?"

The voice was high but somehow thick. A shiver ran through Steph. *Ignore it.*

"Mummy, are you there?"

Ignore it. Ignore it. Ignore it.

The screen lit up and showed a dialogue box with *Password* written above it.

"No."

Steph stared, anger and frustration tightening her stomach. "No, no, no."

She tried "password" and "password1", then again but with a capital P both times. Nothing. She tried "12345" and again nothing, then a new message.

Too many login attempts. Try again in 60 seconds.

A timer started counting down.

"Mummy, please!"

Steph stood back from the computer, fingers interlaced and palms pressed against her forehead. She wanted to scream and smash and rage.

"*Mummy!*"

The need in the child's voice tore at some primal part of her. She'd always imagined being a mother, she wanted kids. Jed had said he did too, but was often little better than a kid himself. She'd spent half her time cleaning up after him, tried time and again to convince him he needed to pull his weight and help with housework, cooking, shopping. They both worked, they should share the rest equally. He always agreed with her, always promised to do better, and never did. He had plenty of time for Lou, though, Steph was pretty sure of that.

"*Mummy!*"

She went to the bedroom door and looked in. The giant baby-man thing was sat up in bed, leaning forward, one pasty arm outstretched. His eyes widened again like before when he saw her, then narrowed. A damp, salty aroma filled the air.

"Mummy?" His voice was softer now, questioning but somehow resigned.

Steph didn't know how to respond.

"Mummy gone again," Xavier said, and tears rolled over his pale cheeks. Then he began to sob.

Every maternal instinct in Steph fired, every human instinct at the sight of someone in pain, in distress. *Again*, he'd said. How many times?

Your turn now.

The hell it was, but she couldn't see Xavier suffer this way. She moved closer and he looked up with big, wet eyes. His head was bigger than hers, but bore a baby's face. A desperate, frightened, needy face.

"It's okay," Steph said. "It'll be okay."

She sat on the edge of the bed and pulled Xavier into a hug. He clamped tightly to her, buried his face in her chest. She felt a tingling sensation through her heart and lungs, that grew quickly into a kind of vibration. She became short of breath and needed to pull away, but Xavier's grip was too strong.

"Let me go!" she said, and his arms tightened further.

Panic rose and Steph began to thrash against him, but Xavier's arms were wrapped around hers, pinning her elbows to her ribs. Her skin throbbed as Xavier seemed to suck something through it. Holding her ever more tightly he leaned back into the pillows, drew her up and onto him, and wrapped his legs around hers as tightly as his arms. She cried out, tried to force her way free, but he was far too strong. Far stronger than he had any right to be, she feared he could easily crush her like kindling if he chose to. And as he held her close, that drawing away sensation, as though he were somehow sucking the life energy right out of her.

"Please let me go." The words slurred between constricted sobs, but he didn't obey. Slowly her vision dimmed and she sank into oblivion.

When Steph woke it was dark. She still lay atop the large soft form of Xavier who slept, breath rasping through his mouth. With a noise of disgust, she pushed away and got off the bed only to fall to the floor. Her vision swam, dizziness nipped at her mind. Her legs were weak, as though she'd run a marathon. She pushed up onto hands and knees and crawled away from the bed, heading for the living room.

Come to us.

The voice in her head was sibilant and wet, like the ocean sucking at stones. Not voice, voices. Many overlapping each other.

Come to us. Be replenished.

"No, no, no." She crawled across the living room floor, heading for the kitchen. She was thirsty as hell, needed to drink her body weight in water. And she craved food to regain her energy.

The voices continued to cajole, entreat, and she knew it was those things beneath the waves. She remembered them lifting Tracy's naked form the first time she saw, imagined them filling her with whatever she needed to sate the ravenous Xavier.

She pulled herself up and put her mouth under the kitchen tap. She drank and drank until nausea made her stomach swim but it didn't slake her thirst at all. She scrabbled around in cupboards and found a pack of Sao crackers and ate them, scattering crumbs, but her hunger didn't change. She saw a loaf of bread on a cutting board on the counter, a serrated bread knife beside it. Ignoring the knife, she grabbed the loaf and bit into it, tearing hunks off with her teeth, wolfing them down. Hunger still tore at her gut.

Come to us.

She was staggering to the door before she realised she was moving. She wanted to resist, to refuse, but weakness drove her on and something in the promise of those voices teased her. Strength beyond normal parameters, power to achieve more, to be more.

She walked, faltering, through the darkness, through the trees. When she reached the water, the spiny giants were already emerging, swaying, from the depths, their hunger as apparent as hers. She pulled her clothes off, knowing they needed contact with her skin.

She shuddered as the cold, hard bristles of their appendages pressed into her and lifted her. Then energy flooded in. Like molten steel injected through her flesh, she heated up and every nerve buzzed. Images of Tracy flying apart with sprays of blood and bone flittered through her mind but she knew it wasn't her time. There was so much in her yet to be exploited. So much for all to gain in circular symbiosis as Xavier grew. Grew into what she wasn't sure, but the creatures gave her fleeting images of his form maturing over too many years, developing from monstrous infant to powerful adolescent, more than human, a bane to humanity. Xavier would be the herald of their rise and she would mother Xavier into their hero.

Steph moaned, charged and filled with the dark, churning energy she needed to pour into Xavier like a seagull regurgitating fish into its young. This was the purpose and it felt wonderful.

She had no idea how long she hung there as they engorged her, but too soon it was over and she was lowered back to the cold ground. They retreated beneath the waves and she returned to Xavier.

As she walked, she saw the Mazda 2 with its tyres slashed. The car reminded her of why she was here. Of Jed and his pathetic needs. Of his life with Lou known about by everyone except her. Steph's so-called friends laughing behind her back just as he fucked Lou in secret only from her, while she cleaned up his mess, cooked his meals to replenish the energy he'd spent on that other woman. Rage built inside her.

Steph went back into Tracy's house – her house? Xavier's house? It didn't matter – through the back door.

"Mummy!" the voice just as needy but joyful now, expectant.

She walked through the kitchen, swollen with the creatures' energy, drawn by Xavier's need, grabbing the serrated bread knife as she went.

He reached for her from the bed, eyes wide, mouth split in a grin. Under his arms she saw the start of bristled chitin, the edges of a carapace at his back. She whipped the knife across one outstretched arm, watched the flesh peel open at his wrist and scarlet blood spill. Xavier stared in disbelief, eyes scrunching in pain. She heard and felt the anguish of the creatures beneath the waves.

"No more," Steph said through gritted teeth.

As Xavier pulled his wounded arm back, pressed it tightly to his chest, looking up at her in shocked confusion, she swept the knife around again, across his throat. She felt the serrations skitter across the bones of his spine and blood flooded Xavier and the bed.

Steph almost collapsed at the screams of fury and despair in her mind from the creatures, but she rallied, reversed her grip on the knife and drove it down into Xavier's chest.

She kept moving, unlocking the front door, striding down the road away from the house, away from the sea. Naked, but not cold, energised, she walked. The essence she'd absorbed, the sustenance she was supposed to pass on to Xavier, stretched her bones, burned under her skin, filled her fit to burst. She had no idea how long she could contain it, if she could survive what they'd done to her or if it would tear her apart, but whatever came next didn't matter.

"I will be used no more."

THE SITTER

Rob Francis

The sitter's house could only be reached by boat. In better times, Charles thought, the island mansion must have stood in manicured grounds lapped by the dancing waters of the upper Thames. Now it stood amidst a throng of bramble and gorse, an occasional willow poking its head above the scrub. A battered wooden skiff lurked amongst the reeds of the backwater shallows, a rope leading from an iron hoop at its prow to another atop a wooden post on the island. The rope was frayed and silt-laden.

A blackbird burst into song nearby. Charles stood, remembering another moment in another world, when the wonder of a blackbird's call amidst the silence of the Western Front was enough reason to live.

But he couldn't linger. The evening was drawing in, and Master James would be waiting.

Charles placed his easel and the canvas sack of brushes and paints into the skiff before clambering in himself. The muscles in his thigh had never fully healed after Cambrai, and he had to consider each movement. He searched the skiff. Perhaps there had once been an oar or pole to help guide the boat across the channel, but no more. He reached back to the riverbank and took up a fallen branch that might serve. It was bent and cracked, but he found that when he pushed it into the sludge of the riverbed he could propel the boat forward a little. It was better than touching the bilious water. With each shove the stink of river mud assailed him.

It took over half an hour to reach the island, and he was damp with perspiration as he pulled the skiff onto the sloping shore, collected his things, and trudged up to the house. It was a sprawling Victorian pile, though why it had been constructed on an ait in one of the busiest, dirtiest rivers in England he couldn't say. Three extensive storeys of dark

Victorian brick under a slate roof looked down on him, leaded windows winking red in the dying light. Streaks of guano ran from under the eaves, and already barbastelles were beginning to flit over the grounds and river. The house wasn't at all as he had imagined.

Charles tugged the letter of commission from his pocket. *Come at the end of the day*, it said. *Master James wishes to sit for a portrait in oils. The door will be open. You will receive further instructions when you arrive. The portrait must be completed in one sitting.* The letter ended by stating he would be paid two hundred and fifty pounds for his labours. He smiled as he read it once again. Enough for he and Milton to live comfortably for several months, or half a year if they were careful.

He was sure he was at the right address, but as he approached the portico he began to consider that perhaps he'd been the victim of an elaborate trick. The door was indeed ajar, but the steps were punctured with tall weeds growing through the cracks, while rampant wisteria drooped from above the lintel. No one had passed this way for some time.

He stepped over the threshold, pushing the door open. A wide entrance hall framed a staircase ascending to the first floor, several doors leading off the hall and a corridor past the stairs leading further back into the house. There was a scent of mildew and rot. The furnishings gave an impression of weight and expense but had become mouldered and layered with dust. Despite the atmosphere of abandonment, a chandelier above blazed with lighted candles. Someone lived here.

"Mr. Swynn." The voice was tinny and seemed to come from nowhere. It took Charles a few moments of searching for its origin, before it spoke again and he discerned a brass horn on the wall near the door, connected to a long pipe. "Thank you for coming, Mr. Swynn." The words reverberated from the horn. "I'm afraid I can't be there to greet you in person, but be assured I can hear you. There are speaking tubes all around the house, so I will be able to communicate as you make your way to the sitting room. You have your professional accoutrements?"

"Yes," said Charles, nodding to his bag and easel before realising no one could see the gesture. "And you are?"

"A servant only," the voice said. "I care for Master James. Now, if you are ready, please progress to the third door on the right down the corridor. It is painted red."

The floorboards shuddered as Charles moved down the corridor, passing grubby but well-executed paintings hung in gilt frames. He winced. With some restorative care a few masterpieces might be revealed, if only he had the time to inspect the artwork.

He halted at a red door and turned the handle, letting himself into a large room that was better maintained than the entrance hall. A thick burgundy carpet matched the dark wallpaper and furnishings. Two gas lamps on the walls illuminated most of the chamber. An empty fireplace stood at the far end, ashes scattered across the hearth. The air was faintly humid, alive.

In the centre of the room stood a red-upholstered chaise longue with a large doll on it. The doll rested against a trio of plump crimson cushions, arms hanging loose, legs stretched out. It wore a blue sailor suit with a fisherman's cap and stared straight ahead with wide, unblinking eyes, a grin contorting its face.

"This is Master James," said the voice from another bronze horn in the corner of the room. "He is pleased to meet you and to sit for you. Please proceed at your convenience."

Charles placed his things on the dusty carpet and approached the doll. A half-dozen paces from the chaise longue, he paused.

The doll had stitches. Its eyes were wide open, the lids sewn to the orbital brow and cheek. Its grin was held in place by thread lacing the corners of the mouth to the upper cheeks. The doll's skin was thick with white powder and a little scarlet blush over the cheekbones, hair lacquered black with polish. Downy hairs caught the lamplight from above to glisten across its face.

Not a doll, then. The corpse of a boy, no older than five when he died.

Charles reached out a hand. Hesitated.

"Please do *not* touch Master James. He does not care for it," warbled the voice.

Charles straightened. He turned to the horn.

"I won't paint a dead child."

He collected his things and was almost out of the room when the voice spoke again.

"Master James knows about Milton, Mr. Swynn. Knows and *understands*. Though the courts, and Mr. Milton Finch's family, may be more judgemental."

Charles stopped. Milton would be in his dismal garret on Wellington Street right now, working by cheap candlelight on a poem, tongue nipped between his teeth in concentration. They'd been so careful. Charles would only visit his lodging house in the early afternoons, when all the other occupants were at work. They rarely went out together, and then only to the safer places – the theatres, and a selection of small, discreet pubs. Discovery would mean hard labour. And Milton's family were devout Catholics.

"I don't know what you're talking about."

The voice exhaled wetly. "Rutting, Mr. Swynn. Fucking. Sodomy. Mutual onanism, as the courts might have it. All kinds of secret acts. *Dangerous* acts. Master James knows."

Charles leaned against the wall for a moment, the scent of wallpaper mould tickling his nose. He could walk away, of course. No one would be able to stop him. But then what?

"Why do you want me to do this? Paint… that?"

"What I want is irrelevant. Master James wants to sit for you. He believes you will both benefit from the experience. Knowledge brings with it such power, Mr. Swynn. Don't you agree?"

Charles grimaced. He set up his easel on the floor a few yards from the chaise longue and its grisly occupant and began to unpack his paints.

"If you require anything, please say," came the voice. "There is a dumb waiter here, on the eastern wall." A faint creaking preceded the arrival of a tray held in place by thin ropes. It held a dusty glass of water.

Charles left it there, despite his raw throat and the sweat that tickled his scalp. He concentrated on beginning to sketch an outline of the chair and Master James. His stomach clenched with every stroke.

"To help you work, I will give you some musical accompaniment."

"No, that's quite—"

A chorus of voices rolled from the horn, a madrigal of chanted words and phrases that swelled and ebbed, their meaning indiscernible. The singing would have been unpleasant at the best of times. In these circumstances, Charles found it almost painful.

He cursed silently. Then returned to the sketch, determined to block out everything else in the world.

★ ★ ★

The singing stopped.

"All is progressing, Mr. Swynn?"

Charles paused, paintbrush hovering over the canvas. The sketch was finished, the painting itself just begun.

"Yes."

"Do you require anything?"

"No. Thank you. Now if you don't mind—"

"You fought at Cambrai."

"Yes. How did—"

"There was another soldier there. David Fitzwilliam. Hated you from the start, didn't he? *Hated* you. Knew you for what you were as soon as he saw you. Always making lewd jokes that you did your best to rise above. He was one of your kind too. Oh yes. And you knew that. But there would be no accepting of it. Not from Fitzwilliam."

Charles concentrated on the chaise longue, layering purple and red to darken the background, the better to contrast with Master James's pale face. *Red and white*, his mum would have said. *Blood and bandages*.

"And then your company went over the top. Fitzwilliam went in the first wave, while you gave some cover from the trenches with your Number 1. Only he broke. Just a few dozen steps into no man's land and he gave up. Turned to scurry back. What did you do, Mr. Swynn, do you remember? Yes. You lie awake at night and dream about it."

The red he'd mixed was too dark. It seemed to swallow the light in the room, as if he were painting the essence of a void. He reached for the tube of scarlet.

"You shot him, Mr. Swynn. In the groin. Nicked an artery, so that he bled to death in minutes, in the thick mud, crying for his mother. Did you do it on purpose? Or was it an accident, an errant shot while you were keeping the Hun down? I'm not sure you even know. But Master James knows."

Charles's lathered brush wavered before the canvas. The wound in his thigh began to ache, a burning that set his knee trembling, so that he had to shift his weight to his other leg to carry on.

"It wasn't like that," he said. "I could hardly see. The sweat, the mud, the smoke. I wasn't aiming for Fitz."

But the madrigal had resumed. The voice remained silent.

* * *

The hour was very late, or very early. The image of Master James was emerging, coalescing. Charles had never felt such revulsion for something he was creating. But it had to be done.

The horn rattled. The singing stopped.

"Your father was a void. Cold and inscrutable. Rarely spoke to you except in admonition. But not so cold to your mother. All *sorts* of things he would do to her, whenever he wanted. Even when you were in the room, until you grew big enough to object. You remember, don't you? It flashes into your mind at the strangest moments."

Acid swirled in Charles's gut and crept up his throat. He nipped his lip and concentrated on getting the azure of Master James's jacket just right.

"And one morning, when the void finally swallowed him whole, you were awake. You went down to the kitchen and saw him in the garden, tying the rope to that old cherry tree you used to love. It was spring, and the blossom fell as he tightened the knot. You pulled the curtains closed and went back to bed. Waited for Mother to find him. Didn't you, Mr. Swynn? Master James knows."

Charles cursed as his brush slipped, bleeding azure into the chaise longue. He stepped back from the painting and drew a breath.

The horn clicked and the awful chanting began to drift from it once more.

* * *

Charles had saved the boy's features until last. He had to force himself to look at them, at the stitches that twisted the young face into a visage of grimacing joy. He gritted his teeth as he made the delicate strokes, his jaw aching almost as much as his leg. When the words came again, they startled him.

"For a while it was just you and your mother. She made a little extra money from reading cards for her friends and neighbours. The Tarot. A battered deck that was passed down from her mother. She taught you to read them, and to read people. Got you to tell them things based on her observations, rumours she had heard."

Charles took some titanium white on his brush, the better to highlight Master James's deathly complexion.

"There was a lady who lived two streets away, a Mrs. Brooks. Her infant son had been ill with rubella, and your mother said the boy was on the mend. Improving by all accounts, but Mrs. Brooks still fretted. She wanted to know what the cards held. You did the reading for her, your mother prompting you. You told her the boy would live. It was the safe bet. Two days later he died. Three days after *that*, Mrs. Brooks drowned in the Thames, not all that far from where we are. Did you know that? I think so. Your mother never told you, but you heard the rumours. That was your fault, Mr. Swynn. Master James knows, and now you do too. You do too!"

Charles swore. The pain in his leg was a spur. He tried to focus on the fine detail before him.

With the final shading of Master James's twisted grin, the portrait was done. Charles had no idea of the time but he had never felt so exhausted, even at Cambrai. He sat on the floor, uncaring of the brush that dropped from his hand to daub the carpet. With numb fingers, he began to gather his things into the sack.

It was a fine painting. The best work he'd ever done. Master James seemed to almost project from the canvas, was animated by the clash of colours and the vibrancy of the brushwork. But it was hideous. Charles wasn't sure that he'd ever want to paint again.

A creaking heralded the arrival of the dumb waiter, bearing a fat brown envelope. Charles shuffled to it on hands and knees. Inside was a stack of grubby five-pound banknotes. He stuffed it into the sack.

"This payment will last you the rest of your long life. Master James knows. You *both* know. You have been given a precious gift, Mr. Swynn. Those with an artistic temperament such as yourself are so much more receptive to it."

Charles hauled himself up and grabbed the easel. With a final glance at the corpse, he fled the room.

The voice followed him along the corridor, as he limped past those paintings that had been filthy when he last saw them, but now appeared slashed and defaced beyond recognition.

"Would you like to know your end, Mr. Swynn? How you die? *When* you die? Master James can oblige."

Charles hurried through the open door and into twilight.

He'd been painting for almost a full day. As he rushed awkwardly to the skiff, he slipped, leg twisting, the easel bouncing down the slope and into the river. Charles ignored it, stumbling to the boat and climbing aboard as his thigh screamed in protest. The branch was where he'd left it, and he frantically paddled towards the opposite shore.

He crawled from the skiff on hands and knees, shoving the boat back into the channel before scrambling through the trees to the nearest street. If the buses were still running, he would be able to get home soon enough, and present Milton with the money he'd earned. It would all have been worth it.

Carshalton Street was lined with large Victorian homes, each with a spacious garden out front. As he hurried towards the bus stop, a young woman looked up, trowel in hand as she tended a bed of roses. She smiled.

This lady is just married, Mr. Swynn. She doesn't know it yet, but she's pregnant. Her son will be killed in the next great war while still a young man. The grief will excoriate her, until there is only a tattered shell left. Then she will swallow all the pills the doctor prescribes to try to make her life more tolerable. She will be buried alone. And since her husband remarries, she will remain that way forever.

Charles slowed. The woman nodded and raised her hand a little. Charles looked away and quickened his pace.

"What?" he hissed. The voice was in the air around him, crawling across him, crackling in his ears.

A gift, Mr. Swynn. Such a gift! To know the fate of everyone you see. What could be more wonderful? What could inspire more empathy and understanding of our fellows?

Up ahead was the bus stop. And next to it, the Lords' Round theatre. As Charles neared, the doors opened and dozens of theatregoers streamed onto the street, chattering to each other.

Ah...

The voice multiplied a dozen-fold, hissing a swarm of fates at him with insistent fury.

The man in the pinstripe suit is having an affair, which will last for ten years before...

The small man losing his hair doesn't know it, but he harbours a cancer...

The tall woman with the red scarf will live a long life, but will be incarcerated in an institution for over thirty years, where she will undergo…

"Stop!" he shrieked, stumbling across the street and into an alley. He leaned against a damp, fetid wall and gasped for air.

Perhaps he'd gone mad. Perhaps he never had painted the corpse of a small boy. Maybe the house didn't exist, and he'd been wandering the streets in a delirium for hours. He could make his way back to Milton through the back streets, however long it took. Milton would look after him.

He dug into his sack. Not a dream. The money was there, crammed into the envelope. But he would be home soon. When Milton was there all could be put behind him. The boy, the painting, the voice.

But only until it whispered his lover's name and fate into his consciousness.

It would be a gift, Mr. Swynn. To know how long you two have left together, so you can make the most of it. Consider the power such knowledge will bring.

No. That couldn't be borne. Not yet.

At the end of the alley was a fence with a pair of iron railings twisted apart to allow access into the small churchyard beyond. There would be no one there at this hour. Charles limped through the gap and into the gloaming, amongst the graves and the yew trees that hung over them. He sat in the stillness, his back to a tombstone, and waited for darkness.

★ ★ ★

The moon cast a glow of molten copper and bone across the churchyard. In the night-time silence, Charles retraced his steps to the small track through the trees, to the river and the waiting skiff. All was deserted. The water was russet and gold in the moonlight. As the pain in his leg flared again, Charles waded into the cold channel to grab the skiff and drag it back to the bank. Then he climbed aboard and took up the twisted branch once more.

You refuse the gift, given so lovingly? A great pity.

Charles began to shake, his arms and legs twitching with exhaustion. It was hard to grip the branch. Progress was slow. Bats whipped the air just above his head.

He forced himself through the scrub and back to the house. Through the open front door.

He climbed the stairs. At the landing he turned left, to a corridor with doors on either side. Still leaning on the branch, he hobbled onwards. At the first door he grabbed the doorknob and turned, sending the door wide. A sparsely furnished room, the blue curtains half-drawn against the moonlight. A painfully thin woman lay on the bed, mouth open, a faint hiss coming from her throat as she slept. This room also contained the same brass horns he'd seen downstairs. He moved along to the next door. Another room, this time with a man naked atop the bedclothes and facing away from Charles. He wasn't sure if the man was asleep or not. Charles opened his mouth to speak, then hesitated. He was sure it would be wrong to break the silence.

The following room was lit by wall lamps. A hooded figure in a dark brown cloak was hunched over someone on the bed. Charles could only see the person's bare feet atop the blanket. The cloaked figure raised a hand and the light glinted from the tip of a long needle, black thread trailing from it. As the hand descended again, the feet spasmed. The room was silent, apart from the whisper of moving thread.

"Next room, Mr. Swynn," said the cloaked figure. "Take some rest. I shall be along presently."

Charles found the next door ajar. He pushed it wide and stumbled to the bed, dropping the branch as he went. He climbed onto the dusty bedspread and set his head on the hard pillow. Somewhere outside a blackbird was singing to the encroaching dawn. He closed his eyes.

He passed from waking to sleeping and back again. His leg burned, then became numb. He saw Milton working on a poem, tongue between his teeth, waiting for him to return. Saw him searching the streets. Saw a hundred different fates for the man he loved. He opened his eyes and stared at the stained ceiling.

Later, he heard singing. The madrigal that had accompanied his painting of Master James swelled around him, lifting him from his dreams and to a place of soft, warm darkness. The words still didn't make sense, but they were familiar to him. Comforting. The others in the house were chanting, either for him or for each other.

After a time, he joined his voice to theirs.

IT HAS EYES NOW

Christopher Golden & Tanya Pell

Hannah woke to the sound of her grandmother screaming. She dragged the blanket up to her throat and looked around her room as the old woman's cries echoed through the house. The orange salt lamp glowed dimly atop her bureau. Her oscillating fan whirred and the curtains billowed with gusts from a rainstorm that had blown in after midnight. The room felt ordinary, familiar, comforting.

Only the screams were new.

"Nana."

The word came out a whisper. Hannah kicked off her covers but caught her foot getting up. The sheet tugged at her ankle and she pulled free, but not before it threw her off balance. She careened into the frame of her bedroom door, getting her hands up just in time to keep from smashing her face on the wood. Then she was out in the hallway, padding barefoot on faded carpet, trying not to think about the bodily fluids that had been spilled on that carpet in the weeks since Nana had moved in with them.

She passed the bathroom, reached for the switchplate that would turn on the overhead light in the hallway, but hesitated.

Nana's scream had faded to a whimper. Another voice came from that room, talking low – Hannah's mother, Eleanor.

"Ma, stop," Hannah's mother rasped. "You'll wake her. Goddammit, mother. Do not wake Hannah with this crazy shit. You know it'll get into her head and the girl will never sleep again."

Hannah's hand remained frozen above the light switch. Silence thrummed in the darkness. She strained to listen for more words, for any sign of whatever passed between her mother and grandmother in that moment. Were they also straining to listen, to see if they had woken her?

She could still hear the rain on the roof and the whir of the fan back in her room, but nothing more. The other end of the hallway had two doorways. The one straight ahead led into the main bedroom, where Hannah's parents had always slept. It was this room she had fled to during stormy nights all through her childhood. This room where she had crept into bed between them for comfort and reassurance, where she had bounced and played, where she had lain to watch television any time she was sick. Where she had wept, inconsolable in the middle of the night, every time her childhood nightmares had driven her, screaming, into wakefulness.

Her parents' room had always been her safe place.

Then her father had left, spoiling it all. He'd always carried the scent of whiskey and cigars, but her mother noticed other smells on him. The aroma of other women. He'd never denied it or tried to defend it – he'd simply left, after which it had been just Hannah and Eleanor, seven years of daughter and mother. That had changed only recently, as Nana approached the end of her life. Hannah was twenty now, halfway through her undergrad business program, and suddenly they were three generations. Except one of them was dying, and soon there would be two generations again.

A slow creak from Nana's room announced a shift of weight. Hannah's mother had risen from the chair by the old woman's bed. Hannah could picture her mom's face, brow knitted in consternation, as it so frequently was. In a moment she would peek out into the hallway and find Hannah eavesdropping – something Hannah would normally never do, but damn it, the scream had worried her and then her mother had said what she'd said, and now…

Hannah ducked into the bathroom. Into the darkness there. Even with the rain on the roof she could hear the drip from the shower head, the plunk of that drip into the tub.

Her grandmother's bedroom door opened. The hinges were silent, but Hannah felt the change in air pressure, saw the bathroom door shudder just a bit. She knew her mother had stepped into the hall. Would she only crane her neck to scan for any motion in Hannah's bedroom, or would she come down the hall to check?

Hannah breathed slowly. Quietly.

Her mother huffed in satisfaction, assuming she remained sleeping. As if anyone could have slept through Nana's scream.

The door clicked shut. Hannah emerged from the bathroom and padded softly along the carpet, stopping just outside Nana's bedroom to listen.

"—back to sleep, Ma. It's okay. I'm right here."

"I won't. I can't," Nana ground out.

She sniffled, and Hannah thought she must be crying. The thought broke her heart.

"I'm sitting right here," Eleanor said.

"I can see you." Nana's reply carried an edge. "Dementia hasn't made me blind, Eleanor."

"For God's sake, Mother—"

"You're not listening. It's the grin—"

"I know. And I know it's scary, Ma, but it's just a dream."

Hannah could hear the exasperated sigh from her grandmother. She could almost feel the wave of emotion radiating through the door.

"Eleanor, I know you mean well," Nana said. Tired, on the verge of surrender. "And I know you don't believe me. I suppose it doesn't matter anymore. Yes, the grin started as a dream. It followed me in dreams for years. But now it lingers a little longer every time I wake up. It's in the darkest corner of the room."

"Ma—"

"It has eyes, now, Eleanor. Used to be I could feel the shape of it, but it was just that grin, the sharp teeth, that godawful fucking smile—"

"Ma, for Christ's sake, we're dropping f-bombs now?"

Nana barked a harsh laugh that turned into a loud coughing fit. Outside the door Hannah put a hand over her heart, wanting to go to her grandmother and comfort her. Instead she could only wait.

Wait, and feel the chill seeping into her bones. Because all of this sounded so familiar.

Familiar enough that she wanted to cry. Or scream.

Instead she only listened.

"You think because I'm old I've forgotten how to swear? This is the problem, Ellie. You look at me with your eyes and you see me so diminished that you don't listen anymore. You think because I forget so easily, because dementia makes me go off with the fairies all the time... you think I'm never in my right mind at all. But I am. Right now, I am. And you don't listen. It's got eyes now and it follows me up from my dreams, and it's watching me. And it's getting closer all the time."

Silence in the room.

Just the rain on the roof, and the whirring of the fan back in Hannah's bedroom, and the plunk of droplets falling from the shower head to land loudly in the tub.

"I don't know what to say to that." Eleanor's voice was a sad, broken rasp. "I wish I could bring you some comfort, Ma. I just... I'm not equipped for this."

Nana began to cry. Softly. "For God's sake, Eleanor. If you can just stay with me and stop trying to make me go to sleep. And let me keep a light on."

"The light—"

"Keeps me awake. Yes. Which is what I want, or are you still not hearing me. When the sun comes up, then I can sleep. Until then—"

"Okay. All right, Mom," Eleanor said. "Whatever you want. Whatever you need."

A beat. An exhale. A thank you.

But outside the door, listening, trembling, Hannah had an idea of how this would really go. Her mother would stay and in time her grandmother would fall asleep, and then her mother would turn out the light and return to her own room. Hannah knew it had happened many times before, but until now she had never intruded upon their privacy like this. She hadn't heard about the grin. The dreadful smile that waited in the dark, full of malice and cruel intention.

Do not wake Hannah with this crazy shit, her mother had warned. *You know it'll get into her head and the girl will never sleep again.*

Because Hannah had suffered childhood nightmares that had plagued her almost from infancy, until puberty. Medication had helped. Therapy had helped. But those nightmares had left scar tissue inside her dreamlife. She barely remembered her dreams now, but they always felt anxious and full of dread, as if her subconscious mind anticipated the arrival of something malignant.

The grin. She'd dreamt of it hundreds of times.

Woken in tears, bathed in sweat, often damp with her own urine.

It had been years. She hadn't endured one of those nightmares since at least the sixth grade. But now—

Her grandmother said it had eyes. That it followed her up out of sleep. That all she wanted was someone to keep her company until the sun rose.

Hannah knew her mother would break her word the moment Nana fell back to sleep. Fear seethed in her own mind, but she moved quietly back to her room, shut the door, and lay on the carpet in silence as she waited for her mother's betrayal. It couldn't have been more than twenty or thirty minutes before Nana's door opened and Eleanor snuck out, and back into her own room. Her door closed with a tiny squeak of the hinges and a click.

Another fifteen minutes passed, as Hannah waited to be sure her mother was asleep. She watched the shadows of her own room but saw nothing there. Eventually she rose and went quietly to her grandmother's bedroom, slipped inside, and sat in the hard, straight-backed wooden chair in the corner. Its rigidity made it nearly impossible to fall asleep, and that was what Hannah needed.

Nana slept, snoring softly.

Hannah shifted uncomfortably, eager for dawn, staring at each dark corner of the room in turn, sure that she would see the grin at any moment. Would she also see its eyes, or were those reserved for Nana alone?

The rain fell. The night wore on.

The need for sleep gnawed at her mind. Dragged her down.

In the corner, something might have stirred.

She nodded off.

"It doesn't sleep, you know."

Hannah jolted awake, neck muscles spasming as her head snapped up. She stifled a cry, reaching for the base of her skull as if she might poke inside her skin and pull the pain out by force. Morning had arrived, and despite her youth, her body was making her pay for hours contorted in that chair.

Beside her, on the bed, Nana was awake and staring into a corner of the room.

"Morning, Nana," she began. "How are you feeling?"

The old woman continued staring into the corner. A string of silvery drool spilled from the corner of her mouth – the facial muscles weakened by age – and pooled into a dark spot on her pillow.

"It doesn't sleep," Nana said again. "I don't know where it goes during the day. But it doesn't sleep. Even though it has eyes now." She spoke as if frustrated by a riddle, desperate to puzzle it out.

Hannah couldn't resist a glance at the corner. The sun shone on the other side of the house in the early hours, so the shadows were still deep, but the morning provided enough illumination for her to see that the corner remained empty. She could see the seam where the walls met. The old, floral wallpaper that her father had always hated had begun to peel along the crown moulding, but otherwise the walls were smooth, the corner vacant.

She rose from the chair and took a tissue from the box on the nightstand.

"What doesn't sleep?" Hannah asked, dabbing at Nana's mouth.

Her grandmother blinked, eyes misty. Nana had grown up in a household ruled by Depression-era toughness. Her generation did not like to waste anything, not food or household goods, and certainly not tears. But as the disease wore away at her memory and personality, Nana had become a person who cried often, at the slightest emotional high. Joy, confusion, sadness, and frustration – any of these might start the tears slipping down her cheeks, following the heavy lines of her wrinkled face. Mornings were always hard, when the veil of sleep had only just lifted and the old woman seemed to straddle two worlds, lost somewhere between. Hannah supposed Nana was lost in that mist most days now, unable to find her way back out again.

"Nana?" she urged, watching her eyes, the thin lashes framing paper-thin lids.

"It has eyes now," Nana repeated quietly, fingers swollen with arthritis, clutching her quilt. "All the better to see you with."

Hannah's gaze strayed back to the corner. Empty.

Not empty.

She forced a thin smile, lips closed because Hannah never smiled with teeth. Never. No one in the family did.

"There's nothing there, Nana. It was just a bad dream." She hated the words so often used by her own mother to dismiss her own childhood nightmares. She hated herself for echoing such feigned comfort, but how could it be otherwise?

"Just a bad dream," she recited, patting Nana's hand.

Nana didn't answer, but her eyes, distant and vacant only a moment before, flashed with disapproval. Hannah almost apologised, chastened by the look, but then it was gone and Nana turned her face away, staring into the shadowed corner. Waiting.

"How about a shower and then breakfast?" Hannah said, too cheery for the chilly morning gloom. "I'll make banana pancakes! Just like you and Mom taught me. Do you remember, Nana? Our pancakes?"

Nana didn't answer. Hannah could see the old woman had gone wandering in the mist again. In those moments Nana seemed shut down, as if someone had unplugged her mind. The faraway gaze and confused rambles were difficult enough to watch, but somehow these unplugged moments disturbed her even more. She needed to be away from the room for a few minutes to clear her head.

"I'll turn the shower on for you," she said. It was important to get the water temperature just right. If Nana turned the shower on herself, she was liable to make it scalding hot.

As Hannah left her grandmother's room, she kept her gaze downcast so she would not be tempted to look again into the corner, or to think about the grin of her own girlhood nightmares. She told herself the eyes she felt watching her depart had to be Nana's. Anything else would be impossible. After all, in her nightmare, the grin never had eyes.

The day passed in a simmering of strange anxiety. After breakfast, Hannah went for a six-mile run. The pancakes had been delicious and comfortingly nostalgic, but by mile three, she regretted the choice. Her physical health and her mental health were inextricably bound, and she needed fresh air and exercise to remind herself that there was more to the world than the atmosphere of decline and madness and grief that slowly ate away at her house and home like black mould. But running after pancakes hurt more than it healed.

When Hannah returned from her run, her mother went out to meet an old friend for coffee and then to the supermarket. They checked on Nana throughout the day, but the old woman had drifted into her pleasant daily rhythm, breathing, napping, watching the cable channels that showed the films or television series from her youth, letting it wash over her because she couldn't keep track of storylines anymore. Sometimes she imagined the actors on the television were in the room with her. Hannah would ask her who she was talking to, only to learn that Nana was in conversation with Lana Turner or Cary Grant, or the entire cast of a show called *The Odd Couple*.

Eleanor grew slightly frantic in those moments, wanting to somehow shake Nana out of these delusions, but Hannah found they warmed her heart. Her grandmother's mind would never be repaired and these illusory interactions were so pleasant, why not be happy for her? If she thought Frank Sinatra was sitting on the end of her bed, drinking coffee and talking to her, serenading her, being kind to her, where was the harm?

Hannah made a small bowl of pasta for Nana, a little after five o'clock. She brought it upstairs with a single meatball, broken up, easy to swallow. Later there would be tea with lemon cookies, which Nana had always loved. She tried to engage Nana in conversation, but the old woman ate listlessly, silently, watching black and white figures haunt her television, the ghosts of another era and another life.

Down in the kitchen, Hannah and her mother ate in similar silence. Hannah glanced at her, desperate to ask about the conversation she'd overheard between her mother and grandmother the night before. *Tell me about the grin, Mom. When I was little you always said I was just having nightmares, but then how do you explain what Nana's seeing? Why were you so afraid she would tell me about it, Mom?*

Tell me about the grin!

Hannah speared a little bit of asparagus with her fork, stared at her mother, and tried to make the words come out of her mouth. Eleanor looked at her. Perhaps she saw something in her daughter's eyes, some sign that Hannah's desperation was about to lead to a conversation Eleanor did not want to have.

So her mother smiled, lips tight across her teeth. She smiled the way they all did, showing barely a glimpse of the inside of her mouth. You couldn't have called it a grin.

"Too quiet around here," Eleanor said with a forced chuckle. "How was your run today, love? How was your day?"

"Nothing to report, Mom. You were here for most of it."

Eleanor shrugged. "You have work tomorrow, though. That's good. You need the stimulation. You can't just hang around here all the time waiting for the old lady to die."

Hannah shivered. "Mom. Come on."

"I'm kidding. Mostly." Eleanor smiled. "She's my mother, Hannah. If I can't joke about our little vigil, who can?"

She was right about that. And Hannah couldn't deny the fact that they were living in the midst of a vigil. Nana's condition would continue to deteriorate, and if there was any mercy in the world, she would die before she diminished to little more than a withered thing shitting and pissing itself in a sickening cycle until its battery finally ran out.

Hannah looked away from her mother, unable to meet her gaze with such thoughts in her head. She felt ashamed, sickened, and also horrified at the truth of it. If she believed in God, she would have prayed for him to take Nana that very night. She did not believe, of course.

And yet, God or no God, prayer or no prayer, that night her hopes were answered.

Hannah woke up choking.

She clawed at invisible hands wrapped round her throat, but only found her own clammy skin. She bolted upright and the opening of her airway sounded like the pop of a champagne bottle.

For a moment there was only blind, heart-thundering panic, but slowly she became aware of herself and her surroundings. The bed, sheets damp and tangled. Her shirt clinging, soaked through and smelling sour. The oscillating fan overhead, drying the sweat at her temples and neck, its chain pinging against the glass dome of the light with a clink, clink.

Just a nightmare. Already it began to blur at the edges, fading even as she tried to turn her inner eye toward it. She puffed out a long breath as she repressed a sob, eyes stinging and hot. Angry as much as terrified. She'd not had such a horrible nightmare in years.

A rustling came from the corner of her room and her head snapped round, neck muscles too tense, the movement too sudden and painful. She blinked rapidly, trying to clear the moisture from her eyes.

"Nana?"

The word came out a strangled rasp.

The figure stood unmoving in the corner by her window, so completely still that Hannah wondered if she was breathing. Weak light leaked in through the curtains, barely enough to illuminate the side of her grandmother's face, but Hannah found her eyes slowly adjusting to the dark. She could see the stiff, grey curls tight against Nana's skull, and the silhouette of the old woman's long nightgown – the one with the little flowers at the collar – swallowed by shadow. Even in the poor light, Hannah could see Nana's hand poking out below the ruffled cuff, her fingers slack, the joints gnarled and swollen with arthritis.

But more frightening than Nana's unusual appearance in her room and her preternatural stillness was the expression on her face. Though half her face was hidden in shadow, her mouth turned up in a toothy smile and her lips were stretched too far, so wide that the heavy lines of her face folded and creased to accommodate that smile. Nana's eyes seemed too big in her head, the whites too bright in the dark. The old woman stared at Hannah.

Grinning.

"Nana?" Hannah said again, the voice of a child speaking to the monsters in the dark, hoping they would not answer back.

There was a crunching like teeth grinding together. Impossibly, Nana's smile grew wider. Slowly. Eyes on Hannah, never blinking, she hinged at the waist, leaning into the light.

Grandma, Hannah thought distantly, what big teeth you have.

Nana's face was contorted and wrong, as if strings had been hooked at the corners of her mouth. Her eyes bulged, her stare keeping Hannah frozen in bed, not daring to move or breathe. Slowly, Nana's hand rose from the shadows, bringing one finger to her lips. A hissing *shhhh* issued from between clenched teeth, her mad grin never shifting.

Not Nana.

Hannah opened her mouth to scream, heedless of the warning, but another sound made the cry catch in her throat. A voice from beyond her door and down the hall – Nana's voice. A call for help that broke into sobs. Despite the horror in the corner, Hannah's eyes moved to the door, drawn to the sound. The cry from her grandmother's room faltered, even as Hannah heard her mother stumble into the hall. Light bloomed through the gaps in Hannah's doorframe, flooding out from her mother's room. The sound of rushing feet on old carpet as Eleanor ran for Nana's room, calling out. Eleanor's cries turning to shouts, then pleading.

Hannah dragged her gaze back to the window, her stomach turning to ice. Not-Nana was gone, but the grin remained. That horrible smile filled with teeth, eyes alight with malice floating above it in the dark. It watched Hannah – those eyes, that smile – until it began to fade.

Not back into shadow, but simply out, like the slow turning down of a gas lamp.

The machinery of death is always running silently in the background of life. All of its quiet mechanisms purr along unnoticed until they are needed. Hannah sat numbly in that same chair in her grandmother's room, while Eleanor spoke softly on the phone to the owner of Arthur J. Fogg Funeral Home – whose name, oddly, was not Arthur J. Fogg. Overhearing the rhythm of their conversation, the sorrowful tones of her mother's voice, Hannah understood that this was not Eleanor's first time speaking with them. A series of events had been prearranged, and would unfold once the wheels had been set in motion by Nana's passing.

Now that moment had come. Her nightmare had driven her from sleep in terror so powerful she still trembled, and now she sat with the hideous reality of loss. She'd never understood grief so well. It was more than sorrow. Much like fear, grief existed in the liminal space between harsh reality and a revised existence that seemed entirely imagined. Certain things could not be real, until they were. Both fear and grief lived in the moment between those truths.

A man named Charles Paxson came from the funeral home. For some reason he could take no action beyond offering a prayer until another visitor arrived, a startlingly tall woman named Angela. She carried herself with a solemnity that might have felt insincere from anyone else, and the kindness in her eyes made the moment painfully real. Hannah would never be sure if Angela was a nurse or a social worker or a doctor, but whatever she was, she signed the paperwork that confirmed Nana had died, and then Hannah and Eleanor each kissed Nana's cooling temple, and Charles Paxson suggested they leave the room.

Men working for Paxson came in with a black bag. Hannah didn't have to see them do it to know they zipped Nana up and carried her away. Paxson told Eleanor that she and Hannah could come to the funeral home in the morning to confirm arrangements Nana had already made, so that everything would be done according to her wishes.

Soon, the house was empty, save for Hannah and her mother.

Though it was the middle of the night, Eleanor made tea for them both. She added amber tea sugar as a treat, put the cups on the kitchen table, and the two of them sat there in silence. Eleanor blinked in apparent surprise as she realised there were tears in her eyes. She wiped them quickly away, as if daughters weren't meant to be caught crying when their mothers had died.

Hannah sat, unwilling to lift her gaze to look at anything but the untouched mug of tea in front of her.

"Suddenly I don't want tea at all," Eleanor said, but of course by that time the tea in both cups had gone from hot to barely warm enough to be palatable.

Hannah's breath hitched in her chest. "Mom?" she asked, without looking up.

What could it possibly have been about the tenor of that single syllable that gave her away? Hannah had no idea, but somehow – in the way that mothers have – Eleanor sensed the question that was coming.

"Don't even think it," Eleanor said. "Don't you dare. Your grandmother was an old woman. She's been sick a long time. It's a blessing that she went like this, instead of lingering in that fog for years. That would have been torture for her."

And for us, Hannah thought. She knew her mother thought so, too. Neither would say it aloud.

Hannah laughed quietly.

"Jesus," Eleanor said. "Something's funny?"

"That was disbelief, not amusement."

"What do you disbelieve?"

Hannah threw up her hands. "Are you joking? I heard you last night. Not tonight, but last night. I heard you both." Finally she lifted her gaze and locked onto her mother's eyes. "Those nightmares I had when I was little—"

"Hannah, stop."

"Fuck that! I had one last night worse than ever! I thought I was insane. I wanted to run screaming from the house, Mom. Then I woke up and…"

Her anger deflated. It might have been justified, but Nana was dead, and here she was shouting at her mom.

For the first time, Hannah noticed that she and her mother were doing the same thing with their eyes. Had been doing it, ever since discovering that Nana had passed away. Eleanor would look at Hannah, she would look down, she would glance at items there in the kitchen. But she wouldn't scan the room, wouldn't look around or peer at the corners.

The truth hit her so hard she could barely breathe. "You see it, too."

"Don't be stupid," Eleanor scoffed, then seemed to regret her harshness. "I love you, kid. I always have. No, I've never seen this bogeyman from your nightmares." Her gaze shifted away, toward the refrigerator. "I've never seen it because it isn't real. Your grandmother had nightmares, too. Hallucinations, ever since she was a little girl. My dad always told me to just hug her and humour her, and that's what I did all my life. It only became a problem when you heard her talking about it. You were so small, only two years old. And then you had your first nightmare about it."

Hannah narrowed her eyes, staring at her mother, fury rising again. She can't say it, Hannah thought.

"The grin. My first nightmare about the grin."

Eleanor stood up from her chair. "It made your grandmother half-crazy, and I had to deal with it my whole life. Trust me, I was not happy when I figured out my baby girl had picked up on it. I was so grateful when you stopped having those nightmares. And now here it is." Her face crumbled with sorrow. "She's got it into your head again, and she's not even here for me to be angry with her."

Hannah stared at her mother's face, trying to read her, trying to decide how much of what Eleanor had said was the truth and how much was denial. After a moment, she rose, chair legs scraping the floor like a shriek.

"I guess neither of us is in the mood for tea," she said.

Eleanor softened, seemingly grateful to be off the subject. "I feel hollowed out. I don't think I could find myself in the mood for much of anything."

Hannah went to her. Grieving, angry, confused, she pulled her mother into an embrace and the two of them wept together, quietly. After a few minutes, they relaxed into that embrace.

"Tomorrow's going to come too soon," Eleanor said. "Let's get some sleep, okay?"

She broke their embrace and started away, but when Hannah remained where she was, Eleanor looked back. "What is it?"

Hannah felt small. Childish. But she remembered the fear that had woken her, just before she heard her mother's cry and realised her grandmother had died.

"Could I climb in with you, just for tonight?" she asked. "I know I'm not a little kid anymore, but it feels so…" Hannah gave a tiny shrug, unable to find the words to continue.

Eleanor went back and wrapped Hannah in her arms again. "Of course. I'd like that. We'll both feel less alone."

There were times when things could get prickly between them, but not just then. Not that night. In that moment, the love of mother and daughter was as simple as it had ever been. After the confusion and fear she had been dealing with, it was a relief to feel safe.

Even just for a moment.

Convinced she would find no sleep, Hannah lay down beside her mother and pulled the covers up to her chin, prepared to do no more than toss and turn and count the seconds till daylight.

Still, exhaustion and loss and the simple comfort of having her mother within arm's reach was enough to lull her into a shallow doze. She drifted, as one does in a strange bed, in and out of consciousness, never fully awake and never fully asleep. She couldn't tell how long this went on. Sleep ignores such crude magicks as clocks.

Within this liminal space, Hannah never opened her eyes, frightened of coming too fully into wakefulness and destroying any chance of rest. Frightened of something more. Something that grinned. Something that now had eyes.

She struggled for unknown hours to remain in slumber, but eventually she found herself growing more aware of the room around her. Her eyes remained closed but she could not have claimed to be sleeping. She felt the crust gathered along her lashes, the gritty sands of sleep. Or perhaps it was salt from tears shed while she dreamed, her body grieving even while she was unconscious. While the sheets were soft and well-worn beneath her, they were not her own. And she could not hear the whir of the fan overhead.

There was, however, another sound. The sound that had dragged her into wakefulness.

A slow inhalation of breath behind her. Then out again.

Her mother. She remembered now. She'd gone to sleep in her mother's bed like she had as a little girl when she'd needed someone to banish the fears of childhood. Those of being taken and those of being left behind. What better comfort than to have someone beside you when you were at your most vulnerable?

Longtime married couples often found it difficult to sleep alone, listening for a breathing pattern they knew better than their own, or too aware of the absence of warmth on the opposite side of the bed. Exhausted new mothers might be so preoccupied with the safety of their infant that they avoided slipping into deeper, more restful sleep. Daughters might be jolted awake in the middle of the night by the cries of a dying parent.

Had Hannah's mother endured her own demons in the dark? Monsters made of sorrow and loss and fear rather than floating grins and eyes?

Another breath was drawn beside her, hitching, hesitant, and Hannah wondered if her mother might be crying in her sleep. She could reach out her hand and—

She was lying on her right side.

This seemed crucially important.

Because if she was lying on her right side, the steady breaths behind her and the eyes she felt on the back of her neck could not possibly belong to her mother.

If Hannah had been in her own bed, alone, she might never have dared open her eyes. But the comfort of her mother's presence lingered. Her heartbeat fluttered, racing. An icy chill prickled her skin. Her mouth went dry. She wanted to scream, but her lungs refused to cooperate. There had been times in her past when she had thought she felt terror, but now she knew how wrong she had been. The shuddering of her heart, the paralysis of her voice, the way her entire body seemed to scream in silence – this was terror.

But she wasn't a child anymore.

Hannah opened her eyes to find her mother, asleep, facing her in the bed. The pale, blue light of just-before-dawn filled the room, illuminating Eleanor's face. Shadows hid in the crevices of early wrinkles and frown lines or pooled in the deep hollows beneath her closed eyes. Eyes shut too tight to be sleeping. Her mother's breathing was so quiet, so shallow, Hannah knew she was already awake.

Betraying every instinct she had, Hannah reached slowly for her mother, telling herself if she could only be quiet, go slowly, the thing breathing in the corner behind her would never notice. Her fingers grazed the back of her mother's hand, and she felt tendons gone taut. Her mother clutched the sheets in a tight fist. Hannah stared at Eleanor's face, mentally pleading with her to open her eyes, so at least she would not be alone with her panic.

Mustering a hitching breath, perhaps gathering her courage, Eleanor opened her lids, meeting Hannah's gaze. Her mother's eyes glistened. Her features were soft, blending into the dark, but her eyes were clear. Hannah felt the weight of her fear, and her focus, just as she felt the weight of the eyes behind her burrowing into the base of her skull. An awareness prey has of a predator.

Hannah thought of divers. Of sharks in the deep. Sharks with permanent grins full of sharp teeth.

She had hoped that if she woke her mother, if the thing in the corner knew she was not alone, the breathing would stop and the terrible grin would be gone and take its terrible eyes with it. But its breath came closer. Hannah's lips parted with an audible pop and she tried to speak, but only managed to mouth the word *Mom*. A plea. A child begging a parent to fulfill her promise to always keep her safe. To keep the monsters away.

But whatever delusions of safety she still harboured were shattered by the look of resignation on her mother's face. Some part of her had believed the truth could never be as horrible as she imagined.

That part of her was wrong.

"I'm sorry, baby," her mother said.

Behind her, Hannah knew the grin widened.

Her mom offered a sad, coaxing smile.

"You're going to have to look eventually."

MIDNIGHT DISEASE
C.J. Leede

We came to the Land of the Midnight Sun to try and cure my writer's block.

Lucas is in Jack's arms as we deboard the plane in Reykjavik. The flight was nothing, five hours from New York, but with a screaming infant, it lasted an eternity. Jack smiled and apologised to our neighbouring passengers, brought them in on the situation. Some of them smiled back, indulgent, children or grandchildren of their own off somewhere in the world. Lucas did not care one way or another. He looked at me as he screamed. Kept his eyes on me, as if to say, *I am yours and I want them to know it.*

Lucas is in the ninetieth percentile of weight and height. His grip is very strong. He likes to take hold of my hair and rip it down toward him, likes to try and take it for himself.

Inside the airport is a Joe's Coffee just like in New York, and it both elates and disappoints me. My moods have been unpredictable post-birth, and I can hardly keep track of them, let alone rein them in. So I've given up trying. Long lines of beautiful, faintly related-looking people spill out from what turn out to be water filling stations, all these cousins-of-cousins' reusable bottles in hand, patiently waiting their turn. Jack rubs at the backs of his eyes, but still smiles beneath the dark circles. We don't sleep anymore, at least not mostly. Like my words, sleep now presents itself as something we perhaps never quite knew how to do. An awkward stilted approximation of something human. *Unlike* my words, in the most desperate moments, sleep still comes to claim us. Even if afterward it feels as though it didn't.

Where the words used to be, now is a vast screaming darkness.

I've read about mothers who can't take the onslaught of hormones and damage to the body and lack of sleep. The myriad ways in which they can snap.

We get smoothies. I try to sort out the transport to our rental car. A lanky teenage boy leads us over to a van. He is not interested in the baby, but he is not disgusted by him either. He is merely indifferent. I like people like this, who allow us to exist. Who still treat us like people, and not only parents.

My husband has given Lucas an empty plastic cup to play with, we Americans who did not even bring reusable bottles. I want to say that it is wasteful, but the baby's hands are already on it. The mess that Lucas produces is profound. I can't seem to keep him clean no matter how often I bathe him. This smell just clings to him, this sour milk afterbirth. Jack's mother comes to our brownstone once a week and holds the child before her face, inhaling forcefully, smiling in a daze.

Because my husband is holding the baby, the teenager and I load the bags into the back of the van. They are large, and heavy, because we will be here for two months, all of July and August before my husband has to return to his professorial duties. I am outwardly healthy again, finally. I can lift bags and carry things. I don't involuntarily piss myself at every turn. My arms are strong because of the weight of the child I lift and rock through the night. I can even have sex now, theoretically.

We get the van loaded up, and I hand the boy a tip. He laughs at the cash in my fingers and shakes his head. He tells me Americans always do this, but it is not customary here. I think about insisting. Another couple gets in with us. They do not have a child. They are our age, thirties, but vibrant youth still shines on their faces, radiates out from their skin. The Icelandic boy gets in the driver's seat, and the couple sit beside him, squeezing in on the front bench seat. I sit behind the driver, and Jack and Lucas sit beside me. The other couple are silent, bright smiles and eyes open in wonder, taking in the sights. Jack, beside me, speaks to Lucas, cooing and bouncing him loudly for all of us to hear.

We arrive at the rental car place, a hut in the middle of a barren field, the smell of sulphur strong in the air. I walk around the van, and I reach for the baby so my husband can step out of the van and deal with the logistics at the counter. I hold my arms out, anticipating the warm, weighty feel of Lucas in my hands, the smell that will once again assault my senses. Instead, something is violently hurled at my face. I flinch back, turn away quickly, on instinct. And just at that moment, the front door of the van opens from the inside and collides, hard, with my skull.

My ears ring, I lose balance. A flurry of movement ensues, and I think the others are rushing toward me, to help. I stumble back, nauseated. Where did this nausea come from? I reach out for someone to catch me. But no one comes. I stumble back into the side of the van, lean hard against it, try to breathe through my nose.

My hearing is the first sense to come back, pinpointing on a scream I know too well, the one that belongs to my baby. Sight comes second, and I stare at the plastic cup on the ground, the one Lucas threw at me, the one that hit me before the van door did.

The female of the couple is coming to me now, apologising for opening the door. She is frantic, and I tell her that it's okay, it wasn't her fault.

I know whose fault it was.

Now crying, now being cooed over by my husband and the couple, the teenager's eyes wide but continuing to unpack our luggage. I am bent over. Hands on my knees.

I stand slowly. Lucas is calming, his volume waning in the Icelandic morning. My husband sighs in relief.

★ ★ ★

We drive toward the city. We will have lunch once we arrive and then continue on to a town called Borgarnes and out into the wilds where we have rented a cabin. The baby sleeps in the back seat, and my husband drives. I stare out the window at the lunar, mostly barren landscape of asphalt, volcanic rock, and low grass. A purple flower crops up here and there, lupin I believe. The sun is bright and hot. The GPS directs us.

"Are you okay?" my husband asks.

"Yes," I say.

"No, you're not. What's wrong?"

I turn and look at him, to see if he's joking. "Did you not see what happened?"

"What, with Lucas?"

"He threw the cup at me, and I hit my head."

"You can hardly blame Lucas for your head hitting the door."

"Are you serious?"

"Yes, I'm serious. You can't blame a six-month-old baby for some tourist opening the door and hitting you in the head."

Writers have experienced this throughout the ages. It's totally normal. You're just tired.

His voice. When did my husband's voice start grating on me? When did I start to associate it with dread?

It's because we aren't sleeping, he said, *as soon as we get past the five times a night phase—*

We follow the GPS into the town that is hardly more than a hamlet, a handful of buildings and maybe twice as many houses. We stop for lunch in a mom-and-pop establishment that looks like someone's living room. Jack finds some Advil for me out of one of our bags. We eat fish soup. I might have a concussion.

"What do you think so far?" Jack says. He tries to take a sip of coffee, but it's too hot, steam wafting up, fogging his glasses. Lucas stares at me from his lap.

"About Iceland?"

"Yeah. Any inspiration striking?"

I turn and look out the window. The landscape is beautiful. The place is otherworldly. I can feel how far north we are, the magic of it. I soften.

"Thank you for coming here," I say. "I really... it's nice."

Jack reaches out and puts his hand over mine. I love the feel of his calluses, a reminder that I found the one academic who takes pride in his physical strength and fitness. I realise I'm looking forward to getting back to our workout routine, running together, tumbling into the shower, sweaty and full of hot blood.

"Do you feel anything?" he asks.

I turn to look back out the window. He's not asking about us, not asking about my head. He's asking if this was a good idea. He's watching me, searching desperately for the woman he fell in love with, any glimpse of her.

And looking out at it all, a sheep ambling by in those purple flowers, a place so unlike home we might as well be on another world entirely, I think...

Yes, I can feel something, maybe. Just a little thread, a small trickle, a—

Lucas knocks over Jack's scalding cup of coffee. It spills over the table and down into my lap.

* * *

The GPS takes us from the town on a dirt road that looks as though no one, let alone foreigners, should ever traverse it. To even call it a road is a generosity I would not have given, but the GPS device insists.

"I'm sure it gets a little better farther up," Jack says.

It says it's going to be forty-seven minutes. The hatchback jumps and lurches over the gravel. Ten minutes in, the dirt road is now covered in rocks ranging from the size of softballs to basketballs. The car rattles and clanks. Lucas is crying.

"Did we get the extra insurance?" I say, metal scraping beneath us as the car clambers over the terrain.

Jack's jaw tightens, just perceptibly. "No."

"We didn't?"

"The travel guides said it wasn't necessary."

"Jack, we may end up paying for this car."

"No, we won't," he says.

His knuckles are white on the wheel.

We drive (bump, jostle, jerk, shake) for thirty more minutes on this road, and navigation says we will now arrive at our destination in another twenty. It is almost unbelievable that we were in any kind of town an hour ago. There is no one in any direction. No buildings, no animals, nothing. Just rocks and dirt and far off hills or mountains. Lucas has not stopped crying. We discuss trying to feed him, but with the car moving as it is, it's not safe to remove him from the car seat. It hardly feels safe to have him in the car at all.

Jack hits the brakes, hard, and I am shot forward, the ancient seatbelt cutting into my always sore breasts, my stomach lurching again. My head is still not right. The skin on my stomach and thighs is burned. Lucas screams.

"Jesus Christ, Jack!"

"Look!"

A small stream of water trickles in front of us. A stream of water across the road, dotted with rocks larger than any we've seen yet.

"Jack, I don't—"

Lucas screams.

"What?"

"I said, I don't think—"

"I don't need your negativity right now. The GPS says this is it, and they gave us the GPS at the rental car place and—"

"Well, can we clear it?"

A new wail from the back, the kind that is always accompanied with fresh piss and spittle and maybe a healthy dribble of vomit. I turn to Jack, to tell him we have to turn around. This isn't safe for anyone.

Then that look. That look of determination my husband gets. The one that says he *will* finish the impossible dissertation. That he *will* run two marathons in two days. It says that if anyone has ever not succeeded it is simply because they chose to quit. Having Lucas did nothing to that ability in him, it made no difference to the sheer force of will that has always been his life's blood. Distinguished, tenured, celebrated. I wonder, if Lucas had grown inside him, would it have ripped that determination from him? I am so nauseated from the car ride, from the headache, now that we are no longer moving. I open the door, lean out over the rocks and sand, and throw up.

We get out. I clean Lucas's face and let him bruise my nipple as Jack clears rocks from the path and places his hands in the water to determine the depth. I stare out over the landscape, in the flat bright sunlight. It is silent out here. The only sounds the unfathomable continued rumbling idle of the hatchback and Jack's huffs and grunts.

The colours are strange. Sometime during our violent drive, they have shifted from blacks, greys and greens, to an alien sort of orange and blue. Mountains in the distance, a low orange shrub all around, seemingly the only living thing. Desert, but with periodic pools of water, small ones reflecting the sky. Everything blue, tan and orange. I check my watch. It is noon. The sun has not moved in the sky since we have been here. Just a steady stream of bright light over an indifferent land. I like it here. I inhale the air, dusty but clean. Not polluted, not city air. And the way the light shines down over the mountains, the sharp jagged slope of them—

Lucas bites down, hard, on my nipple. I suck in a breath. He's drawn blood. I hold him in front of me at arm's length.

He looks content. He looks as though he might just drop off into a blessed nap. Then he blinks his eyes open. We stare at each other.

★ ★ ★

The block didn't come all at once. It came on slowly at first, a nudge, a gentle shudder.

I found out I was pregnant after an uncharacteristically bad reaction to our favourite Chinese takeout back in Brooklyn. I stood at the window of our brownstone, and I rested my hand on my stomach, the other clutching the test I would show Jack minutes later. I took that moment, though, just for the two of us. This child and me. As the night breeze blew a plastic bag into the spring-blooming cherry blossom outside the window, I realised I had created something tangible. For the whole of my career I had generated ideas, stories, theoretical worlds. But for the first time, *this*.

I had made something real. A person. Jack and I had made a person.

He cried when I told him. Then he kissed me hard, and backed me up against a wall. Everything we had ever wanted, had ever dreamed of, we had achieved. So delirious, so heady and impossible, this joy. Our careers were in great places, we had a community and friends and a home and a life. And now we had a baby.

It came on slowly at first. Quietly.

It snuck in beneath the floorboards and between breaths. Small, nearly insignificant.

Blank half-moments. Tiny gaps in a train of thought.

Two months in, and I sat at my desk, mid-thought, mid-sentence, hands poised on the keys, and the words just... disappeared. For just a moment, just a second. I reached for them, and they were gone.

Then I blinked, and they returned. And I forgot it had even happened.

Jack decided to learn tangible skills. He took it upon himself to build the crib, painted and repainted the nursery with paints he had researched to be as non-toxic as possible. We selected fabric swatches and relished in revealing the news at intervals to family and friends.

By the fourth month, my belly swollen and shockingly alive with our baby inside, it happened nearly once a day. Just a moment, accompanied by a kick to the stomach. It was like running. I was running fast and free and limitless, and then suddenly the ground dropped out from below me. And I was falling. Down, deep down, into a dark and endless pit.

I ran to the bathroom to vomit, and the steady nausea of the pregnancy would clear for just a moment. But the feeling, the knowing that for that moment the words had not been there. It crawled its way beneath my skin.

It happened again.

It happened four times, five, six.

By the end of the third trimester, there were hours, sometimes an entire afternoon, in which I could produce nothing. I grasped and groped for any words, for anything. My friends, my companions for the whole of my life and career, for the whole of a solitary childhood. They were abandoning me. What even was I without them?

And when Lucas came, the day he ripped himself free of the confines of my body, took his first triumphant terrified screaming breaths in this world, at first I did not realise.

Our little boy was here, and he was so beautiful. No words will ever describe the joy. Nothing could possibly convey it. Our pride.

He was healthy, and he was strong. He was everything we had dreamed of. The nurse cleaned him and handed him to Jack, and I had never seen my husband so full of purpose, so complete. He was so stunningly radiant that it nearly hurt to watch him. Jack and this precious little person we created. I was the happiest I had ever been. It was more than finishing a book, more than sparking a new idea. This was something else entirely.

Jack handed Lucas over to me. I reached for him, and I held him so tight against me.

And that was when I felt it.

The sick feeling, the destabilising terrifying tilt.

No. No, I pushed it aside.

The doctor stitched me up and cleaned the mess. I held my perfect child, my child who I loved. My wonderful elated husband stood beside me, squeezing my arm, crying and taking pictures.

But I knew.

No. I didn't want—

But I *knew*. Of course I did.

It was the feeling of an organ having been ripped from me. A limb. My whole self.

Not the birth, not the thing I had grown here. But something I had carried with me for as long as I could remember. The indescribable and otherworldly beating heart of my life. My identity. My everything.

My words.

His eyes were scrunched up tight, his face still pink.

Lucas, my little boy, the one I created from my own flesh and blood, he came into this world kicking and screaming.

And he took my words with him.

★ ★ ★

I stand now with this child, in the middle of this arctic desert. I look into his eyes.

And I think...

This little boy, unformed and dependent as he is, he *knows* what he took from me. He did it on purpose. But then I think, that can't be... can it?

He smiles, an eerie smile. It doesn't look like Jack's, or mine. A shiver runs down my arms. Why does he frighten me so much? My own child should not frighten me.

Only my hands keep him from falling. Only my two hands between this life and the rocky ground below. What if I just dropped him now? What if I simply... let go?

And yet he smiles still. Because he knows I can't. He knows that he owns us now, that we are beholden to him, whether we like it or not.

He knows.

"Honey! I got it! I freakin' got it!"

Jack. Boyish, triumphant. He's found a way for us to pass the stream. But Lucas and I do not look at him. We stare only at each other.

★ ★ ★

We come upon our cabin so suddenly I think I've imagined it. There is no cabin, and then there is one. Just sitting there behind some rocks. A black wooden structure with white trim on the porch and a bright yellow front door. I squint and can now see that maybe ten minutes' walk from us are another few cabins, intermittently placed among the rocks and pools. We've happened upon a community, of sorts.

Jack and I are shaking. We don't realise it until we both stand beside the car and find each other shades paler than usual. We will undoubtedly have to pay for the hatchback. But we made it. I smile at my husband, just a little. He smiles back, and it is so young, so silly on this nearly forty-year-old professor's face that I let out a small laugh.

Love is such a funny thing. Just when you begin to fear you may have lost it, you realise you never could.

A warm, wet liquid spreads beneath Lucas in my arms. He is smiling too.

★ ★ ★

Inside, there is one small living room/kitchen, a port-o-head style bathroom that one adult human can stand in, arms at their sides, and a bedroom that just accommodates one full-sized bed and no bedside tables. The space is very tight, in that European way. But the living room opens onto a front porch that looks out over the expanse of the Martian wastes. We can see for miles and miles, the other cabins behind us, so that our front porch view is completely uninterrupted. It's gorgeous.

I hand Lucas over to Jack and do not meet his eyes. I step into the bathroom to clean myself up.

"Well, that was eventful," Jack says when I am out. "Should we, uh…" He looks at me suggestively and indicates the tiny bedroom. The door can't open all the way against the foot of the bed. Lucas is in his travel cradle on the couch, sitting up and looking at me.

Thief. The word pushes its way in to my still-aching head.

Insidious little creature, who has charmed and tricked and fooled us.

Thief. He knows what he took. I see it now, suddenly. Standing here in this cabin.

Why couldn't I see it before?

A knife glints over on the magnetic knife rack, the sun shining against it. I don't know why my eyes catch on it. My heart pounds through my chest.

I—

"I'm going to take a walk," I say.

"Oh. Okay. Well, don't you want to at least feed Lucas first?"

"He just ate." I shake my shirt out against my chest. I'm having trouble breathing. The nausea is pressing in again on me.

"He seems hungry to me."

My eyes cut to the child, now in Jack's arms. How did he get there so fast? Jack so quick to move to him, so attentive to his needs. Lucas watches me. It does not matter what I want.

I sit on the couch and wait for Jack to lower him into my arms. I stare out over the expanse outside as the child sucks from me, as he draws more blood. His eyes on mine. I keep my eyes on the horizon.

★ ★ ★

We go into town for dinner and groceries. A different town on the other side, small and cute with a small cute restaurant, a little glass atrium inside with flowers and plants, in stark contrast to the seemingly barren world outside. We eat fish and fresh baked bread, and I am permitted one glass of wine. We discuss the landscape and business opportunities. We discuss what we think it would be like to live here. I have shaken off the anxiety of earlier, chalked it up to the headache and car ride.

I feel better now. I am enjoying myself, my time with my husband. Lucas sits in my lap.

I lean over him to take bites of food, and he swings back with his arm repeatedly and hits me, his fists pounding my chest. Jack thinks it's cute. I watch him watch Lucas. I watch him watch me. The woman he made a mother.

We stand to leave at the end of our meal, and a family comes in as we are exiting.

"Oh, I'm so sorry!" the husband of the family says, backing out to make room for me.

"It's fine," I say, and wait for him to pass. "No problem."
"No, no, please, you go first, I insist."
"It really is fine, thank you," I say.
"No, it's only right for a new mother. Please, go on."
Finally, I agree, and I step past him, back into the light. A cat runs across the parking lot in front of us.
"What was that about?" Jack says.
"What?"
"Why wouldn't you just take him up on it?"
"I didn't need to. I was fine waiting."
"Yeah, but he wanted to let you go first, with Lucas. The whole thing could have taken less time."
"But I'm not an invalid."
"No, but you're a mother."

I stop, halfway through the lot, my legs nearly buckling.

"Are you okay?" Jack says. He is there at my shoulder,stroking my back, taking Lucas from me.

★ ★ ★

At night, I sit on the porch, staring at a blank notebook page. The laptop is too much, the bright blank screen a taunting too harsh to face. I will myself to think of anything, any words to dredge forth. I will take *anything*.

But there is nothing. Jack comes out with two mugs of tea with whiskey, and he massages my shoulders. I lean back into him.

"What do you need?" he says.

"I don't know." I don't want to talk about me. Don't want to talk about this, sitting here and staring at a screen. Reaching and reaching, every second. "How are you?"

"I'm great," he says, rubbing my shoulders, the muscles on either side of my spine. "I'm happy. I like it here. Lucas is doing great, and work is finally leaving me alone. I'm just happy to be here, and to be all about you." His hands move up and over my shoulders, one of them down to cup one of my breasts. He kneads it, still sore, always sore, but the attention from him is more welcome. I lean back, and I stare up at a bright blue sky. It's a relief, being here with the perpetual sun. The pressure is off to sleep, to live on a normal schedule again. My breath comes quicker, my heart picking up its pace, just a little.

"What if—" My voice falters.

"Don't go there," he says, leaning into my ear, brushing my hair back. "Don't go there. It's coming back, I promise."

"But—"

"Hey," he says, and he leans forward and tilts my face to him. He kisses me, long and slow. I lean into his kiss. I am so empty, so hollowed out and bereft, it feels as though I am dying. I can't explain to him what it means to have lost it. I can't explain it to anyone. Only someone like me will understand. Only someone whose whole self is what they create. But Jack knows as much as anyone else can. Jack knows, and he picked me. He chose me, knowing who I was, what I was. He has stayed with me, even while I am no longer a person, am no longer myself. When I have been reduced to one thing, one singular thing that has nothing to do with me at all. I want his kiss to take it from me, all of it. All the pain, the reaching, the endless gaping void. I want—

Lucas wails. Jack stiffens.

★ ★ ★

"I'm going to make a local speciality!" Jack announces when I wake. I don't know what time it is. Still, that sun, hovering.

"Oh?" I pad over to the kitchen and reach for the French press.

"Kjötsupa. I got some locals to teach me how to make it."

"Wow," I say.

"Yes." He lifts the large knife he is cutting with, the same one the sun shone so brightly on before, and points it to me. "And I am convinced, this is going to fix you."

"The Kjötsupa?"

"Yes. The people at the market said they swear by it. Said it's the best dish and the only thing to eat when you aren't feeling yourself, and is very traditional here. It's going to be great."

"Maybe we should go explore today, after you cook," I say.

He looks up at me. "You don't want to write?"

I turn away from him, blink a few times, my insides turning as though he plunged that knife into them.

"I just thought exploring might be fun," I say. "But we don't have to. I mean I know we're here for—"

"I think exploring sounds great," he says. He smiles, and he cuts his vegetables, and he tries to hide it, but I see it there. The disappointment. He doesn't know how to help me, and he doesn't know why I'm not helping myself. He thinks I am choosing this. Disappointment on my husband's face.

I walk over to where Lucas sleeps in the travel carrier. I lift him to me and let him take.

★ ★ ★

"Hey," Jack says, "he's out. No one's around. I think, maybe, if we're fast, and we can leave one of our phones on speaker with him and take one with us, maybe we can go for a walk together." His look is hopeful and charming and everything I fell in love with. "I mean, if it would be all right with you. If you want that."

I nod. At this man who is my husband. This man who I fell for the moment I laid eyes on him so many years ago now.

Outside in the late afternoon, it is so quiet, save for the crunch of our shoes in the gravel and dirt, the wind blowing through the low brambles and shrubs.

"Hey, you remember that night?"

"Which one?"

"At your parents, the first time."

My body heats, a little, at the memory. The sounds and images and the feel of him. It was a two-hour drive to my parents' house from the city, and we couldn't even make it to the front door. It was dark out, and I texted and said we'd be late. Jack laid me down on the driveway, so close to the house we could hear them talking and walking around inside. There were wounds up and down my spine for weeks from the concrete, on every single vertebra. I loved those wounds, loved the flex of the skin healing, delicious as I stretched awake in bed beside him the next morning, and the next, and all the nexts after that.

"I remember."

He stops walking and grabs hold of my arm. He spins me toward him, pulls me close. We stand on the dirt road in the northern reaches of the world, desert shrubland sprawling around us, cabins ahead, mountains behind. And here, just him and me, just us.

I reach up on my toes and grab for the back of his head, pressing my lips to his. Searching his mouth with my tongue. I remember thinking on the day he proposed, *I get to do this forever. How could I ever have gotten so lucky?* He pulls back, and he tucks my hair behind my ear. "I'm sorry," he says. "I know it's hard. I think this is going to help, though, and I'm here."

He drops his forehead to mine, and we stand here a moment, the breeze pushing against us. "I love you," I say.

He says it back.

I pull my husband to the side of the road. The low-lying shrubs and bushes come up to my hips, large brambling things, but without thorns. Like giant open tumbleweeds.

"Think we can swing it?" I say.

He eyes the bushes and then me. The phone is still silent. Jack smiles.

We get as low as we can, laughing as our heads come up above the top of the vegetation, straining to rip our clothes off in the brambly dirty undergrowth. Finally, I lie down like I did that night, and my husband moves over me. And I am here. I am here with the sticks and roots in my back, against my hips and shoulder blades, I am here with his skin and mine, and we are a team and a unit and a support system. And even if something terrible has happened, even if I am struggling to remember the feel of who and what I am, desperately groping in the dark to find it once again, I am not alone. I have him, we have each other.

He moves, and—

There. Oh god, there, yes. I can't believe it. I feel it, the tiny first glimmer of a spark, an idea. Just at the edges of my mind, just tentative and half-formed, but—

Oh my god. I let out a sob of a laugh.

There are words here.

In him, in us, in this low underbrush beneath an unrelenting strange sun.

He moves, and I move, and his groans turn into a growl, and I am close, so close to feeling some kind of release, some kind of force of life again. The words are there, close enough to see, to feel, and Jack is here, and I am here, flickering but alive. Barely, almost. Inches away, seconds, climbing toward that blessed oblivion that will make me truly and completely forget what it is I have lost. To maybe even get it back, to feel all of it moving through me and within me and—

Jack stops. He pulls back.

"Did you hear that?"

"What? No, keep going, please—"

"Shit. Where's the phone?"

The words, dying embers, drifting, fading.

"What?" I say.

"The phone, where is it? I must have dropped it when—" Jack pulls out of me, falling back into the brush and sweeps his hands over the ground. "Where is the phone? We need to be able to hear Lucas. We need—"

He is frantic. Desperate. This searching and groping. I know the feeling. I know it.

My eyes catch on something, shining in the dappled sun. "Here," I say, as if in a dream. Not really here. I hand it over. The call hasn't been disconnected. Jack turns the volume up, and we hear the soft cooing of a not-yet-but-almost screaming child.

Jack laughs, something like tears shining in his eyes. He relaxes back down on top of me. His shirt is halfway on. He is no longer hard. His breaths come heavy and fast. "Fuck, are we the worst parents?" he says.

"I don't know."

"Oh," he says. "Time to get back."

I look down at my breasts where he is looking. The milk squeezing from them at the sounds the child makes through the phone. This child and this body in some kind of mutually determined agreement that I have been left out of. I was never alerted, or asked. The words—

"Hey," Jack says. "You're beautiful like this." He means with my breasts leaking milk.

He means as a mother.

He turns to pull on his pants, and I have seconds only, with his back to me, to cry.

★ ★ ★

It is night time, but Jack leaves to head to a store and get one final item for his meal. I sit with the notebook and stare at its blank taunting pages and grip the pen so tight and squeeze my eyes shut and beg, plead, tell the universe that I will do anything, anything at all to get it back. To remember who I am, to find a purpose again, a real purpose. To want to live at all. Anything.

I think for the first time in a long time of my mother. We were close once, but now we talk over the phone only every once in a while. I imagine her standing here, in this too small room.

She was an artist, before she met her husband. Her paintings filled our life and home with colour and wonder. My early memories of her always with paint on her face, beneath her nails.

She met her husband when I was five, and he was an artist too, but more traditional, from a different kind of life than ours. He thought I needed structure, needed solidity to rely on growing up. That the late night fast food runs that struck my mother on a whim and the way we spoke in the even-levelled discourse of friends would negatively impact me in the long run. It was time for her to be more of a parent and me more of a child, for all of us to properly assume our roles.

My mother stopped painting when they got married. She sold her car, a bright orange Thunderbird that she loved nearly as much as she loved me, bought something practical and bland. They built a home together, and they designed it so that his painting studio was the largest space, off on its own. And hers was tiny, a walk-through built into the kitchen so she could always tend to us at the same time. She took up odd jobs, showed up for her husband and for me. At first she was so happy, was so eager to take on this new role and personality. Of course that didn't last for long.

I asked her once why she didn't paint anymore, and she told me that her creative energy had been transferred to something else, something better. Her life's work, being a proper mother and wife. She said this with full belief. She convinced herself that these words were true, that he and I fulfilled the creative need in her.

And yet.

The dynamic changed. So much frustration. There was so much frustration in our house, all the time. She was tired now, always tired. Moody, tempestuous. If I asked a question too many times, if I had emotional tumult of my own, it was met with increased volume, a snapped response and often more. My voice that had once mattered, our back and forth in which I felt as though even if we weren't quite equals, our ideas were equally important, equally valid. My voice was silenced. Children are meant to listen. And I was a child now. I transformed from a person to a child, and she transformed from a person to a wife. Our new roles took over everything, trumped anything else. And there was no room for the emotional turmoil of two. She had claimed that space as her own because she had given up her art. She had given up everything for *us*.

An artist is inherently selfish. An artist nurtures something inside the self, or ignores it. But it is always the self that rules us, always the spark within. Even now, sometimes I call her for advice or during a crisis, but her crises often take precedence. She gave up her creative self for me, so it is my turn to hold the space for her.

The baby's crying becomes a wail. It runs through me in this miniscule space like poison, like venom, like electric shock. I did not mean to create this thing. I did not know what I was handing over, what I stood to lose. Why did I think I would be exempt? Why did I think I could do it all, that I had such a deep and overflowing well that I could pour myself into two children? My human baby and my art.

I scoop the child up and take him into the kitchen. I set him down on the little table, and he looks up at me and cries and cries. He sees the breasts and the arms and the skin and warmth, and that is all. He sees nothing more. This volatile, knowing parasite.

There is spit up on my shirt. I peel it off and cast it aside.

And I know I can't take it anymore. I cannot bear one more second of this life. A life without words, without any sense of self.

The sun shining into the cabin and into my eyes.

Glinting off the blade of the knife.

I can't do one more second. I realise it with a clarity so profound, even Lucas is silent for a moment.

And I do what I've wanted to since we arrived in this place.

I step to the rack and wrap my fingers around the base of the knife.

I walk back to Lucas, trying to remember what it felt like to love waking up in the mornings, what it was to feel my presence on this earth could matter to more than one human.

In this little cabin in the middle of nowhere in Iceland, in the silence of the ever-bright night, I hold the knife up above the baby, and he cries now, again, and the blinding sun is reflected in the metal.

As I begin to cut.

★ ★ ★

The knife slices into the flesh of my skin.

I barely feel it. My breasts, now so abused, so accustomed to pain.

I start with just one. I slice deep in, down and around, getting all the tissue. Blood spills from my chest down over my stomach. I cut until I have freed myself of the left one entirely.

I do the same on the right. An incision, a circular arc, a great sawing sweep.

These things that cause cancer and pain and exist not for me but for men and children, the child before me. They have never existed for me. But I stand here, and I hold them in my hands, these fleshy food bags that used to be something of mine.

I drop them to the table next to the child. He screams. I am so sick of the screaming. If I have to endure one more second of it—

I can't. I can't do it.

I raise the knife again.

★ ★ ★

I cut off my ears. Both of them.

But I still hear, can still hear that infernal screaming that will fill my senses forever.

I stab at my ear drums, dig in with this knife until blood pours from there too, but there is only the whirring pool of it, the rushing and dripping of my blood. I stuff my ears, the holes that were once my ears, up with paper towels.

★ ★ ★

What does one need to write?

Eyes, hands, brain, seat, torso. Legs, for pacing.

* * *

I undress completely. Lucas is still crying, tears still leaking from his eyes, but he is watching me. I make sure to hold his eyes now. Make sure he is watching as I squat down, the same way I did for the birth, the same way I did when I pushed him out of me. And I reach inside. I push the knife deep in, all the way. I undo the work of the birthing doctor, all the careful stitching. Reopen the tears and gaping wounds.

This easy bake oven, human growing bag. Another part I never asked for, never chose to carry. This internal built-in Russian roulette game that brings monthly pain, pregnancy pain, birthing pain, all the various hells of afterbirth.

The one I don't even get to make decisions over because that's a job for men in suits who have never met me and never will.

* * *

And...

I laugh. A sob of a laugh.

I feel a hundred pounds lighter. I feel like a self. A true self, existing for no other.

Not a mother, not a child, not a wife.

A person.

* * *

But I am not finished. I am not ready yet. I just need one more thing.

No more consoling, no more cooing, singing, affirming, advising, commiserating, agreeing. No more giving away freely what needs to be saved for the paper and ink.

My words are mine, and no one else's.

I open my mouth and cut out my tongue.

* * *

I stand in the cabin in Borgarnes, bloody and dripping and barren.

But I am not barren.

Not anymore. Never again.

I put the baby back in bed, and I leave him the breasts to play with. My husband will be home soon, and he will see what I have done. He will see the woman that he knows he married.

And here, alone, there stands a *person*.

I step outside into the bright light of the midnight sun, the porch boards creaking below me, the blue and orange panorama shining and full of such stillness and life, so full of wonder. Of potential.

I sit down on the edge of the porch, bleeding. I reach for my notebook.

I smile, and I laugh.

As the words seep up from beneath the lunar surface of this land and skitter over the floorboards, up my bare feet and legs and into my core.

Words in the blood on the cabin floor, making their way toward me, sliding out from Lucas's crib, too fast for him to hold onto.

Rushing back.

I smile so wide.

As I bleed on the page.

BIOGRAPHIES

Caolán Mac an Aircinn is a translator, classicist and independent scholar who lives in Dublin, Ireland with his fiancée, Shannon. He has been writing on and off since he was six, and has published short stories in the genres of science fiction and horror as well as a translation to Irish of a section of the *Iliad*. He writes both in English and in his native Irish. When he is not working or writing, he enjoys teaching the Irish language, playing traditional Irish music and bothering his two cats, Uwe and Cathal Brugha.

Alan Baxter is a multi-award-winning British-Australian author of horror and weird fiction. His books include *Blood Covenant*, *Sallow Bend*, *The Roo*, *The Gulp*, *The Fall*, *Served Cold* and *The Leaves Forget*. *This Is Horror* podcast calls him 'Australia's master of literary darkness' and the *Talking Scared* podcast dubbed him 'The Lord of Weird Australia'. He's also a martial artist, whisky-soaked swear monkey, metalhead and dog lover. He writes his darkly strange tales deep in the valleys of southern Tasmania. Find him online at alanbaxter.com.au.

A.K. Benedict is an award-winning writer of *USA Today* bestselling novels, short stories and scripts. As Alexandra Benedict, she writes Golden Age-inspired mysteries with contemporary darkness. *The Christmas Murder Game* was longlisted for the Gold Dagger Award and both *Murder on the Christmas Express* and *The Christmas Jigsaw Murders* are international bestsellers. As A.K. Benedict, she writes high concept, speculative fiction and scripts. Shortlisted for the BBC Audio Drama Award and other prizes, she won the Scribe Award for her *Doctor Who* audio drama, *The Calendar Man*. Her critically acclaimed short stories feature in many anthologies including *Best British Short Stories*, *Best British*

Horror, New Fears, Phantoms, Uncertainties 6, Reports from the Deep End and *Bound in Blood*. Her debut high concept thriller, *The Beauty of Murder*, was nominated for the eDunnit Award, and her latest, *Little Red Death*, has to date been sold into fifteen territories. Alexandra now lives in Eastbourne with her husband, writer Guy Adams; their daughter, Verity; and their dog, Dame Margaret Rutherford.

Clay McLeod Chapman writes books, comic books and YA/middle grade books, as well as scripts for film and television. His novels include *Ghost Eaters*, *Whisper Down the Lane* and *What Kind of Mother*, and his most recent novel is *Wake Up and Open Your Eyes*. You can find him at claymcleodchapman.com.

Kay Chronister is the author of the novel *The Bog Wife* (2024), along with the collection *Thin Places* (2020) and the novel *Desert Creatures* (2022). Her short stories have appeared in *Clarkesworld*, *Beneath Ceaseless Skies*, *Strange Horizons*, *The Dark*, and elsewhere, and her work has been nominated for the Shirley Jackson and World Fantasy Awards. She lives in Pennsylvania.

Ryan Cole is a speculative fiction writer who lives in Virginia with his husband and snuggly pug child. His work has appeared or is forthcoming in *Clarkesworld*, *PodCastle*, *Escape Pod*, *Cast of Wonders*, *This Way Lies Madness* and *Voyage YA by Uncharted*, among others, and has been nominated for the Pushcart Prize. Find out more at ryancolewrites.com.

Craig DiLouie is an author of horror, military/historical and speculative fiction. Published by Hachette Book Group and Simon & Schuster, his most notable works include *Episode Thirteen*, *Suffer the Children* and *The Children of Red Peak*, among other novels. His latest, *My Ex, The Antichrist*, was published in July 2025. Learn more at CraigDiLouie.com.

Tracy Fahey is the Irish author of six books, three of which – *The Unheimlich Manoeuvre*, *I Spit Myself Out* and *They Shut Me Up* –

have been finalists at the British Fantasy Awards. In 2024 she won the Paul Cave Prize for Literature, and in 2023 she was granted a Saari Fellowship by the Kone Foundation. Her short fiction, which examines the interface of folklore and the Gothic, has been published in over forty anthologies. She has been awarded writing residencies in Ireland, Scotland, Greece and Finland.

Jeffrey Ford is the author of the novels *The Physiognomy*, *Memoranda*, *The Beyond*, *The Portrait of Mrs. Charbuque*, *The Girl in the Glass*, *The Cosmology of the Wider World*, *The Shadow Year*, *The Twilight Pariah*, *Ahab's Return* and *Out of Body*. His short story collections are *The Fantasy Writer's Assistant*, *The Empire of Ice Cream*, *The Drowned Life*, *Crackpot Palace*, *A Natural History of Hell*, *The Best of Jeffrey Ford* and *Big Dark Hole*. Ford's fiction has appeared in numerous magazines and anthologies, from *Tor.com* to *Magazine of Fantasy and Science Fiction* to *McSweeney's* to *The Oxford Book of American Short Stories*, and has been widely translated. He has won World Fantasy, Edgar Allan Poe, Shirley Jackson, and Nebula awards, and *The Physiognomy* was decreed a *New York Times* Notable Book of the Year.

Philip Fracassi is the Bram Stoker and British Fantasy Award-nominated author of the novels *A Child Alone with Strangers*, *Gothic*, *Boys in the Valley* and *The Third Rule of Time Travel*, as well as the award-winning story collections *Behold the Void*, *Beneath a Pale Sky*, and *No One Is Safe!* Philip's stories have been published in numerous magazines and anthologies, including *Best Horror of the Year*, *Nightmare Magazine*, *Southwest Review* and *Interzone*. He lives in Los Angeles and is represented by Copps Literary Services, Circle of Confusion, and WME. Visit his website at pfracassi.com.

Rob Francis is an academic and writer based in London. He mainly writes short fantasy and horror, usually in the middle of the night or on the train to work. His stories have appeared in magazines including *The Arcanist*, *Apparition Lit*, *Metaphorosis*, *Tales to Terrify* and *Weird Horror Magazine*. Rob has also had stories published in various anthologies, including *Alternative War* (B Cubed Press), *The*

Old Ways (Eerie River) and *Costs of Living* (Whisper Hour Press). He lurks on X (formerly Twitter) @RAFurbaneco

Christopher Golden is the *New York Times* bestselling author of such novels as *Road of Bones, All Hallows, The Night Birds* and *The House of Last Resort*. With Mike Mignola, he is the co-creator of the *Outerverse* comic book universe, including such series as *Baltimore* and *Joe Golem: Occult Detective*. He has also written for film, television, video games, and animation, and he co-wrote and co-directed the Audible original series *Slayers: A Buffyverse Story*. Golden has been nominated for the Bram Stoker Award eleven times in eight different categories, and won twice. He has also won the Shirley Jackson Award and the Audie Award, and his work has been nominated for the British Fantasy Award and the Eisner Award, among others. Golden lives in Massachusetts.

Rebecca Harrison sneezes like Donald Duck and her best friend is a dog who can count. Her first book, *The White Horse*, a gothic folk horror that the author describes as *Jane Eyre* meets *The Wicker Man*, is published by Salt Heart Press.

C.J. Leede is the *USA Today* bestselling author of *Maeve Fly* and *American Rapture*. Her debut novel *Maeve Fly* won the Golden Poppy Octavia E. Butler Award and the Splatterpunk Award, and earned a Bram Stoker Award nomination. When she is not driving around America, C.J. can be found in LA with her boyfriend and rescue dogs.

Full-time family man, artist, musician and ferret owner with twenty-plus books under his belt, **Chad Lutzke** dips his toe into all things dark: crime, thrillers, noir, slice-of-life and horror – all smothered in heartache, with the occasional sliver of hope. Some of his books include *Of Foster Homes & Flies, Stirring the Sheets, The Pale White, Skullface Boy, Bruises on a Butterfly, Three-Smile Mile,* and *The Neon Owl* series. Lutzke's work has been praised by authors Jack Ketchum, Richard Chizmar, Joe R. Lansdale, Stephen Graham Jones, Tim Waggoner, and his own mother.

BIOGRAPHIES • 261

Gary McMahon writes intensely personal and introspective horror stories. His short fiction has appeared in countless anthologies and magazines and has been reprinted in *The Best Horror of the Year*, *The Year's Best Fantasy & Horror* and *Best New Horror*. He's been nominated for several awards and has even won a couple of obscure ones. He is the author of the *Thomas Usher* novels, *The Concrete Grove* trilogy, *The End* and *The Bones of You*, and his novella *The Grieving Stones* was recently adapted into a feature film. He lives with his family in Yorkshire, UK, where he reads, writes, watches far too many films, lifts weights, and trains in Shotokan karate. His website can be found at: garymcmahon.com.

Mark Morris (Editor) has written and edited over fifty novels, novellas, short story collections and anthologies. His script work includes audio dramas for *Doctor Who*, *Jago & Litefoot* and the *Hammer Chillers* series. Mark's recent work includes the *Obsidian Heart* trilogy, the original *Predator* novel *Stalking Shadows* (co-written with James A. Moore), the official novelisation of the *Doctor Who* sixtieth anniversary special *Wild Blue Yonder*, and the anthologies *New Fears* (winner of the British Fantasy Award for Best Anthology) and *New Fears 2* as editor. He's also written award-winning audio adaptations of the classic 1971 horror movie *Blood on Satan's Claw* and the M.R. James ghost story 'A View from a Hill'. His novel *That Which Stands Outside* was published in 2024 by Flame Tree Press.

Tanya Pell is a narcoleptic horror author living in the American South. Her works include the Gothic horror novel *Her Wicked Roots* and *Cicada*, a creature-feature novella. Her short fiction can be found in anthologies like *Mother Knows Best*, *Obsolescence*, and in the forthcoming novel *DEAD FM* with Alan Lastufka.

Priya Sharma writes short stories and novellas. She is the recipient of several British Fantasy Awards and Shirley Jackson Awards, and a World Fantasy Award. She is a Locus Award and a Grand Prix de l'Imaginaire finalist. Her books include *All the Fabulous Beasts*, *Ormeshadow* and *Pomegranates*, and her short fiction has appeared in publications such as *Tor.com* (now *Reactor*), *Interzone*, *Black Static* and *Weird Tales*. She has been translated into Spanish, French, Italian, Czech and Polish. She lives in the UK where she works as a medical doctor. More information can be found at priyasharmafiction.wordpress.com.

Lucy A. Snyder is the Shirley Jackson Award-nominated and five-time Bram Stoker Award-winning author of fifteen books and over one hundred published short stories. Her most recent title is the Lovecraftian body horror novel *Sister, Maiden, Monster*. She lives near Columbus, Ohio, with a small jungle of houseplants, a fleet of aquariums, a clowder of cats, a shed of reptiles, and an insomnia of housemates. You can learn more about her at lucysnyder.com.

Tim Waggoner has published over sixty novels and eight collections of short stories. He writes original dark fantasy and horror, as well as media tie-ins, and his articles on writing have appeared in numerous publications. His books include the novels *Lord of the Feast*, *We Will Rise*, *They Kill* and *The Mouth of the Dark*, and the movie novelisations *Halloween Kills*, *Terrifier 2*, *X*, *Pearl* and *MaXXXine*. He's a four-time winner of the Bram Stoker Award, a one-time winner of the Scribe award, and he's been a two-time finalist for the Shirley Jackson Award and a one-time finalist for the Splatterpunk Award. He's also a full-time tenured professor who teaches creative writing and composition at Sinclair College in Dayton, Ohio. His papers are collected by the University of Pittsburgh's Horror Studies Program.

Shirley Jackson award-winner **Kaaron Warren** published her first short story in 1993 and has had fiction in print every year since. She has published six multi-award-winning novels: *Slights*, *Walking the Tree*, *Mistification*, *The Grief Hole*, *Tide of Stone* and *The Underhistory*, and seven short story collections, her most recent being *Calvaria Fell*, with Cat Sparks, from Meerkat Press. Her stories have been shortlisted for the World Fantasy Award and the Stoker, and have appeared in both Ellen Datlow's and Paula Guran's *Year's Best* anthologies. Her writing podcast *Let the Cat In* showcases ideas, objects, and inspirations. Her latest novel *The Underhistory*, from Viper Books, was described in *The Guardian* as 'a beautifully constructed, suspenseful gothic tale'.

FLAME TREE PRESS
FICTION WITHOUT FRONTIERS
Award-Winning Authors & Original Voices

Flame Tree Press is the trade fiction imprint of Flame Tree Publishing, focusing on excellent writing in horror and the supernatural, crime and mystery, science fiction and fantasy. Our aim is to explore beyond the boundaries of the everyday, with tales from both award-winning authors and original voices.

•

Other titles in this series:
After Sundown
Beyond the Veil
Close to Midnight
Darkness Beckons
Elemental Forces

Flame Tree Press novels by Mark Morris:
That Which Stands Outside

Other horror and suspense titles available include:
October by Gregory Bastianelli
Sebastian by P.D. Cacek
The Incubations by Ramsey Campbell
The Queen of the Cicadas by V. Castro
The Stones of Landane by Catherine Cavendish
Five Deaths for Seven Songbirds by John Everson
The Wakening by JG Faherty
Dead Ends by Marc E. Fitch
One by One by D.W. Gillespie
Stoker's Wilde by Steven Hopstaken & Melissa Prusi
Demon Dagger by Russell James
The Raven by Jonathan Janz
Hearthstone Cottage by Frazer Lee
Those Who Came Before by J.H. Moncrieff
They Stalk the Night by Brian Moreland
August's Eyes by Glenn Rolfe
Misfits by Hunter Shea
Lord of the Feast by Tim Waggoner
The Gaia Chime by Johnny Worthen

•

Join our mailing list for free short stories, new release details, news about our authors and special promotions:

flametreepress.com